D0436870

THE HIDDEN MEMORY OF OBJECTS

DANIELLE MAGES AMATO

THE HIDDEN MEMORY OF OBJECTS

BALZER + BRAY
An Imprint of HarperCollins*Publishers*

Balzer + Bray is an imprint of HarperCollins Publishers.

The Hidden Memory of Objects

www.epicreads.com

ISBN978-0-06-244588-9 (trade bdg.)

Typography by Sarah Creech

17 18 19 20 21 PC/LSCH 10 9 8 7 6 5 4 3 2 1

First Edition

TO MY BROTHERS

AND TO PHIL,
FOR DOING ALL THE DISHES

CHAPTER 1

MY BROTHER, TYLER, DIED THREE TIMES: FIRST IN AN abandoned building in Washington, DC; then in the back hall of a funeral home in McLean, Virginia; and finally on the stage of Ford's Theatre, just a few feet from where Abraham Lincoln was assassinated. I couldn't blame myself for the first two, but the third one? That was entirely my fault.

On the day of my brother's funeral, I sat outside the viewing room in a pink upholstered chair, hoping the cops would show up. Not the young ones, those freshly shaven go-getters who respected my parents' wishes and told me nothing. I wanted an old-timer, a chatty veteran on the brink of retirement, who might let a few things slip.

The instant I spotted their dark cookie-cutter suits, I was on my feet. The tall one, I could have sliced a finger on the clean line of his jaw. But the other one—he had grizzle. I needed to move fast. I ducked past two girls tangled in a hug by a photo of Tyler in his varsity baseball uniform. I narrowly avoided a collision with his ex-girlfriend, Emma. But before I could reach the cops, a warm hand on my shoulder stopped me, and Squarejaw and Grizzle pushed open the door of the viewing room. The people inside glanced toward me, their faces stiff and lacquered over with grief. I jerked back and closed my eyes. I couldn't go in there. I wouldn't.

"You okay, Brown?" asked the boy who'd stopped me.

"Don't call me Brown," I said, glaring up at him. He seemed familiar, although he didn't look like anyone else in the room. He was all rich colors and textures—an oil painting in a room full of charcoal sketches. His skin gleamed a dark Vandyke brown, his eyes umber. His chunky, oversized glasses were indigo blue, and his bow tie blazed scarlet. He wore his hair natural, not that he needed the few extra inches of height.

"Not Brown," he said. "Megan. That's right. Sorry."

He knew my nickname *and* my real name, but I didn't recognize him at all? "Do I know you?"

"You don't remember me?" He looked down at his feet with a slight smile. "Of course you don't."

"Do you go to Westside?"

"I go to school in DC." He shifted the messenger bag slung across his chest and stuck out a hand. "Nathan. Nathan Lee." I stared at the pattern of lines on his palm. By the time it occurred to me to shake it, he'd dropped it back by his side. "I'm a friend of Tyler's. I heard what happened, and . . ." He shifted from one foot to the other. "I don't know. I guess I wanted to make sure you were all right."

All right? Tears burned behind my eyes, and anger turned my stomach. *Keep quiet,* I thought. *He's trying to be nice,* I thought. *I want to knock the nice right off his face,* I thought.

"Is there anything you need?" he asked, nicer than ever, and I knew I wasn't going to keep quiet. I could hear Tyler's voice in my head: *Watch it, Brown. When you're upset, you forget how to talk like a normal person.*

But I didn't listen.

"I need to know how Tyler died," I said. "Because no one will tell me."

Nathan's face froze. "Whoa. That's . . . I don't know."

"Also a lamb kebab."

He shook his head, confused.

"A lamb kebab," I repeated. "From Moby Dick's. With a side of cucumber sauce? That would be great."

"Are you serious?"

My anger drained away in an instant, and I covered my face with both hands. Even dead, Tyler was always right. "Please, just go."

And after a long moment, he did.

I felt heavy and sick, like I'd swallowed a stone. And I couldn't escape. I was trapped in this room full of familiar strangers, all moving in slow motion through an invisible sea of sorrow. I longed for the feel of scissors in my hand, for the smell of paints and pencils and glue. I'd tear this whole scene apart and remake it on paper: a collage of flowers, perhaps, each one elegant and waxy as death. And there I'd be, tucked away in one corner, my face a blur, my mouth open in a silent scream, a figure of horror like something out of a Francis Bacon painting.

A funeral-home official in gray pinstripes descended on me. "Miss Brown? Megan Brown?"

I nodded.

"The service will be starting in a few minutes." He looked down his nose at my baggy sweater and black knit skirt. "Now might be a good time to change your clothes. You can use the family services room."

"Family services room" turned out to be a euphemism for "large closet with mirror and tissues." A framed photo of Tyler sat on a shelf, even here, his red hair a blaze of color in the fluorescent light. He grinned up at me from the picture, his letter jacket slung over one shoulder, looking more like an American Eagle model than like the colossal goofball who thought it was funny to wear my bras to the breakfast table.

On a hook behind the door, the navy blazer and skirt my mother had chosen for me hung waiting, still sealed in their dry-cleaning bags. A small table by the mirror held the other items she'd left me. Apparently, she expected me to wear panty hose. And makeup.

We couldn't just mourn, I guess. We had to look the part.

I yanked on the outfit and stepped into toe-pinching pumps I hadn't worn in at least a year. As I picked up Mom's makeup bag, I heard my father's voice outside in the hall. Raised. Angry.

"He's my son, and I'll decide when it's time for us to talk about it!"

I cracked open the door. My father towered over a female detective who couldn't have been more than five feet tall. I'd seen her once before: at our house, the night Tyler died. Johnson—that was her name. Her deep brown skin was unwrinkled, and her tight curls showed no sign of gray, but given her badass expression, no one would dare mistake her for a rookie.

Adrenaline raced through me, and I pressed my face to the doorjamb, determined to catch every single word.

"I'm only here to pay my respects, sir," she said. "We can talk about the autopsy results another time."

An icy shock raced through me. She had the autopsy results? I held my breath, hoping she would say more.

I could see Dad's hands shaking. He balled them into fists, and his face hardened. "I can't believe you would even bring up the investigation today. And here, of all places. Don't you follow any kind of protocol?"

Detective Johnson nodded grimly, as though having a distinguished history professor get up in her face was a routine part of her job, though not one she liked very much. "You're absolutely right. I should go."

As she turned to leave, I saw my best chance of finding out what had happened to Tyler walking out with her.

"No!" I shoved open the door and stepped into the hall. They both turned toward me, and I froze in place, my confidence deserting me in an instant.

My father raised a hand. "Megan, I want you to stay out of this."

I forced my chin up, fighting the hated tears. "If the autopsy results are back, I have every right to know what's in them." Dad looked down at his feet, but Badass fixed me with a laser glare, sizing me up. "Please, Dad," I choked out. "I need to know."

But Dad said nothing. He didn't even glance at me.

After a short pause, Johnson spoke. "As I told your father, the autopsy was inconclusive. We're still waiting on toxicology results."

"Toxicology?" I asked. "Isn't that, like, drugs?"

She nodded.

"But that doesn't . . ." I shook my head. "I thought maybe he fell.

He was in a condemned building, right? And he was on crutches. He didn't fall?"

"He did have a head wound, but it appears that was not the cause of death," Johnson said. "And the initial blood screen came back positive for opiates."

Dad lifted his head. "Opiates? You mean like morphine?"

"In this case, I mean heroin."

I stopped breathing for a moment, then started up again with a gasp. Tyler? Taking heroin? That was impossible. Ridiculous, even.

But Badass couldn't have been more serious.

Dad looked every bit as gut-punched as I felt. "I don't understand. He was graduating in three months. He had a full ride at UVa, playing baseball. He wouldn't jeopardize that by doing drugs."

Johnson's voice was matter-of-fact. "Officers canvasing the area found several witnesses who saw a boy matching Tyler's description in the parking lot of a McDonald's on New York Avenue, a known open-air market for heroin and methadone in that neighborhood."

She said it so easily, like it would be just as easy to believe. It wasn't. Anger and confusion gripped my throat, and I fought to get the words out. "But . . . Tyler . . . he didn't drink."

"Miss Brown, I'm not talking about alcohol."

"No, I mean . . ." My voice choked off, and I clenched my skirt in frustration.

"He didn't *even* drink, is what she means." I turned and saw Nathan Lee hovering at the end of the hall, looking vaguely embarrassed. "I'm sorry, I was just . . ." He gestured to the men's room door behind him. "I should leave." He took a few steps, then turned back. "But Megan's right. Red was totally clean. Heroin?" He shook his head. "Doesn't make any sense."

Ten minutes ago, I'd never seen this Nathan guy before, but now he felt like a lifeline.

And he wasn't finished. "Besides, why would he have gone to some McDonald's in DC to buy drugs? I guarantee you, there are plenty of drugs right here in Virginia." He caught the look in Johnson's eye and finished, "Ma'am."

"This is enough," my father said. "I've told you, my wife and I don't want Megan pulled into the investigation." He looked over at Nathan. "And you . . . I'm sorry, I have no idea who you are."

"He's with me," I said. Nathan glanced over at me in surprise, and a corner of his mouth turned up.

"We do have to talk to Megan, I'm afraid. And all of Tyler's friends." The detective gave Nathan a significant look. "But remember, this is only preliminary. We still have to wait for the full toxicology report."

"How long?" my father asked.

"Four weeks. Minimum." She must have seen the look of disbelief cross my face. "I'm sorry, but that's how long it takes."

"And if it was an overdose?" Dad asked.

"Well, then we'll do our best to determine if it was accidental or intentional."

Suicide. She was talking about suicide. Even unspoken, the word landed like a blow. I shook my head, as though I could knock it loose, but it burrowed deep and stung hard. *Suicide.* I glanced over at Dad. He looked like a papier-mâché version of himself, hollowed out and thin.

"Heroin?" he breathed at last. "Are you sure? There hasn't been some kind of mistake?"

"No mistake." Detective Johnson's face softened, and her voice took on a gentler tone. "I'm sorry. I know this is hard. But you can't blame yourself for not knowing. Addicts hide things. Especially from the people who love them best."

I swayed on my feet, suddenly dizzy. I thought Tyler's death had been *it*—the kind of once-in-a-lifetime event that broke everything into "before" and "after"—but now here I stood, teetering on the edge of yet another cliff. I turned to my father, searching his face, hoping he'd protect me, somehow, from whatever came next.

But Dad just . . . crumpled. He let out a breath that seemed to make him shorter, and his chin dropped. "He *had* been withdrawn for the past few weeks."

I let out a low cry.

"He was moody. Distracted," Dad continued. "Not acting like himself. That whole story about how he broke his leg? Climbing the backstop on the baseball field?" He shook his head. Tears were running down his cheeks now, and he didn't bother to wipe them away. They panicked me. "I knew it sounded off, but I didn't even bother to—" His voice broke, and he fell silent, jaw clenching.

And that was the moment. The moment Tyler died all over again. It was bad enough that I'd never see him again, but now . . . he wouldn't even be the person I remembered. My brother wasn't just going to die; I was going to lose everything I had left of him.

"Dad—" I began.

"It doesn't change anything. We won't love him any less. Just because . . ." He trailed off, rubbing his face with his hands. "I have to find your mother." He turned to Johnson. "I think you should go. I'll see you out." The two of them walked away, leaving Nathan and me alone.

I pushed the heels of my hands into my eyes, as though I could keep the hot, bitter tears from spilling out. It didn't work. I gave in, slumped back against the wall, and cried.

Nathan came closer and leaned against the wall beside me. He didn't speak.

When I finally opened my eyes, I saw that his were closed. He had taken off his glasses, and I realized I'd been wrong about the color of his bow tie—it wasn't scarlet. It was carmine, a red with less green, more blue. And in the fluorescent hallway light, his skinny black suit had a hint of sheen to it. Very retro, like something that had come through a time machine.

He opened his eyes and caught me looking at him, his face a mirror of my own sadness and confusion. I pushed off the wall and stepped away.

"You know, you're not at all how Tyler described you," he said.

I turned toward him. "How did he describe me?"

"Shy. Quiet. Standoffish."

"I'm quiet."

His lips quirked in a half smile.

"Ordinarily," I said.

His smile grew, transforming his face, giving rise to new shapes and shadows. "No, I don't think so. You may be hard to get going. But when you go, you go."

I wasn't sure what to say. So I said nothing.

"And I'm sorry I crashed that major family moment," he said. "I didn't mean to make things awkward or—"

"No, I'm glad you were there." I rubbed my arms against a sudden chill, and I studied the lines and angles of Nathan's face. After the way he'd stood up for Tyler—and for me—he seemed less like a stranger and more like a friend I'd just met. "I thought I wanted answers, you know? About what happened to him. But now . . ." Tears clogged my throat. "It's like they're trying to take him away from me."

Nathan was silent for a few seconds. Then he held out his hand. "Give me your phone."

"What?"

"I'm going to send you something. A video. Did Red show you the videos?"

"What videos?"

"That's what I thought."

I gave him my phone, and he dialed. A muffled ringing came from his bag. "Now I've got your number. And you've got mine." He tapped away on my phone for another few seconds, then held it up to snap his own picture. "I'll save that with my number. In case you forget who I am."

I snorted, wiping at my face. "Unlikely."

He handed it back to me. "I'll send you that video. Just watch it, okay?" He reached out a tentative hand and rested it on my shoulder. "And listen, no matter what happened to Tyler, or how he died, no one can take him away from you. Okay?"

I was suddenly overwhelmed again, drowning in missing Tyler, overcome by the words pounding in my head. *Heroin. Overdose. Suicide.*

Nathan stepped back. "I actually brought you something else, if you want it. I meant to give it to you before, but . . ." He reached into his bag and pulled out a tattered paperback with a sepia-toned photograph on the cover. "Tyler was carrying that around for months. Left it at my place. I figured you might want it. Sentimental value and all."

I nodded, my eyes blurring with tears again.

"Okay. I guess I should go." He took a few steps, but then he stopped. "You have my number, if there's anything you need." He made a kind of bowing gesture and disappeared down the hall.

I ducked into the family services room, shut the door behind me, and dropped the book Nathan had given me into my backpack. I still had to force myself through the funeral. My arm felt heavy as I reached for Mom's makeup bag, and I thought, *My entire body is filling up with stones.* Instead of going to the mirror, I picked up Tyler's picture.

I remembered standing at the edge of a swimming pool at maybe five years old, my bare toes curled around the rounded lip, watching him flash through the water like a seal. He made it look effortless, like something people just *did.* I wanted to do that, look like that, be like him. But when I flung myself into the pool, I flailed and gasped and sank, until he swam over and pulled my head above water.

He'd been doing the same thing ever since. My brother sailed through life like it was one long sock slide. No matter how hard I tried, all I seemed to do was skid. So Tyler did his best to pull me with him. But he couldn't do anything about what I called the Look: that expression of surprise and disappointment I always got when I told people I was Tyler Brown's little sister.

"Really?" they'd say, staring at my mud-colored hair and my paint-stained fingers. The Look was usually followed by the Pause, as they waited for me to act like him, to do something outrageous

or entertaining. I excelled at defying that expectation. People called him Red Brown, so gradually I became known as Brown Brown. It was more than a nickname; it was a self-fulfilling prophecy. They called me Brown, so I gave them Brown. Life was easier that way. Part of me might have hated Tyler for it. But mostly, I still just wanted to be like him.

My phone beeped. I fished it out of my bag to find two new messages. One was from Elena. It read: *Can't believe I'm so far away. Thinking of you. Good vibes from Texas.*

I thought about all the things I wanted to tell her, all the things I couldn't fit into a text. I wrote, If you're not over here in fifteen minutes, you can find a new best friend.

Seconds later, her response: *You've been saying that since the fifth grade.* I breathed a little easier. Obscure *Ferris Bueller's Day Off* reference identified and answered. Infinitely more comforting than a funeral hall full of sympathetic looks.

The other text was from Nathan. No message, just a link to a YouTube video. I hesitated, my finger hovering over the phone. Then I took a breath and clicked the link.

The video that came up was titled "You Are My Sunshine." Posted by a user called TwoRedCents, it had racked up 305 views—hardly viral, but not a secret, either. The video started, and I gasped when I saw myself, sitting next to Tyler on his bed. His guitar rested on my lap, and he positioned my fingers on the strings.

"Okay, so this is A," he said. Then he moved my fingers. "Here's D." He moved my fingers again. "E. And back to A. Now you start singing, and I'll tell you when to switch."

I gripped the phone a little tighter. This had been shot almost two years ago, right after all the crap Elena went through in eighth grade. The crap that made moving away seem like the best thing that could possibly happen to her. The morning after she'd left, Tyler had dragged me out of my room and declared I needed to learn to play guitar. That's how we got along best: me learning and him teaching.

In the video—ugh, I still had my awful eighth-grade bangs—I strummed the guitar a few times, then started singing softly, staring at my fingers. "You are my sunshine, my only sunshine. You make me—"

"Now D," Tyler said.

I grimaced as I tried to twist my fingers into the new position. Tyler helped me, laughing. "When it starts to sound like actual music," he said, "you'll know you're getting somewhere."

I began to sing again. The video cut to another lesson, but the same point in the song. I was incrementally better. As the song continued, the video progressed in a kind of time lapse of me mastering some basic chords. Now and then, the song was interrupted by short scenes of me and Tyler doing other things: thumb wrestling, eating potato chips, looking at our phones. By the end of the song, I wasn't half bad. We sang the final words together: "Please don't take my sunshine away."

"Awesome," Tyler said, and the video ended.

My chest ached so hard that I rubbed it with one hand. That was Tyler as I'd always known him. Whatever the police or the medical examiner said, he wasn't a figment of my imagination. But how did the boy in this video turn into the boy in Detective Johnson's police report? And how had I not even noticed? Dad and Nathan seemed as shocked as I was. But maybe Mom knew something. And maybe she could help me figure out how the hell I was supposed to deal with it.

As I was forwarding the video to Elena, I heard three quick knocks at the door. "Miss Brown?" The funeral-home gestapo had found me. "The service is beginning."

"I'll be right there."

I looked around the room. Mom would notice if I didn't put on lipstick, at the very least. I dug through her makeup bag and came up with a tube of bright red. Carmine—a perfect match for the color of Nathan's bow tie. I opened the tube and considered wearing it like an invitation, a flipped middle finger, a badge of courage. But when the knocks at the door sounded again, I shoved it back in the bag and looked for something a little more brown.

CHAPTER 2

AFTER THE SERVICE, I WAS TRAPPED IN THE HORROR of something called the condolence line. Another funeral-home euphemism. The reality of the experience called to mind the way they used to press witches to death by adding rock after rock to a board on their chests. There I stood, with everyone else's heartbreak piled on top of me, rock after rock, when I could hardly bear the weight of my own. My head buzzed with unshed tears, and I fought to keep my breathing steady.

My mother stood beside me, poised and perfect, every inch the gracious Virginia lady. People always said we looked alike—except for the poise and perfection, I guess. She worked in fundraising for Ford's Theatre in DC, planning swanky events for even swankier people. I knew she must be on autopilot today, hosting this event she never dreamed she'd have to plan. She greeted every guest with shatterproof politeness. She shook the hands of my classmates' parents, a power parade of congress members and judges, lobbyists and think tankers. She remembered their names without a single hesitation. How could she be so utterly composed, when I felt two inches from total collapse? I tried to read her expression, but I couldn't tell whether Dad had told her yet, whether he'd repeated all those things Detective Johnson had said about Tyler.

Stuck in the line, not willing to look anyone in the eye, I stared at an endless stream of cleavage and neckties and tried to distract myself with a game I called Three Things. For years, I'd been an obsessive gatherer of little objects. My father called me his magpie, always bringing home shiny bits of paper and string. And ever since I could hold a pair of scissors, I'd been cutting up things that appealed to me and arranging them in tiny, intricate collages. The thing about *things* is: each one has a voice. Every little object has its own special something to say. And when you put them together, the right things in the right way, they tell a story.

But there are places where scissors and glue are inappropriate. Like the dentist's chair. English class. Your brother's funeral. So I came up with Three Things. I look around, wherever I am, and pick out the three objects that best tell the story of that moment, like a living collage. No scissors necessary.

Three Things from the condolence line at Tyler's funeral: a girl in a somber black dress and a jeweled Hello Kitty necklace. A photograph, pressed into my mother's hand by his kindergarten teacher, of Tyler at five years old. My own face, reflected in the gleaming wood and brass of my brother's coffin.

Finally the last miserable person came through that long and miserable line. I turned to my mother, desperate to ask her about Tyler, but she was already in motion, grabbing her purse and pulling out a list. "Megan, you and your father are riding home with Mrs. Koss."

I struggled for calm. "I really need to talk to you. Right now."

She didn't meet my eye but instead continued to scan the paper in her hand. "At home, I promise. I'm having the flowers donated, and I need to follow up with the staff here. I don't want you to wait." She squeezed my father's shoulder and walked out of the chapel.

I turned to my father. "Did you tell her? About the detective?"

Dad held up a hand. "Please don't talk about that here." He followed my mother out the door.

I snapped the head off a white carnation and shredded the petals into my pocket. *Raw materials,* I thought. *For later.*

Mrs. Koss cried the whole way home. She apologized for crying, then cried again, then apologized again, then apologized for apologizing. When she pulled her Volvo wagon into our driveway, Dad's door was open before the car even stopped moving. "Thank you, Judy, I really . . . ," he managed, and he made his escape into the house.

As I climbed out of the backseat, Mrs. Koss rolled down the driver's window. Her faded blue eyes were rimmed with red, and wisps of dyed blond hair stuck to her cheeks. After her own kids had gone off to college, she had babysat Tyler and me for years, until we were old enough to be home by ourselves after school. She reached out a hand through the open car window, shaky and uncertain, and I hesitated to take it, not wanting to be anchored to her grief. But I did it anyway.

"If I can help, I'm right across the street. Come find me anytime."

I nodded. She held my hand in both of hers now, turning it over and studying it.

"Are you going to be okay?" I asked.

"Sweet girl, worrying about me." She pressed my hand to her

cheek before letting it go. “I’m praying for you, all right? You don’t have to tell your folks that; I know they don’t go in for that kind of thing. But I wanted you to know.”

“Thanks.”

“Now go in there and tell your father I’m sorry. Again.”

I choked out a laugh. “I think he knows.”

Mrs. Koss gave a damp wave as she pulled out of the driveway, and I went through the back door into the kitchen. Dad was already sitting on the deck outside, swirling a glass of Scotch in one hand and staring off into the distance. I changed out of my hateful funeral suit and headed for the front porch to wait for Mom.

I stopped short in the doorway. On the front mat, someone had left a plastic takeout bag. I untied the knot and cracked open the Styrofoam clamshell, releasing the familiar smell of lamb kebab, rice, and grilled tomato. There was even a side of cucumber sauce.

Nathan. It could only be from Nathan. The food in my hands seemed to warm my entire body. My chest unclenched, and some of the tension in my neck melted away. I curled up with the container on our front porch swing and sent a message to Elena.

This day blows, I wrote.

God so sorry, came the reply.

Need to talk? Not just text?

Because the phone has a feature that allows us to do that.

I hate talking. Just distract me?

Are you meeting with the counselor?

I rolled my eyes. Terrible distraction. You suck at this.

Talk to the counselor. It helps, trust me.

Saw her once. She wore two different colors of black at the same time.

Snob.

Stop trying to do this alone.

Go back to see her.

Sure thing, I wrote. I will absolutely do that.

We are men of action. Lies do not become us.

I sent her the poop emoji.

I watched the video you sent. So sweet!!! Where did you get it?

New Boy.

WHAT?

I went off on him and he brought me food.

I don't know what that means, but I like it. Keep him.

Thinking about it.

Yes, I know: think first.

That will be your slogan when you run for office.

Megan Brown: She Thinks First.

It's solid life advice.

An inspiring philosophy, Elena replied.

Exactly what you want on your tombstone.

And with that, the reality of the day came crashing in again. My stomach clenched, and my heart turned to ice.

Oh my god, she wrote.

So so so sorry.

Elena Rodriguez: She Does Not Think First.

You still there?

I really do suck at this.

I set down the takeout container, no longer hungry. It had felt so good to forget, even for a moment, but forgetting made remembering that much worse.

I paused, wondering whether or not I should tell her.

They're saying Tyler died of an overdose, I typed.

WHAT? WHO?

The police.

OMG

Not Tyler

How is that possible?

I don't know, I sent back, as my mother's car pulled up in front of the house. But I want to find out. I slipped the phone into my pocket.

Mom emerged from the car with two reusable shopping bags. She held them up to show me. "Good news. More casseroles."

I followed her inside as she brought the bags to the kitchen. "Mom," I began, "about Tyler—"

"I saw you on your phone. Was that Elena?"

"Yes."

"Oh, good." But the disapproval crept into her body language immediately. Her lips pursed, like they always did when Elena's name was mentioned.

"Don't worry," I said. "She's still a thousand miles away."

Mom sighed. "You know I don't have a problem with Elena."

I managed to hold my tongue. Despite Elena's wild clothes, her lack of indoor voice, and the fact that she could spout off a passionate rant about absolutely *anything*, Mom had always liked her. Mom's real problem was with *me*, or at least it had been, for that tiny window of time when I'd acted more like Elena and less like the quiet daughter she preferred.

She opened the freezer, revealing a nearly solid wall of food. "Huh. We should eat these, I guess."

But she didn't move. She stood there with the freezer door open, staring blankly as the cold mist curled around her. In the unforgiving kitchen light, the lines around her eyes cut deep beneath her makeup, and her cheeks looked sunken and hollow. Her brown hair, as stick straight as mine, hung limp around her face, and I could even see a hint of silver creeping in at the roots.

I started pulling plastic containers and jars out of the bags. "Listen, I don't know if Dad has talked to you yet, about the detective—" As I turned toward her, a jar slipped from my fingers, hit the floor on its side, and cracked, releasing a slow creep of tomato sauce onto the tile.

Mom didn't even flinch; her mind was someplace else. She closed the freezer door and lowered herself onto a barstool. "When you were a baby . . . ," she began.

Worst opening line of a story ever, I thought, reaching for a dish towel.

"You were a holy terror. I mean, you were colicky, you didn't sleep, you didn't like tags touching your skin. Sometimes I would think you were crying just to mess with me." A half smile crossed her face. "Tyler, though, he was *easy.* Even in elementary school. I used to say to him, 'Kid, you know it's not actually your job to make my life easier. You're allowed to screw up every now and then.'" She shook her head. "But he wouldn't listen."

She knew.

I moved to the barstool next to her, tomato sauce still dripping from the towel in my hand. "Mom, did you have any idea? Did you notice anything weird going on with him?"

Her face hardened. "Nothing weird *was* going on with him."

"Um, did Dad not tell you? The detective said—"

"Your father told me what the detective said." Mom clasped her hands in front of her. Despite her bland expression, I could see her fingers clench, her knuckles whiten. "But it's obviously some kind of mistake."

I leaned back, taking a moment to consider what to say next. "Mom, they did tests. They got results. I think it's pretty unlikely they made a mistake."

She stood and tugged her clothes firmly into place. "Those are *preliminary* results. I'm sure the final report will show that no drugs were involved, because what happened—" Her voice caught in her throat, and she took a slow breath to steady herself. "What happened to Tyler was a tragic accident."

"Mom, can't we at least talk about this?"

She shook her head. I could see her careful facade splintering now, like cracks spiderwebbed in broken glass. She was holding the pieces together by force of will, but I thought the smallest tap might shatter her. "I don't need to talk about it," she said. "Tyler was a good boy. There's no way this was anything but an accident."

I wished I could agree with her, if only to make her feel better. But what would happen when the police stormed in here in four weeks with their final reports and their scientific certainties and broke my mother into a thousand pieces? "We can't pretend this isn't happening," I said. "Don't you want to know the truth?"

For an instant, she cracked. Tears spilled over and ran down her cheeks. "The truth is . . . he's gone, Megan," she said. "Nothing will ever change that. And nothing will ever bring him back."

I wanted to go to her, to close my eyes and curl into her lap like I did when I was small, to cry myself safe in the citrusy smell of her perfume. But when I took a step toward her, her hands flew up defensively, and she stepped away from me.

Like a blow to the chest, it knocked the wind right out of me. *I'm not gone, Mom,* I thought. *I'm right here. What about me?*

I bent down and scooped up the jar of pasta sauce, throwing the whole mess, dish towel and all, in the trash. "You should eat something," I said, and I walked out of the kitchen.

I went to Tyler's room, because that's where I always went when I needed help. My feet took me straight to his door, and I had to force myself not to knock. Instead, I rested my hand against the wood. I could so clearly picture him whipping the door open and leaning on the doorframe.

"You've got sad face," he'd say. "Go away. I'm not your therapist."

"But Elena's halfway across the country."

"So make new friends."

"I don't need new friends," I'd say. "I have you."

He'd groan. He'd roll his eyes. And he'd let me in. Every time.

Except this one.

I took a deep breath and opened the door, but I froze before I could take a single step. Gone were the piles of dirty clothes and the chaos of cables and headphones. The carpet was visible, and it even had vacuum cleaner tracks in it. Mom must have done this, somewhere in the obsessive cleaning and organizing stage of grief. I stepped into the room, feeling like a trespasser in a place I didn't belong. What was Mom thinking? Was she going to turn Tyler's room into a shrine, keep everything exactly as he'd left it? Minus the mess, of course.

It was a terrible thought. I did a quick calculation of how much longer I had to live in this house: two more years before college, and then all those summers and Christmases. I was *not* going to live in the Tyler Brown Memorial Museum.

And which Tyler Brown was she memorializing, anyway? Some guy who didn't just play varsity baseball and get named Best All-Around Senior, but was also neat and clean and always took out the trash? It was like whitewashing an already-white picket fence. This spotless room did not belong to the brother I remembered. And it sure as hell didn't belong to that other Tyler, the one Detective Johnson had described, the kid who OD'd in an abandoned building forty-five minutes from home.

The Tyler my mother saw, the one I saw, the one the police saw . . . they were like puzzle pieces that didn't fit together. Like a bad collage. Or an exquisite corpse. The surrealists invented those, a hundred years ago. They'd fold up a piece of paper, and each artist would draw part of a body—one the head, one the torso, and one the legs—without showing the others what they'd done. But because they were surrealists, they might draw a hand for a head, or a machine for a chest, or fish fins for legs. And when they opened the paper, they'd find this bizarre Frankenstein creature, assembled from parts that didn't belong.

That's what was happening to Tyler. Everyone thought they had a piece of him, but when you tried to put the pieces together, you didn't get a whole person anymore.

I retreated slowly, leaving Tyler's room. I knew I couldn't bring him back, but I wished I could make him *whole* again. I wished I could make all those different pieces tell the same story. I went down the hall to my own room and threw myself onto the bed, shoving aside the bag of clothes I'd brought back from the funeral home. It hit the floor with a loud *thunk.*

I leaned over to see what had made the noise—and then I remembered. The book Nathan had given me. The one Tyler had been carrying around with him for months.

I snatched up the bag and dug through until I found it. The cover, which had been worn when Nathan gave it to me, was now ripped nearly in half. I held the two pieces together and read the title. *Disasters in the Sun: The True History of John Wilkes Booth in Seven Objects.*

A little jolt of shock ran through me. "Seven Objects?" Sure, I preferred my own game of Three Things, but the similarity felt too strong to ignore.

On the cover, a brooding, surly-faced man showed off his curly hair and Civil War mustache. I flipped the book over and read.

> In this revelatory new survey, acclaimed historian Dr. David Brightman journeys through the life of the most reviled man in American history. Using seven objects that once belonged to Lincoln assassin John Wilkes Booth—including a letter written in code, a sumptuous theatrical costume, and the infamous derringer pistol Booth used to kill the president—Brightman delves deep into the heart and mind of a killer. His groundbreaking approach promises to forever transform our understanding of a pivotal figure in nineteenth-century history.

Standard-issue academic gobbledygook. My dad wrote books like this—about a different time period, but the same general idea. I flipped it open. The pages were flagged with brightly colored Post-it notes, highlighted in neon pink and yellow, and marked with scrawled handwriting that I recognized immediately as Tyler's. "Lincoln as both hero and villain," one note said. "JWB rocking the ladies," read another.

It looked like the work of a history grad student. Or a deeply obsessive weirdo.

Neither of those descriptions fit the Tyler I knew. I closed the book and studied the photograph of Booth on the cover.

I thought I knew all of Tyler's secrets. He wasn't shy about sharing gross locker-room stories or embarrassing facts about his ex-girlfriends. And in return, he'd listened to all my complaints about teachers and my thoughts about art. I'd even, in a moment of weakness, confessed my ill-fated crush on his best friend, Bobby Drake.

But apparently Nathan—a guy I'd never even met—knew things about Tyler that I did not. And Nathan had brought me food, which meant he knew where we lived. Why had Tyler never mentioned him?

I closed the book again and studied it. *The True History of John Wilkes Booth in Seven Objects.* If this Brightman person could uncover the history of a long-dead killer by going through the stuff he left behind, then surely I could use Tyler's things to figure out what had been happening with him over the last few months, and how he had ended up in that abandoned building.

After all, I was really good with objects.

Armed with the book, I returned to Tyler's room. I stood in the doorway and assessed it for a moment. Where to begin? His laptop seemed the obvious choice. When it booted up, I tried to get into his email, but I couldn't figure out the password. The more times I guessed wrong, the tighter the knot in my stomach became. I tried names of sports teams and ex-girlfriends. I even tried hacker bait like "password" and "12345" before giving up completely and going to his browser history.

It was full of John Wilkes Booth. Pages and pages about Booth's childhood and his famous family and the conspiracy to kill Abraham Lincoln.

And then there were guns. So many pages about guns, especially ones from the Civil War and the late 1800s. He'd read stories about replica guns and gun auctions, watched videos about loading them and firing them.

I closed the laptop and rubbed at my arms, trying to chase away the chill spreading through my body. What the hell was all this? I'd never thought of Tyler as a gun lover. But then, I'd never thought of him as a heroin user, either.

Restless, I walked over to Tyler's dresser and flipped through his shoe box full of ticket stubs and band stickers. Most of the bands I'd never heard of, but I found a ticket from last fall's Mountain Goats show at the Black Cat on Fourteenth Street. As I held the ticket in my hand, I could almost see Tyler leaning on the kitchen table, begging Mom and Dad to let him go, blathering on and on about the genius of John Darnielle, until they finally looked at each other with a smile that said, "We were always going to say yes, but we liked watching you fight for it." Tyler's face had broken open with the biggest grin I'd ever seen. He'd let out a whoop, kissed my mother on top of her head, and physically lifted my father off the ground.

The memory warmed me. But then I thought: *Did he buy drugs after the show? Did he skip it altogether to go shoot up with his friends? Or did all that come later?*

I shoved the ticket stub into my pocket, where my hand brushed against my scissors. They were my constant companion: a pair of little gold embroidery shears shaped like a stork. The blades were his beak, the handles his feathers and feet. The scissors even had a leather sheath that prevented embarrassing injuries. As I looked at all the things Tyler had left behind, I pulled out the shears and turned them over in my hand. *Why the hell not?* I thought. Tyler was gone. Mom had said it herself. Whatever had made these things special was gone with him. And like Mom said, nothing would bring him back.

I started with his clothes, dragging T-shirts and pants out of his dresser drawers and cutting out pieces that spoke to me—the collisions of color, the interesting textures. Everything I didn't want, I threw on the floor. I liked the contrast of my mess against Mom's orderly vacuum tracks, so I knocked down the ticket stubs too. In the closet, I dug around for Tyler's favorite coat, slicing off a big black button and tucking it safely into my pocket. I found a braided lanyard hanging on the back of the closet door, a gift I'd made for him during my one miserable summer at Girl Scout camp. When I touched it, I could almost smell bug repellent and cherry lip gloss, could almost hear the camp songs echoing in my ears. I cut the lanyard in half.

He'd left a glass bowl on one of the shelves, filled with coins and safety pins and other odds and ends. I plucked a metal ball from the bowl. It was about the size of a marble and pitted like a tiny moon. What was it? I couldn't cut it, but I rolled it around in my hand and decided to keep it, too.

When I was through with the closet, I turned to Tyler's bed. He still used the quilt my grandmother had made him, piecing together clothes he'd loved as a kid. I was starting to feel a little dizzy, and I rested one hand on the quilt. I had a sudden mental image of Tyler and me jumping on this very bed, eight and six years old, shrieking at the tops of our lungs. I sank down onto the carpet, breathing heavily. No way was I cutting up the quilt.

This was all too much. My chest heaved; my head spun. *Tyler, Tyler, Tyler.* His name sang through my mind. He was gone, but he was here, hiding inside every object he'd left behind, reflected in a hundred secret mirrors where no one but me would think to look for him.

What about under the bed? I thought. *Did Mom clean under the bed?* I leaned over to look. Plenty of stuff still there. Game cases, hangers, a dirty plate—I tossed them over my shoulder and out into the room. Then my hand closed around Tyler's keys. He'd spent a frantic half hour searching for them on the night that he disappeared. He hadn't found them; he'd been forced to take the spare set. I sat up, thinking, *Oh, good. He'll need these.*

And then I remembered: no. He wouldn't.

And then I started to cry.

My head was pounding, like I'd spent too long upside down. Yellow lights blinked at the edges of my vision, and a bitter smell burned my nose—something harsh, like melting plastic. Just as I realized that something might really be wrong with me, I saw a flash of what looked like Tyler standing in the doorway of his room. But as I slumped to the floor, it was my father's arms that closed around me.

CHAPTER 3

"I STILL THINK WE SHOULD HAVE GOTTEN THE CT scan." My mother's voice filtered through the darkness that surrounded me.

"The doctors said it wasn't necessary," Dad replied, "and Megan didn't want it. She wanted to come home."

I forced one eye open. In the days since my collapse, every sound and sliver of light had driven needles through my brain, but for the moment, my head seemed clear. From my position on the bed, I could barely make out my parents, standing in the doorway of my darkened bedroom. I tried not to move or even breathe, for fear I'd trigger the headache again. No pleasure could be sweeter than this absence of pain.

"They said it was probably a migraine," my father said. "From all the stress."

"She's never had a migraine before."

"Exactly. If it happens again, *then* maybe we have something to worry about."

"Robert, if anything were to happen to her . . ." My mother trailed off, the silence stretching out between them. She leaned back against the doorframe. "I went to that bereavement group this afternoon. The one Detective Johnson suggested? The one for parents."

"So soon? Are you sure?"

"I had to try *something*. I can't sit around, never leaving the house."

My father turned away from her at that, but she kept talking.

"Everyone sat in a circle, and the first woman who spoke, her son was killed by a drunk driver. 'He was a good kid,' the woman said. 'He wasn't in a gang; he wasn't using drugs. He didn't deserve to die.'" Mom paused. "And I thought, *The police are saying my son might have overdosed. Would that mean he* did *deserve to die?* I stood up and walked out." Her voice quaked. "I don't think I can do this."

My father tried to wrap his arms around her, but she shrugged him off and disappeared down the hall. He stood frozen for a moment, his hands still outstretched. Then he followed her.

I forced myself to sit up, and the pain arrowed through my head again. Our family needed Tyler. He smoothed over the rough edges and generally made things all right. He would never have put Mom and Dad through all this pain and confusion. Not on purpose. Not if he could help it. So what had happened?

Tears threatened, burning my nose and the back of my throat. I recalled the moment, scissor sharp in my memory, when Detective Johnson had first told us Tyler was dead. It had seemed impossible that everything could change so completely in an instant, and I'd felt my mind skid into reverse, as though I could step back in time just five seconds and undo what she'd said. But the past is the past. Five seconds ago feels *so close*, but it might as well be five years or five centuries ago. Yesterday is already history.

But tomorrow is a blank page. I still had more of Tyler's objects to examine, more truths to uncover. If I couldn't change the past, maybe I could force it to make sense.

Three days later, I walked into school for the first time since Tyler died—and for the first time ever by myself. In the two years I'd been going to Westside, Tyler had driven me to school every single day, and pushing open those doors without him left me feeling small and vulnerable and abandoned. I came to an abrupt stop in the front hall, where the school's name was blazoned in big letters above the photographs in our alumni hall of fame. These astronauts and elected officials, famous scientists and wealthy entrepreneurs reminded us every day of what Westside High School expected us to achieve. A few months back, someone had painted over the first S in Westside, and even though a fresh S had been installed in days, Tyler still joked about it every morning.

"It's that time again," he'd say.

"What time is it?" I'd be forced to reply.

"Time to take a walk on the Wet Side."

A stupid inside joke. I hadn't given it a second's thought until now, when I stood in the school hallway holding the slack end of a gag that would never be funny again. How was I supposed to navigate my life when even the most ordinary things had the power to take me right back to the way I had felt the moment I lost him?

I reached up to rub the talisman I wore around my neck: the black button I'd cut off Tyler's coat. I'd lacquered the back of it with a triple coat of Frankly Scarlet nail polish I'd taken from my mother's bathroom, creating the backdrop for a mini collage. On a hill made of cut-up ticket stubs, under a sky dotted with flower-petal clouds, a tiny figure set off on a journey. I'd sealed the collage with glue and strung the button on a thin black cord. Now I clutched it in my hand and tried to remember what I wanted to do first. Get Tyler's locker combination from the main office. Then check his locker for more objects. Then, I guess, complete the pointless ritual of going to class?

When I emerged from the main office, I learned the unpleasant truth: I had become some sort of celebrity. All eyes followed me. Boys steered clear, but girls who hadn't spoken to me since middle school found it necessary to grab my arm or pat my hand, sometimes nodding sympathetically, sometimes bursting into tears.

Even worse than the girls I hardly knew were the ones I knew for sure didn't like me. Like Emma Herndon, Tyler's most recent ex-girlfriend. I crossed back past the main doors just in time to see her outside, stepping from a big black town car. As always, her clothes were crisp and unwrinkled, and her hair was aggressively perfect, like she'd walked out of a shampoo ad. I'd seen her on television with her senator father as often as I'd seen her at our house. But today, even from where I stood, her face looked red and splotchy, and her hands were shaking. I stood frozen, watching her.

The driver leaped out and ran around to help her. Barely older than me, he looked like a kid playing dress-up in his navy suit, his skin pale as paste against his tousled dark hair. He fidgeted with his striped tie as he held open Emma's door. She waved him off and hurried instead into the arms of two sympathetic friends. As they walked into the building, the driver followed them.

She stopped and turned to him. "I'm fine, Matty," she said, clearly not fine.

"Well, I'll be here after school to pick you up."

"Hailey can give me a ride."

"Sorry, senator's orders," he said. "And you know what that means."

She blanched, and I remembered what Tyler always used to call Emma's father: the Tyrant. But making sure your grieving kid got home from school safely didn't sound so terrible to me. "Whatever," she said. She walked away from the driver—and straight toward me.

I tried to avoid her by ducking behind a group of guys from the baseball team, all of whom were wearing black armbands with Tyler's jersey number on them. But every head swiveled as I went by, and Emma spotted me.

"Oh my god, Brown!" she called out, rushing over. She rested her forehead on my shoulder, and after a moment, her whole body shook with sobs. This was awkward, to say the least, because my own eyes were bone dry. When she'd dated Tyler, she'd barely spoken to me, but it was hard to resent her now, when she seemed genuinely destroyed. Instead of obeying my natural instinct to smack her hands away, I tried to follow Tyler's most important piece of advice for fitting in at Westside: "Go along to get along." I leaned into her perfumed hug and squeezed back when she held my hand.

"Everything feels wrong without him," she said.

I couldn't muster a response, but she didn't seem to require much input from me. I just nodded and nodded until her pit crew whisked her away.

As I rounded the corner by Tyler's locker, grief prevented me from getting too close. Literally. Other people's grief. An elaborate memorial had built up in the hallway, starting at Tyler's locker and spilling out across the floor. Notes and balloons. Flowers. A cross. Even an American flag. It was like walking headfirst into a wall of mourning. I closed my eyes and concentrated on pulling air into my lungs.

It's a piece of art, I told myself, rubbing Tyler's button. *Like a kitschy postmodern assemblage.* I pushed my way through to the locker. *It's accidental, crowdsourced sculpture,* I repeated to myself, but still, my hands shook.

I cleared off Tyler's locker so I could open it, tucking a few pieces of paper—notes and drawings—into the pockets of the art journal I kept in my bag. *Raw materials,* I thought. *For later.*

As I spun the dial on the lock, the overpowering smell of flowers made my stomach turn, and I felt another headache coming on. The lights overhead seemed to get brighter and brighter, and I struggled to see Tyler's locker combination on the little slip of paper the vice principal had given me. Just as I opened the door, a group of guys pushed past me to get to their lockers.

One of them was Tyler.

Suddenly I was plunged into darkness. I pressed myself closer to the locker, desperate for something solid to hold on to. Had the power gone out? My head swam and my heart galloped in my chest. Had that really been Tyler, or was I imagining things?

Through the darkness, I began to see flashes of light, dim at first, as though I were looking through a pane of glass painted an oily copper green. On the other side of the glass, the flashes illuminated Tyler.

It's him. It's him. It's him. The words echoed in my head.

Tyler's face blurred, then shuddered like old-fashioned film catching in a projector before it started moving again. He reached into his locker and took out a wooden box, a little smaller and flatter than a shoe box. Abraham Lincoln's face was carved into the lid.

Again, darkness. Again, the tidal wave of panic consumed me.

When the sickly green flashes returned, I saw Tyler, and this time, Bobby Drake was standing beside him. My knees began to tremble, and my legs threatened to give way. Tyler threw back his head and laughed, though I heard no sound.

For an instant, his features seemed to shift and change, and I thought I saw another face stretch beneath his skin.

Then the image settled, and he was Tyler again. He opened the wooden box and took out two cigars. Then he reached into his locker and lifted the square of metal that made up the locker floor, putting the cigars underneath. As he slammed the door shut, my knees buckled. I caught myself before I fell, staggering backward a few steps.

With a bang, the power slammed back on, and the fluorescent lights dazzled my eyes. As my vision cleared, I looked around frantically, hoping to see my brother. Afraid I *would* see him, because that would mean something was really wrong with me. But the whole area was empty, and the only sound I heard were voices, far away, echoing down the hall.

My hands shook with the aftermath of adrenaline, and I blew out a shuddery breath. What had just happened? Was that a side effect of the migraine medication? The result of not enough sleep? Maybe Mom had been right. Maybe I should have gotten that CT scan after all. I tilted my head experimentally. It felt foggy and disoriented, but otherwise okay.

Tyler's locker stood open in front of me, full of ordinary, comforting things: textbooks, a jacket, a couple of baseballs. But I couldn't shake the images I'd seen, like that blurry vision of Tyler opening the floor of his locker. I bent down and started dumping his stuff onto the ground by my feet. When the bottom of the locker was clear, sure enough, way at the back, I spotted a tiny indentation in the metal. I inserted my fingernail and pulled, and the floor lifted up. Two cigars sat on the linoleum beneath it, right where Tyler had put them.

In my hallucination.

Beside the cigars lay a few more of those pitted metal marbles like the one I'd found in his bedroom, along with a fat roll of cash, wrapped in a rubber band.

My ears buzzed, and the edges of my vision started closing in. I stumbled and tripped over a stuffed bear, going down hard on my butt and scattering the memorial in all directions.

Someone rushed over and squatted down next to me. "Crapdogs!" he said. "Are you okay?"

"I don't know. I think I might be having a stroke?"

I shook my head to clear it and peered up at Eric Bowling. We'd been friends once, back in junior high, before his dad had gotten sick and he'd missed all that school. When he had finally come back, it had been a whole year since we'd seen each other, and I was kind of afraid to talk to him. I wasn't sure what to say to someone whose dad had just died. The irony of that wasn't lost on me now.

He examined me. "Well, your face doesn't look droopy or anything, and you're talking okay. Can you smile?"

I forced the corners of my mouth upward.

"I don't think you're having a stroke. But you really do look terrible." I shot him a glare. "No offense!" He reached down and helped me back to my feet. Eric had the look of a seasoned nonathlete, like he'd been working for years to build arms that scrawny, but he was stronger than he seemed. And he had an energy about him, as if motion lines trailed his floppy dark hair and quick hands. "So tell me," he went on, "have you been experiencing any blackouts or periods of missing time?"

"I doubt I was abducted by aliens, if that's what you're getting at."

"No, seriously, when my grandfather started having seizures, that was one of the first questions they asked him."

"Seizures?" I swallowed hard. "No. No missing time."

"What about weird smells, like burning rubber? Or maybe oranges?" he asked. "You know, when there aren't any oranges."

I thought about my collapse in Tyler's bedroom—the lights I'd seen, the smell of plastic. "I'm sure it's nothing." I looked him over. "Could you maybe do something for me?"

"What is it?"

"Could you look in that locker and tell me if you see cigars?"

"I don't think you're supposed to have tobacco products on school . . ." He looked. "Nope. Nothing there. Were you having some kind of hallucination?"

"Lift up the floor—it comes out."

Eric did as I asked, a look of delight crossing his face. "A secret compartment? Well, that's awesome. And there they are. Two cigars." He whistled when he saw the money. "And that's not all." He looked up at me. "How did you know they were in there?"

I let out a breath. I could see the next few weeks stretching out in front of me. There would be more doctors, more tests. And then what? What was routine procedure for this kind of thing? I looked at the cigars, then over at Eric. How weird would this really sound?

"So before I opened this locker," I said haltingly, "I had a vision . . . a seizure—whatever you want to call it. I saw my— Well, I saw a lot of things. But I also saw that secret compartment, and those two cigars. And then, when I opened the locker, there they were. For real."

Eric let out a slow breath. "Do you think, maybe . . . I mean . . ." He stopped and tried again. "Maybe you came back to school too soon? Because all that grief and stress can really mess you up."

My stomach clenched. "Maybe. But that doesn't explain how I saw something my brother did when I wasn't even here."

Eric's face brightened. "Wait, check it out, maybe we're not talking about stress or seizures at all," he said. "Maybe we're talking about something else. Maybe we're talking about"—he punctuated his final word with both hands—*"superpowers."*

"O-o-o-okay." I took a step away from him. "And on that note, I have to go." I picked up Tyler's gym bag, which I had brought to carry his things home in, and quickly dumped the contents of his locker into it. Then I grabbed the cigars, the marbles, and the cash, slammed the locker door, and nodded at Eric. "I appreciate the help." I started to walk away.

"Think about it! That's all I'm saying!" he called after me.

I waved good-bye without turning around. *Note to self,* I thought. *Never talk to Eric Bowling again.*

The bag full of things from Tyler's locker never left my side while I suffered through my three morning classes. Finally the bell rang for lunch, and I ducked outside into a wooded spot dotted with picnic tables that were strictly reserved for seniors. Given my newfound celebrity status, no one questioned me. I took out the roll of cash first, my heart heavy in my chest. I couldn't think of a single reason for Tyler to have this—a single good reason, at any rate. I thought him doing drugs was bad, but was he dealing as well?

I removed the rubber band that circled the money and discovered a well-worn pink ticket, the kind you might get at a carnival, which read *Glen Echo Park: Dentzel Carousel. Good for one ride.* The ticket brought back instant memories of summers in the park, watching puppet shows and grinning at my brother from the back of a brightly painted wooden horse. On the other side of the ticket, Tyler had written the name Leigh in black ink.

I set the ticket aside and counted the money. Nearly four thousand dollars, in hundreds and fifties.

Anger burned through me. How could Tyler have been acting so normal and yet been hiding all of this? He had always told me to go along to get along, but I thought that meant with strangers or people you didn't actually like. I never thought he might be playing that game with *me*.

Maybe there was some other explanation for this money, something better than my worst-case imaginings. If anyone would know, it would be Bobby. When the bell rang again, I headed inside to find him.

I didn't have long to wait before he appeared from the between-class crowd. Objectively, I'd have to describe Bobby as tall and gorgeous—the kind of gorgeous that knows precisely how gorgeous it is. He wore jeans and a Yale polo shirt, the one that used to be my favorite: a gorgeous deep azure. Yale blue, he called it, as blue as the blood that ran through his family's four generations of Yalies. He looked straight over my head, and I had to step into his path to get his attention.

"Hey," I said.

"Brown." He stepped neatly around me and kept walking, as if I were the world's easiest obstacle course.

I blew out a long breath and considered abandoning this plan altogether. But I forced my shoulders down and my chin up and followed him to his locker, which was right beside Tyler's. I stood there until he finally looked over at me, running a hand through his mess of curly brown hair. Six months ago, that look would have set my heart racing and scattered my thoughts like loose paper. Six months ago, I was a fool.

"Yeah?" he said.

I held up the cigars I had taken from Tyler's locker. "What are these?"

Bobby's eyes sparked. "Yes!" He plucked them from my hand. "Senator Herndon's Cubans. I thought we were all out." He pulled a box covered with faded labels out of his locker; the cardboard lid read *Paradise* in an elaborate, vintage script. He opened the box and put the two cigars inside, beneath a faded black-and-white picture of a naked woman lying in a hammock.

I did my best to go along, but I couldn't quite pull it off. "You know, that woman is probably somebody's grandmother."

"Well then, she's a total GILF." He traced a finger across the photograph, lingering on the curve of the woman's rear end.

I shuddered. My mind shot back all those months, to the night that marked the end of my crush on Bobby. I remembered the party, remembered drinking three—possibly four—glasses of mystery punch. As for the rest, I was grateful for the gaps in my memory. I had a vague recollection of sitting on Bobby's lap. I remembered the scratch of his jaw against my cheek, the biting scent of his cologne. I wasn't sure exactly what had happened next. Had I kissed him? Had he kissed me? But the sound of his laughter, the way he'd stood up and let me fall to the ground—those things I wouldn't forget. "A little advice," he'd said. "No guy likes it too easy."

I shook off those thoughts and tried to focus on the task at hand. "I found some other stuff, in Tyler's locker." I took the carousel ticket out of my bag and showed Bobby the writing on the back. "Do you know anything about—"

He laughed. "That girl was so pathetic."

"What girl?"

"Her dad was a rent-a-cop who used to work here." He snorted. "She would gladly have given Tyler a ride on *her* carousel, if you know what I mean."

I knew what he meant. "But Tyler didn't like her?"

"He liked getting into the school with her dad's access key."

I pulled out the roll of money, shielding it with my body so it wasn't visible to everyone in the hallway. "When I found the ticket, it was attached to *this*."

Bobby's face shifted, and for a second, I saw anger in his eyes. "Yeah, that's mine," he said, and he reached for the cash.

I tucked it in my bag before he could touch it. "So where did it come from?"

"We— I earned it."

I gave him a look.

"That's all you need to know." He held up a hand. "Wait, the ticket with her name on it was with the money?" Bobby shook his head, his mouth a thin line. "Oh, Red, you little shit."

"But how did he—" I stopped talking as a jolt of pain arced upward from my eye, shot across my skull, and settled behind my ear. I clutched at my head and leaned back against the lockers with a thud. Fear sank its claws into my chest. What was going on? Was something really wrong with me?

"You okay?" Bobby was standing way too close.

"Fine." I scooted away from him. "I've got to go."

He didn't try to stop me as I pushed off the lockers and headed for the nurse's office. "Seriously, though," he called after me. "That money is mine."

I didn't turn around.

I told the nurse it was my stomach. I didn't mention that I probably had a brain tumor, or tell her about the migraine or the weird smells. I didn't say it was existential angst, brought on by questioning everything I ever knew about my brother. And I didn't tell her that I was hallucinating things that weren't real but were somehow . . . true.

When my dad arrived to pick me up, I dragged myself into the passenger seat, glancing over at him. He looked as bad as I felt. His red hair, darker than Tyler's, stuck up in thin, crazy tufts in the back, and he wore a Saturday sweatshirt and jeans, even though it was Tuesday.

"Are you okay, Dad?"

"That's supposed to be my line."

"I mean, aren't you teaching today?"

Dad scrubbed his face with his hand. "I didn't want to worry you. But I decided I'm not going back to George Mason this semester."

"What about your classes? It's only April."

"Some colleagues are covering my classes," he said. "I tried to go back. But I couldn't do it. You know Mom; it's good for her to be at work. Just try to keep her away. But me . . ." He sighed, and the sound set my stomach churning. I thought he'd stayed home with me after my collapse because *I* was sick, but maybe he'd been there because *he* was. "I hope I'll be okay to teach again in the fall," he said. "I mean, I will. I will be okay." He looked over at me. "What about you? Is it your head?"

I couldn't look him in the eye. "No. It was all . . . too overwhelming, you know?"

"Do you want to tell me about it?"

I stared at his tired blue eyes and the one reddish tuft that stuck straight up on top of his head. He looked like a little boy whose parents had dragged him out of bed for school and forgotten to comb his hair.

Tyler would know exactly what joke to make at this moment. He'd know whether to suggest a run to the batting cages or whether to make Dad his famous three-layer Jell-O surprise. "No. I'm okay." I rubbed Tyler's button on the cord around my neck. I wanted to go straight home and hide under my covers forever, but didn't our family need a Tyler?

"Hey, Dad? Want to get some coffee at Greenberry's on the way home?"

Dad reached over and squeezed my hand.

I smiled for him and tried to make him laugh with our long-standing joke about the word "macchiato." But the stone in my chest grew heavier and heavier, and when I finally got back to my room, I slumped into the chair at my worktable, unable to stand.

I rested my forehead on the rough, paint-stained surface and forced air into my lungs. After a few breaths, I reached for my backpack, digging through it for the notes and cards I'd taken from Tyler's locker. I tried not to read them, blurring my eyes to everything but the color and shape of the words, but a few stood out: "friend," "miss," "soon," "Tyler." I pulled out my scissors and started cutting. The shapes looked like flower petals, long and elegant, so I made leaves out of them, coating each piece with watercolors to dim the knife-edged words. By the time I could breathe freely again, I had a tiny bouquet of paper lilies, each one graceful and sorrowful and mine.

CHAPTER 4

THAT NIGHT I CURLED UNDER THE COVERS WEARING my warmest flannel pajamas, bone weary and cold all over. My phone chirped, and I brought it into bed with me. Elena had sent a picture of the *Goonies* movie poster.

Feel like a watch-along? she wrote.

We can spend the whole movie texting. . . .

Sorry, I wrote.

It's been a day.

No apologies, she wrote back.

What flavor of day?

You know. The usual.

Human sacrifice.

Dogs and cats, living together.

Mass hysteria.

Whoa. Ghostbusters day.

That's not effing around.

There will be stories.

I hope so.

Later.

I'll be here.

I rested my phone on the pillow beside me and watched the video of me and Tyler that Nathan had sent for maybe the dozenth time. At first, it had seemed so sweet, but the more I watched it, the more it troubled me. I had no idea he'd recorded our guitar lessons. In some shots I'd been wearing school clothes, but in others, I was in ratty pajama bottoms and a T-shirt with no bra. And he'd put me out there for anyone to see, with no warning, without asking. He clearly valued his own privacy, but didn't he think I deserved the same?

And when had he even started a YouTube channel? Had he considered himself an amateur filmmaker, or was he just trying to get internet famous like everyone else with a cell-phone camera?

When the video ended, the screen bounced back to Nathan's original message, and I could see his picture, small and smiling, beside the link that he had sent. I clicked on the photo, and Nathan's face filled the screen. I studied the curve of his chin and the shadow in the hollow of his cheek, tinged with a hint of violet.

How had Nathan known my brother? How well? For how long? I replayed our two short conversations in my mind, wincing at every awkward, rude comment I'd made, and I remembered that he'd asked if Tyler had shown me "the videos."

As in more than one.

I sat up in bed and clicked on Tyler's YouTube username, TwoRedCents, but I didn't see any other videos on the channel.

Well, maybe Nathan had more he could share.

I sat up and quickly typed out a message. More videos, I wrote, and hit send.

Ugh. Ugh ugh ugh. No matter what Elena said, I was terrible at thinking first. My fingers practically tripped over one another trying to correct my mistake.

I mean, are there more videos?

And if so please send?

Videos of Tyler.

Not videos of you.

No offense.

I'd definitely watch videos of you.

I smacked myself in the forehead with the phone. *Oh my god, stop hitting send!* Before I could figure out a plan for damage control, he wrote back.

Best series of msgs ever.

Thanks.

My fingers hovered over the screen, and my mind raced through a dozen possible responses, but I didn't type any of them. After a long pause, Nathan texted again.

No more videos. That I know of.

But how are you? You okay?

I let myself fall back onto the pillow. Did Nathan know anything about the money in Tyler's locker? I didn't want to bring it up over text—I wanted to see his face when I asked him.

Or maybe I just wanted to see his face.

Lots of questions, I wrote. Can we talk? A blast of nerves shot through my stomach, and I couldn't quite tell if I was excited or terrified. In person?

Sure, I guess so.

Tomorrow? Here? Or I can come to you.

Another pause, and then he wrote back: *In a hurry, huh?*

I buried my face in my hands. This whole exchange had been beyond humiliating. Before I could tell him to forget the whole thing, he wrote:

Tomorrow might work. Your place. If I can.

Great, I replied, trying for casual. See you then.

My mom dropped me off at school the next morning, and I walked through the parking lot with the carousel ticket clasped in my fingers, turning it over and over until the paper felt soft as fabric. I was on the lookout for Leigh Barry, the only Leigh I could find in last year's yearbook. It wasn't much to go on, but I was going on anyway.

A car horn sounded, and Eric Bowling pulled up beside me in a little blue Geo Metro that must have been twenty years old. He rolled down his window and hooked one elbow out.

"Well, well, well! Exactly the person I was looking for!"

I kept walking.

"I wanted to talk to you," he said, driving slowly alongside me. "You know, about yesterday. The *incident*"—he managed to italicize the word with his voice—"by the lockers?"

He waited for some response. I offered none.

"You know which *incident* I mean?"

I stopped walking and turned to him. "Yes. I know which *incident* you mean. The *incident* was fairly memorable to me."

"Anyhow," he went on, "I think we should talk. I've taken the liberty of preparing some research for you to look at." He glanced around to make sure no one could hear us. "It's to help you figure out your next step. You know, as you move forward with your powers."

"What is your *problem*? I do not have . . ." I dropped my voice to a whisper. "I am not some kind of superhero."

He smiled. "Isn't that exactly what a superhero *would* say?"

"You are infuriating. Has anyone ever told you that?"

"Oh, yes," he said. "You, personally, used to tell me that all the time." It didn't sound like an accusation, but still, I felt a pang of guilt for not doing more to stay in touch with Eric. "Now back to the subject at hand. There are a lot of things you should consider." He reached into his backpack and pulled out a three-ring binder. "I thought about what happened to you, and I decided what you basically did was See the Past." The phrase "See the Past" got verbal capitals and its own hand gesture. "So I made a list of some local experts who can do that, in different ways. I also pulled some articles and information about each one."

"You did all that *last night*?"

"Sure. You can take a look if you want." He offered me the binder.

I started walking again.

"Or I could just tell you." He pulled the car forward to keep up with me. "There's that famous psychic, Denise Chambers? She used to live in Phoenix, but I looked for her in property sales records and figured out that she lives in Virginia now. Not far from here. She wrote a ton of books about how she helped the police by communicating with murder victims. And there's this other woman, Rebecca Tattenbaum; she runs an antique shop on Capitol Hill, and rumor has it the building is haunted—"

"Sorry," I said, cutting him off. "Thanks but no thanks." I ducked between two parked cars and made a beeline for the main doors.

* * *

I spotted Leigh Barry at lunchtime, eating at a table with a couple of other girls. Anxiety curled in my stomach as I watched them. If there was anything I hated more than talking to people, it was talking to *new* people. I reached up and tugged at my hair. Tyler had always acted like talking to people was easy. It was *supposed* to be easy. I mean, it was called small talk. The word "small" was right there in the name. So why did it feel so massive and unmanageable instead?

Leigh didn't look particularly intimidating. She wore a rose-pink cardigan over a ratty gray band shirt—the kind that was genuinely worn out, not the kind most Westsiders seemed to have, the ones that cost more because you bought them prefaded. Her pale hair hung down her back in two long braids, and when she laughed, she turned her face toward the ceiling and let out an oversize "Ha!" I waited for her friends to leave before approaching her table.

"Um . . . hi! Leigh, right?"

Behind her rectangular glasses, Leigh's eyelashes were so pale they nearly glowed. "That's me." She flashed a bright smile. "What's up?"

She had no idea who I was. Not a promising beginning.

"I'm Megan. Megan Brown? I'm—"

I watched the surprise and recognition move across her face, and her smile collapsed. "Oh, you're Red's sister." She looked around, as though hoping for reinforcements. "Are you . . . I mean, is there anything you need?"

A double scoop of the salted caramel ice cream from Larry's, I thought, but I stopped myself. *Go along to get along.* I mustered a smile. "No, thanks." I'd been practicing a few smooth, casual questions about Tyler that I could ask, but now that the moment was upon me, my brain was having trouble sending signals to my mouth. I sat down next to Leigh and pulled the ticket out of my pocket. I turned it so she could see her own name on the back. "Do you recognize this?"

She let out a little hum, and her hand went to her mouth, but I could see that she was smiling. I'd found the right girl.

I slid the ticket across the table toward her. "You guys were friends?"

Her mouth went hard. "I thought so."

"What happened?"

She let out a harsh laugh. "Um, the baseball team's senior prank happened."

A few months ago, Tyler and his teammates had broken into the school and set up a Slip 'N Slide, complete with sprinklers, right outside the principal's office. But what did that have to do with Leigh?

Leigh stood and reached for her backpack. "Anyway, if you want to know more about it, talk to Bobby Drake." She spit out his name like bad milk. "I'm sure he'll brag for days."

"Oh, god," I shot back without thinking. "Please don't make me talk to *him* again."

She stopped with her bag over one shoulder and stared at me for a second. Then she busted out a laugh and sat down again.

"Listen," she said, "it was my own fault. I helped them get into the building. Red said it was no big deal. And I believed him." She sighed and picked up the carousel ticket. "He just lit things up, you know? Like Christmas every day." Her chin crumpled, but she didn't cry.

Her emotion washed through me. Then I remembered: Bobby had said that Leigh's dad *used to* work here.

"The prank . . . did your dad lose his job over it?"

One harsh nod from Leigh. "Because he took the blame for the missing access key. He covered for *me.*"

I thought about the roll of money in Tyler's locker, and the pieces fell into place in my mind. He'd been saving the money for Leigh, because he felt bad about her father. I unzipped my backpack and took out the roll of cash.

"When I found that ticket, it was attached to this." I held it out to Leigh, but she recoiled as though I'd offered her a spider. I tried again. "Seriously. I think he meant it for you."

She pushed my hand away. "Yeah, he tried to pay me off months ago. And I told him I didn't want his guilt money."

"I'm sure he wanted to do what was right."

"No, Tyler just wanted to be the good guy. He couldn't accept that this time—he wasn't. He was the bad guy. And he couldn't talk his way out of it. Or buy his way out of it. But that's how all of you think."

I shook my head. "All of us?"

"My dad took this job in the first place so I could go to this *amazing* school." Her voice was laced with sarcasm. "But it didn't take me long to figure out that everyone who goes here is, like, Richie Rich, and they have no concept of what real life is like. Or they *feel sorry* for me."

"I don't—" I began.

"Save it." She shook her head. "Do you even realize how messed up this place is? I mean, sixteen-year-olds get cars that cost more than my dad used to make in a year. And those weekly assemblies where they announce who got into what fancy college? It's like they're actually *trying* to rub it in."

"Yeah, those assemblies suck," I tried.

But Leigh wasn't listening. "So I'll tell you what I told your brother: I don't want your charity. I feel sorry for *you*, for living in this privileged little bubble and having no idea what life is like in the real world."

As she grabbed her backpack, I sat stunned, tears in my eyes.

She looked back at me, and I watched her realize that I was the girl whose brother had just died. Her shoulders sagged, and her face twisted into a wince. "Aw, fuck," she said. "I'm really sorry. I'm really . . ." She dashed away without finishing her sentence, leaving me once again the center of curious stares from everyone in the room.

I shoved the money back into my bag. Leigh's words stung, because there was truth to what she'd said. This school was an unforgiving place for people who weren't on the "right track," or who didn't fit into the Westside mold. And no matter how harmless Tyler might have thought that team prank was, he had used Leigh. He'd hurt her, and he'd hurt her family. I understood why he'd been looking for any way to make it right. But even if that's what the money was *for*, I still didn't know where it was *from*, or how Tyler and Bobby had managed to "earn" more than four thousand dollars.

I watched Leigh's braids flying as she disappeared through the cafeteria doors. I took out my art journal and did a quick sketch of her in pen: her head thrown back, laughing full out at the sky.

When Dad and I came home that night with Chinese takeout for dinner, Detective Johnson was sitting at our kitchen table.

Her leather jacket hung over the back of a chair, and a knotty black tattoo peeked out from under the cuff of her white dress shirt. My mother perched on a barstool, just back from her evening run, her hair in a sweaty ponytail and her posture rigid and stiff. Johnson looked up when I came through the door, and her keen eyes met mine.

I glanced at my bag, as though she could see the roll of cash right through the canvas. Should I tell Detective Johnson about the money? It felt disloyal, somehow, like ratting Tyler out, but on the other hand, why should I keep it a secret?

Mom turned and spotted me, and her body immediately relaxed. She held out a hand, and I walked to stand beside her.

"Detective Johnson is here," she said unnecessarily.

"Detective Johnson is leaving." The officer pulled on her jacket, and relief washed over me. "But I do have a question for Megan before I go."

I sank down on a stool next to my mother, letting my bag thunk to the floor at my feet. Mom rested a hand on my arm. Her fingers were trembling, and I curled my hand around hers.

"We're investigating the possibility that Tyler was at a party in northeast DC the week before he died," Johnson said. "Not far from where his body was found."

"A party?" I shook my head, confused. On one level, it made sense. Tyler at a party—that always made sense. Part of his plan to make sure I fit in at Westside—or at least got by—was to drag me to a lot of excruciating parties. But I'd never heard him talk about going to one in DC. "Is that bad?"

"Not necessarily. But if he went to that neighborhood regularly, to meet with friends, that might help us understand what Tyler was doing there the night he was found."

"Did you know anything about this party, Megan?" my father asked. "You can tell us. You don't have to protect him."

I don't? I thought. *But that's what he would have done for me.*

But then I paused.

At least, I think he would.

Mom's hand tightened in mine. She hated the police asking me questions. She might call that "being protective," but to me, it felt like babying, as though she thought my poor childlike brain would be scarred by the harsh facts of the police investigation. Mom and Dad would shuffle Detective Johnson out the front door as fast as they could. But Johnson might know things about Tyler that I didn't, and as long as she was still here, maybe I could do some investigating of my own.

"I went to some parties with Tyler," I said. "Where was it? I mean, do you have the address?"

Johnson looked a bit suspicious, but she pulled up the information on her phone and showed it to me. "Well?"

I repeated the address in my head a few times so I would remember it, then shook my head. "No. It's not familiar."

Johnson cocked her head to one side and gave me the eye. "We're looking for whoever sold him the drugs. Depending on the toxicology results, we may be able to charge them in Tyler's death." She stared at me for a few more moments, but when I didn't speak, she just nodded and turned to shake my father's hand. "All right. You have my number if there's anything else you need."

"Wait! I have a question for you." I could feel my mother stiffen beside me as I spoke.

Johnson paused, her gaze shifting between my parents. Whatever she saw in their faces didn't deter her. "Go ahead."

"The police officer who found Tyler's body," I said, "why did he go into that building in the first place?"

"You don't know?"

I shook my head.

"We got an anonymous call." She shrugged slightly. "We're investigating that as well. There may have been someone with him who was afraid to stay and face the authorities."

It turned my stomach to think that somewhere in the world, there might be a person who knew exactly what happened to Tyler, who might even have been with him when he died. Someone who wasn't coming forward.

My father stood, bringing the conversation to an end. "I'll walk you to the door, detective."

Mom also rose to her feet, formal and polite in every circumstance. "Thank you again for bringing Tyler's things."

"Not a problem," Johnson replied. She gave me one last searching look before disappearing with my father down the hall.

I turned to my mother. "Tyler's things?"

She picked up a clear plastic bag, the size of a kitchen trash bag. A jumble of random objects shifted inside as she set it down on the countertop. "Tyler's personal effects," she said. "Stuff from his car, and the things they found with his . . ." She trailed off. *His body,* I thought with a sharp pang.

"His cell phone?"

"Missing."

I reached for the bag, then stopped myself as a thought occurred to me. "Wait, so if they're returning all this stuff to us, does this mean they're done investigating? Is that the end of it?"

She closed her eyes and shook her head. Her expression didn't change, but the twitch in her cheek betrayed her.

You're making it harder for her, I thought. I remembered the look on her face when she had told my dad about the support group, and how she'd walked away when he tried to comfort her. She wanted to pretend all this had been an accident, and she wasn't going to let us convince her otherwise. I bit down hard on the side of my tongue and said nothing. The two of us stood together for a moment, staring at the plastic bag.

Part of me thought, *Let it go.* But only part of me.

"Do you mind if I take a look?"

She opened her eyes again. "Go ahead." I reached for the bag, but she took my arm. "You'll talk to me, right? If there's anything going on? Anything you need?"

"Sure, Mom." I grabbed hold of the bag and edged free from her grip. "I'll talk to you."

Instead of going to my own room, I headed instinctively for Tyler's. I sat down on his bed and upended the bag, spilling the contents out onto the quilt. All these things might hold his secrets: *The True History of Tyler Brown in Seven Objects.* Or they might only amount to a pile of junk. I pushed aside a blue sweatshirt and some crumpled receipts, and finally, at the bottom of the pile, I uncovered a wooden box with Abraham Lincoln's head carved into the lid.

It was the same box I'd seen in my hallucination, when I had almost passed out by Tyler's locker. My pulse sped up, and my mouth went dry. The box was *real.* And it had been with him when he died.

I sat staring at it for a few moments. It was far more elaborate than I remembered, and I felt drawn to it in a way I couldn't explain. Ornate metal feet curled around the bottom corners of the box, and a brass clasp held it closed. The lid was intricately carved with curves and scrolls surrounding a central diamond shape, which framed Lincoln's head. His face was in profile, like on the penny. He had the usual beard, but his hair was swept up and away from his forehead in a cool wooden pompadour. He looked like the James Dean of Abe Lincolns.

I reached out to run a fingertip over the scrollwork on the lid.

As soon as I touched it, a sharp heat seared across the center of my forehead. I jerked my hand back and rubbed at the pain, squinting at the box through narrowed eyes. I could hear my own breath, jagged and uneven, far too loud in the quiet room. My mind raced. What was going on?

Still gripping my forehead with one hand, I stretched the other out slowly. If I touched the box again, would the same thing happen? Before my trembling fingers made contact with the wood, I stopped myself. If this was really happening to me, I should proceed carefully. Methodically.

I went through all the other objects from the bag, handling each one carefully, but nothing unusual happened. Finally only the box was left. I stared at it for a moment, looking for answers in Lincoln's face, but he gazed inscrutably into the distance.

No more excuses, no more delays. I took a deep breath and seized the box in both hands. The pain drilled into me again, as though my head were splitting in half. It felt like the headache I had gotten before—turned up to eleven. I rocked backward onto the bed, still clutching the box, swamped by waves of nausea that barreled through me, one after the other. Somewhere beyond the pain, I could hear a rush of sound, words so indistinct I couldn't make them out. At the edges of my vision, shadowy figures moved across a black and threatening landscape. I dropped the box and grabbed at my head with my hands, but the crushing ache did not fade.

What was happening to me? The fear overwhelmed even the pain, as I started to think again about all those scenarios that didn't involve superpowers. Things like brain trauma. And cancer. And aneurysms.

I needed help. Wincing against the sudden, overwhelming brightness of the room, I staggered to the door. As I stepped out into the hallway, I saw a figure coming up the stairs. Tyler?

"No . . . I can't . . ." I stumbled backward to escape the vision descending on me.

But this vision actually caught me before I hit the ground. It had strong arms and big chunky eyeglasses and smelled so good I wanted to cry.

"Nathan?"

I lost my balance, my eyes burning with tears of relief. Nathan dropped awkwardly to the rug with me half on his lap.

"Hey, hey, what's wrong?" he asked, still cradling me.

"Thank god you're real," I whispered.

"Okay, let me get your parents. They're right downstairs. They told me to come up."

"No! Please. I'm fine." I tried to untangle myself, but he tightened his arms around me, scrutinizing my face.

"You don't look fine."

"Get my painkillers. Please."

"Are you sure you don't want me to get—"

I grabbed a handful of his shirt. "No. Just help me? Please?"

He searched my eyes for a moment. "Okay," he said. "Where are your pills?"

"Bathroom." I tried to pull myself up. "Prescription bottle."

"Easy there. Sit a minute." He unwound himself from my body and headed down the hall. Without his warmth, I began to shiver. He brought me the migraine meds the doctor had prescribed, along with a glass of water, and I managed to choke down two tablets.

"Do you need to lie down?"

I nodded, and he hooked an arm around my waist to help me up. We stumbled down the hall to my room, where I kicked off my shoes and collapsed onto the bed.

Nathan looked around, his eyes going to the old drafting table I used as a workspace for my art. I liked to mix media, combining paint and fabric and paper, and all those supplies lay scattered across the table: acrylics, watercolors, and oils; Mod Podge and colored tissue; tiny triangles of paper in a dozen colors that I hadn't bothered to sweep away. I had tacked a few finished collages on a corkboard above the table, and Nathan's eyes lingered on them. They looked so small and vulnerable up there, and I half expected him to say, "You think you're some kind of artist? Who do you think you're fooling, Brown Brown?"

"So." I forced out a laugh that sounded more like a cough. "You made it. Thanks for coming by."

"Listen," he said, "I'm gonna go."

"Wait." The back of my head still ached, and Nathan looked blurry around the edges. He tugged nervously at the bottom of his shirt, a short-sleeved black button-down with white panels in the front. He looked like he'd spent the afternoon bowling—in 1964.

I knew I should let him leave before I did something embarrassing, like passing out or throwing up all over him, but I wasn't sure I had the guts to ask him to meet with me again. And I needed to figure out if he was one of those people Detective Johnson was looking for . . . the ones who knew more about Tyler's death than they were telling.

"My backpack," I said. "It's in Tyler's room. Would you get it for me?" He returned with it in a matter of seconds. "The front pouch. Pull out what's in there."

Nathan reached into my bag and came out with the roll of money. He held it up and turned to me, wide-eyed. "Holy shit, Megan. What are you into?"

My snort of laughter left me gripping my forehead in pain. "It's not mine. It's Tyler's."

Nathan didn't respond. He turned the money over and over in his hands, a deep crease between his eyebrows. Finally he looked back at me. "I don't get it. What was he . . ." Sadness flickered across his face, and he blew out a deep breath to steady himself.

My heart lurched toward him in that moment, and the rest of me wanted to follow. I didn't know whether to be disappointed or relieved that he had no idea where the money had come from.

He held up the roll. "That detective said drugs. Heroin. You think this is related?"

"I don't know."

"'Cause this doesn't look like buying. This looks like dealing." He sat down on the edge of my bed.

"I know." I stared at his hand, which rested a few inches from mine. My vision clouded over again, and I could feel myself getting woozy. I wasn't sure if it was the migraine meds or some kind of aftereffect from the pain, but I was going to pass out, and soon. Even if Nathan couldn't explain the money, I still wanted some answers.

"How did you meet my brother?"

Nathan glanced back over at my artwork. "Oh, you know, the usual places."

"Was it at a party? A party in DC?"

His eyes were back on me in a second, and I felt like he was sizing me up. "I should go."

I grabbed his hand as he stood to leave. "Are you a liar?" I asked.

He froze, his hand still in mine, and he didn't answer.

"Because you don't seem like a liar. You seem like someone who cared about my brother. But then, I've been known to have really bad judgment."

After a moment, Nathan let go of my hand and sat back down. "Yeah," he said. "We met at a party."

"Did he go to a lot of parties in DC?"

"A few."

I tried to concentrate, but the thoughts kept slipping away from me. "Why didn't he ever take me with him?"

Nathan shook his head, rubbing his hands on his thighs. "It's a long story."

I let my head fall back onto the pillow. "I'm not going anywhere." But the dizziness was getting worse. My stomach turned, and I could barely keep my eyes open.

"DC has a curfew. If you're under seventeen, you can't be out after eleven. So a lot of the parties are underground."

"Like in someone's basement?"

Nathan snorted. "Not literally underground. They throw them in businesses after hours, or in closed-up buildings."

I fought to keep talking. "So Tyler was sneaking out and driving across state lines to break the law and dance in a boarded-up building?"

"Pretty much, yeah."

I gave in to the vertigo and let my eyes drift shut. "I'm listening. Keep talking."

Nathan took my hand in his. His thumb drifted across my knuckles, warm and comforting. And that was the last thing I remembered.

CHAPTER 5

I WOKE WITH A START, DISORIENTED, IN PITCH-darkness. Through bleary eyes, I checked the clock on my nightstand. It was four a.m. Nathan was gone.

My headache had faded, but I still wore my clothes from the day before, and by the time I had peeled off my stiff, wrinkled jeans, I was wide-awake. I pulled on a robe and padded out into the hallway. My parents' door was ajar, and I could hear the muffled sounds of late-night talk radio.

My father had always been very opposed to watching television or even reading in bed. He had a firm policy about such things: "No shortcuts, no crutches." Relying on coffee to wake you up in the morning or music to put you to sleep at night—those were lazy habits, he always said. And lazy habits made lazy minds.

But that was before.

Now we needed all the help we could get. Anything to ease us through the days, to shorten the endless hours. As I got closer to their door, I could hear someone crying inside their room, so softly that I couldn't even tell which one of them it was. I leaned my back against the wall and slid down to sit on the carpet. Were they huddled together in there, comforting each other? Or was one of them crying into a pillow so the other one wouldn't hear?

I hugged my legs tightly to my chest and tucked my face into my knees. I knew I shouldn't keep listening, but somehow the sound kept me company, made me feel less alone. Sorrow tugged on me again, calling me down to where everything was cold and dark. I was drowning, and I dug my fingernails into the skin of my legs, trying to give myself something to hold on to. My body felt thick with exhaustion. Moving seemed impossible, but staying still was unbearable. I forced myself to my feet and back to my room, where I sat on the floor, my back leaning against the bed.

When I closed my eyes, I could see Abraham Lincoln's face, just as it had looked on the lid of that wooden box. With one touch, it had knocked me flat. This made it official: what I'd experienced by Tyler's locker was not a fluke, something brought on by grief and stress and migraine medication. I was really seeing images—and suffering pain—when I touched some of Tyler's belongings. It had started that night when I trashed his room, when I collapsed and thought I saw him in the doorway. It had happened again in the hallway at school. But this box took things to a whole new level.

So why did Tyler have a Lincoln box? Our dad was the history buff in the family, not Tyler. But maybe he had it because he was so obsessed with that book about John Wilkes Booth.

The book.

Heart pounding, I dug around under my bed until I found it. I flipped to the back cover and studied David Brightman's author bio. It described his education and two lofty-sounding awards, ending with the sentence: "Dr. Brightman works in the division of political history at the Smithsonian's National Museum of American History."

The Smithsonian? That was right across the river in DC. Maybe I could email the guy and see if he could tell me something about the box, something that might be important.

Maybe Tyler had even done the same.

I went online to find an email address for Dr. Brightman, but there was no sign of him on the staff page at the American History museum. If he had worked there when his book had been published, he didn't seem to work there anymore. I tried a general search on his name, but all I got was review after review of his book, which had apparently been very popular. No sign of where he worked now or how to get in touch with him.

I rubbed at my eyes. I could feel an ominous headache starting to build again. I wasn't going to be able to spend hours on the computer trying to track down one random guy who might have moved anywhere in the country by now. Who had the patience for that kind of research, or the ability?

And then it hit me: I knew who.

The next day, after the final bell, I headed to the parking lot to hunt down Eric Bowling's car. Luckily for me, it was both brightly colored and junky and therefore stood out in the crowd of white BMWs and silver Mercedeses. I leaned against the hood, hoping he didn't have some kind of club after school. But a few minutes later, I spotted him. These days, he sported a backpack on wheels, which made him look a bit like a flight attendant rushing for a plane. He wheeled his way through the narrow spaces between the cars.

I didn't wait for him to speak. "Come have coffee with me."

He just stared.

"Coffee," I spoke slowly this time. "With me." Maybe I wasn't being clear enough. "I want to go someplace and talk. I need a favor."

He held my gaze for a moment before he answered. "Can I go through my research binder with you on the way?"

I considered this for a moment. "No."

"It was worth a try." He reached into his pocket for his keys. "Whenever you're ready." As we got into the car, he set his backpack on the console between us. The bag was decorated with a scattering of little pink and purple jewels.

I eyed it. "Sparkly."

He shrugged. "Katie strikes again." His little sister had been in preschool the last time I'd seen her. "She got a Bedazzler for her birthday. Everything we own is now covered in them." He pulled out the same three-ring binder I'd seen earlier and set it on top of the backpack, patting it with a smile. "In case you change your mind." He started the car. "Where to?"

"Cemetery Starbucks?"

"Yes, ma'am."

The Cemetery Starbucks had earned its name from the little green hill in the parking lot with two faded tombstones on it. The spot had once been a family graveyard, but as the years passed, a strip mall had sprung up around it. The family wouldn't sell the land, so Armistead Thompson and Amana Abigail Tobin—and the others whose stones had been lost or stolen long ago—shared their final resting place with three banks, two nail salons, and Lo's

Szechuan. And a Starbucks, of course.

Coffee cups in hand, Eric and I dropped our bags under a tree and walked over to the gravestones. It had never seemed like a strange place to hang out, just kitschy, a little piece of Old Virginia peeking through the new. But now, as I read the familiar inscriptions, I didn't think about the dead but the people they had left behind.

Amana had died in 1904, when she was twenty-eight. Her stone held her name, her dates of birth and death, and a single line: *The lost in sight are to memory dear.* Armistead's life had been more colorful. According to his tombstone, he had fought for the South during the Civil War, was captured at Gettysburg, and died at twenty-seven, after spending more than a year in a Union prison camp. His marker also featured a poem, which began:

Mouldering though thy body be
Yet in our dreams thy form we see.

A chill shot through me. *Thy form we see.*

You, too? I thought.

These stones didn't commemorate long lives and easy good-byes. They held the grief-stricken cries of parents who longed to see their children one last time. I made my way gingerly over the grass, conscious of what lay beneath, and joined Eric, who was sitting on his research binder.

He finally asked the question I'd been waiting for. "I'm guessing this is about your brother?"

My breath hitched in my chest, and I nodded.

"I won't say I know how you feel, but I do know this: it sucks."

I cracked a tiny smile. As far as I was concerned, "it sucks" beat "I'm sorry" any day.

Eric took a sip of coffee before he spoke again. "I keep thinking about that time when you and I were in the sixth grade, and we were all hanging out at the club pool, and Tyler snuck into the room with the audio equipment. Do you remember?"

I shook my head.

"Come on, you have to remember. He figured out how to work the PA system, and he made it blast that old Pink song?"

The memory popped into my mind, as whole and complete as if it had happened yesterday, and I had to smile. "Oh, god. 'Get the Party Started.'"

"And then while everyone at the pool was standing around confused, he strutted on out, climbed up the high dive, and did that awesome flip. I thought he was the coolest person ever." Eric grinned. "But you know what I remember most? After pulling that killer stunt, he spent the rest of the day hanging out with *us*."

The ache in my chest was bittersweet. *Nothing will ever be that fun again,* I thought. It felt incredibly selfish and petty to be sad about that, about all the fun we wouldn't have together, but there it was.

Eric shook his head. "That's why, when I hear the things people are saying about him—"

"What are people saying?"

Judging by the look on Eric's face, my tone had been harsher than I intended. He paused. "I'm sorry, I shouldn't have . . . Are you sure you want me to tell you?"

I nodded.

Eric shifted on his binder. "A few people told me he got killed when a building collapsed on him. A guy in my world history class said he knew *for absolute certain* that Tyler was shot. I think most people are waiting for someone official to say what happened one way or the other."

I let out the breath I'd been holding. "Aren't you going to ask *me* what happened?"

"What? No, I would never presume to—"

"He overdosed. On heroin."

Eric's whole body froze. "No way. How is that possible?"

"That's what I'm trying to figure out."

"Whoa," he said. "So what do you need from me?"

"I need to find this guy." I pulled out Dr. Brightman's book and showed Eric the bio on the back cover. "It says here he works at the Smithsonian, but I don't think that's true. Or at least, I couldn't find any record of him."

"Okay," Eric said. "I'm sure I can do that. Do you mind if I ask why?"

I flipped through the pages, showing Eric the writing inside. "Tyler was really into his book for some reason. Plus, there was a box—a wooden box with Abraham Lincoln's picture on it—in the bag of things the police gave us. The things that were with Tyler when he . . ." I trailed off. "I want to find out whether it's important. And whether it's got anything to do with what happened to him."

My phone beeped, and I fished it out of my bag. Eric craned his neck to see the screen. "Who's Nathan Lee?"

"A friend of my brother's. From DC." I shielded the phone from Eric so he couldn't see Nathan's text.

Hey. How are you? Better I hope.

As I was reading, a second text came in.

Didn't get a chance to tell you, but your art is rockin it.

I smiled. I may even have blushed.

"A friend of Tyler's who makes you smile," Eric said. "I like him already."

I turned off the screen and met Eric's eye. "And back to the box."

"Of course, the box," he said, a smile lurking around the corners of his mouth. "What's it for, do you know? Papers?"

I thought about the flashes I'd seen at Tyler's locker, and about the cigars that Bobby had taken from me. "I think it's a cigar box."

"That's right, you had those cigars the other day, when you freaked out in the hallway."

"I did not freak out in the hallway."

"Okay, when you had a supernatural episode in the hallway. Better?"

"Not better." *But probably accurate,* said a little voice in my head.

"Well, you describe it, then."

"I can't." I huffed out a breath. "I only know I've started seeing things when I touch certain objects. Like when I touched Tyler's locker, I saw that Lincoln box. Then it sort of, you know, showed up at my house. And when I touched it, I basically passed out."

"Wait wait wait," Eric said. "You saw that box in a vision and then it showed up at your house?" He pulled the fat three-ring binder out from where he was sitting on it. "I think it may be time to go through some of this superhero research."

"Put that away."

Eric did not put the binder away. "Let me get fanciful for a minute here. Maybe you've got a connection to your brother still. And he's trying to communicate with you. Like, from beyond the grave." A new idea struck him. "Or hey! Tyler used that locker every day, right? Maybe it's haunted a little bit. Like he's still lingering around it? And that's what you saw."

"But he used a lot of things every day," I said. "So why aren't all of them haunted? I've gotten visions from only a few objects. And what's so special about that box? When I touched it . . . I've never felt anything like that."

"What do you know about it?"

I put a hand on Eric's arm, remembering. "Tyler's friend Bobby—he called the cigars Senator Herndon's Cubans. Maybe the box came from Senator Herndon too."

"Pretty generous of the senator to give them away."

Pretty generous was right. *Unbelievably* generous, in fact, for the Tyrant to invite Bobby and Tyler to help themselves to his expensive cigars. But how else would they have gotten their hands on them, and the cigar box as well? The Tyler I knew wouldn't steal. There was no way.

Not if he'd really been the Tyler I knew.

"So you think this Dr. Brightman can help you figure out why the box is so important?"

"Maybe," I said. "It's worth a try."

"Well, let's find him, then." Eric reached into his bag, pulled out an iPad, and started tapping away madly. "Okay, so here's a *Washington Post* article on David Brightman from a few years back." He tilted the tablet so I could see. "It says he's an expert on all things Abe Lincoln—his own private collection is supposed to be amazing, but he also helps other people research and authenticate Lincoln stuff, particularly stuff from the assassination." He whistled, scrolling farther down the page. "Look at these prices! I never realized how *obsessed* people are with the Lincoln assassination."

"Yeah. I know."

"It's actually kind of disturbing. I heard that this museum up in Maryland has an exhibit where you can see the bullet they dug out of Lincoln's head—along with *pieces of his actual skull.*" Eric shuddered. "On the one hand, I'm like, 'Who would ever want to go see that?' On the other hand, I'm like, 'I totally want to go see that.'"

I made a face. "Count me out."

"Anyhow, if it has to do with Lincoln, it looks like Dr. Brightman's your guy."

"Great. So, what, does he have an office somewhere? Can we email him and ask him to take the case? Like an artifact detective?"

"This article still says he works at the Smithsonian's American History musuem. Let me see if there's anything more recent. . . ." Eric's brow furrowed, and then he actually flinched away from the screen, half shielding his face with one hand. "Oh my god."

"What?"

"His wife and son were killed in an automobile accident. Like three years ago. There's a picture of the car, and . . ." He quickly scrolled away. "Wow. That's awful."

"Maybe he left the Smithsonian then? Moved someplace else?"

"Could be. Let me check one more thing." He kept tapping, then raised a fist in triumph. "Yes!"

"What?"

"His name came up in connection with this major auction of Lincoln memorabilia that's going on in New York later this year.

Apparently, Ford's Theatre in DC, where Lincoln was assassinated, is hosting a preview of the auction. It's like an exhibit of all the items that are going up for sale. And Dr. Brightman is speaking at the opening reception this Saturday."

I stared at him for a moment. "Eric Bowling," I said, "research truly is your superpower."

If he'd had feathers, he would have preened.

"And," I continued, "it seems today is my lucky day."

"Why is that?"

"Ford's Theatre? My mother just happens to work there."

CHAPTER 6

I TOLD MY MOTHER I WAS WORKING ON AN EXTRA-credit history project. Given the weeks of school I'd missed, all my unfinished assignments, and what she had begun calling my "isolation," a school project—and the old friend who came with it—were all the reasons I needed for Mom to put us on the guest list for the opening of the exhibit.

I figured we would take the Metro, but Eric preferred his own car. "Are you sure your mom doesn't mind you driving me around so much?" I asked when he picked me up to head into DC. "I can kick in some gas money." Even in elementary school, Eric's mom had been big on conservation and teaching the value of a dollar.

"She's cool with it," Eric said. "She likes me to have life experiences."

I raised my eyebrows at that. "If you say so. . . ."

Eric navigated us into the city, and we left the car in an ungodly expensive parking garage by the Verizon Center, where the Washington Wizards played. We wove through the milling tourist crowds, past the blindingly bright marquee flashing ads for upcoming events (Barry Manilow! Disney on Ice!), and two blocks over to Ford's Theatre.

From the outside, it looked like all the other old buildings in DC, redbricked and many windowed. It might have been an office building. The exhibit guests spilled out the front doors and onto the sidewalk, a mingling, chatting blur of power ties and designer perfume. I stopped short, my gaze caught by one particular dress, and Eric crashed into me from behind. I couldn't help but stare; the flowing fabric was a true Tyrian purple—a color I'd seen only once, in a Roman mosaic at the Natural History museum. In my mind, it was reserved for ancient emperors. I took in all the rich fabrics and expensive patterns around me. I supposed if we had emperors today, these people were them.

We went into the lobby—gold and white with marble floors—where I spotted my mom right away. I felt a sudden urge to hug her, but I knew how she felt about keeping professional spaces professional. She shook Eric's hand and walked us past two park rangers in full uniform scanning tickets. In the narrow hallway outside the theater, a woman in a black pencil skirt and matching sweater set greeted exhibit guests.

"Genevieve," my mother said, resting a hand on the woman's sleeve, "have you met my daughter? Megan, this is Genevieve Herndon, our head curator here at Ford's. But you probably know her as Emma's mom."

My heart stuttered in my chest, and I forced a smile. Emma's mother. The wife of Senator Herndon—the owner of the box Tyler had probably stolen. Eric took one look at my face and jumped to my rescue, quickly introducing himself. Mrs. Herndon shook his hand before turning back to me.

"It's nice to see you again, Megan," Mrs. Herndon said. "I met you at the funeral, of course, but I'm sure you don't remember. I can't tell you how sorry I am." Her face was creased with concern, her sleek brown bob sharp edged enough to cut paper. "Emma is still recovering from the shock of it all, and I know it's been so hard on your family. I'm just glad I got to spend time with Tyler before he passed."

My mother blinked. "You did?"

"Well, yes," Mrs. Herndon replied. "He'd been volunteering in the museum on the weekends for the last few months. Every so often, when his baseball schedule allowed. I assumed you knew about that."

Mom's eyes widened, her jaw clenching. She clearly had not known about that. "I'd like to speak to Mrs. Herndon for a moment," she said to me. "Why don't you two go look around? We're displaying the artifacts on the stage of the theater itself, but Eric, have you ever seen the permanent exhibit downstairs?" I opened my mouth to protest, but Mom held up a hand. "I know. You've seen it all before. But humor me. Take Eric downstairs. I'll meet you in the theater in fifteen minutes."

"Nice to meet you, Mrs. Herndon," Eric said, as I grabbed his arm and pulled him toward the staircase that led down to the museum.

Eric was instantly captivated by the exhibit, which traced Lincoln's presidency from his arrival in DC through his assassination. I tugged on his arm. "Hurry up! We've got to get upstairs before this Brightman guy leaves."

"I'm sure he'll still be . . ." Eric trailed off, his attention caught by a printed sign. "Wait, Lincoln's first vice president was named *Hannibal*? That's hilarious!"

"Ten minutes," I warned him. "That's all the geek-out time I'm giving you."

I would rather have been in the Hirshhorn, surrounded by a gallery of Joseph Cornell boxes, but the museum at Ford's was not without its pleasures. When I came to see my mother, I usually wandered around, looking at the photographs, playing a game of Who's Got the Worst Civil War Facial Hair. But today, I only had eyes for John Wilkes Booth.

Of course Tyler had been coming here, I thought. If you're obsessed with Booth, where better to come than a museum chock-full of his belongings? Right over there was his diary, there was the boot he wore the night of the assassination, and along that wall was a whole collection of photographs of him working his day job as an actor.

I walked over to look at the photos: Booth in a toga, Booth in a silky top hat, Booth with a walking cane. I pulled Dr. Brightman's book out of my bag to compare the image on the cover to the ones on display. He was a good-looking guy, that John Wilkes Booth, with his piercing eyes and artfully tousled hair. And if Brightman was to be believed, he was also athletic, charismatic, and a bit of a playboy.

He sounded a lot like my brother, to be honest. Was that what made Tyler so interested in him? Did Tyler see, in the handsome face of this actor-turned-assassin, something dark that he recognized in himself?

The thought sickened me. Tyler might have had secrets, and he might have gotten involved with drugs, but he hadn't hurt anyone, and he hadn't planned to. Had he? I shook my head, trying to wipe my traitorous mind clean.

I walked past the life-size statues of all the conspirators who'd been involved in the assassination plot, pausing to stare into Booth's white, unmoving face. A small crowd had gathered in front of the gun that Booth had used to kill Lincoln, a pocket dueling pistol called a derringer. It floated in its case, held up by nearly invisible supports. So tiny—no longer than my hand—and yet no matter how many times I walked past it, my eye always wandered back to its curved wooden handle, its ornate silver barrel, its round, looping trigger. It was . . . pretty. You know, for the world's most famous murder weapon.

That's where Eric found me. Staring at a gun, daydreaming about my brother.

He came up beside me and nudged my shoulder with his own. "Ready to go find this Brightman guy?"

"Finally. Yes. Let's—" A series of beeps from my phone stopped me. Messages from Nathan.

Trying to think of a good reason to text.

So it won't look like I'm just checking up on you.

No luck so far.

When I looked up from the phone, Eric was grinning, his head cocked to one side. "Nathan Lee from DC, I presume?"

I forced the cheesy smile off my face. "Okay, smartass. Let's go."

Eric and I walked up the staircase from the museum and entered the theater. My mother waved us down the aisle and up a short flight of stairs to join her on the stage. The mingling of the bright and the fancy continued here, as people wandered among long rows of display cases, browsing the auction items on exhibit.

"Well, that was quick," my mother said.

Eric grinned at her. "Don't worry. I'll come back."

My mother patted his arm. "Good boy. The artifacts downstairs belong to the National Park Service, but these are all part of a private collection that's being auctioned off in a few months." She shook her head. "I have to admit, these auctions always make me feel a bit sad. I guess, when it comes right down to it, I think history should belong to everyone, not just people who can pay top dollar to take home a piece of it." She sighed. "Do you want me to stay and walk you through the exhibit?"

Eric was already scouring the crowd with narrowed eyes, stretching up on his toes to get a better view, on the lookout for David Brightman.

"No, that's okay," I said quickly. "This is great. Thanks, Mom."

"I've got work to do here all afternoon, so I'll see you at home tonight." She squeezed my arm and disappeared into the crowd.

"Any sign of him?" I whispered to Eric.

He clutched my arm. "There he is!"

I followed his gaze. Whatever I might have been expecting, Dr. Brightman was no rumpled history professor. He looked like a white guy who'd stepped out of a Japanese fashion show. The legs of his close-fitting gray suit ended an inch above his ankles, and his black boots were crisscrossed with silver buckles. He'd pushed up the sleeves of his suit jacket, and underneath it he wore a black T-shirt that looked effortlessly expensive. And he was wearing sunglasses. Weird ones. The lenses were completely opaque, and a wire ran down from one earpiece of the thick black frame, disappearing into the collar of his coat.

My mind went as blank as a fresh sheet of paper. The speech

I'd been mentally rehearsing for days vanished in an instant. Without a glance in my direction, Eric set off across the stage toward Dr. Brightman. I tried to hold him back, but his shirtsleeve slipped through my fingers. I hurried after him, a sick feeling growing in my stomach.

Eric stopped a few feet from Dr. Brightman and gestured for me to go ahead. I shook my head, and he gave me a little shove, as if I were a reluctant toddler.

I forced out a fake cough, hoping to get Dr. Brightman's attention. Then I inhaled some spit and genuinely couldn't stop coughing. He turned and glared at me.

"Dr. Brightman," I sputtered, gasping for breath. "I'm . . . Megan Brown. Camille Brown is my mother—she helped organize this event?"

"Yes, of course." His face radiated disinterest. Not trusting my voice, I reached out to shake his hand before he could turn away. He wore thin black gloves, and the silky fabric slid against my palm.

"I was hoping you might be able to help us with an artifact. A wooden cigar box. We've been trying to figure out its history."

Dr. Brightman spared me only a half glance. "I'm afraid I can't help you."

"It's important."

"I don't deal in ordinary objects," he said. "The city is full of reputable dealers who handle that kind of thing."

I gaped at him. "But if you could just—"

"I told you, I'm not interested." His tone was final. "Excuse me."

He turned away from us toward one of the display cases. Inside was a small square of yellowed cloth, stained with age. The case was labeled *Clara Harris: Assassination Dress, 1865*. As we watched, Dr. Brightman removed his sunglasses and rested them on top of his head. Then he reached down and opened the case.

"I don't think you're supposed to open the . . . ," Eric began.

Dr. Brightman ignored him and pulled off one of his gloves.

Eric spoke up again. "And I *really* don't think you're supposed to touch the . . ."

"Please, Dr. Brightman," I said, "I'll only take a minute of your time." As he picked up the piece of cloth, I reached out to get his attention, and my hand brushed the tiny square of fabric.

The pain hit instantly, dark and blinding, with a shock like plunging into cold water. The dim lights flickered, sickly green, and the world around me congealed into a thick, dense fog.

But then the pain dialed back, as if controlled with a knob. The flashes of light stabilized, and my vision began to clear.

I heard voices, talking in that stilted way actors do when they're performing for a crowd. Then laughter, very close by. I looked around for the source, and what I saw disoriented me completely. I was no longer on the stage, where I'd been moments before. I was high above it instead, standing on one of the balconies.

I glanced to my left, where a bright shaft of light fell across a man in a red-upholstered rocking chair. His back was to me; all I could see were his broad shoulders and a head of dark, curly hair. He laughed again—a warm, deep laugh, the kind that makes everyone else want to laugh too.

A woman sat near him in an elaborate, old-fashioned white dress, like those reenactors my mother sometimes hired to work this kind of event. Then the woman stood abruptly, and the box erupted in a blur of sound and movement. I couldn't see anything clearly, except for her. She glowed brightly, casting everything else into darkness. All of a sudden she turned toward me, as though she was looking right into my eyes, and she screamed, reaching out to me for help. Her dress was covered in blood.

I jerked my head away from the sight and found myself looking directly into Dr. Brightman's eyes. They were such a dark brown that I could barely see the outlines of his pupils. He stared long and hard at me before reaching up and snapping his glasses down onto his face. I squeezed my eyes shut, and when I opened them again, I was back on the stage of the theater. The world looked normal, and the woman and the man in the chair were gone.

The pain—the visions. I'd experienced them again. And that tiny piece of cloth was the source.

I stepped back, shaking hard, and grabbed hold of Eric's arm. I pointed to the fabric in Dr. Brightman's hand. "What is that?"

I expected him to brush me off, to dismiss me as rudely as he had before. But Dr. Brightman's entire demeanor had changed. He paused a moment, considering; then a slow smile spread across his face. "This," he said, holding up the scrap of fabric, "is a piece of the dress that Clara Harris was wearing on the night Lincoln was assassinated." He returned it to the display case before tugging his glove back on. "Remnants of the dress are rare, and there have been some questions about the provenance of this piece, but now that I've examined it, I'll encourage my client to move forward with a purchase."

"Who's Clara Harris?" Eric asked.

Dr. Brightman stopped and looked at Eric for the first time.

"Apparently a high school education is not what it used to be," he said. "Clara Harris was the daughter of Senator Ira Harris." We stared at him blankly. "She and her fiancé were here with the Lincolns on the night of the assassination."

"Of course," I said. I knew there had been another couple with them, but I hadn't remembered their names.

"The dress she was wearing became a blood artifact," he continued, "stained by the violent events of that night. Of course, most of it was probably Henry Rathbone's blood—her fiancé. After Booth shot Lincoln, he stabbed Henry seven times before leaping from there"—he pointed out the presidential box, where Lincoln had been sitting that night, watching a play unfold on this very stage—"to here. Actually, he landed just about where we're standing now."

"Ouch." Eric winced.

I eyed the square of fabric in the exhibit case. It looked like a ratty, yellowed scrap of paper, like one of the fingerprint-darkened fragments that littered my drafting table after I finished a collage. Not like my idea of an important historical artifact.

"Did you call it a *blood* artifact?" Eric asked. "Is that a thing?"

"Oh, yes," Dr. Brightman said. "When Lincoln was shot, people combed this whole theater for relics, and if they could, they dipped what they found into his blood."

Eric's face was half horror, half fascination. "Why?"

"Powerful things, blood artifacts." Dr. Brightman said. "For instance, take Clara Harris's dress. She never washed it. Hung it in a closet, out of sight. But whenever people stayed in that house, they claimed to see visions of the president, rocking back in his chair and laughing, just as he was doing the moment he was shot." Dr.

Brightman rested a hand on the glass case and fixed me with a look. I couldn't see his eyes behind the sunglasses, but I remembered their piercing black stare. "As though the dress itself held the memory of that awful night."

I was barely breathing. *Every object has a voice,* I thought. *Every object tells a story.* The things I'd found in Tyler's room—the ticket stubs, the lanyard I had made him—they held so many strong memories for me. Memories I could almost see and hear and touch. "Do you think that's possible?" I asked.

Dr. Brightman shrugged. "Clara's family certainly thought so. They bricked up the closet with the dress still in it. Finally, Clara's son tore down the wall and burned the dress in a final desperate attempt to make the visions stop."

Eric and I stared at him, spellbound.

"Is that true?" Eric choked out.

"I specialize in true," Dr. Brightman said. He took out his wallet and handed me a business card. "I've changed my mind. Call me at this number, and my assistant will find a time for us to meet. Bring your Lincoln box." He smiled that same slow smile. "I think we may be able to help each other."

He examined me for a moment longer and then walked off down the row of display cases.

My knees started to shake, and I felt a sudden, desperate need for air. I rushed down from the stage, with Eric at my heels. He followed me out into the lobby, where I slumped down onto a bench, dropping my face into my hands.

"You saw something!" he said. "When you touched that cloth. What did you see?"

I described the woman in the white dress, the man laughing. The blood.

"Megan, from where I was standing, it looked like—did Dr. Brightman see it too?"

"Yes." I nodded. "I'm sure he did."

Eric dropped onto the bench beside me. "Crapdogs," he said. "What are you going to do?"

I let out a long breath. "I think it may be time to break out that binder you've been carrying around."

CHAPTER 7

AS WE WALKED DOWN TENTH STREET TOWARD THE car, Eric called the number on the card to make an appointment with Dr. Brightman, while I tried to wrestle my body back under control. My thoughts churned; my muscles ached. Everything around me looked brighter and crisper than it had an hour ago, as though I'd tweaked the focus settings in my brain. I squinted and stuck close to Eric.

"You're all set for Monday afternoon," Eric said, putting his phone away.

I took a deep breath. "A weird thing happened back there."

"Only *one*?"

I rolled my eyes. "I mean, a weird thing happened when Dr. Brightman and I touched that fabric. For a second, all I got from it was pain, like when I touched the Lincoln box. But then everything went super clear. Clearer than anything else I've seen so far."

"Why is that?"

I rubbed at the nagging ache that gnawed behind my eyes, wishing I'd brought my painkillers. "I think it was because of him. Dr. Brightman. What if he was right? What if there *was* a memory attached to that piece of cloth, but I couldn't see it until he touched it too?"

I looked over at Eric, watching him take the mental leap I'd already made.

"The Lincoln box," he breathed.

"Maybe there's a memory attached to it too. But for some reason, I can't see it by myself."

Eric maneuvered me around a tour group that was blocking the entire sidewalk in front of the International Spy Museum. "I think the time has finally come to pursue another line of inquiry."

I sighed. "Superheroes?"

"Superheroes," he confirmed. "Granted, most of the information I have to offer comes from comic books, but here's the gist—"

"But you never even liked comic books."

"Lucky for you, I live for a good research project. So." He shook his shoulders loose before embarking on the next bit. "The story of how a superhero becomes a superhero, that's called their origin story." He looked at me intently. "What's yours?"

"What?"

"How did this happen? Were you bombarded by cosmic rays? Bitten by a spider? Hit by lightning?"

I shrugged. "I don't think so."

"I hope you would have *noticed*."

I thought for a moment. "I got sad." I forced the words past the lump in my throat. "Really, really sad."

"Huh." Eric nodded, and I got the sense that he was choosing his next words very carefully. "Well. That seems significant. But maybe not sufficient."

I wiped away a tear with the back of my hand.

"Let's put that question aside for a moment," he said. "Once a superhero has their powers, they basically have to do two things: figure out the extents and limits of those powers, and find someone to help them, to guide them on their path. Like a mentor. Okay, so some of them don't have mentors, but then they end up living in a trailer park for years, or hanging out in the woods in Canada until they figure it all out, and I wouldn't recommend you do either of those things."

"Crossing them off my list."

"In the *X-Men* comics, they have a whole school with a special room where they put the new superheroes to learn what they can do." His eyes lit up. "Hey, maybe we should experiment? Get some things that belonged to your brother. Everyday things, or things he had with him when he . . ." Eric went quiet.

"I've touched all those things," I said. "Nothing happened. And I've been through his room. And his locker."

"So where else did he spend time?"

My head snapped up, and I met Eric's eyes. "What about here in DC?" I thought of all the places that I knew Tyler had gone: the party Detective Johnson thought he went to, the McDonald's where the cops said he might have bought drugs. The abandoned building in northeast DC where his body had been found. "I know some places we could try."

"Well, let's get going!" Eric rubbed his hands together gleefully. Then he looked over at me, and his face changed. "Um, Megan . . ." He pointed at me. "Your nose is . . . You're bleeding."

I jerked a hand up, and it came away bloody. "It's nothing." I wiped at it, but the blood kept coming. "No big deal."

"Wait here." Eric ducked into a burger joint on the corner and grabbed a big wad of napkins, more than I could possibly use. He handed them to me. "Are you sure you're okay?"

"I'm fine," I said. "Let's go."

Back in the car, I mapped out the first address I wanted to visit. With the phone's robo voice guiding us on our way, I sat back and watched the city blur by. Our route took us past stretches of beautifully restored buildings, then rows of run-down storefronts, then gleaming new office buildings plopped down awkwardly in the landscape of the city.

Three Things from a DC afternoon: the screaming yellow-and-red sign of Yum's Chinese. The slow surrender of white paint peeling off brick. A tiny, bright-purple house with a sign that read *Faith and Hope Tabernacle Church.*

We stopped at a red light along New York Avenue Northeast, and a blur of movement surrounded the car. Six or seven plainclothes police officers swarmed across the street in front of us, drawing their weapons and pulling on black jackets with *POLICE* emblazoned across the backs. They descended on a convenience store with the focus and intensity of a swarm of piranha. Even through the closed car windows, I could hear shouting inside. When our light turned green, Eric hit the gas so hard the tires squealed as we went through the intersection. He turned and gave me a concerned look. "Where exactly are we going? Are you sure we should be driving around here by ourselves?"

Adrenaline coursed through me, and my headache lessened for the first time since we'd walked out of Ford's Theatre. It left me feeling shaky and kind of elated. "You want to turn around?" I craned my neck to look back toward the convenience store. "Maybe we could ask one of those cops for a police escort."

"Okay, I'm not saying that, it's just . . ." His chin dipped toward his chest, and he shifted in his seat. "I've never been to DC before."

"What? I seem to remember you on those endless field trips to the Smithsonian in middle school."

"I mean the *real* DC," he said. "I've never been beyond the tourist stops. I've never been *here*." He gestured around us.

On any other day, I would have agreed with him. I could see my usual anxiety mirrored in his face. But what had happened today proved I wasn't losing my mind. I'd seen a 150-year-old woman covered in Abraham Lincoln's blood—*really* seen it, and I wasn't the only one. Dr. Brightman had seen it too. I wasn't going to rest until I learned more. "I think we can handle it," I said.

"What about Nathan Lee from DC? Maybe we should give him a call."

"No," I said. "Absolutely not. We are not giving him a call."

"I'm sure a friend of Tyler's would be willing to help us. He might even have some other ideas about where Tyler hung out in the city."

Eric was right. Nathan would *definitely* be able to take us places Tyler had been. But he also might want to know why we wanted to go there, and I wasn't willing to spread the whole superhero story around just yet.

The phone spoke up again. "Your destination is on the right."

"Oh good," I said. "We're here. Pull into the parking lot."

Eric parked and looked around, confused. "But . . . this is a McDonald's."

"Exactly." I opened my door. "Hungry?"

As we got out of the car, Eric held up his phone and waved it around. "I'm not getting any reception here. Can I borrow yours to send a message to my mom? Since a police escort is out of the question, I figure someone should know where we are."

I handed it to him and looked around. Of all the places Tyler had been in DC, a restaurant full of people had seemed like the least painful spot to start this little adventure. And this wasn't the shady, run-down place I had imagined; instead I'd have to call it a fairly fancy McDonald's. It was two stories tall, with actual landscaping. A bright new condo building stood across the street, with a Starbucks and a farm-to-table restaurant on the first floor. Beyond that, construction cranes loomed high against the sky, assembling the metal shells of apartment buildings. If this was a drug hangout, I had a feeling it wouldn't be for long.

I surveyed the parking lot. I don't know what I had expected—significant objects lying around that I could just pick up?—but the lot was surprisingly clean. Some students in school uniforms cut through, heading toward the nearby Metro, and a couple of homeless guys hunched on the curb beside the building. I walked in circles around the Dumpster in the far corner of the lot before resting a cautious hand on its rusted surface. Nothing happened.

Eric joined me at last, rolling his wheeled backpack behind him, and we went inside. I didn't get any visions when I touched the front door, or the backs of the chairs I passed, or the napkin and ketchup dispensers at the drink station. No trace of Tyler anywhere. At least, none that I could find.

"Hellooo," said the woman behind the counter, drawing out the word. She gave us a pointed stare. "Can I take your order?"

We got a couple of milk shakes and more fries than two people should ever eat. We took them upstairs, sat by a window, and stared out at New York Avenue below us. I pulled out my scissors, cut up the paper place mat that had come on the tray, and tucked the pieces I liked into my journal.

Eric, to his credit, didn't say much. He didn't chatter; he didn't ask questions. He just chewed and looked out the window. I watched him for a minute, studying his profile as he ate.

One of Tyler's other rules for fitting in at Westside had been "Stay away from targets." He meant people who drew attention to themselves. People who stood out for some reason as weird or different or strange. We both knew he meant Elena, though he never said it out loud.

With Elena, it had started with name-calling. "The Mouth," kids called her, because she always had her hand up, always had something to say. Then they started carrying sunglasses to put on whenever they passed her in the hall. Because, they said, her clothes were too bright. Once, she walked into Civics Eight to find the whole class wearing them.

Elena tried to laugh it off. She even got one of those *Rocky Horror Picture Show* T-shirts with the lips on it, just to show them, to throw "the Mouth" back in their faces. No way were they going to change *her*. But the brighter she shone, the harder they tried to wear her down. And the more I stuck by her, the more my other friends quietly drifted away.

Elena never broke. She just got tougher. Still, by the time her dad got the job offer in Dallas, her parents had watched her struggle long enough. They moved a month later.

"We can't let what happened to Elena happen to you," Tyler had said. "You have to be careful. First rule: stay away from targets."

I'd rolled my eyes. "Stay away from targets? That's just mean. Plus it's probably racist, sizeist, ableist, and a dozen other ists."

"Screw that," he'd said. "It's practical. It's for your own good. I don't care about the damn ists."

I remembered that rule now, sitting across from Eric. And I realized that, no matter how much Tyler might have wanted me to steer clear of them, targets seemed to be my kind of people. And the only friends who stuck.

"So are you dating anyone?" I asked.

He choked on a fry. "Whoa. Non sequitur. Are you conversationally challenged or something?"

"Apparently."

"Um, okay. No." He scratched his nose. "Are you?"

"No." I paused, considering. "Any chance you're gay?"

Eric leaned back in his chair. "Jeez, Megan, this is not how most people interact."

"Well, you are wheeling around a rhinestone-covered backpack."

"Hey. That kind of stereotype is really damaging," Eric said, his chin high. "Sorry if it disappoints you, but I happen to be a skinny, sparkly straight guy who isn't dating anyone."

"Fair enough." I popped my last fry into my mouth and dusted off my hands. We couldn't hide out in this McDonald's forever. I still had two other DC stops on my list. I tucked my journal into my bag and stood. "Let's move."

"Where are we going now?"

"To a party."

When we walked out the door of the restaurant into the bright afternoon sunlight, we found Nathan Lee leaning against Eric's passenger door.

He wore dark sunglasses today, and his shirt was a vivid titanium yellow, which brought out the warm undertones in his skin. The shirt also had a black collar, black buttons, and *Buzzy* embroidered on one pocket.

I turned to Eric, bristling with accusation. "You texted him, didn't you? All that 'I've got no reception here' crap. You took my phone and you *texted* him."

Eric shrugged. "What can I say? I believe in the power of reinforcements."

Nathan spotted us and broke out in a dazzling grin. "Megan Brown." He lifted his sunglasses to the top of his head. "Look at you. Running around on the wrong side of the Potomac. What excuse do you have for this wild behavior?"

I felt a glow in my chest, and I tried not to smile. "What can I say? I'm bereaved."

"How about you, Sparky?" he asked Eric.

Eric held up his backpack. "I'm Bedazzled." He and Nathan shook hands.

I turned to Nathan. "Why did you come? I mean, I know the traitor called you," I said, gesturing to Eric. "But why did you come?"

"I wanted to make sure you were okay. Last time I saw you, you were flat on your back in bed."

Eric turned to me, his wide-eyed silence louder than words.

"I'm fine." I shook myself free from the spell Nathan's smile had cast. Eric and I had things to do. Potentially embarrassing things. And I was not about to let Nathan find out what those things were.

"Anyhow," I said, "it was nice of you to come all this way, but—"

"Oh, I wasn't far. A few blocks from here. Getting my hair cut."

"Regardless. We're running a little bit late right now, so we should probably go."

"Where are you off to?"

Eric spoke up. "We're tracking down some of the places Tyler might have gone in DC."

I gave him the dirtiest look I could muster, forbidding him with my eyeballs to say a single word about superheroes. "Yes, that's right. And we should get going." I tugged on Eric's door handle. He took the hint and unlocked the car.

I got into the passenger seat, and Nathan climbed into the seat behind me.

I turned around to look at him. "What are you doing?"

He made himself comfortable in the backseat, propping one foot up on the center console. "I'm coming with you."

"You so aren't."

"I so am," he said. "Fine by you, Sparky?"

"Fine by me," Eric said, starting the car.

I turned to Eric. "Exactly whose side are you on?"

"Yours," he said. "You need all the help you can get." Eric put the car in gear. "Buckle up, Nathan. We're going to a party."

The address Detective Johnson had shown me was less than a mile away from the restaurant. As we drove, residential streets gave way to faded, peeling commercial buildings. Next to a shop that rented heavy equipment, we found the place we were looking for. I had expected a house, but this was an abandoned industrial building, with a whole wall of rolling metal doors that locked shut at the bottom.

The three of us got out of the car and walked down to where the street dead-ended in a low concrete wall, brightly marked with graffiti, stickers, and wheat-paste posters. Pretty damn cool wheat-paste posters too: laughing faces in graphic black-and-white, an Asian girl with a machine gun, a few different ads for bands. Beyond the wall was a stretch of dirt, and beyond that, railroad tracks. We watched a Metro train clatter by.

"This party sucks," Eric said.

"It was weeks ago," I replied. "But it was here." I turned to Nathan, who was intently studying some graffiti on the side of the building. "Were you here? At the party?"

"No." Nathan pulled down his sunglasses, so I couldn't see his eyes. "Not that night."

"Well," Eric said, looking around, "if you could get into that building, and you opened all those doors, and you added some music and alcohol . . . it would be crankin'. Party in the cut, you know?"

Nathan and I both turned to look at him.

"What? I googled 'DC slang' back at the McDonald's."

Nathan shook his head. "Just . . . no."

"So these underground parties. How long have they been going on?" I asked.

"Maybe six months?" Nathan shrugged. "The story is that Cedric Williams—he goes to Trinidad High—went to this thing last summer, like a model United Nations, and there were high school students from the whole area there. Not only DC, but Maryland and Virginia too."

"Model UN?" I said. "Fascinating."

"While he was there, he met this guy who lives in McLean. They . . . well, I guess you could say they hit it off, and they got this idea to swap parties every month: one in DC, one in Virginia. It's kind of like an exchange program. A United Nations . . ." Nathan paused for effect. "Of fun."

I rolled my eyes, pressing my lips together so I wouldn't smile.

He was getting into it now. "They send delegates to our parties, we send delegates to their parties, and together, we make a better DMV for everyone."

"DMV?" Eric asked.

"DC, Maryland, Virginia," Nathan explained. "You should know these things, Slim."

"Yeah, yeah, I get it," I said, twirling a finger. "Move on."

Nathan's phone rang, and he reached into his pocket to check it. "Give me a second, you guys." He walked back toward the car, laughing as he answered the phone.

While I was trying to piece together Nathan's conversation from the bits that I could overhear, Eric leaned over to me and whispered loudly. "As long as we're here, do you wanna try a training exercise?"

"So now you're Professor Magneto all of a sudden?"

"Okay, that is just . . . wrong. But never mind." An assortment of trash had gathered along the Jersey barrier at the end of the street. Eric bent down and picked up an old shoe, handing it out to me. "Take it. See what you see."

I recoiled. "Shouldn't you use a glove with that?"

"I've got hand sanitizer in my bag. Come on."

I scrunched up my face and touched the tip of the shoe with my fingers. Then I reluctantly curled my hand around the whole thing. Nothing. I shook my head.

"Okay," Eric said. "Let's keep trying. Maybe there's something here that will work."

I poked at random trash for a minute or two, getting nothing but dirty. I was about to give up when Eric jogged over with a muddy baseball cap in his hand.

"The only interesting thing I found was this." He held the cap out toward me, and I saw our school logo—the Westside Wildcats—on the front.

Excitement pinged through me. I took the cap from Eric, and all the lights went out.

In the darkness, I heard the squeal of car tires. I tried to keep a firm hold on the cap, afraid that if I dropped it, whatever secrets it held would be gone forever.

A flash of light cut through the blackness: a streetlight reflecting off a car windshield. I squinted through the blinding glare, trying to see something, anything, even as the light burned my eyes and splotches of purple and yellow obscured my vision. Finally I could make out the car, speeding around the corner and screeching to a halt—it was Tyler's dark-blue Audi. The hazy figure of a boy stood in front of the car, waving for it to stop. He yelled and slammed a hand down onto the hood, but I couldn't tell what he was saying. His voice was distorted, like it had been run through an audio filter. He clutched the baseball cap in his fist, shaking it furiously.

I squeezed my eyes shut and opened them again, and for an

instant, the guy's face became perfectly clear. He was a few years older than me, with blond hair buzzed short against freckled skin. He reached up to wipe blood from a cut above his eyebrow; his face was red and one eye looked swollen.

Then the light throbbed and pulsed, and I lost sight of him, but the *wah-wah-wah* of his voice continued. I concentrated on what he was saying, and it sounded like: "Give it back. Give it back."

I caught a glimpse of Tyler behind the wheel of the car, clearly upset. Bobby sat beside him in the passenger seat, a fierce scowl twisting his face. On the dashboard in front of them lay the Lincoln cigar box. From the lid, Honest Abe watched the proceedings with disapproval. Tyler got out of the car and came around to talk to the guy. He reached out a calming hand, but the guy slapped it away. Bobby joined them, and I thought I heard the guy say something about his dad. He was seriously pissed off. And maybe a little terrified.

Then the light began to fade. The last thing I saw was the guy standing in the road, alone. The car was nowhere to be seen. He tried to straighten his arm, but it looked seriously painful, like it might be broken. He bent over, breathing hard, and then he started to cry. He just stood there, his hands on his knees, sobbing.

I closed my eyes, swamped by a wall of pain that swept up from the back of my head. When I opened them again, the scene was gone. I sagged against Eric, who supported me with one arm as I sat down hard on the asphalt. Nathan saw the commotion, put his phone away, and came running over.

"It happened again, didn't it?" Eric asked. "You got all glazed over for a few seconds. I wasn't sure if I should try to snap you out of it, or leave you alone. What did you see?"

"Please." I looked up at Eric, tears filling my eyes. "Not in front of him." I jerked my thumb toward Nathan.

"Hold the hell on," Nathan said. "What happened?" He squatted down beside me and rested a warm hand on my arm.

"Nothing." I shrugged it off.

"She saw something," Eric said.

Nathan turned to me. "You saw something? Like what something?" When I didn't respond, he turned to Eric with a bite in his voice. "Tell me."

"She's been seeing things, since Tyler died," Eric said. I slumped down in defeat, putting my face in my hands. "She's been having . . . visions. Or something. Like when she touches things that belonged to Tyler, she can see a memory of where he'd been or when he touched them last." His eyes lit up. "Oh! It's like a Pensieve. Except the memories are attached to objects. So it's like a Pensieve crossed with a Portkey."

Nathan stared at him. "I have no idea what you're talking about right now."

I looked out from behind my hands. "First you give me comic books, now Harry Potter?"

"The secrets of *life* are in Harry Potter," Eric said. "Gryffindor for the win."

"Wait." Nathan held up his hands, his face confused. "You're serious?" He sat down on the ground next to me. "You're totally serious right now? You're having, like, visions? About Red?"

I nodded.

"Visions that are real? You're not having a nervous breakdown?"

I shrugged. "Jury's still out on that one."

"Is that why you've been having those headaches?"

"Or the other way around."

Nathan studied me hard for a moment, his total focus on me. Then he spoke. "Okay, so, I think . . ." He stopped himself, then started again, haltingly. "Maybe you should go back to the doctor."

I closed my eyes so he wouldn't see the tears welling up in them.

"After what you've been through? Anyone would be stressed. Anyone might . . ." He paused. "Lose touch with reality a little bit."

"Yeah." I nodded. "Yeah, okay."

I kept my eyes on my shoes, not willing to look Nathan in the face. He stood, and I felt the distance between us open up. *Very practical of you, Nathan,* I thought. *Stay away from targets.*

I reached for Eric's hand. I hadn't visited all the places in DC where I knew Tyler had gone. At least one remained: the building where his body had been found. But I couldn't make myself do it. Not today. Maybe not ever. I looked Eric in the eye. "Take me home? Please?"

He tried to help me stand, but I sank down to the asphalt, holding my head.

"In a minute," I gasped. "I need a minute."

The three of us stayed there together in silence for a while, watching the Metro trains go by.

"Are you going to tell your mom and dad what's going on?" Eric asked on the drive home, after I told him what I'd seen.

"I don't know." With shaking hands, I brushed at the tears that ran down my face. They wouldn't stop. I'd cried so much in the last few weeks. If I kept this up, I'd evaporate completely, and there'd be nothing left of me but a pile of salt.

"Well, are you going to the doctor?"

"Apparently I should." I could hear the hurt in my own voice. We'd dropped Nathan off at the Metro. He'd been all sympathy and kind concern, and I still hadn't gotten the bitter taste of it out of my mouth.

Eric paused. "That guy who stopped Tyler's car," he said. "Did you know who he was?"

I leaned my head against the cool glass of the car window and didn't say a word. I watched the lights on the Capitol dome come on as the dusk spread. The world always looked melancholy to me at this time of day, and the ache in my chest made me wish I were home. I rolled down the window, and the car filled with the smell of a warm day turned chilly.

Even through all the glare and distortion, it had been a painful joy to see Tyler again. The first time it had happened, in the hallway by his locker, I'd been so overwhelmed by the whole experience that I hadn't been able to focus on anything specific. But this time, the little details had hit me: that chunk of red hair that always fell down over his left eye. The way he rested one wrist on his steering wheel when he drove—I had already forgotten that. How could I have already forgotten that?

"Damn it." I sat up straight, caught by a sudden realization. "I didn't collect anything from the party site. No raw materials. I should have grabbed a gum wrapper. Anything."

"Oh, right." Eric took one hand off the wheel and reached into his back pocket. "I got you this." He held out a ripped but neatly folded piece of paper.

I opened it to see two striking eyes in a dark face—part of one of the street-art posters that had surrounded the site. The man in the stylized black-and-white photograph wore a bowler hat, big round glasses, and a steampunk-looking coat with a high collar that covered his ears.

"Sorry it's torn," he said. "The glue on those things is not messing around."

I looked up at Eric, puzzled. "How did you know?"

"Are you kidding? As long as I've known you, you've been shoving scraps of paper in your pockets."

I pulled out my art journal. I meant to tuck the page away for later, but a compulsion seized me. I fished out my scissors and my supply pouch, carefully cut out the man's hat and glasses, and pasted them onto a clean page of the book. With a black watercolor pencil, I began to sketch Eric's face in the style of the man from the poster. I put in his long nose, curious eyes, and floppy hair, flattened against his forehead beneath the bowler hat.

"Thanks," I said.

"For the poster?"

"For the ride."

Eric gave a half laugh. "You're welcome." He was quiet for a minute. "And I have to say, what you did back there? That was pretty frakking cool. I mean, I'm sure it's scary and overwhelming and all that. But also? Pretty frakking cool."

"Thanks."

"Let me know whenever you're ready to talk superhero names," Eric said. "I've got a whole other binder for that."

CHAPTER 8

ON MONDAY, AFTER SCHOOL, I SAT AT MY WORK-table, sorting collage materials and watching out my bedroom window for Eric's car to come around the corner. He wasn't due to pick me up for the appointment with Dr. Brightman for another half hour, but I couldn't focus on anything else. The tabletop in front of me overflowed with the papers and other objects I'd been collecting for the past few weeks. I kept trying to organize them in the envelopes and cubbies I normally used, but these objects defied me, refusing to be classified and tucked away.

My heart jittered as I picked up a brochure from the auction preview at Ford's. When Dr. Brightman and I had touched that piece of fabric and had seen Clara Harris, screaming and covered in blood, he hadn't seemed surprised. He must know how all this worked: the objects, the visions. He might be able to tell me what it meant and why it was happening.

But would I like the answers he gave? And what would happen when we put the Lincoln box in his hands? Was I right about there being something—some memory—attached to the box that I just couldn't see?

That I didn't *want* to see?

I jerked my head up at the sound of voices outside, but it was only a pair of joggers, laughing their way through an ordinary Monday afternoon.

I moved aside the cards and papers from Tyler's locker, uncovering the program from his funeral. In stark black letters, his years of birth and death appeared below the phrase *A Celebration of Life.* In a poorly reproduced photograph, Tyler smiled at me across time, across the gulf that now separated us, from some forgotten day when he was still with us. I looked for answers in the line of his neck, the curve of his shoulder. I didn't feel any closer to understanding how he had ended up the way he did, or why. The underground parties might explain what he had been doing in DC, and drugs might explain the money I'd found in his locker, but I still hadn't seen anything that explained how he had ever gotten involved with drugs.

I picked up the program and stared into Tyler's eyes. I'd leaned on him so heavily after Elena left. I'd done everything he asked without question. He said he wanted me to be careful, but *he* had not been careful. He said he was helping me fly under the radar, but maybe that was just code for lying and pretending to be someone you weren't. And maybe that was something we had both gotten good at.

A blur of movement outside caught my eye, and I stepped to the window. A dark sedan pulled up in front of our house. Not Eric. I took a half step back, then froze when I saw who was getting out of the car: Detective Johnson, briefcase in hand.

I tore out of my room and ran down the stairs, throwing open the door as she rang the bell. She smiled at me, and my stomach twisted. Whatever she was here for, it couldn't be good.

"Hello," she said with a nod. "I came to update your parents on some details of the investigation."

"What details?" I asked.

My mother appeared, removing my hand from the door and opening it all the way. She wore good manners like a suit of armor. "Detective Johnson. Come in." She turned to me. "Megan, please give us some privacy." She walked the detective into the living room, and I dogged their heels the entire way.

Johnson took a seat on our couch, her sharp eyes taking in all corners of the room. "Will your husband be joining us?"

Mom sighed when she spotted me lurking in the corner. "No. He's . . . not available at the moment."

I looked around too—where *was* Dad? Mom had picked me up after school, and I hadn't seen him anywhere. He must have gone out. Good for him. Lately it felt like he never left the house.

"All right," Johnson began, reaching for her briefcase. "I'll just—"

The doorbell rang again.

"Megan," my mother said coolly, "would you get that?"

"But . . . ," I spluttered, gesturing to Detective Johnson.

Her voice was firm. "Megan, go."

I raced to the door and threw it open. Eric stood on our porch, wearing a red oven mitt on each hand. He held them up as if in surrender. "Hey! I thought if you had any trouble touching the Lincoln box, we could try these." He waggled them.

"The detective is here. Right now. Telling my mom some kind of news."

Eric's eyes went wide. "Got it. Your room?" When I nodded, he took off the oven mitts and disappeared upstairs.

I returned to the living room. Mom sat beside Detective Johnson, her eyes glassy and dull. She reached for my hand, which sent a jolt of fear racing through me. I sat on the arm of the couch. "What is it?" I demanded.

"We've been in touch with the admissions office at UVa," Detective Johnson said.

"And?"

"And it appears that Tyler withdrew his acceptance. Two weeks before he passed away."

I looked to Mom for confirmation, but she seemed dazed, staring straight ahead. "But . . . how is that possible?"

Detective Johnson didn't waver. "He was in contact with the admissions director via email, and he told her he was not planning to attend. He released his scholarship money, as well."

My mother took a piece of paper from the coffee table; it trembled as she handed it to me. Sure enough, it was a printout of an email from Tyler, saying that due to "unforeseen circumstances," he had decided not to attend the University of Virginia in the fall.

"What does this mean?" I asked, utterly confused. "Was he going somewhere else?"

Detective Johnson shook her head. "We can't find any evidence of that."

"But . . ." I stared blankly at the paper in my hand. A flush of heat spread up my neck, and I came shakily to my feet. "Are you saying he killed himself?"

"It's not conclusive," Johnson continued, "but it does speak to his state of mind in the weeks preceding his death."

Mom finally lifted her head. Tears welled in her eyes. I wanted to comfort her. I wanted her to comfort me. But she stood abruptly and said, "This is complete nonsense. Detective, I'd like you to leave."

Neither of them tried to stop me as I ran off to my room.

Eric was sitting cross-legged on the floor, and he looked at me in surprise as I slammed the door and tumbled onto the bed.

"Are you okay?" he asked.

I shook my head and buried my face in the pillow. I'd thought it couldn't hurt worse than it already did. But if Tyler had really left us on purpose? Calculated the date and time? Made detailed plans? All while he'd been driving me to school every morning, telling me the same stupid jokes, making the daily unspoken promise that things would always be that way? I wasn't sure I could bear it.

Someone knocked on the door, and I stormed over and threw it open, already talking. "Mom, we have to—"

Detective Johnson stood in the doorway. "It's not Mom," she said. "Not your mom, anyway. Can I . . ." She gestured toward my room.

I stepped back and held the door open for her.

As she came in, Eric looked back and forth between us. "I'll be in the bathroom." He left quickly and closed the door behind him.

Detective Johnson headed straight for my worktable. "These are really good," she said, reaching out a hand to touch the corner of one of my finished pieces. "I like the way the leaves look like lace in this one."

"Thanks." I leaned against the wall and crossed my arms. "Mom let you come up here?"

She smiled slightly. "I can be persuasive when I want to be."

I bet she could. I offered her the only chair.

"I'm sorry," she said. "I know this is hard. But I think it's better to let you know what's going on." She hesitated, examining me closely. "I think you want all the information you can get."

I kept my chin high, hoping the tears in my eyes didn't show. "I do."

She nodded. "So I wanted to tell you . . . we've been getting a lot of calls. From journalists. About your brother. They're sniffing around for a big story, trying to be the first one to break it, whatever *it* turns out to be. And they will. Even without the formal autopsy report. Someone will say something, and it will come out."

I lowered myself unsteadily onto the bed. She was right. This would be a huge story. Something Westside High would never stop talking about. My mom's friends . . . she wouldn't be able to escape this. We'd never get out from under what had happened to Tyler. It wouldn't just define him, it would define all of us.

She rested her hands on her knees. "So what I'm asking is this. Do you want me to tell you? If I hear when it's going to hit? Do you want to know?"

I looked into her calm, serious face. "Yeah," I said. "I do."

"Okay." She stood. "And one more thing." She handed me a business card, her eyes knowing. "If there's anything you're not telling me. Anything at all." She gestured to the card. "I hope you'll reconsider. Help me get this right."

As Johnson left my room and walked down the stairs, Eric stuck his head in the bedroom door. "Is the coast clear?"

I nodded and jumped to my feet. I had to get out of this house. Away from my mother, away from the detective, away from all of it.

"Oh my god," Eric said. "Your life is crazy."

"Just grab the oven mitts and help me with the damn box."

"A comment that illustrates my point."

I led Eric down the hall to Tyler's room. The bag of personal effects was still sitting on Tyler's bed, but the box was nowhere to be seen.

"Are you sure you left it here?" Eric asked.

"I didn't touch it again after that night." I emptied the bag again, going through the contents with growing anxiety. After looking under the bed and in the closet, I went to the door and stuck my head out. "Mom!" I yelled. "Mom, are you here?"

She didn't answer, but my dad came out of their bedroom wearing pajama pants and a white undershirt, rubbing at his face. "What's happening? Are you hurt?"

"Were you asleep?" I asked. "It's like four o'clock. The police were just here. Didn't Mom try to—"

"Is that why you're screaming?"

"I left something in Tyler's room, and I can't find it," I said. "A wooden box. Have you been in there lately?"

"Is that all?" Dad let out a breath. His face was marked with sleep lines. "I haven't seen any box. And I don't think your mother has been in there in weeks. Seriously, Megan," he said, walking back toward their room. "Don't scare me like that again."

I turned to Eric. "It's gone. The box is gone."

"Clearly we need a new plan." Eric was pacing back and forth in Tyler's room, plotting out our next move with a ballpoint pen and a spiral notebook.

"We're supposed to leave for Dr. Brightman's office in ten minutes.

With a box we don't have. Exactly what kind of plan is going to help us here?" I sat on Tyler's bed, my eyes still searching the room for the missing box. I'd asked my mother, and she had no idea what I was talking about either. "It's like the box just disappeared."

I stood and started pacing the room. What were we supposed to do now? From the pile on Tyler's bed, I scooped up the metal marbles I'd found in his room and in his locker. I fidgeted with them, rolling them back and forth in my hands.

"Maybe," Eric said, holding his pen in the air, "somebody else wanted that box."

"Do you mean someone stole it?"

Eric shrugged. "It's a possibility."

"Sure, forget all the electronics and my mom's jewelry. Somebody broke into our house and thought, *Hey, check out this cigar box*."

"It was important," Eric insisted. "You didn't see anything when you touched the other objects in the bag." He gestured to the things strewn across Tyler's bed from my wild search. "You tore through them like they were nothing." He stepped closer. "There's got to be a reason that some things trigger your visions and not others. Maybe Tyler's death left a trail of marked objects, somehow, and the box was important because it had something to do with what happened to him."

My thoughts raced. Eric's theory that the box had been stolen was ridiculous; almost no way could it be true. Mom or Dad must have moved it, and they were so stressed out and distracted they'd forgotten. But Eric was right about one thing: the visions seemed to be triggered only by certain objects, and I had no control over what I saw and when.

But *could* I control them? If I learned more about this ability, maybe I could see more, from more objects. Maybe I could really use the visions as a tool to help me figure out what had been going on with Tyler these last few months.

I stopped my pacing and faced Eric. "We're going to see Dr. Brightman. Box or no box, I think maybe he can help me."

Dr. Brightman's office was in a brick row house on Capitol Hill. Like its neighbors, the house had a little square of green lawn in front, surrounded by a low wrought-iron fence. The sidewalk bustled with pedestrians: moms with fancy strollers, couples making their way toward Eastern Market, older folks walking their dogs.

A short flight of steps led to a bright-blue door. Eric bounded up the stairs first, and we crowded together on the small stoop. I pressed the bell, and moments later, Dr. Brightman himself answered the door. He was dressed more casually today, in dark jeans and a black sweater. Far from ordinary, though, the sweater had a tall, slouchy collar and bright silver zippers that slashed across each sleeve. He wore gloves but no sunglasses, and his eyes were sharp.

"Miss Brown. And . . . friend. Please come in."

He gestured us through the door and into a room that was nothing like I'd expected. The historical building had been completely gutted and renovated with an eye toward ultramodern design. A glossy black monolith of a desk stood in one corner of the main room; in front of it, two dark leather couches formed a sitting area. All the tables and decorative touches were made of metal and smoky glass. The walls had been papered in an understated stripe, and thick gray carpet covered every inch of the floor. A staircase led up to . . . where? Living quarters? Rooms filled with the historical artifacts and polished antiques I'd expected?

Eric eyed the room's only personal-looking object, a set of car keys hanging on a hook by the front door, with a goofy plastic key chain in the shape of Abraham Lincoln's head.

"Have a seat," Dr. Brightman said. We did. The furniture was less comfortable than it looked. He sat on the couch opposite us. "So you have a box to show me?"

I shared a look with Eric. "I ran into a little trouble with the box."

"Trouble?"

Eric jumped in. "It was stolen."

I gave him a warning glare. "We don't know for sure that it was stolen."

"But it's a possibility," he said.

I took a deep breath before plunging forward with my prepared speech. "I'm pretty sure the box belonged to Senator Gary Herndon, and my brother took it before he died." Even as I said the word, it choked me a bit. "My brother, that is. Died. Not Senator Herndon." I steadied my voice. "And I want to figure out what happened to him."

Interest sparked in Dr. Brightman's eyes. "The Herndon family has been collecting Lincoln artifacts for generations. The senator's own father spent years—and hundreds of thousands of dollars—assembling one of the nation's best private collections." He leaned toward me. "But if you don't have the box, why did you come?"

"Because of what I saw when I touched that piece of fabric at the exhibit." I looked him in the eye. "Because of what *you* saw. I thought you might still be able to help me." I hesitated. "I've seen things like that before. Visions, or whatever you want to call them. And when I touched the box, I . . ." My hand went involuntarily to my head as the memory of how it felt pulsed through me.

"It was painful?" he asked.

"That's putting it lightly."

"Was the box the only object that you've . . . had that reaction to?"

I thought of the baseball cap we'd found, and how long it had taken me to recover after touching it. "Not quite."

Dr. Brightman nodded. A slight smile began to play at the corners of his mouth. He was silent for a long time before he spoke.

"Every object has a history." He picked up a clear glass bowl from a side table. It was spun through with black threads, like ink spilled in water. He weighed it in his hand. "Someone made it. Someone packaged it, shipped it, sold it. Maybe someone used it for years, every day, before you ever owned it. Maybe not." He put the bowl back down. "Most of the time, that history is invisible to us. Or we don't care. But sometimes, history gives the most ordinary objects special meaning. They become not just eyeglasses, but *Benjamin Franklin's* eyeglasses. Thomas Jefferson's fountain pen. The flag that covered Abraham Lincoln's coffin. They connect us to people and moments from the past, and we hunger for that connection." He shrugged. "Of course, an object doesn't have to be worthy of a museum to have a history. And some histories are more painful than others." He stood. "Do you want to try an experiment?"

"What kind of experiment?" Eric asked. I nudged him with my elbow, and he made an apologetic face.

Dr. Brightman went to his desk and opened a drawer. He took

out a small card and returned to the couch, laying it down on the glass table. It was a photograph of a young woman in profile, the paper curled at the corners and yellowed with age. She wasn't particularly pretty, but she looked stylish. You know, for the 1800s.

"So, how to describe this. . . ." Dr. Brightman thought a moment. "Have you ever heard of slow glass?"

I shook my head.

"Purely science fiction, of course. But a fascinating idea." He ran a finger over the surface of the coffee table. "When light enters glass, it bends. It slows down, bounces around, before coming back out. But what if we could slow down the light even more, so it became trapped for years? When it finally emerged, you would essentially be seeing the past." He tapped the photograph with one gloved finger. "Imagine artifacts the same way. As though there were memories bent and bouncing inside them, waiting to be seen again. Some memories are brighter than others. Some burn like staring at the sun."

I lowered my hands and rested my fingers on the photograph.

Nothing happened.

Memories like lights, I thought. I squeezed my eyes shut. Lights did glimmer behind my eyelids, but they might have been nothing more than an illusion.

"You need to keep your eyes open," Dr. Brightman told me. "Look at the object, but look beyond what you see."

I tried to look beyond the photograph, but I had no idea what I was doing. And still, nothing happened. Until Dr. Brightman's bare hand closed over mine.

A light rushed toward me, and the world around me shifted.

Instead of Dr. Brightman's impeccable office, I found myself in a green-and-gold restaurant, lit by hanging lamps and brightened by the clink of silverware on china. Dr. Brightman stood beside me, his hand still on mine. The woman from the photograph sat at the table in front of us, her cheeks flushed pink and a spark of mischief in her blue eyes that the camera hadn't captured. Across from her sat a young man with a shock of dark tousled hair and a mustache that grew down toward his chin. He had one arm hooked over the back of his chair. His eyes were locked on the young woman, and a wolfish grin split his face.

She tossed her head, and her long curls bounced against one shoulder. "I won't wait for my father's approval to marry. If I let him make my decisions, then nothing in my life will belong to me. Not even my mistakes." She beamed at the young man. "Or my joys. I count you among the latter, of course."

He smiled indulgently, pulled out a pocket watch, and checked the time. Then his face altered, as though a mask had dropped down over his features—or as though one had been pulled away. He stood, suddenly stiff and rigid.

The young woman laughed up at him. "Johnnie," she said warningly, "don't tell me you're leaving so soon. I might have been at six or seven other engagements this morning."

The man's expression did not soften. With some ceremony, he reached down and took the woman's hand, lifting it to his mouth and kissing it. "'Nymph, in thy orisons be all my sins remembered.'" As he turned to leave, I saw him reach into his pocket and pull out a card. The photograph. He gripped it in his hand as he walked away from the table.

The woman called after him, surprise and confusion coloring her face. "*Hamlet?* That's your exit line? At least give me some *Romeo and Juliet*." Despite her irritation, he disappeared through the door, swallowed up by the light.

Dr. Brightman shifted beside me, pulling the photograph from between our linked hands. The world went dark.

When I could see again, we were back on the couch in Dr. Brightman's office. He had a slight smile on his face. "You found it."

Eric rested a hand on my arm. "What did you find?"

"A memory." I raised my hand to the back of my head, where a dull ache had started to grow. "That man . . . it was John Wilkes Booth, wasn't it?"

Dr. Brightman nodded. "Very good. The assassin, on the morning of his famous crime."

I shuddered. "And who was she?" I nodded toward the picture.

"Booth's fiancée. Lucy Lambert Hale."

"Her father didn't want them together?"

Dr. Brightman picked up the photograph in his still-gloved right hand and carried it back to his desk. "Like Clara Harris's father, John Parker Hale was a powerful senator. In fact, he'd been named ambassador to Spain. Some historians believe Hale requested the assignment just to end his daughter's engagement to an *actor*, of all things."

"And the photograph?"

"Found on Booth's body after his death. Along with images of several other women."

I rubbed my neck where the ache had started to spread.

Eric spoke up. "Wait, isn't that card in the museum at Ford's

Theatre? I think we saw it there the other day."

Dr. Brightman put the photograph back into its drawer and locked it. "You might be surprised how many artifacts in museums are not as genuine as they appear."

Eric flopped back against the couch, flabbergasted. "Is this a normal afternoon for you, sir?" he asked Dr. Brightman. "Do you meet a lot of people like Megan?"

"I've met a few." Dr. Brightman said. "Now and again."

"The others you've met . . . ," Eric began hesitantly, "do they all eventually need the same . . . aids that you do?" He gestured to Dr. Brightman's glove. "Is this the natural progression of the dise—" He stopped himself. "I mean, of the ability?"

Dr. Brightman evaluated him for a moment. "No," he said at last. "It isn't." But he didn't elaborate.

My head buzzed with dozens of questions, so many I could hardly string words together to ask them. "Why does it hurt sometimes?" I asked. "And why does it work like that—why could I see that memory when you helped me, but not on my own?"

"I can only speculate as to why," Dr. Brightman said. "But that does seem to be the effect: two people coming together clarifies the memory and lessens whatever pain might be associated with it."

Eric perked up. "Pain shared is pain halved." We turned to look at him. "My grandmother says that. It's a proverb." He paused. "She's German."

"All right," Dr. Brightman said. "Enough time to recover?" He returned to sit opposite us. "Good. Let's move on to something of your brother's."

"But I don't have the box."

"Surely you have something of his. Anything."

I thought for a moment, then pulled the button on its string from around my neck and set it down on the glass coffee table.

I reached into the pocket of my jeans and pulled out the rough metal marbles I'd collected from Tyler's things. I had tucked them into my pocket that morning, for good luck. They joined the necklace on the table.

Finally I dug through my bag until I found Tyler's copy of Dr. Brightman's book, *Disasters in the Sun*, with all its dog-eared, scribbled-on pages. I set that before him as well.

"Interesting," Dr. Brightman said, picking up one of the marbles. He put it back on the table and loosened the fingers of his remaining glove. "Let's try the necklace."

Eric sat forward on the couch. "Are you going to touch it?"

"That is precisely what I am going to do. After Miss Brown touches it first."

My hand hovered over the button. "What am I looking for?"

"The strongest memories. The brightest lights," Dr. Brightman replied.

I held the button in the palm of my hand. I kept my eyes open but unfocused, trying to imagine a beam of memory, caught inside the small black plastic circle.

And then it hit me. Light, like a hood covering my face, so bright I couldn't see. I dropped the button on the glass table with a clatter, gasping in panic like the time I'd tried to go snorkeling but couldn't convince my brain that it was okay to breathe underwater.

"Good," Dr. Brightman said. "Try again."

I hesitated, and he intertwined his fingers with mine. We rested our joined hands on the button.

This time, the light lasted only a few seconds before it ebbed away. As it withdrew, the dim shape of a boy came into focus: Tyler, sitting at a glossy wooden table with a wine bottle beside him, brooding over something on his cell phone. He was wearing his coat, worrying a button in his fingers. As the image cleared, I could see that he was in a wine cellar, lined with cherry-wood shelves and stocked with hundreds of bottles. Music and voices drifted toward him from somewhere else in the house.

"Yo, Red!" someone called. Tyler didn't even look up. Bobby staggered down a steep flight of stairs, red plastic cup in hand. He spotted Tyler and stopped short. "Dude." He shook his head. "Dude, dude, dude. There is a *party* going on."

Tyler held up the wine bottle at his elbow. "Any idea how much this cost?"

Bobby shrugged. "A lot? Zach's dad likes wine."

"I looked it up." Tyler showed Bobby his phone. "Almost *five thousand dollars*." He gestured around them at the wine cellar. "I mean, is this necessary? We're basically sitting in a bank vault here."

Bobby's eyebrows went up. "So?"

"Nothing." With a sigh, Tyler slumped back in his chair. "Just thinking about something a friend said to me."

Bobby whacked him in the chest with the back of his hand. "Well, stop thinking and start partying. Be fun. That's why I bring you places."

Anger flashed across Tyler's face. If I hadn't been watching him so closely, I might have missed it, because almost instantly, his usual lazy grin was in place, his body language laid-back and mellow. "I have a better idea," he said. "Wanna take one of these home?"

Bobby stretched out a hand, and Tyler high-fived him. With the sound of the slap, the image seemed to fall away, sliding down my field of vision as Dr. Brightman's office replaced it. I blinked, dazed and dizzy, and then I realized that Dr. Brightman had removed his hand from mine.

He picked up his gloves. "Well. You've certainly got a talent for this. But perhaps that's enough for one day." He stood and walked back to his desk.

I put the cord with Tyler's button around my neck, trying to process everything I'd just seen. The "friend" Tyler had mentioned must have been Leigh. She'd really gotten under his skin. I'd never heard him talk about money that way before.

Dr. Brightman spoke again. "So. Now that I've helped you, I have a favor to ask in return."

"Wait." This change of subject bewildered me. "What kind of favor?"

"The same kind of favor I just did for you," he said evenly. "My own ability can be a bit . . . unpredictable. I'm investigating some unusual artifacts at the moment, and I could use your help."

"Unusual?" I asked. "Unusual how?"

"Over the last few years, I've made my living in blood artifacts—and I don't just mean artifacts from Lincoln's assassination. There's a whole network of collectors who specialize in what they call murderabilia."

The word sent a cold shock through me, and I shared a significant look with Eric. "Murdera*what*?"

"Memorabilia from crime scenes, particularly violent crimes,"

Dr. Brightman explained. "And while most artifacts require documentation—some proof of the history and provenance of the object—collectors of murderabilia are often willing to rely on the word of an expert. Like myself." Dr. Brightman smiled slightly. "So I started tracking down objects that were associated with other assassinations. And other crimes. There's good money in it. But those objects can be . . . *unpleasant* to authenticate."

That sounded like an understatement.

"When you say 'unpleasant,'" Eric said, "do you mean it hurts when you touch them?"

Dr. Brightman raised one shoulder in a half shrug. "The authentic ones, yes. And I've grown a bit oversensitized over the years." He held up his gloves as though to illustrate his point. "With that kind of artifact, the pain is too intense for me to see any details."

I had a mental image of myself backing away from him all the way home to Virginia. "I'm not so sure that I—"

"Call it payment for the help I've given you today." His gaze was level, and his eyes stayed locked on mine. "And perhaps, in the future, you'll need my help again?"

My stomach twisted, but I couldn't let go of my link to Dr. Brightman. He knew what this was, this thing that was happening to me. He knew how it worked, and how to control it. And the Lincoln box—I might still be able to find it, and if I did, he could help me see what memories it held. I nodded.

"Wonderful," he said. "I'll be in touch."

As Dr. Brightman came around the coffee table to see us to the door, his still-bare hand brushed Eric's sleeve. Dr. Brightman hissed in pain, raising a hand to his forehead.

"What is it?" Eric asked.

"Your jacket," Dr. Brightman said. "The girl who made it lost a hand in one of the factory machines. You should be more careful where you buy clothing."

Eric's face slackened and his mouth fell open. He shrugged out of the jacket and held it by his fingertips, like it was something unclean, as he walked out the door. I had a feeling I wouldn't see that jacket again.

I locked eyes with Dr. Brightman. "That's amazing. Did you really just see that?"

Dr. Brightman paused a moment. "No. But he should thank me. That was a truly awful jacket."

CHAPTER 9

AN HOUR LATER, I WAS BACK AT MY WORKTABLE, staring out my window at the street below. But now, the flutter in my chest wasn't nervous anticipation. It was fear.

Eric and I hadn't spoken much on the trip back from the city. Every time he'd started a sentence, I'd told him I wasn't ready. Now he lay on his back on my bedroom floor, knees bent, one oven mitt behind his head, the other covering his eyes. His chest rose and fell in a steady, even rhythm, but I knew he wasn't asleep.

I swung around in my chair to face him. He must have sensed my movement, because he popped up to a sitting position, the oven mitt falling to the carpet at his side.

"Now?" he asked. "Are you ready now?"

I rubbed my hands over my face and sat up straight. "I think so. Yes."

"So first, *oh my god*, I have to—" He stopped himself, and I could almost see him forcibly reeling that sentence back into his body. "No. Wait. Sorry." He breathed once, slow and deep. "You talk. I'll listen."

The weight of my fear lessened a bit. "You go."

He grinned. "Okay, so the first thing I have to say is: this is *real.* Seriously. I mean, I believed you before, and I knew you weren't making it up, but somehow, when we were sitting in that house with Dr. Brightman, it all just . . ." He trailed off and threw up his hands, at a loss for words.

"You mean, when we were sitting in that strange, sterile house with that murderabilia professional, shit got real?"

"Yes, and the second thing I have to say is: you never, ever have to go back there. You know that, right?"

"What else can I do?" I asked. "Tyler's gone. My brain is self-destructing. I can't tell anyone what's happening to me. I don't even totally believe it myself. And I don't know what to do next. I can't find the box. My mom will barely let me talk to the police. I can't use my advanced crime-fighting skills to sweep Tyler's room for hair and fibers. I can't get my conveniently placed friend in the police department to run fingerprints for me or steal the files on Tyler's case. I have no skills. And I have no friends."

Eric let out an offended huff. "Well, that's not exactly—"

"You know what I mean. I need Dr. Brightman. I have no choice."

Eric reached out and put a hand on my knee. "You *do*, though. You do have a choice. And you have skills." He smiled slightly. "And you have friends."

I squeezed his hand, and my breath hitched in my chest. "But what if I never go back to see him, and then I never find out what happened to Tyler?" A worse idea struck me. "Or what if I *do* go back to see him, and I *become* him? What if that's me in two years? Or six months? What if I end up wearing gloves and weirdo sunglasses and keeping Charles Manson's bloody sock in a velvet box in my freezer?"

"In that case, I'd suggest you go with a plain old plastic bag. Velvet crumples."

I hit him with one of his own oven mitts. "I'm serious."

"Well, you don't have to decide right now, do you? Give it some time."

"I just . . ." I struggled to find the words to articulate what I wanted to say. "I can't stand still. Not right now. I can't sit back and wait for everyone else to tell me who my brother was and what happened to him. It's like, if I stop, I'll just—" I twisted my fingers together and squeezed until it hurt. Everything I wanted to say sounded so melodramatic. *I'll explode. I'll fly apart into a million pieces. I'll die.*

Eric nodded, his face serious. "Okay. I hear you. Well, what about that guy?"

"What guy?"

"The guy you saw fighting with Tyler in your vision. At the party in DC. Maybe he knows something about what was going on."

I spun back toward my worktable and dug through the cabinet beneath it until I found a pad of paper. Eric eased up behind me to watch over my shoulder as I slapped the paper down on the table and started drawing. Beneath my pencil, a face started to take shape. Short blond hair, freckles: the guy from my vision.

"Whoa," Eric said.

"What?" I didn't look up, my focus entirely on the page.

"That's just . . . impressive. I've never seen anyone do that before."

"It's going to take a little while."

"I can wait." I could sense Eric moving around the room, ping-ponging from one spot to the next until I set down my pencil. Then he came up behind me again.

"Do you know him?" I asked.

Eric studied the guy's face. "No, I don't think so. But can I take this with me? I can check it against my yearbook; see if I can find him."

"You do that."

Drawing had calmed me a bit, centered me, as it always did, but my chest still ached and sweat prickled the back of my neck. After I walked Eric out, I sat on the front porch and listened to the neighborhood sprinklers come on, filling the cool early-evening air with a smell like rain.

Detective Johnson thought Tyler had dropped out of school to take his own life, and Dad couldn't be bothered to get out of bed to hear the bad news. The Lincoln box was missing, and my next best hope of figuring out what had happened to Tyler seemed to rest on my questionable skills as a police sketch artist. Or on my connection to a murder-happy historian who'd offered me what had to be the world's weirdest after-school job. I closed my eyes and breathed in deeply.

My phone chimed, and I pulled it out of my pocket. Messages from Elena.

How was your day?

Better, I hope.

I'm hoping it was a Ferris Bueller kind of day.

You stayed home sick. Drove a Ferrari. Danced in the streets of Chicago.

The weight on my chest lifted a bit, and I smiled. All work and no play makes Jack a dull boy, I replied.

No. Tell me you're kidding.

Redrum.

Stop it. I'll have Shining nightmares for a week.

Was it that bad?

Take away the ax, and you have my day.

Take away the ax? Well at least that's something!

I snorted.

How's New Boy?

For a moment I was back on that dead-end DC street, and I felt Nathan step away from me again, that small distance gaping wide between us.

New Boy is old news.

Elena sent a frown. *Sorry.*

Me too.

Maybe aim for a slightly better day tomorrow, okay?

Okay, I wrote.

Nightmare on Elm Street?

Good night, you.

Eric was already at school when I arrived the next morning, leaning against a flagpole by the main entrance with my drawing in one hand. "Any luck?" I asked.

"Yearbook was a bust," he said. "But I've been here since six a.m., watching people show up for school. You said the guy's arm was hurt pretty badly—I thought if I couldn't match the sketch, I might at least see somebody in a cast. But no luck. Not so far."

"So what do we do next?"

Eric handed me the drawing and pulled the research binder out of his backpack. "I thought we might return to the question of how you got this power." He started flipping pages.

"Does it matter how I got it? It's here."

Eric paused midflip to fix me with a look. "Origins are important. How we got to be who we are? It matters." He continued flipping. "And maybe we can find someone else to help you. Someone a *leetle* less murder obsessed."

"Sounds good to me." I leaned over to look at the binder. "What have you got?"

"Not much. But I was thinking about what you said about, you know, getting sad. We know Dr. Brightman was sad too—he lost his family in a car accident." He found the page he was looking for and held out the binder to show me. "You remember what I said about Rebecca Tattenbaum? She owns that antique shop on the Hill. Well, it was her parents' store. They were killed in a robbery when she was twenty-one, and she was the one who found their bodies. She had some kind of mental break—a delivery man discovered her, almost catatonic, sitting beside her parents' bodies in a pile of broken wood and glass."

"That's terrible."

"But now the store is incredibly successful. Partly because people think it's haunted. But also because she's got"—he pointed out a sentence in the article we were looking at—"'an uncanny eye for valuable antiques, finding rare treasures in the most unexpected places.'" He gave me a significant look, eyebrows raised.

"But millions of people lose parents. And brothers. And wives."

"I know," Eric said, shrugging. "It's not really a theory yet. More a work in progress."

The parking lot was filling up now, and people were making their way into the building for the start of another day. I spotted Bobby Drake in the crowd, wearing a brown leather jacket and that same damn blue shirt. I ducked behind Eric's shoulder and covered my face with one hand.

"What the . . ." Eric looked around. "Who are you hiding from?"

"Shhh," I hissed. "Leather jacket. Tyler's best friend."

"Well, let's show him your drawing," Eric said. "He was there, right? He probably knows the guy."

"I really don't want to—" I began, but Eric was already flagging Bobby down.

"Good morning. Mind if I ask you a quick question?" Eric held up the drawing. "Do you know this person?"

Bobby rolled his eyes. "Who wants to know?"

I stepped out from behind Eric.

Bobby glanced from me to the drawing, and his face shifted from boredom to fury in an instant. "What have you heard?"

"Nothing."

Bobby moved in close. His eyes glittered strangely, and his voice was hushed. "Seriously. What has Kyle been saying?"

I blinked at him, confused.

"Tell me." He grabbed my wrist. Hard. More shocked than hurt, I tried to pull away, but he held on.

Eric leaned between us and threw a kind of John Wayne bravado into his voice. "Hey now," he said. "Take it down a notch."

Bobby let go but showed no signs of calming down. I rubbed at my wrist.

"Did he go to the police? Is that what's going on? Because we didn't lay a hand on him. He was bleeding before we ever saw him that night."

My whole body had tensed up, ready to bolt, and I struggled to force words out. "No police. We just wanted to know who he was."

Bobby let out a loud breath and shook his head. "Listen, Brown. There are things the cops don't need to know about, okay? So you'd better not go poking around in—" He stopped himself and fixed me with a glare. "You're Red's sister," he said at last. "Act like it." He slouched off.

I turned to Eric. "He just totally lost it." I swallowed hard, my throat dry. Bobby was hiding stuff from me, and from the police—stuff about Tyler—and I was going to find out what it was. No matter how much he threatened me.

"I don't know what all that was about," Eric said, "but I'm concluding that this guy"—he held up the drawing—"is named Kyle. I can work with that." He pulled out his phone and took off toward the main entrance. "I'll text you when I have news."

Eric's message didn't arrive until just before the last period of the day. *Meet me at the track after school,* it said. *ASAP.*

When the final bell rang, I dashed outside to find Eric leaning on the chain-link fence that surrounded Westside's athletic field. I collapsed against the fence next to him, breathing heavily. "What's up?"

"Right there." Eric pointed to a few guys on the lacrosse team who were straggling out onto the field for practice. "With his arm in the sling. Kyle Davis. I'm pretty sure that's him."

"Yep," I breathed. "That's him." I watched Kyle warm up and

stretch with his teammates. He had the same hair, the same freckles, the same nose as the guy I'd seen in my vision. It was as if I'd conjured him up wholesale from my own mind, and now here he was, breathing and walking around like everyone else. When the other guys set off to run some kind of passing-and-shooting drill, Kyle sat on the bleachers and tightened his sling.

"Now's our chance." Eric strode off toward an opening in the fence.

"Wait," I called after him in a loud whisper. "What are you doing?" But once again, Eric had left me behind. By the time I caught up with him, he had already climbed three steps up into the bleachers and was introducing himself to Kyle.

"Eric Bowling. Sophomore. And this is Megan Brown. Her brother was—"

"Red Brown," Kyle said, understanding dawning across his face. He glanced over at his teammates, who were all the way across the field, and then leaned in closer to us. "Listen, I'm sorry about what happened to him. He was a good guy."

Eric cocked his head to one side. "Really? I heard you were screaming at him at a party a few weeks back. People don't usually scream at good guys."

Kyle looked surprised and ran a hand across his arm. "He just . . . took something from me, and I needed it back, that's all. But he made it right. End of story."

I thought back to Senator Herndon's cigars, and to Bobby and Tyler in the wine cellar. Exactly how many people had Tyler been stealing from? "What did he take?"

"Yeah." Kyle stood to go. "I'm not going to tell you that."

"Are you worried about the police?" I persisted. "I won't go to them. I just need to know what happened."

"Sorry, kid." Kyle stepped off the bleachers and onto the field.

Eric clambered down quickly and blocked Kyle's path. "Wait," he said. "She can see things."

I stared at Eric in disbelief. "What are you doing?" I mouthed.

"Yeah, me too," Kyle said, opening both eyes wide and looking around.

Eric dropped his voice to a dramatic whisper. "No, like *psychic* things. Things no one else can see. Things you wouldn't want anyone to know." He gestured to me. "Show him, Megan."

Show him? I wanted to show Eric Bowling a thing or two.

Kyle turned around and looked at me expectantly. "Okay, I'll bite," he said. "Show me." He waited, eyebrows raised.

I sent Eric one last dagger-filled look before walking over to Kyle and resting my hand on the sling that covered his arm.

Nothing happened. I tried to see the lights. No luck. I closed my eyes, attempting to buy myself some time.

"Does it normally take this long?" Kyle asked.

He sounded like every jerk I'd ever known, every stupid, entitled ass who'd made me duck into a girls' bathroom when I saw him coming, for fear of being noticed—and once noticed, targeted. I thought of the Kyle I'd seen in my vision. That Kyle hadn't been a jerk. He'd been a scared little boy.

I snapped my head up and stared Kyle straight in the eye. "I know what happened to you that night," I said. "The night of the party. I can see you. Standing next to Tyler's car. Begging him to help you."

Kyle looked uncomfortable now, and he glanced between me and Eric. "Okay, Tyler told you that. So what?"

I didn't flinch. I didn't blink. I just let a smile cross my lips and tried to channel Jack Nicholson in *The Shining*. "I'm not finished. After everyone else was gone, you cried." I shook my head. "You stood in the dirt by the side of the road, crying like a little boy."

Kyle stepped away from me, his eyes wide. "How did you—"

"I bet I can see what you were doing last weekend too." I reached for him again. "You want me to try?"

"Enough," Kyle said. "Stop it. Freak." He checked the location of his teammates, then led us off the field and around to the other side of the fence. "The thing Red took from me. It was one of my dad's watches."

I tried to puzzle that through. "When did he do this?"

"About a month ago. I had a party while my folks were out of town. A real rager, you know?" He smiled a bit, remembering. "Sometime during, or after, I don't know, Red lifted it. I mean, my dad collects watches. He has dozens of them. But if he'd realized it was missing, he would have killed me."

"So you went after Tyler to get it back," Eric said.

"No, I went after Park." He held up his broken arm. "That didn't turn out so well."

"Who the hell is Park?" I asked.

"Eugene Park. The guy who DJs at all the undergrounds," Kyle said. "Tyler sold the watch to him." I must have looked completely dumbfounded, because Kyle shook his head at the expression on my face. "Seriously," he said. "For a psychic, you don't know shit."

My head swam. Tyler was selling the stuff he sold? So maybe

there *was* something other than drugs that would explain the money in his locker.

"Where is it now?" I asked.

"The watch? I don't know. Park has it, I guess. But Red bought me a new one. Identical. I put it back before my dad noticed, so we were cool." His freckled face turned serious. "Look, I don't want the cops thinking I had a grudge against Tyler or something, okay?"

"So how can we find this Eugene guy?" Eric asked.

"Yeah, I'd stay away from Park if I were you. I heard his dad is Korean mafia out of Annandale." He snorted. "And don't call him Eugene."

"Thanks for the advice," I said. "When's the next underground?"

"I'm done with those parties. And with you." Kyle left us and jogged back toward the field.

"Hey, Kyle," Eric called.

He turned.

"How much would you say that watch was worth?"

He shrugged. "I don't know. Six thousand?" He went back through the fence to rejoin his teammates.

I leaned against the fence for support. "Six *thousand* dollars?" I exhaled. "Where the hell would Tyler have gotten the money to replace it?"

Eric leaned beside me. "I don't know—maybe from the Korean mafia?"

"That's ridiculous," I said. "Tyler was not mixed up with the Korean mafia."

"O-o-okay. If you say so."

My mind raced. "I'm betting this guy Park will be at the next underground," I said. "Which means *we* need to be at the next underground."

"You know I support you in this, right?" Eric said. "I want you to find out what was happening with Tyler. I'm cheering you on."

"I hear a 'but' coming."

"But there's no way you should go to that party by yourself. And I'm not exactly cut out for the role of bodyguard."

I had a pretty good idea where he was going with this. "You want me to talk to Nathan, don't you?"

"You *have* to," he said. "We need reinforcements. Besides, you don't even know where the party is, and he totally will. If you get him to go, I'm in too." He nudged me with his elbow. "I even promise to leave the Bedazzled backpack at home."

I looked at him for a moment. He might as well have had a bright red bull's-eye painted on his shirt. "Don't you ever want to be more normal?" I asked.

"Normal is a statistical invention. *Not* a desirable personality trait."

I snorted. "Fine. I'll talk to Nathan, see how he feels about the role of bodyguard." My stomach lurched, and I couldn't tell if it was excitement or dread. Anticipation, I decided. One way or the other, I was going to see Nathan again.

That night I curled up in bed with my phone to write Nathan a message. It took me a good twenty minutes to compose, and in the end, it said:

Want to go to a party with me?

Right after I hit send, the phone rang, and I jumped, startled.

It was him.

I sat up and stared at the phone in horror. He wasn't supposed to call. He was breaking all the rules I had carefully put in place to avoid this. Okay, so maybe he wasn't aware of the rules, but that was no excuse. I let it go to voice mail.

Within seconds, he sent me a message:

I know you're there. You just texted me.

I'm not really a phone-talking kind of person.

You have a phone. You talk. You are a person.

Not on the phone, I'm not.

Please pick up.

I really want to hear your voice.

The phone rang again. I sat for a moment with my finger hovering over it, uncertain. Then I thought, *What the hell? He already thinks I'm delusional. How much worse can I make this?* So I answered.

"Hello," I said.

"There you are. See, I feel better already."

"Me, not so much."

He laughed. "Tell me about this party."

"I was actually hoping you would tell *me* about the party. I heard there's another underground coming up?"

"Really?" he said. "I don't know much about it."

"I want to go."

"Why?"

"Do you want the long answer or the short answer?"

"Always, *always*, the long answer."

So I told him about Kyle, and the watch, and the Korean mafia.

He was quiet for a long minute. "So Red was *stealing* stuff? And selling it to Park? I don't . . ." His voice shook. "How did I not know that?"

"I'm as surprised as you are."

"I'm not just surprised, I'm *pissed.* Why would he—" I heard rustling and banging on Nathan's end of the line. "I knew he had money, but I thought he, you know, had money. How long was that going on?"

"That's what I'm going to that party to find out."

"No way."

"Look me in the eye, Nathan Lee . . . ," I began.

Even as upset as he was, I heard him snort out a laugh.

"Metaphorically," I said. "Look me in the metaphorical eye and tell me that it makes sense to you that my brother died the way the police say he did. That he drove to DC, bought some heroin, went to an abandoned building, and overdosed." Nathan didn't speak, but I could tell from his silence I was getting somewhere. "Don't you see? I deserve to know how that happened. Why that happened. More than that, *Tyler* deserves it."

"How about this option, Megan?" he said at last. "Let it go."

A chill shot through me. "What?"

"I mean, what would happen if you *didn't* try to figure out what happened? If you stopped trying to put together all the pieces and, you know, let yourself grieve?"

I fell quiet. I listened to the sound of Nathan's breathing and thought about it. I tried to imagine living with what had happened. Accepting that I'd never truly understand why.

"I don't think I can. Because Tyler isn't who I thought he was. And that means I'm not who *I* thought I was." I fought to keep my voice steady. "I know this might not make sense to you. But I have to put him back together. Or I can't put myself back together."

Nathan let out a little hum, and I swore I could feel it vibrate through my own chest. "I think you underestimate your phone-talking skills," he said.

I breathed out a laugh.

"How about this," he said. "I'll find out where the party is, and I'll talk to Park for you."

"That sounds great. I'll be standing right next to you when you do."

Nathan let out an exasperated sigh. "Megan."

Before he could say another word, I jumped in. "I know you don't think going to that party is a good idea. But you can't stop me. No matter what you say, no matter whether I have to ask every damn student at Westside where and when it is, no matter whether you come with me or not, I'm going to that party."

Nathan paused for a moment before answering. "Give me ten minutes." He hung up.

Five minutes later, he texted me.

Saturday night.

The old Barnes and Noble at Bailey's Crossroads.

I pumped my fist in triumph.

One condition.

What's that?

I get to drive.

CHAPTER 10

NATHAN PULLED UP IN FRONT OF MY HOUSE ON Saturday at midnight, right on time. As he approached, he turned off his headlights and rolled down his window. I ran down the front walk, glancing up at my parents' darkened bedroom as I went.

"Need a lift?" he asked.

I grinned at him, jittery with nerves and excitement. "I see you've done this before."

As I walked around to the passenger side, I ran my fingers over the hood of his car. It was old—not like clunker old, more like classic old. I couldn't make out the color, but its chrome stripes and silver bumper glinted in the yellow glow of the streetlight. It had small round headlights and a tall front grill with the word *RAMBLER* underneath it. "What's a Rambler?" I asked, sliding onto the wide bench seat. No gear shift separated me from Nathan, which made me oddly uncomfortable.

"*This* is a Rambler." Nathan caressed the skinny steering wheel. "A 1961 AMC Rambler. The perfect car." He used a gear stick by the steering wheel to put the car in drive.

"If you say so." I reached up for my seatbelt, but there wasn't one.

Or at least, there wasn't one that went across my shoulder. As I fastened the lap belt, I thought, *Well, that's risky.* And the thought was so ridiculous that I laughed out loud.

"This car is no laughing matter," Nathan said. "The Rambler was the 1963 *Motor Trend* Car of the Year."

I laughed again.

Nathan watched me, his eyes warm. "You look nice tonight."

"Sure, okay," I mumbled. I'd thrown on a black T-shirt and jeans, figuring that would make me as inconspicuous as possible. I reached up to rub Tyler's button, which I still wore on the string around my neck. I'd also stashed Tyler's pitted metal marbles in my pocket, just to have another little bit of him with us tonight.

Nathan and I lapsed into silence. I glanced over at him. He looked different tonight. He'd set aside his usual retro clothes, with all their vivid colors, in favor of a denim jacket over a gray zippered hoodie. He took occasional sips from a travel coffee mug that he kept in a cup holder on the floor. As we drove, the car took on a quiet closeness. The streetlights slid over us, one after the other, and everything outside was hushed and dark. Nathan slung an arm across the back of the bench seat, and I tried to ignore how much this felt like a date.

That got easier once we picked up Eric. He slid into the backseat wearing a Sex Pistols T-shirt and a pair of skinny jeans. His hair was spiked every which way with gel.

"Nice look," Nathan said.

"I lead a secret double life as a punk guitarist," Eric said. Nathan and I both turned around to stare at him.

As we pulled away from the curb, Eric leaned forward, resting his arms on the front seat. "What did you tell your parents?"

"Nothing," I said.

"What? You couldn't come up with some kind of cover story?"

"Like what?"

Eric made a face. "I don't know, that you're sleeping over at someone's house?"

"Whose? Yours? Nathan's?"

"We are seriously your only options? I'm very sad for you right now."

"I left a note," I said. "In case they wake up. Told them you and I went to that twenty-four-hour diner in Tyson's Corner." Tyler might have been the good boy, the glue that kept our family together, but apparently there was nothing he liked better than a lie and a secret Saturday night out. I could do that too.

We drove past the bookstore, which was in a typical Virginia strip mall, but we didn't park in the lot out front. Instead, Nathan found a spot several blocks away on a residential street.

"You ready?" Nathan took a final sip of his coffee, and I reached for it, hoping the caffeine would balance out the adrenaline buzzing through my system. He handed it to me.

I took a swig, then choked and spluttered on the contents. It wasn't coffee.

"Is this . . . tea?"

"Oolong," Nathan replied.

"Who drinks oolong?"

"Literally a billion people," he said, pulling on a baseball cap. "Ready now?"

I nodded, wiping at my mouth with the back of my hand.

We avoided the well-lit parking lot and walked down the dark alley behind the store.

"How'd they get into this place?" Eric asked.

"Some kid who goes to Westside—his dad owns the building, and he jacked the keys." Nathan paused. "Or so they told me."

I edged closer to Nathan. "Doesn't this shopping center have security guards?"

"Sure does," he said. "Want to know how much they make an hour? A hell of a lot less than they're making tonight."

We passed the store's delivery entrance and kept going until we reached a narrow door with a single lightbulb above it. I spotted a couple of kids in the shadows, the chrome-orange tips of their cigarettes glowing in the dark. Nathan knocked. I could make out the pounding rhythm of music on the other side of the door. A guy stuck his head out, releasing a blast of sound into the night. He looked around before grudgingly letting us in.

As we walked through the empty back room and into the bookstore, the music hit me like a physical thing, a hum that traveled up my legs and settled in my chest. It took a moment for my eyes to adjust to the darkness. Most of the light in the room came from the dancing bodies, people wearing glow-stick bracelets and flashing LED lights strung around their necks or attached to their clothing. A few lights were aimed up at the walls, illuminating empty bookshelves in flashing blue and green and purple. All the freestanding shelves in the middle of the room were gone, but signs still hung overhead to divide the store into sections. People thrashed around in Self Help and Young Adult, and where the Children's section had been, someone had hung a makeshift sign that read *The End Is Near.*

I tried to imagine how I might re-create it all on paper when I got home: the shapes, colors, textures. But even if I sprayed a coat of fixative over the whole scene and hung it on my wall, I couldn't possibly capture it.

"Whoa," Eric said. He had a humongous grin on his face, and he bounced slightly, like he was about to jump out of his skin. "This is totally old school." He looked over at us. "Tonight, you must call me by my rave name. Gambit."

"Let's just find Park," I said.

Nathan greeted friend after friend with shouts and complicated handshakes, and I realized his clothes weren't the only thing different about him tonight. His step bounced, his shoulders slouched, and he unleashed a sly smile I hadn't seen before. I left him to his friends and scoured the crowd for Park. The store was large enough to have a lower level for music and DVDs, and I walked over to the railing and leaned on it, looking down. People thronged around a central DJ station where a dark-haired figure stood, performing for his adoring fans.

Was that Park?

A small stage was set up beside him with drums, a couple of guitars, and microphones, but no band played. Around him, an ecstatic crowd throbbed and churned, flashes of skin gleaming in the dim light. Faces flickered into view, then disappeared again into the darkness.

For a moment, I felt dizzy, as though all this was just another vision—the flashing lights, the distorted sounds, the hazy people all around me. I found myself looking for Tyler in the crowd. *He isn't here,* I told myself. But I searched the faces anyway, hoping for a glimpse of him, an image from another time. Had he spent these parties dancing like a wild man? Manning the back door? Flirting with girls in dark corners?

That's when I saw it: a tiny white envelope, passed from one person to another, tucked into a pocket. Something handed back in exchange. Drugs, for sure. I couldn't tell what kind—my experience was limited to smoking pot once at summer arts camp. But all of a sudden, I wanted that envelope, whatever it was. Wanted to lose myself in the party, to turn up the volume on the lights, the music, the crowd. Wanted to be someone else—anyone else—and not the person I had been when I walked through the door. And the sinking thought occurred to me: Tyler might have come to these parties with something similar in mind.

The music seemed too loud inside my head, and I started breathing way too fast. I reached instinctively for my scissors, but I had forgotten to tuck them into the pocket of my jeans. All I could find in my pockets were the marbles. I clutched them as panic threatened, blurring the edges of my vision. *I need to cut something,* I thought.

At that moment, Nathan walked up behind me, leaning over my shoulder to speak right in my ear. "That's Park," he murmured, pointing out the DJ.

I was so wound up that when he touched me, I nearly jumped out of my skin.

He took my shoulders and turned me around to face him. I looked down, afraid he'd see the panic written across my face. He tilted his head down until he finally caught my eye.

"Hey, what is it? What happened?" I could hear the concern in his voice even over the music.

I shook my head, unable to answer, and he pulled me into a hug. Beneath his zippered hoodie, he wore a plain white T-shirt that smelled like tea and fabric softener. His chin fit perfectly on top of my head, and I rested my cheek against the warm plane of his chest.

"I miss him too," Nathan said. "It's not the same without him."

I wanted to pack my bags and move into that hug. I wanted to build a little den there and hibernate until winter was over. My fingers trailed up under his jacket, across the muscles of his back, and curled into fists by his shoulder blades. I hadn't been held like this in . . . I couldn't remember how long—and the heat and comfort of it was shocking. I felt something crack open inside me, and I was suddenly scared that whatever that was, it might have been the only thing holding me together.

I pulled away. Nathan studied my face, his eyes searching and intense.

"I'm fine." I steadied myself, trying to make that true. "Let's go."

We collected Eric, who was dancing at the edge of a small crowd in Classics, and headed downstairs. Somehow, in the five minutes we'd been there, Eric had acquired a pair of eyeglasses made of glow sticks, which made him look like a rave Harry Potter.

We made our way through the crowd. The closer we got to the DJ station, the better I could see Park, who wore a white baseball cap and a screen-printed T-shirt that had faded to illegibility.

"Wait, what's the plan?" I asked, as Nathan raised his hand to get Park's attention.

"We don't know enough to have a plan," Nathan said. "First we talk to him. Evaluate the situation. Then we make a plan."

Before I could answer, a guy stepped between us and Park. He was barely taller than me, with a short afro and a grin almost as large as the headphones he wore. He uncovered one ear and greeted Nathan.

"Hey, Sinatra! What up?" He went to hug Nathan at the same time Nathan tried to shake his hand, and they bumped chests awkwardly.

"What was that, bruh?" Nathan said, laughing. "We hugging now?" He turned to me, one hand gripping the guy's shoulder. "This here is Cedric Williams."

I smiled. "One of the underground masterminds, I hear."

Cedric grinned. "Ooh, so formal." He smacked Nathan's chest. "You hear that? I'm a mastermind. What's that make you?"

"Shit, man, next to you?" Nathan said, still laughing. "Nothing at all."

Cedric gave me a quick once-over and a wink. "Nathan brung the bait!"

"Okay, back up," Nathan said, slinging a possessive arm around my neck. "Listen, I need Park." He spoke louder as the music crested. "Tell him Red sent me."

Cedric's eyebrows went up, and he nodded. "Sure thing." He walked around the DJ table to yell something in Park's ear. As Cedric spoke, Park glanced over at us, but his face showed no emotion. He slipped his own headphones down to his neck, and Cedric took his place at the tables. Park came around and gestured for us to follow him. He took us to a corner where the music wasn't quite so loud.

"Red sent you?" Park said. Colored lights flashed, leaving his face alternately bright and shadowed. "Fucked up, what happened to him."

"Yeah," Nathan agreed. "Fucked up."

"Who're these two?" Park indicated us.

"Eric Bowling. Punk guitarist." Eric stuck out his hand.

Park didn't shake it. "Sure thing, bama." He turned to me. "And you?"

"I'm Meg—" Nathan shook his head slightly, and I stopped myself. "Just Meg. Meg White." I paused awkwardly. "I'm with his band," I finished, pointing to Eric.

"Come on. These two fakin'," Park said. "They stink of the five seven one."

Nathan shook his head. "Naw, man, they're cool."

Park rolled his eyes. "Okay, Slim, what you want?" He pulled off his cap with one hand and ruffled his dark hair with the other. On his left arm, a silver-and-gold wristwatch caught the light.

My eyes locked onto the watch. Was that it? The one Tyler had stolen from Kyle?

"Red said you helped each other out sometimes. He brought you stuff?"

"Maybe," Park acknowledged. "Sometimes."

A single diamond glinted on the face of the watch. I couldn't keep my eyes off it. I couldn't stop wondering what memories it might hold.

"How long you guys . . ." Nathan waved a hand back and forth. "When'd he start selling to you?"

Park's face went instantly suspicious. "You messin' with me? You some kind of narc?"

Nathan looked offended. "I wouldn't do you like that. I heard what happened to Kyle."

Park twisted the watch on his wrist and eyed Nathan for a moment. "How 'bout this? You want in with me, you do me a favor."

Nathan shifted his weight, not dropping his eyes from Park's. "Favor?"

Park gestured to the stage that was set up behind him. "I had a band tonight. They came, they set up, they got smacked. Left me hanging. What say you play something for me?"

"Play?" Nathan choked out. "Like a song? Oh, hell no . . ."

"Why not?" Park said. "If you're being straight with me? If they are who they say they are?" He pointed at Eric. "Punk guitarist." And at me. "Girl in band." He gave Nathan a taunting smile. "That's my deal, Sinatra. Play first, talk later."

Nathan slowly turned toward Eric, fixing him with a look of distilled death.

Eric smiled at Park. "Of course. No problem at all."

The three of us made our way over to the tiny stage as Park headed back to talk to Cedric. "We can totally pull this off," Eric said, slinging a guitar around his neck.

"Are you high?" I asked. "Have you been licking glow sticks?"

"Nathan, can you sing?" Eric asked him.

"Sure, I guess . . ." Nathan trailed off as Eric walked toward him with the bass guitar. He held both hands out in front of him. "I can-*not*, however, play bass."

"You don't have to play it," Eric said. "You just have to look good holding it." Nathan took the bass with a glare that promised severe punishment at a later date. He shrugged out of his jacket and hoodie and slung the bass across his chest. Eric turned to me. "That leaves you on drums, Megan."

I laughed a little wildly. "Okay, I play a little guitar. A *little.* But I have never in my life played the drums."

"I'll tell you a secret," Eric said. "Playing the drums well is a skill that takes years to learn and a certain degree of innate talent. Playing the drums badly?" He shrugged. "Even a monkey can do that."

"Not me." I shook my head. "I. Can. Not."

"Then you have to sing."

I plodded over to the drum set and picked up the sticks. "Where do I start?"

"I'll stand next to you and go *bum badda-bum badda-bum* and you keep time."

I gestured in confusion at the array of drums in front of me.

"Just hit the middle one." Eric pointed to it.

This was the most ridiculous thing I'd ever heard in my life. And yet I tried out a few *badda-bum*s. "What if I can't hear you?"

"We'll figure it out." Eric turned to Nathan. "Okay, we just have to fake our way through one song. What do you feel comfortable singing?"

"Nothing." Nathan said, fear lighting his eyes.

"But who's your favorite singer?" Eric pressed. "I mean, one where you know all their lyrics without having to think about them."

Nathan rattled off a list of names.

Eric shook his head. "Seriously? I've never heard of any of those." For the first time, he looked a bit panicked. "That guy called you Sinatra. Do you know any Sinatra?"

"Doesn't everyone?" Nathan said. "But only the Capitol years. I can't stand the later stuff."

Eric paced a little. "Okay. Okay. The Chairman of the Board. We can make this work. . . ." He thought for a minute. "'Fly Me to the Moon'?"

"Yeah, I know that one."

"Okay. Follow my lead. And be ready to sing fast."

The music from the DJ station faded out, and Park gestured to us to get going. Faces in the crowd turned toward us. Park leaned back against his tables, arms crossed, a curious light in his eyes.

As Eric started toward the microphone, Nathan stopped him with a hand on his arm. "This might be a good time to ask if you can actually play the guitar."

A slow grin spread across Eric's face. "Oh, yes. Yes I can." He stepped up to the mic, then covered it with one hand and turned back to us. "Wait. We need a band name."

"Exquisite Corpse," I threw out.

Seconds later, Eric was greeting the crowd. Nathan gripped the neck of the bass so hard, I thought the strings would cut through his skin. As I heard the first notes from Eric's guitar, I felt a giddy, unexpected joy shoot through my chest, and I wanted to laugh out loud. Then Eric walked over and stepped on my foot. Hard. *Oh, yeah,* I thought. *I have a job to do here.* I started to beat out the rhythm he indicated, feeling like a two-year-old banging pots and pans.

Nathan leaned into the microphone and began to sing "Fly Me to the Moon." He had undersold his singing voice, which was deep and resonant. My heart beat faster as he made his way through the first verse in a slow, leisurely way.

Then Eric peeled out a few fast, driving notes on the guitar. He stepped on my foot faster and faster, and I sped up in response. Nathan turned and stared at Eric in disbelief, but he quickly launched into the next verse at this new pace. It sounded fun and unexpected and . . . cool. Nathan had the voice, but it was Eric who was making it all work, surprisingly completely in his element. It was one of those moments that stretched out and seemed to defy time, as I watched my friends do this amazing thing that I had no idea they were capable of.

Three Things from the unanticipated bookstore concert: Eric's hair moving against his forehead as his fingers flew, Nathan's shirt stretching against his shoulder blades under the strap of his unplayed bass, colored lights flashing against my eyelids when I closed my eyes.

It almost felt like Tyler was there with us, playing along.

Nathan finished the last verse, and I lifted the drumsticks as Eric gave one final lick on the guitar and held up an arm in triumph.

The crowd was, well, underwhelmed. I heard some halfhearted applause. Most of them didn't seem sure what to do. Park looked satisfied, though. He gave us a thumbs-up and jumped back on the mic. He started a song that was better for dancing, and the crowd came alive again. As the guys set down their instruments, I grabbed them both by the shoulders. "That was freaking awesome." They grinned back at me. We climbed down from the stage, but not before I peeled a sticker off one of the guitar cases and tucked it into my purse. *Raw materials, for later.*

Cedric bounced over. "I saw that! Not bad, bruh." He nudged up next to me, bumping my hip with his. "Hey, Meg, right? You *have* to come to the DC underground next month."

I grinned at him. "That sounds great." I gestured to his headphones. "Is music, like, your thing?"

"Naw, not really." His eyes glowed. "I'm more into politics, myself."

Park walked over and clapped a hand on Nathan's shoulder. The watch glinted in the light, calling to me. "Okay, Sinatra," Park said. "Let's talk."

At that moment, over the loud dance music, I heard the squeal and pop of a megaphone turning on. "Everyone stay where you are," a voice called out.

The cops had arrived.

I could have run. I probably should have run. But instead, as I watched the party disintegrate around me, I grabbed hold of Park's arm and closed my hand around the watch.

CHAPTER 11

THE WATCH BURNED LIKE A BRAND, BUT I HELD ON as the pain streaked up my arm to settle behind my eyes. The flashing party lights smeared and blurred, dimming to a soft, warm glow. I found myself in a darkened room, where the only light came from a glass display case filled with watches. The case stood as tall as my shoulder, and inside it, each watch rested on its own plush stand. Some of them gently spun and rotated. For a moment, I thought I was in a jewelry store, but as my eyes adjusted, I could make out a bed, a nightstand, a dresser, and a flat-screen TV. Someone's bedroom.

And Tyler was there, alone. Through the viewfinder of a small handheld video camera, he studied the watches, slowly panning across the collection. He spoke softly to himself, like he was practicing a voice-over to lay in later.

"Time is money," he said. "Or so the saying goes. And some people don't just keep time, they hoard it." He broke off. "No, not hoard. Stockpile. That's better. They stockpile more time and money than any one person could ever use. And they'll keep right on—"

With a stomach-wrenching drop, the scene was ripped away. Park had yanked his arm from my grasp, and I tumbled to the ground. He stood above me, his eyes burning with a cold fire. He opened his mouth to speak, but the police megaphone blared again. "Stay where you are," the amplified voice repeated.

Park gave me one last glare and disappeared into the crowd. The entire room was a tumble of frantic movement. Instead of saying "Stay where you are," the officer should just have said, "Completely freak out for a second, then run like hell while we try to apprehend you."

People knocked into us from all sides. Nathan pulled me to my feet, and I grabbed a handful of Eric's shirt to keep him close. Cedric had left the DJ station, but the music kept playing, and the lights kept flashing, so the panic of the crowd seemed almost like another dance. Bodies thronged the staircase leading up to the main level. It looked like a death by trampling waiting to happen, and yet I started toward it.

Nathan stopped me. "Through here! The back room!" He pulled me along behind him, so I pulled Eric. Nathan led us away from the crowd and along one wall until we came to a swinging door marked *Authorized Personnel Only*. We ducked inside, out of the semidarkness of the party into the full-on darkness of an unknown room. Eric dug out his cell phone and turned on the flashlight, revealing a wall of Occupational Safety and Health posters, a water fountain, and a tattered couch. He reached for the light switch.

"Don't turn on the overheads," Nathan said. "Do you want to advertise that we're in here?"

My ears were ringing from the music, and in the quiet room, Nathan's voice sounded tinny and recorded. "How did you know to come back here?" I asked.

"There's always a storeroom." Nathan shielded his eyes when Eric swung the light toward him. "And a fire exit." He pointed.

Past the towering rows of storeroom shelves, now bare, a red exit sign hovered in the distance. The door was blocked by a rolling metal book cart and a pile of empty cardboard boxes. Nathan and I cleared a path, and Eric opened the door, his light revealing a grim concrete stairwell leading up. Horror-movie warning bells sounded in my mind, but a loud crash from the other side of the storeroom sent me pushing past Nathan and Eric and climbing the stairs two at a time. When we reached the top, Nathan opened the metal door a crack and peered out. He gestured for us to stay quiet, and we emerged into a long, narrow alley between the bookstore and the sporting-goods warehouse next door.

At one end of the alley, the flashing lights of police cars painted the walls blue and red, a *Law & Order* echo of the party lights inside. A uniformed cop ushered two crying girls into the back of his patrol car. He shut the door and was approached by another officer, a smaller figure in a leather jacket. The lights hit her face. Detective Johnson.

I spun back toward the door. There was no handle on the outside, just a smooth surface that offered no escape. Johnson turned to look down the alley. "You there! Stop! Police!"

Once again, unless she'd said, "You there! Flee the scene of the crime!" she was asking for disappointment.

We ran for the opposite end of the alley, cop footsteps echoing behind us. We hadn't gone far when I heard a cry. Eric collapsed to the ground behind me. I froze, not sure what to do, and Nathan skidded to a stop as well.

Sprawled on the pavement, Eric glanced at Detective Johnson

and the two other officers, who were gaining rapidly. "Go!" he cried. "I'm fine! Go!"

Nathan and I locked eyes. I couldn't read his expression, but there was no time to take a vote. I sprinted back toward Eric, but Nathan got there first. He had Eric half on his feet by the time I reached them, and the police were almost on top of us.

Then the door from the stairwell flew open again, and a group of five or six guys tumbled out into the alley, right in front of the cops. Johnson stopped herself in time, but the other two took the boys down like bowling pins. Before they could recover, Nathan had hauled Eric the rest of the way up, and we escaped into the night.

"Are you okay?" I asked Eric as we circled back through the neighborhood toward Nathan's car.

"Fine." Eric ducked his head. "That was a stunning display of my natural athletic ability. You like?"

Nathan slapped Eric on the back. "I cannot believe you on that guitar. Seriously, man. That was *ridiculous*."

"Yes, well," Eric said. "I dabble."

Then Nathan stopped short, and he threw out an arm to block us. "Wait." He ushered us off the sidewalk and into the shadows. A police car blocked the street where we had parked. The interior light was on, and it illuminated a lone cop, his head bent low over a clipboard. We backtracked until the car was out of sight.

"Can't we go around him?" I asked. "I really should get home."

"It's a cul-de-sac," Nathan said. "No other way in, unless we climb someone's fence." He looked over at Eric and me, clearly deciding that, given the company, that was a bad idea. "Even then, we'd have to drive right past him. We'd better hang out for a while."

We found a tiny neighborhood park. It had no streetlamps, but the playground sand glowed in the moonlight. Eric and Nathan claimed the only two swings, their faces hidden in shadow. I sat on the end of a plastic slide and rubbed my face with my hands. All this effort, all this risk, and we had nothing new.

Eric pulled out his phone and began typing a message.

"Updating your many Twitter followers?" I asked.

"No, I'm texting my mom to let her know I'm going to be later than I thought."

Nathan and I stared at him in pointed silence.

"What?" Eric said. "I told you. She likes me to have life experiences."

I snort-laughed so loudly that they both shushed me, which of course made me laugh harder. Eric smiled at me, his face lit by his phone, the only bright spot in the dark.

"You are so strange," I told him, "that you make everything else seem normal."

"I take that as a compliment."

I leaned back against the slide and listened to the creak of the swings as the guys rocked back and forth. The images of Tyler that I'd seen when I'd touched the watch loomed heavy in my mind, but they had to compete with the still-fresh surge of exhilaration I'd felt on that stage, standing beside Nathan and Eric, *badda-bumm*ing my sad little heart out. I dug into my pocket for my phone so I could text Elena.

Your fondest wish for me has come true, I wrote.

Today was an Adventures in Babysitting kind of day.

* * *

The next thing I knew, Nathan was shaking me gently. "Megan, let's move. Cops are gone, and it's after four a.m. I need to be home for breakfast."

I stood up, stretching the kinks out of my back. "The two of you have very weird families. Do you know that?"

Nathan shot a quick glance over at Eric, who was walking toward the street. He stepped closer to me. "Hey, are you hungry?" he asked. "I mean, do you want to come over?"

I knew I should go straight home. I knew my parents would freak if they woke up and found me gone, even with the note I'd left. I knew Detective Johnson might have recognized me, might even have told my parents where I was.

But my body was still lit up from adrenaline, and I wasn't ready for the night to be over yet.

"I could eat."

We dropped Eric at his house, but instead of taking us across the river into DC, Nathan drove down a quiet, tree-lined street in McLean. He parked in front of a two-story colonial with massive pillars in the front. He turned off the car, and I looked around, confused.

"Wait. Where are we?"

"My house," Nathan said.

"You live here? But you said you lived in DC."

"No, I said I went to school in DC," he corrected.

I looked up at the white-framed windows, at the ivy crawling up the brick, and understanding dawned. "You go to a *private* school in DC. Probably some expensive prep school in—"

"Georgetown. Yes."

I pointed a finger at him. "But when we were at that McDonald's in Northeast, you said you were already in the neighborhood."

"I was getting my hair cut. You don't think I'm trusting all this gorgeousness"—he used both hands to indicate his hair—"to some white salon in Georgetown?"

I crossed my arms and gave him a look. "All along, you knew exactly what I thought, and you didn't correct me. You knew I assumed you lived in that neighborhood because . . ."

". . . because I'm black," he finished for me.

I felt a surge of defensiveness, like he was accusing me of something. But there it was. He was right. "Wow, um. Yeah," I managed. "I did think that."

He shook his head, his mouth a thin line. "Happens to every black kid in this neighborhood." His eyes were tired. That look—I'd helped put that look on his face.

"It's not okay," I said quietly, "for me to, you know, add to that. I'm sorry."

He smiled a little and bumped me with his shoulder. "Come inside?"

A hint of indigo touched the sky, the barest tinge of daylight, as we walked up the long driveway to the back door. Nathan walked close enough that his hand brushed mine, and I fought the urge to grab it and hold on for dear life.

He let us into the kitchen, where he put a teakettle on to boil. He set his eyeglasses on the marble countertop and started rummaging through the cupboards, his long arms easily reaching the tallest cabinets, pulling out mixing bowls and ingredients.

"What are you doing?"

"Um . . . making pancakes?"

"You cook?"

He smiled. "Every single day. My grandmother counts on me for breakfast in the mornings. She wakes up super early, so I have to get up even earlier to beat her in here."

As he worked, I snooped. A doorway off the kitchen led to a little family room, filled with casual furniture and mismatched shelves that overflowed with books and knickknacks. I examined a small wooden Buddha and ran my fingers through a bowl of foreign coins, as varied in color and size as the different languages that marked them. A framed family photo hung above the slouchy sofa.

"Um, Nathan," I called out to him, "could I ask you a personal question?"

"Sure."

"Are your parents, like, Asian?"

He appeared in the doorway. "Chinese, yeah."

"But . . . you aren't."

"True enough," Nathan said. "They fostered me when my mom took off, and I got to stay. They legally adopted me when I was three." The teakettle whistled from the kitchen, and Nathan ducked back inside.

"And your grandmother lives with you?"

"Yeah. My dad's mom. She moved down here from Rockville." Nathan stepped out into the living room. "Just so you know, before you meet her, she has Alzheimer's."

"Oh."

"She usually thinks I'm my grandfather. He died a few years ago, which is when she came to live with us. And if you needed one more reason to believe that Alzheimer's is a totally messed-up disease, it's that it would make *anyone* believe I'm a seventy-year-old Chinese man."

"Well," I said, "you do usually *dress* like a seventy-year-old man."

Nathan smiled. "I wear a lot of his clothes."

"Aha." Things started clicking into place in my head. "You drive his car?"

"Yes."

"And Frank Sinatra?"

"My grandparents immigrated here in the sixties," Nathan said. "Apparently my grandfather thought that to be a good American, you had to act like a member of the Rat Pack. When my grandmother moved in with us, his stuff came with her: the albums, the clothes, the car. I fell in love with all of it. Kinda became my thing." He glanced over his shoulder. "Tea should be ready."

I flopped down onto the sofa and let out a long breath. My muscles relaxed, as though my whole body was melting into the cushions, pulling me toward sleep. I could see Nathan in the kitchen, one narrow hip leaning against the countertop, pouring tea from a clay pot into small matching cups. His hair looked taller than usual, and my gaze lingered on the contours of his face. I felt a tug in my chest, a physical sensation, pulling me toward him.

He came back into the family room with the teacups and offered me one. I took it, cupping its warmth in both hands and bringing it to my nose. I breathed in the scent of bitter grass and raisins and flowers—a smell I associated with Nathan himself—and stared into the bottom of the cup, where tiny leaves swirled.

He lowered himself onto the sofa beside me with a yawn and propped his feet on the coffee table. "The batter's done," he said. "Now we wait for my grandmother to wake up." He sipped his tea, then let his head fall back against the cushions.

I mirrored him, resting my head and closing my eyes.

I must have fallen asleep, because the next thing I knew, my eyes fluttered open, and I was staring at the ceiling. The teacup in my hand hadn't spilled, and it was still warm, so I couldn't have been out for more than a few minutes.

I turned to look at Nathan and found his sleeping face only inches from my own. As though he sensed me there, his eyes opened, and he smiled.

I felt my breathing go shallow.

Nathan closed the tiny gap between us and brushed my nose with his. Then he inched away from me, and his eyes locked on mine.

Footsteps sounded in another part of the house. Nathan and I sat up with a guilty start as an older Asian woman emerged down the stairs into the living room. Her steps were hesitant, her hair streaked with gray. But her small smile bloomed into a larger one when she spotted her grandson.

Nathan jumped up and rushed to greet her. *"Hai, mĕi lì."* I followed them into the kitchen as he walked her over to the table and helped her into a seat. Pleased, his grandmother studied his face closely, patting his cheek with one hand. Nathan kissed the top of her head. He went to the stove and turned on the heat, pouring pancake batter into a pan with a secret, faraway smile.

I had a sudden sensation of falling, like I'd dropped through a wormhole and come out in another world. Everything looked the same, but it all felt different. This was not the Nathan I knew. Or, rather, it was the face I knew, but not the Nathan I'd imagined. And I'd spent a lot of time over the last few weeks imagining him. I tried to shake off this new Nathan, to go back to the moment before and shut the door against him. But he stayed, stubbornly glued in place, and I couldn't seem to remove him without tearing away something essential. I leaned back against the pantry door and sipped my tea.

As the sun came up, tinting the kitchen with rose-colored light, we ate pancakes seasoned with ginger and drank hot tea until I almost liked the taste. After we'd loaded the last dish into the dishwasher, Nathan and I climbed into the front seat of his car so he could take me home. In the dawning light, the car's exterior paint glowed a bright cadmium orange.

"So this is a Rambler, huh?" I ran my hands over the pale-orange dashboard studded with mysterious silver buttons and knobs. I looked up at him and grinned. "Well, let's ramble."

As Nathan fished out his keys, I shifted uncomfortably in my seat. The marbles in my pocket were poking into my hip bone. I pulled one out and held it up to examine it more closely. With the light behind it, it looked like a tiny moon, putting the morning sun into eclipse.

Where did you come from, little marbles? I thought.

Maybe I could find out.

It had been easy to see the memories with Dr. Brightman's help, but everything I'd seen on my own had come to me without my even trying. I hadn't really tried to control the ability, to unlock a memory from an object that didn't give up its secrets with a single touch. I held the marble in the palm of my hand, and like Dr. Brightman had suggested, I unfocused my eyes and imagined myself traveling deep within its metal core, unlocking the light.

A flash. A needlelike pain behind my eyes, so sharp it snapped my head back. And the world around me disappeared in a blaze of light.

CHAPTER 12

AS THE LIGHT FADED, I COULD SEE TYLER AND BOBBY standing in a luxurious wood-paneled study, where bookshelves lined the walls and a portrait of Abraham Lincoln hung behind a massive desk. Tyler pulled Dr. Brightman's book about John Wilkes Booth off one of the shelves and started paging through it. Across the room, Bobby opened the door of an elaborately carved wooden cabinet, and his face lit with delight. He reached in and took out a cigar, which he smelled deeply, drawing it across his face under his nose.

"Leave it," Tyler said.

Bobby's jaw dropped in a parody of shock. "But you're trolling the shelves for first editions."

"No, I'm not. Park told me he wouldn't buy any more books." He put *Disasters in the Sun* down on the desk. "And besides, I wouldn't take anything from here. The Tyrant would bust Emma's ass."

The high-backed leather office chair behind the desk spun around, revealing Emma, drinking from a bottle of vodka she held in one hand. "And it's such a gorgeous ass, wouldn't you say?"

Tyler smoothed a hand across the top of Herndon's desk. "So is this where your dad comes up with all his political decrees?" He pounded a fist on the wood. "Eliminate the capital gains tax! People worked hard for that money!"

Emma rolled her eyes and swatted at him. "God, you're so obsessed with politics now. Just leave it, okay?"

Bobby leaned on an overstuffed armchair, the cigar still in his hand. "So where's the good stuff? Brittany's dad had all those high-end bottles of cognac. I figured Herndon would be stocking something at least as impressive as that." He wandered over to a sleek black safe that stood in one corner. "What's in here?"

"Guns, I think." Emma shrugged. "Daddy loves his guns."

Tyler picked up an object from the desk, and my heart lurched when I saw it was the Lincoln box. "He doesn't collect rare Chinese stamps? Hundred-thousand-dollar comic books? Come on, Em, what's his secret?"

"Nothing," Emma snorted. "He's perfect. We all are. Anything less will not be tolerated." She took another long pull off the vodka, scrunching up her nose. "All he's got are closets full of Abe Lincoln's underwear." She put on a fake deep voice. "What ho! Four score! Gettysburg!" Slumping down onto the desk, she dissolved into giggles.

Then the door slammed open, and all three jumped, their heads jerking guiltily toward the sound.

It was Matty, the guy I'd seen drop Emma off at school on my first day back. He looked exhausted, his black hair as rumpled as his suit and tie. "What are you . . . You know no one is allowed back here." He spotted the bottle in Emma's hand. "Is that *alcohol*?"

"Oh my god, Charity Case," Emma snapped, "chill out. You're

like a sixty-five-year-old Republican trapped in a twenty-one-year-old body."

Matty stiffened. "I'm not a charity case."

She laughed. "Are you kidding me? If it weren't for my dad, you'd be shipped straight back to Hyattsville."

"Hey." Tyler put a hand on her shoulder. "Not cool, Em."

"Is that what you think?" Matty said. "Well, let's see what he makes of this little scene." He gestured to the three of them.

Emma stood, a look of panic on her face. "You wouldn't."

"Watch me." Matty turned and left.

Emma looked back and forth between Tyler and Bobby. "I can't . . . The last time he caught me drinking . . ." Tyler reached out to her, but she dodged him and walked to the door. "I just . . . I have to stop Matty before he gets to my dad." She paused in the doorway without looking back. "You know what?" she said. "Take whatever you want." And she left.

Bobby immediately grabbed a cigar box off a shelf—the one I'd seen in his locker, the one with the naked woman on it—and started loading cigars into it.

Tyler sat down at Senator Herndon's desk, his expression dark. Beside a brass pen holder sat a glass bowl full of the same pitted metal marbles I was holding. He ran his fingers through them and put a handful in his pocket. Then he turned and stared at the portrait of Lincoln hanging over Herndon's desk.

The desk lamp flickered, and I thought of what Dr. Brightman had said. *The strongest memories. The brightest lights.* I gripped the marble in my hand and stared at the lamp until it grew blinding bright.

The image shifted, and I saw Tyler sitting in Nathan's kitchen, the same room where I'd eaten pancakes a few minutes before. He was rolling a marble in one hand, staring off into the distance. Then he bent over Dr. Brightman's book, which lay open on the table in front of him, and wrote furiously in the margins.

Nathan came into view, carrying a camera and a tripod. "Red. Dude," he said. "Stop reading the damn book. I thought we were making a video for The District this afternoon." He snatched the book out from under Tyler's pen and tossed it onto the counter.

"Did you know," Tyler said, "that John Wilkes Booth targeted Lincoln because he was operating above the law? Suspending the writ of habeus corpus, tossing his critics in jail. Basically abusing his privilege and running this country into the ground."

"Did *you* know," Nathan shot back, "that John Wilkes Booth was a murderer? Not to mention a racist asshole who wanted slavery to go on forever?" He gave Tyler a significant look and picked up the marble. "Your fave is problematic, is what I'm saying."

Tyler looked up at Nathan. He seemed tense, his usual carefree energy gone. "He's not my *fave*." He scrubbed his face with his hands. "I just mean—all along, Booth thought he was the good guy. Thought he was gonna be this big hero for what he did. Then he finds out . . . nope. He was the bad guy. For all time, that's how he'd be remembered."

Nathan drew his fingertips down his cheeks, one after the other.

Tyler shook his head. "What are you doing?"

"Crying some white, slavery-loving assassin tears."

Tyler busted out a laugh. "Okay, okay. I'm not looking for a role model here. I'm looking for a *symbol*." His mouth disappeared into a grim line. "Senator Herndon wants to pretend he's this modern-day

Abe Lincoln, but the truth is he's just another entitled bully. His whole political philosophy is basically 'more for me and everyone like me.' He's way overdue for a little poetic justice." Tyler picked up Dr. Brightman's book again, examining the photograph of Booth on the cover.

Then a slow smile spread across his face.

"Well, *sic semper tyrannis*, motherfucker."

Nathan snorted. "What's your obsession with Herndon, anyway? He's no worse than any other politician. And why focus on taking someone down? I thought we were about letting new voices be heard." He tossed the marble back to Tyler, who caught it. "Don't be John Wilkes Booth, man. Be, like, Frederick Douglass instead. Don't take the other guy out. Influence his opinion."

Tyler opened his mouth to argue, but then he shut it again. "He's got—" He paused. "I'm working on something. Not ready to talk about it yet, but I'll tell you more later." He held up the metal marble. "Anyway, if it makes you feel better, I promise I won't shoot anyone to get what I'm after."

All at once, the pieces fit into place: the bowl of marbles in Senator Herndon's study, the safe that Emma said had guns in it. Those weren't marbles after all. They were bullets. I'd been carrying bullets around in my pocket. Probably antiques, given how old they looked, but still. A shudder of revulsion ran through me, but I didn't let go of the small hunk of metal in my hand.

Tyler stood, shaking out his hands and arms as though he could throw off whatever was bothering him. He grabbed the crutches that were leaning against the table. He'd broken his leg only a few weeks before he died, so this scene couldn't have happened very long ago. He hobbled over to Nathan. "We got some great footage in Northeast yesterday. Do you want to head back there?"

"First," Nathan said, "I want to swing by Bailey's Crossroads. I'll show you the site I chose for the next underground. It's gonna be a killer."

Tyler gestured to his cast. "Yeah, well, the last site you chose was a killer too. It killed my entire preseason."

Nathan laughed. "My bad." And he held out a hand. Tyler slapped it, setting off a complex series of high-fives that escalated to ridiculous proportions. They were like boys on the playground, unself-conscious but totally in sync, members of the same team. I had a sudden thought: even though Tyler was gone, Nathan and I had become a kind of team too. I wondered if Tyler might have been happy about that.

I could sense the vision slipping away, gently this time, and I blinked at Nathan's car re-forming around me. My eyes felt crusty and my head foggy, as though I'd woken up from a heavy sleep—and an intense dream. Nathan was holding my hand, and I could hear him saying my name.

"Megan. Megan, thank god," he said. "Are you okay? You glazed over and . . . Man, you scared the crap out of me."

I leaned my forehead against his shoulder, breathing deeply as I shook off the effects of the vision. Then something Nathan had said to Tyler came back to me.

"I'll show you the site I chose for the next underground."

The site *Nathan* chose? Nathan had acted like he barely knew anything about the parties. And Tyler had told all of us he'd broken his leg climbing some kind of cage on the baseball field. But it sounded like he'd been with Nathan instead.

And Nathan had been making videos with him. In secret.

I pulled away from Nathan and looked him in the face. He'd been lying to me. It was as though I'd fallen through another wormhole, and he'd become a stranger to me yet again.

"How could you?"

I got out of the car. I looked around, not sure what to do next; then I started walking.

Behind me I heard Nathan's door slam, and he caught up to me. "What is going on? Is this about your . . . visions . . . or whatever?"

"It's about you. Lying to me."

Nathan didn't look confused. He looked *caught*. I kept walking.

"I don't know what you think you saw," he said, "but I'm sure it's not how it looks."

I turned on him. "Oh, really? Because it *looks* like you knew a hell of a lot about what was going on with Tyler that you never told me. Like how he broke his leg? And how he went around exploring buildings for these underground parties that were *all your idea*."

Nathan froze. "Well. Then I guess it *is* how it looks. But how did you—" Nathan pointed to the bullet in my hand. "Are you telling me this vision thing is real? You actually saw that?"

I gave him a thin smile and shoved the bullet into my pocket. "I'm sorry. Were you happier when you thought I was losing touch with reality?" Beneath my anger, I was beginning to feel something else: embarrassment. I'd actually started to believe Nathan might feel something for me. But clearly he'd been lying to me all along.

"Listen, Megan," Nathan said. "There were things I couldn't tell you. If my parents found out I was planning those parties . . . I couldn't disappoint them like that." He held out a hand toward me, but I stepped away.

"And the videos!" I said as the vision washed back over me. "I want to see all the videos. The ones you were making with Tyler but *you supposedly knew nothing about*. The ones you've got hidden away somewhere. For The District, whatever that is." My voice broke, and I struggled under the weight of yet another blow, of losing once again someone I never had in the first place. "Why didn't you tell me?"

"It was stupid," he said, speaking quickly now. "When I first saw you, at the funeral, I only wanted to make sure you were okay. I didn't think I'd ever see you again. And with the police asking you a million questions all the time, I figured it was safer for me to tell you as little as possible. I never knew that we'd get to be . . . and then we were, and I didn't know how to—"

I cut him off with a gesture. The real question burned in my chest, demanding to be let out. "How long was he doing drugs?" I asked. "What made him start? And were you with him when he . . ."

"God. No. I swear to you, I didn't know about any drugs. When you showed me that roll of cash, I was as shocked as you were."

A sinking feeling spread through my body as I connected all the dots. The pieces fell together with a click that felt like an ending, like the final closing of a door.

"Where is the Lincoln box?" I asked slowly.

"What are you talking about?"

"You took it, didn't you? From Tyler's room, last week. It *was* stolen, just like Eric thought. And it was you." I shook my head.

Nathan's face turned ashen. "I didn't."

"You were there." I struggled to keep my voice steady. "The last night I saw it. I fell asleep; you were alone upstairs. Who else could have done it?"

"You think I, like, burgled your house?" He let out a long breath. "I'm not a thief." For an instant, I thought I saw tears in his eyes. Then he smiled bitterly. "Apparently that was more Tyler's thing."

That stung, and I struck back at him in response. "But you are a liar."

"Fine." Nathan nodded. "So that's what you think of me." He headed back toward his car. "Come on. I'll take you home."

"I'll get another ride."

He stared at me a moment, deliberating. Then he began to walk away.

I yelled after him, "And I want it back."

He turned to me, his face blank.

"The box. I want it back."

"Well, good luck with that," he said. And he was gone.

CHAPTER 13

"I CAN'T BELIEVE NATHAN STOLE THAT BOX FROM you," Eric said. He'd still been awake when I texted him, and it had only taken him a few minutes to come and get me. "Did you see why he did it? In your vision?"

I shook my head, distracted. My mind was back on the sidewalk in front of Nathan's house, his voice echoing in my ears: *"I'm not a thief. Apparently that was more Tyler's thing."* I wanted to shove those words down his throat. But I couldn't deny what I'd seen: my own brother, standing in Senator Herndon's study, chatting about expensive cognac, cigars, and first editions. He'd been stealing, and lying. And Nathan right along with him.

The more I tried to put Tyler back together, the more everything seemed to fall apart.

"Okay, well . . ." Eric kept glancing over at me, his face full of concern. "You don't have to talk about it, but if there's anything you want on the way home, just say the word."

"You know what I want?" I let my head fall back, exhausted. "Not to go home."

"Coffee?" Eric suggested. "We could get coffee? Or, wait—you told your mom we were going to that twenty-four-hour diner, right? Let's do that! We'll turn your lie into the truth."

Eric changed direction, heading toward the Beltway, but his words played over in my mind: *turn your lie into the truth.*

Wasn't that what I'd been trying to do for years?

Since the first day of high school, I'd played the role of Brown Brown. I'd followed all of Tyler's rules, because I'd seen firsthand what might happen if I didn't. I'd laid low. Stayed small. Kept out of sight. Even my art felt brown these days. I held up the button I wore around my neck and flipped it over to study my collage. Did all my pieces have to be so tiny? Why was I limiting myself to buttons and artist trading cards and decorated matchbooks? I *hated* playing it safe.

It's for your own good, Tyler had said.

All this time, I'd thought it was concern. But now it felt more like control. And maybe even a lack of respect.

He'd had no faith in me. Or he'd thought something was wrong with me, deep down. He'd made me lie about myself until it became the truth.

Well, now he was gone. And I was done lying.

We drove past a massive shopping center anchored by a big-box hardware store, and an irresistible urge took hold of me.

"Right here," I said to Eric, making him jump in surprise. "Pull in here."

"Whoa. Okay, here I go," Eric checked his rearview mirror and turned the wheel sharply.

"Park by the hardware store."

I marched inside, Eric trailing behind me, and came out ten

minutes later with three large sheets of galvanized steel. We struggled to fit them in the backseat of Eric's Geo, and when we finally got the door closed, he looked at me, wide-eyed.

"Anything else?"

Without answering him, I crossed the parking lot toward a small beauty supply store. I prowled the aisles until I found what I was looking for: an entire shelf of neon hair dye.

Screw Brown, I thought. *I'm going Red.*

Back home, Mom's car was gone, and Dad was nowhere to be seen. All the better for me. In my bedroom, Eric helped me tear down the tiny corkboard that hung on my wall. Together, we moved my worktable out of the way and wrestled the sheet metal into place. I'd raided the garage for some nails and a hammer, so when I figured out how I wanted the metal arranged, Eric held it in place, and I started pounding.

Barely one nail in, I heard my dad's groggy voice from my parents' bedroom down the hall. "Megan! Is everything okay in there?"

"Just hanging some things on the wall," I yelled. "It may take a while."

There was a pause. "Carry on."

With the third nail, I hit a stud. The shock of the wood traveled up my arm to my shoulder, and I gritted my teeth with the pure satisfaction of it. From then on, I sought out the studs, savoring the feeling of knocking those nails through the metal and straight into the frame of the house itself.

When I was done hammering, my breathing ragged and my arm sore, Eric and I stood back and admired our work.

Eric hadn't said much during this whole process, but now he put a hand on my shoulder. "It's frakking awesome. Now what?"

"Now we add the raw materials."

I pulled out everything I'd gathered since Tyler's death: scraps of clothing, paper place mats, weepy notes written in purple ink. I hung them on the metal wall with magnets, arranging and re-arranging them as I went.

Eric took his research binder out of his backpack and almost shyly offered me a few pages to add to the wall. He paused as he was handing over one particular sheet, caught up in reading what was on the page.

"What is it?" I asked.

"More of my research, trying to track down other people like you and Dr. Brightman." He showed me the paper. "Did you ever see that TV show *Letters from the Other Side*?"

"Definitely not."

"People bring this guy objects that belonged to their loved ones, and he gives them messages from the dead. But *before* he was a TV psychic, he was an archaeologist. See?" He indicated the paper. "And he also suffered a major loss. His wife was killed while they were on a dig together in India."

"And he ended up a TV psychic?"

"He got prosecuted for destroying some artifacts. Guess that kind of put the kibosh on future archaeology jobs."

I took the page from him, scanning the article. "Why does it matter so much to you?" I asked. "My origin story or whatever?"

Eric shrugged. "I don't know. I guess I just wonder . . . something big happens, changes your whole understanding of who you are.

Was it lurking inside you all along? Or did you trigger it somehow?"

He ducked his head, embarrassed. "Or something like that. Listen, take this." He handed me the whole binder. "Use all of it if you want. I'd better get home. You going to be okay?"

I nodded, and as Eric left, I turned back to the metal wall. I sensed a massive artwork lurking in all these pieces, a major mixed-media collage, but I couldn't really see it, didn't understand how to begin it. I started to organize the pieces by color, building a palette, hoping it would help me see the final image. As I worked, the colored groups began to resemble shapes, but it was like looking for animals in the clouds. The blue group looked kind of like a hat, the brown group like a guitar. Or maybe a gun. Instead of fading to a manageable level, my anger grew. That wasn't supposed to happen. My art was supposed to center me.

I abandoned the collage wall and headed for the bathroom. I stared at myself in the mirror for a long time, turning my head this way and that, until my own face became an optical illusion, like the rabbit that turns into a duck, or the old woman and the young woman both trapped in the same drawing. From some angles I thought I could see the sister Tyler wanted me to be. From others, my parents' daughter. And sometimes I caught a glimpse of the girl I had thought Nathan might like.

But where was I?

I went to my room and got my big scissors—no pocket pair this time. Back in the bathroom, I grabbed a section of my hair and sliced through it at the jawline. Once the first cut had been made, the others came more easily, until chunks of hair littered the sink and the floor. I cut the back so short I couldn't see it, but I left a long asymmetrical piece in front that fell to my chin. When I was done, I wasn't entirely sure who that girl in the mirror was, but she looked fearless. I liked her. And I'd discovered a new favorite canvas: me.

Now I just needed color.

I had intended to dye my whole head, but the smell of the bleach made my eyes water. I changed my mind and opted for a fat streak in the front. While I waited for the bleach to take effect, I went down the hall to Tyler's room, hoping I'd been wrong about Nathan taking the box, and somehow it would be sitting right there on Tyler's bed, where I'd last seen it.

But, of course, it wasn't. Once again, I went through all the places where I might have put it, but the box was nowhere to be found. I even searched my own room, just in case. Nothing. After going through all those objects, I had a sense that there were other items missing too—I was sure there had been more things in the bag of Tyler's personal effects than there were now.

Then I had a terrible thought: the roll of cash. I'd showed it to Nathan. Had he taken that too?

I emptied out the contents of my backpack. The money wasn't there. I went back to Tyler's room, but there was no place left to search. The money, the box, the rest of it—all stolen. I felt queasy with anger and betrayal.

Staring down at the objects on Tyler's bed, I wondered if there might be other memories hidden there, memories I could now unlock, the same way I'd done with the bullet from my pocket. But even though I tried, I wasn't able to force a vision from any other objects. Maybe my ability didn't work when I was totally exhausted.

My eyes fell on Tyler's laptop. He'd been making videos with Nathan. A lot of videos, judging by the way they'd been talking. I'd checked his browser history weeks ago, but might there be videos lurking on his hard drive that I hadn't seen yet? I booted it up.

I scoured the list of applications until I spotted some video editing software and clicked on it. A list of projects popped up on the left side of the screen. I had hoped to see dozens, but there were only a few. I recognized Guitar Lessons, but the second project in the list was called Thoughts from Bathrooms.

I hit play.

When the video began, Tyler was standing in a bathroom in someone's house, holding up his phone and recording himself in the mirror.

Then a voice-over began. "Public spaces," Tyler's voice said. "Private spaces. Private spaces inside private spaces, where you can lock yourself away."

The video began to make quick cuts, a different background behind Tyler in the mirror each time, while he remained motionless in the middle. He had clearly shot a few seconds of himself standing in dozens of different bathrooms and edited them all together. The result was almost hypnotic—watching the different wallpaper flash by, watching the walls expand and shrink around him depending on the size of the bathroom he was in.

"And in these private spaces," his voice-over said, "people sometimes keep private things."

In the mirror, he held up a toilet paper cozy that looked like a chicken, then a whole armful of identical bottles of aspirin.

And then the video ended. He hadn't finished it.

The fact of that struck me like a blow, and tears sprang to my eyes.

I looked in the folder called Thoughts from Bathrooms and found a whole list of clips, each one named for a different object. I saw T.P. Chicken and Aspirin, which I figured I'd already seen, but there were also Peacock Feathers, Rainbow Tampons, Tapeworm Medicine, and a whole host of others.

Oh, god, I thought. *Tyler was a collector. Of objects. Of stories. Just like me.*

I decided to add one of the clips to the end of the unfinished video. It took me a few tries to figure it out, but when I got the hang of it, I kept going. The knot in my chest finally loosened, and my breathing relaxed. I arranged and rearranged the clips, inserting and deleting them, telling a slightly different story with each edit. Like making a collage.

I locked the door and lost myself in the work, not leaving Tyler's room when my father knocked, or when my mother called up that she'd brought home Thai food for dinner. I only paused to rinse the bleach out of my hair and put in the InfraRed dye.

There was music in the Thoughts from Bathrooms folder, so I added that to the video too. I didn't know how Tyler would have ended it, so I settled for a return to the beginning, finishing with a long shot of Tyler in the same bathroom he had shown in the first moments of the video.

When it was finally done, I returned to my room and collapsed into bed. My body begged for sleep, but my mind still whirled. All my efforts to figure out what had happened with Tyler—I'd been trying to keep them quiet. Not tell my parents, not rock the boat.

But I was done with that. It was time to get loud. To expose Brown Brown for the lie she was.

I just wasn't sure how.

The next thing I knew, morning light streamed into the room, and my mother was sitting beside me, shaking me gently.

A look of shock and horror distorted her face.

I sat up, instantly awake and panicked. "What is it? What happened?"

Her mouth moved for a moment, no sound coming out. Finally she spoke. "What have you done to your hair?"

Then she looked past me and let out an involuntary scream. I flopped back onto the bed. She had noticed the metal sheeting on the wall.

CHAPTER 14

WE ATE BREAKFAST THAT MORNING IN AWKWARD silence. My mom had insisted that I dye my hair back and tear down the metal wall, but I'd refused. To my surprise, Dad took my side.

"The damage is already done," he'd said. "You'll only make things worse if you try to force her to do things your way."

My mother's lips had flattened and her nostrils flared, sure signs that she was seething mad. But she'd clenched her jaw and said nothing, and now here we sat. In silence.

The angry charge in the air was new, but the silence was not. I'd expected things to get better as time went on. Instead, as the days had passed, the air in the house seemed to grow thicker, and my parents got quieter and quieter, until the rooms themselves rang with stillness. We went through our days like three strangers in an elevator, trying not to catch one another's eye.

Before Tyler died, meals had never been quiet affairs at our house. The kitchen table had always been a place for heated arguments about sports, for merciless sister teasing, and for never-ending stories about the Bay of Pigs, the Kennedys, or whatever else my dad happened to be teaching that semester. Now, the silence echoed.

"Hey, Dad, President Kennedy was assassinated, right?" My father turned to me in disbelief. "No, I mean, I *know* he was assassinated. I was just . . . thinking about it."

The old professor spark lit his eyes for the first time in weeks. "Is this for school? What do you need to know?" He leaned forward, his elbows on the table. "Do you want to watch my TED Talk? Kennedy 2.0: Rebooting Camelot?"

I rolled my eyes. "No. I was wondering . . . what makes someone do that? Target someone like that?"

"Fame." Dad sat back in his chair, settling in for one of his speeches. "Almost always fame. Very rarely, they want to make a political point. As if one person's death could change the whole world."

Mom's head jerked up, and the words seemed to linger in the air around us, echoing off the fridge and cabinets. The glimmer in Dad's eyes went dark, and his features slid back into blankness, his animated expression melting away.

A long, silent moment passed. Then Dad stood and turned on the radio. My eyes widened in shock. "No media during meals" was a sacrosanct rule of the Brown house. Mom didn't react. She just kept pushing cereal around her bowl with a spoon.

The soothing voice of a public-radio host filled the room, and I was grateful for the distraction. Until I realized what he was talking about.

"Authorities say the party was one of several held in illegal locations across northern Virginia in recent months. The building's owner could not be reached for comment."

I let my toast drop to my plate and strained to catch every word.

"Police won't reveal exactly how many students were taken into custody following the event, but sources put the number at more than ten. Arrests were made in three cases, and drug charges are pending."

Drug charges. I blew out a slow breath.

"The story has become a rallying point for local politicians who hope it will shine a light on the growing problem of teenage drug abuse across the DC area, from its poorest to its wealthiest communities. Virginia Senator Gary Herndon, a McLean resident, spoke out on the issue yesterday afternoon."

Hearing Senator Herndon's voice made me want to slide down on my chair and hide under the table.

"As my constituents know, I'm a plain speaker, so I'll put it out there. We can't afford to be lenient on drug crimes. Even when the offenders are our own children. I hear a lot of talk about addressing the root cause of drug crime. I'll tell you what the root cause is. Drugs. Find the source, and prosecute the criminals. No matter who they are."

My mind went to Nathan. He'd been so concerned that someone would find out he was organizing those parties, and it seemed his fears were well founded. Even if he wasn't selling drugs himself, the police were clearly taking this very seriously.

"Please turn that off," my mother said.

"I'm listening to it," Dad replied.

On the radio, Senator Herndon was still talking. "That's why I've been such a vocal supporter of the new crime bill. We need to put more power in the hands of the police to break up and—"

Mom went to the radio and clicked it off. Then she took a deep breath and aggressively changed the subject. "Robert, would you dig your tuxedo out of the back closet for me? We need to get it cleaned before the gala next weekend."

Dad stared at her in disbelief. "You're going to the gala?"

"I'm *running* the gala. A big part of that is actually attending the event, yes."

"Don't you think you should take some time off? Give yourself some space?"

She took her cereal bowl from the table and dropped it into the sink with a crash that made me wince. She stood there for a moment, her back to us, before turning around. All her tightly held control was gone, and her eyes burned. She was a woman drowning, and there was nothing I could do to save her.

"So I'm doing this wrong?" she demanded.

"Of course not."

"I'm sorry that I'm still able to function while you are not. There *are* bills to pay and things to get done."

"We could be getting help with all that. So many people have offered to help."

"You think I need help?"

"Well—"

"You've been wearing the same pair of pajamas for three days, and you want to give me coping advice?"

Dad looked stunned. "I want you to stop pretending," he said. "I know you were listening to that radio story. I know you heard what the detective said—about Tyler dropping out of school." He shook his head. "It's eating me alive, and I can't even talk about it. He *told* us he wanted to take some time off, maybe do a gap year. And we shut him down."

"He did?" I asked.

My mother gritted her teeth. "Not in front of Megan," she ground out.

"I'm done trying to keep her out of it." He gestured to me. "Look at her hair! Clearly it's not working for her, either."

"So that act of self-sabotage is my fault too?"

"Guys, it's just hair," I said. But by the way they stared me down, I could tell it meant much more than that at this point.

"You make it so hard for me to keep it together, Robert." Mom's voice shook. "Sometimes I can hardly stand to look at you." And she walked out of the kitchen.

Dad didn't move. He sat there, spoon in hand, watching the doorway where she'd disappeared.

I stared at him for a moment, trying to figure out what to say. And then I fled. I ran up the stairs to my bedroom and shut the door behind me. I was done trying to put out my family's emotional fires with kind words and cappuccinos. From now on, let them burn.

Slumping to the floor beside the bed, I ran a hand through my newly short hair, tugging on the long chunk in front, and it occurred to me that I hadn't shown it to Elena. I took a quick shot with the metal wall behind me and sent it to her with the message:

New look caused full-on parent breakdown.

It took Elena only seconds to reply.

OMG your hair!

Like it?

It's perfection.

It's so you.

I never would have guessed.

Mom totally lost it.

I'm kind of glad?

I am an awful person.

No, I get it. You wanted a response.

You got a response.

I tugged on the front of my hair.

Yes!

I can't wait to walk into school today and basically say: screw you all.

If you didn't already know, I'm a freak. No more pretending.

There was a long pause before she responded.

I want to say: hooray, go girl, etc.

And I feel like I should.

But truth is, I'm worried about you.

Are you going to the counselor?

I gripped the phone hard. I'd wanted her support. And this felt like a betrayal.

MY MOTHER isn't going to the counselor.

That's a whole other problem.

I'm only saying, and I speak from experience

This may be some self-destructive behavior.

"Megan," my mother yelled from downstairs. "If you're coming with me, come now!"

I stared at the phone in my hand, my heart pounding with frustration.

Maybe my self could use some destructing, I typed back, and I turned off the phone.

I reached for the necklace I'd made from Tyler's button. I'd worn it every day, but it didn't feel right anymore. Instead, I dug out the jeans I'd worn to the rave and went through the pockets until I found the bullets. Now these . . . these were just what I needed.

On my way out the door, my gaze fell on Tyler's copy of *Disasters in the Sun*, with its torn cover and its dog-eared pages. Tyler had been looking for some kind of symbol in that book. Maybe he'd found what he was after. I grabbed it and shoved it into my bag.

I pored over Dr. Brightman's book the whole way to school. The title came from Shakespeare; as an actor, Booth saw the assassination as some kind of heroic action in a play. But what kind of role did Tyler think *he* was taking on, playing at John Wilkes Booth? *"Sic semper tyrannis,"* he'd said at Nathan's house. That was what Booth had said immediately after he killed Lincoln: "Thus always to tyrants." Tyler had been targeting Herndon, that much was clear. But why?

The illustrations were the real treasure of the book for me: photos of Booth, of course, but also mysterious letters written in code, playbills from a dozen different theatrical productions, and image after image of that infamous gun. I tilted the book at different angles, holding it up to the light, trying to see the photographs as clearly as I could. Then I closed the book and stared at it cross-eyed, to see if I could find a memory attached to it, but nothing. My ability had gone quiet.

"Earth to Megan," my mother said, and I tore my gaze from the page.

"Huh?"

"We're here."

I hadn't even noticed that the car had stopped, or that she'd pulled into a space in the school parking lot.

"You know what?" She cocked her head. "It's not so bad."

"What isn't?"

"Your hair."

I smiled.

"But let me make you an appointment at the salon." She crinkled her nose. "It's so sloppy in the back."

My smile dropped. "See you later, Mom." I got out of the car.

My hair made a definite impression. Heads turned as I walked through the main doors, and girls whispered to one another behind cupped hands. When it came to Westside, only a certain kind of "different," practiced by a certain kind of person, was celebrated and accepted. And given Tyler's death, my new appearance was sure to set off a gossip firestorm.

Eric was out of school that day—some kind of doctor's appointment, he'd said—and I felt the lack of any friendly face in the crowd. When the attention started getting to me, I ducked into the ladies' room to hide. I leaned over a sink, turning on the cold water and letting it run over my wrists. I hadn't even made it to first period, and I was already exhausted. I checked the mirror. In the harsh fluorescent light, my hair looked more sloppy than bold. Maybe this had been a terrible idea. Maybe Tyler had been right, after all.

"It looks great."

I looked up. Leigh Barry was washing her hands at the sink beside mine. Her blond braids twisted up and around her head, milkmaid style, and behind her glasses, her eyes crinkled in a smile—one with a hint of apology in it.

"Your hair, I mean. It looks great."

"Thanks." I reached up instinctively to touch it, forgetting that my hands were wet. Water dripped down my nose. "I'm questioning the whole thing at this point. Ready to make a run for it."

She laughed and handed me a paper towel. "Don't. Stay and

fight." Before I could reply, she pushed her way through the swinging door and back out into the hall.

I spent most of the morning reading *Disasters in the Sun* under my desk, brooding over the color plates, until I was more familiar with John Wilkes Booth's mustache than any other person alive. My biggest disappointment was that Brightman didn't include more information about Booth's fiancée, Lucy Hale, the girl I'd seen in the restaurant. I knew what had become of Booth and Lincoln, of course, but what had happened to her? Between classes, I Googled her on my phone. She'd lived to be seventy-four. Ten years after the assassination, she'd finally married. I felt a surge of relief that she'd gone on to live a normal life.

The most shocking chapter of Dr. Brightman's book discussed the modern value of the artifacts he was describing. Tyler had underlined and highlighted that section heavily, and the numbers he'd circled were staggering. Ten thousand for a letter in Booth's handwriting. Fifteen thousand for a pair of Lincoln's eyeglasses. Two million dollars for a signed copy of the Emancipation Proclamation. Those price tags took things to a level beyond watches and cigars. The numbers made my eyelids twitch.

Dr. Brightman had said that Senator Herndon's family had a massive collection of Lincoln artifacts. Had Bobby and Tyler been stealing things that were even more valuable than I'd realized? What could they possibly want with that kind of money? And if Tyler was having some kind of political awakening—this new awareness of how well off we were compared to so many others—why was he stealing and selling stuff to get even *more* money?

I knew only one person who might have answers about that: Bobby Drake. And if anything would test my new self-expressive, self-destructive project, he was it.

After class, I made my way to Bobby's locker. Next to it, most of Tyler's makeshift memorial was gone now, but a few notes remained, still taped to the door. I wondered when the school would assign it to someone else.

At last Bobby appeared. He looked almost ragged. A hint of blue-black darkened the skin under his eyes, and without his leather jacket, he seemed thinner than I remembered. It caught me off guard; I hadn't even considered the fact that he might be grieving too. He headed straight to his locker, barely glancing at me as he spun the lock. "I hope they caught the guy," he said.

I stopped breathing for a moment. Did Bobby have new information about Tyler? "What guy?"

"The guy who did that to your hair." He barked out a loud laugh, his face beyond smug.

Any sympathy I might have felt for him evaporated. "I did it myself."

He looked me over. "Of course you did."

And there she was: Brown Brown still. I cursed myself for letting Bobby undermine my confidence so quickly, and I tried to rally my Red.

"I want to know why you and Tyler were stealing things," I said. "Did you need money?"

He snorted and turned his attention back to the lock. The hollows of his cheeks looked deeper, almost sunken. Was he doing something to himself?

Then I caught my breath. Was it heroin? Detective Johnson was looking for the person who had made the anonymous 911 call. She'd speculated that whoever it was might have been using too. Was it Bobby?

"What were you doing on the night Tyler died?" I asked.

"Did you buy a two-dollar badge to go with that two-dollar haircut? I already talked to the police."

Bobby popped open his locker, and there, sitting on the shelf, was the Lincoln cigar box.

I gasped, and my hand flew to my mouth. *Bobby* had had the box all this time?

He narrowed his eyes. "What's your problem?"

I pointed. "That box. It was in my house."

Bobby grabbed a textbook from his locker and slammed the door. It seemed to close in slow motion, and I stepped forward to grab the box before it latched. But I was not fast enough. The bang of metal on metal echoed through the hall.

"I don't know what you're talking about," he said, spinning the lock.

And then it hit me. "Our spare key," I said. "You know where it is." A sinking certainty rushed through me. I'd been so focused on Nathan having access to the box, I hadn't even considered Bobby.

He tried to leave, but I blocked his path.

"I mean, my dad is almost always home these days. Did you watch the house? Wait until he finally left?"

Bobby crossed his arms and said nothing.

"Why did you do it? Were you hoping to find more cigars? Or no . . ." My brain was turning faster than my mouth could follow.

"That roll of cash. You wanted the money."

Bobby's face went stony. The money had been in *my* room the last time I'd seen it, which meant that Bobby must have gone through my things as well as Tyler's. The very thought made me shudder.

"So once you found the money, why did you take the box? Were you hoping to sell it too? Or were you just afraid the police would figure out that you and Tyler had been stealing?" Last night, I had thought other things were missing . . . Bobby must have cleared out any evidence of his and Tyler's little thieving habit. "What else did you take?"

He advanced on me, close enough that I could smell his gum and aftershave. "Those things were rightfully mine," he spit. "Tyler and I split everything fifty-fifty. Now that he's gone, it's only fair that stuff should come to me." He looked me up and down and made a sweeping gesture that encompassed all of me. "Look at you. You're an infant. Prancing around, drawing attention to yourself. To Tyler." He shook his head. "Grow up, Brown. And back off."

He strode away, and I stared after him, shaking and embarrassed and furious. I slammed my fist into his closed locker door. The box was in there, just two inches away. Two inches and a nice strong crowbar. And possibly expulsion.

I dropped my backpack to the floor right there in the hallway and dug around until I found my wallet. I pulled out Detective Johnson's business card and gripped it tight.

It was time I drew a lot *more* attention to myself. And to Bobby. And to exactly what he and Tyler had been up to. I was turning him over to the police.

I walked outside and tried to find a quiet spot where I could call the number on Johnson's card. Rounding a corner, out of sight of the main doors, I almost ran into Emma Herndon. She was leaning against the brick wall, smoking a cigarette. A big white envelope lay on the cement at her feet, and she was paging through what looked like a college brochure. When she saw me, she choked and spluttered, tossing the cigarette to the ground.

"You didn't see that." She used one of her delicate strappy sandals to grind the cigarette to ash and tobacco leaves.

Fury at Bobby still churned in my stomach, making me feel risky and unmoored. I didn't want to think, I wanted to act. So I started talking. "My brother took something from you—or from your dad. A wooden cigar box. With Abraham Lincoln's picture on it. And I want you to have it back."

Emma's face went slack; she blinked but said nothing.

I plowed on. "Okay, so I don't actually have the box right *now*, but I know where it is. And when I get it, I want to give it back to you. Because it was wrong, what Tyler did. And I'm sorry."

She bent down to pick up the envelope, her face stony. "My dad's got a million of those Abe Lincoln things that Grandpa collected, just lying around his office. He probably hasn't even noticed that it's missing." Her eyes locked onto mine. "Keep it."

She tried to stuff the brochure back into the envelope, but her hands were shaking, and a few pieces of loose paper blew away toward the parking lot.

I ran to retrieve them. A purple NYU logo was blazoned across the tops of the pages. "Heading to New York next year?" I asked, handing them over.

She shook her head. "William and Mary. Where my dad went."

She wrestled the papers back into the envelope. "Go Tribe," she said, her voice flat.

Her eyes darted back and forth between me and the parking lot, and I was seized by an irresistible impulse to keep pushing her.

"Sounds like your dad can be a bit of a tyrant."

For an instant, Emma went as pale and fragile as tissue paper. Then she tossed her hair over one shoulder and summoned back the calm, collected version of herself that I knew best. "I've got gym. See you around, all right?" She smiled, the corners of her lips trembling, and disappeared, clutching her envelope in one hand.

I stared after her, then shook myself back to the present. I still had Detective Johnson's card clutched in my hand. I called the number, talked to the officer on duty, then texted Eric.

Tomorrow morning.

Nine am.

You and I are skipping school and going to the police.

He sent me back the policeman emoji.

Then two different police car emojis.

Then a picture of himself giving a thumbs-up.

You're kind of ruining this moment for me, I wrote.

Oops. Sorry.

That night, I bolted awake from a blood-soaked nightmare that I couldn't quite remember. All I knew was that I'd been wearing a long white dress. I checked my clock—not even midnight, and no chance I'd be going back to sleep anytime soon. I lay awake, my mind turning in restless, never-ending circles.

My first thoughts were of Nathan. I'd been such a jerk to accuse him of stealing the box. I wanted to duck down under my covers and never come out. And I was adding stupid on top of stupid to be thinking about him now. I needed to put him out of my mind entirely. This had always been about Tyler, and Tyler was who I needed to focus on.

What did he want with all that money? Could the stealing have gotten him into trouble somehow? Or the videos? Or maybe it had been one of Nathan's parties that had led him to that abandoned building where he died. . . .

I clearly wasn't getting any more information from Bobby. He could answer to the police. I was going to tell Detective Johnson everything I knew about what Bobby and Tyler had done, and she could sort it out. Wasn't that her job? And as for Nathan . . . I winced at the thought of us on the couch in his family room, at the thought of what I had *thought* was about to happen. Had that only been in my imagination?

Stop. Enough. I folded my pillow in half in an effort to get comfortable. Every time I closed my eyes, images gathered in the darkness. Tyler and Nathan slapping hands. John Wilkes Booth's flirtatious smile. Clara Harris's face, splattered with blood.

I crawled out of bed and turned on the lamp that was clipped to the edge of my worktable. The metal wall gleamed dully in the lamplight, and all my raw materials hung where I had left them. Instead of inspired, the artwork left me feeling lonely. My old button necklace hung from the lamp switch, and I put it around my neck, enjoying its familiar weight once again. I dug out my phone to text Elena.

Today's film: She's Out of Control.

Uh-oh. Do you want to talk about it?

I heard my name, soft and far away. "Megan!"

A finger of fear traced up my spine.

But is that really an 80s movie?

I thought we only did 80s movies.

It came louder this time, a male voice. "Megan!"

Did you hear that?

Hear what?

You do realize I'm a thousand miles away, right?

I dropped the phone onto my bed and raised both hands. Was this what had happened to Dr. Brightman? The visions started taking over? But I didn't see anything. I stood and glanced around, looking for the light.

"Yoooo-hooooo! Megan!"

I walked over to my bedroom window and yanked back the curtain. Down below, standing on the street in front of my house, was Nathan Lee, pretty obviously wasted. He tripped on the curb as he tried to step up onto the sidewalk. A big grin split his face.

"There you are!" he said, delighted.

From down the hall, I heard my mother's voice. "Megan? What's going on out there?"

"Nothing, Mom. I'll take care of it," I called back.

I opened my bedroom window and whisper yelled through the screen. "Go away!"

"I have something to say," Nathan announced. "Not leaving till I do."

"Megan." I heard the note of warning in my father's voice.

I sighed. "Stay right there," I called to Nathan. "And shut up!"

My phone beeped. Elena again.

Are you okay?

You're scaring me.

It's New Boy!

Outside my window.

Totally, completely trashed.

She sent me the emoji with its eyes bugging out.

SEND DETAILS

Or I will haunt you forever like something out of Poltergeist.

I pulled on a faded green hoodie and started for the door.

I zipped up my sweatshirt as I stepped onto the front porch. It was a cool night for early May, and the lightest sprinkle of rain was falling. Nathan made his way up the walk and stopped at the porch steps. With the streetlight behind him, I could see tiny droplets of water sparkling in his hair, catching the light in a whole spectrum of different colors. I felt that same old tug in my chest, but I shut it down. He'd lied to me, and I'd wrongly accused him. Anything there might have been between us was surely over.

His glasses were fogged and dotted with rain. He took them off and stuck them in his back pocket, and his eyes went wide. "Oh, Megan, check you out!"

My hand went instinctively to my hair, and I resisted the urge to ask, "Do you like it?"

He barked out a laugh. "It's vicious. In a good way."

I dropped my hand to my side. "You can't be here. It's late. And it's a freaking Monday night. How are you running around drunk on a *freaking Monday night?*"

"I have something to say, and it couldn't wait."

My face blazed hot with shame, and I ducked into my hood. "I have something to say to you too."

He raised a hand, winding up for a big speech. "I didn't steal anything from you. And before you argue, hear me—"

"I know you didn't," I said. "I was totally wrong about that. And I'm sorry. I can't tell you how sorry."

Nathan froze, his arm still outstretched, his face puzzled. "You . . . What? Really?"

I nodded, my face hot, and turned to go back inside.

"You were right about one thing," he said. "I did lie to you."

I stopped, not turning around.

"At least, I didn't tell you the whole truth. About a lot of things."

I faced him at last.

"Cedric Williams. The guy you met at the underground? The one you called the mastermind of all those parties? He's my little brother."

I thought about their matching grins. Their awkward happiness to see each other. Brothers.

"Half-brother, technically. Different dads. He didn't end up in the system like I did. He was born when I was already in foster care, and his dad's family took him." Nathan looked down at his feet, then up at me. "You know how I told you Cedric went to Model UN, and he met this guy from Virginia, and together they came up with the idea for the underground parties?"

I nodded.

"That guy he met? That was me." He came up a few steps toward me and leaned on the stair railing for balance. "I knew about Cedric, that he existed. But I'd never met him. And then I was talking to this random guy in a dorm cafeteria, and it was him." His laugh was harsh. "I mean, we go to school, like, five miles apart. In the same city. But I never knew him. Or his friends, or the rest of his family." He paused. "Or who I might have been, if the situation was reversed."

I tugged hard on the front of my hair. I didn't want to feel for him, didn't want to forgive him for lying to me. Being angry felt so much better than being sad, and I wanted to hold on to it for a while longer. And if I wasn't angry at him, I might have to deal with all the other things I felt about him, and I absolutely wasn't ready to do that yet.

"I'm a fuck-up," he said. "I should have told you about the parties. But with the cops investigating Red's death, I was scared they would find out, and tell my parents." He paused, his face serious. "My birth mom . . . she just couldn't get her life together. And I know my parents don't think I'm going to end up like her, but I always kind of feel like I have to prove to them that I'm not going to end up like her." He stopped to catch his breath.

"And that's where you met Tyler? At one of your parties?"

Nathan smiled. "Red had his phone in his hand, shooting video. And I was like, 'Hey, Moe. You can't do that in here.' But then somehow he talked me into it." Nathan shook his head. "I don't really know how he talked me into it."

I snorted. Tyler could always talk people into it.

"We had this idea to start a YouTube channel," he continued, "called it The District. We were going to make it a place for teens to talk about politics in DC—and the politics *of* DC." Nathan cocked his head, remembering. "We brought Cedric on board too. He's seriously brilliant, that kid. We would all, like, hole up in a corner at parties and talk—about making videos, about how to get attention for them." Nathan snorted. "At least it gave me and Cedric something to say to each other. He could blab to Red about anything. But when it came to his own brother . . ." He trailed off.

"Huh." I spoke carefully, sensing the emotion beneath Nathan's smooth surface. "Less pressure with Tyler, maybe?"

"Yeah." Nathan's lips quirked in a smile. "Maybe." He shifted, leaning a hand on the porch railing. "Anyhow, after a while, Red started spouting all these half-assed ideas. Like, his heart was in the right place, but he didn't always know what he was talking about. 'The tyranny of privilege!' he'd say. Or what was that other one . . . 'Talk may be cheap, but the rich can't afford it.'" He shook his head, still smiling. "I was like, 'Fool, we *are* rich!' But I really thought we could make it work." He met my eyes. "I'll send you the videos. I promise." He climbed the last two steps and joined me on the porch at last.

I backed away from him, unnerved by his serious face, by the quiet intimacy of this little porch with the rain falling beyond the railing. "Okay. I get it," I said. "You should probably go somewhere and sober up now. . . ."

"Wait." Nathan curled a gentle hand around my arm. "I've got something to show you." He reached into his back pocket and pulled out an old Greyhound ticket, creased and worn. He held it up to show me.

"The first video we ever made for The District," he said, "we took a bus with this friend of Cedric's who was visiting her mom in prison. It had been like ten years since she'd seen her—you know, because DC doesn't have a prison and people from there get sent all over the country. That was the first time I realized our videos could be important."

I swallowed hard, tears welling in my eyes.

"Ever since he . . ." Nathan rubbed the ticket with his thumb. "I've been carrying it in my pocket. It's like I need to have it with me, all the time." He hooked one finger through my necklace and held up the button. "We're not so different, you and I." He ran his finger back and forth along the cord, brushing the side of my neck.

My breath caught in my throat. "Is this what you and Tyler used to do when I wasn't around?" I swallowed hard. "Get smashed and hit on random girls?"

Nathan looked hurt. "You're not random. Ever since the first time I met you, I thought you were—" He stopped himself. "And when he died, I couldn't stop thinking about you, wondering if you were okay."

I shook my head. "But I never met you before the funeral."

"You don't remember." He looked around a bit dizzily. "Like I may not remember any of this." His eyes focused again, and they focused on me. "But remembering is important. You're right to fight for how he'll be remembered."

The silence stretched out between us for a moment. Finally Nathan spoke again, so quietly that I could hardly hear him.

"I think maybe it was my fault," he said. "If I'd known what was going on at my own damn parties . . . if I'd paid more attention. I didn't know about the drugs; I didn't know Red was selling things to Park. Cedric mostly planned things, while I ran around like it was some big game. And now Red's gone."

His face crumpled, and tears mixed with the rain on his cheeks.

In my mind's eye, I could see him and Tyler together in my vision: their easy laughter, their sense of fun. My heart ached for him, and for myself, and for everything wrong about this that could never be put right. I couldn't resist. I wrapped my arms around his waist and rested my cheek on his chest.

"Thank you," he said.

His voice rumbled through my body and sent a spike of sensation straight through me. I felt as drunk as he was. I wanted to run away. I wanted to lean into him. He shifted my arms up so that my wrists rested on his shoulders, and he began to sway, as though we were dancing. He sang softly, little whispered lines from "Fly Me to the Moon."

I was swamped by that same overwhelming feeling I'd had at the underground, that urge to dive in, let go, cut loose. I pulled back slightly so I could see his face. His skin gleamed in the dim light, and the familiar landscape of his face made my wrists hurt with longing.

I grabbed his shirt in both my fists and kissed him.

He froze for a moment. Then he tightened his hold on my hips and pulled me close. His mouth was hot against mine, and he tasted of alcohol. I leaned forward, wanting more, wanting to lose myself in the feel of him against me, and he lost his balance, breaking the kiss.

Cool air hit my face. *What was I doing?* He hadn't come here for this. Or had he? My mind spun, and I had a hazy image of Bobby standing above me at that party, laughing. Embarrassment churned in my stomach, and confusion, and I blinked back tears.

I backed a few steps away from Nathan, and he caught sight of the look on my face. "God, I'm sorry," he said. "I didn't mean to . . ."

"No, it was me. I made a mistake." I felt wrung out, stiff, and brittle. "I should go."

Nathan nodded and sagged down onto the steps.

I stopped at the door and turned, my heart twisted by his forlorn shape silhouetted against the streetlight. As I walked into the house, I pulled my phone out of my pocket.

"Eric," I said when he answered, "I need a really big favor. Again."

Ten minutes later, Eric loaded Nathan into his car while I watched from the front porch. Eric stopped to rub a kink out of his back before he walked across the grass to say good-bye.

"Megan," he scolded, "you told me you weren't into the whole superhero thing. And now here you go, behind my back—"

"What are you talking about? I am not superheroing behind your back."

"Oh no? Your hair says otherwise."

I ran my hand down the red streak, a smile tugging at my lips. "You're trying to make me feel better."

"Yes, I am," he said. "And in exchange, you're making me drive that sneak thief home for you."

Regret fanged into me. "Yeah, about that . . ."

"Don't worry, I let him know exactly what I think of him, in no uncertain terms." Eric smiled proudly. "He said he didn't do it, but, I mean, you've never seen anything in one of your visions that didn't turn out to be true, right?" He shook his head. "Jerk."

"I kind of forgot to mention . . . ," I began.

"Mention what?"

"That he didn't take the box?"

Eric's face froze. "I thought you saw that in your vision?"

"Not exactly."

"So you're telling me you just *assumed* it was him?" Eric started pacing, covering the same few feet of porch over and over again. "Oh, god," he said. "*Oh, god.* I called him a lying weasel!"

"Well, I didn't force you to say that!" I craned my neck, trying to catch a glimpse of Nathan's face through the passenger-side window. "I'm sorry—I saw the box in Bobby's locker. I was going to tell you all about it on the way to the police station tomorrow."

"Wait, what?" Eric's jaw dropped. "You found out what happened to the box, and you didn't call and tell me?"

"I guess it didn't occur to me."

"But it occurred to you to call me in the middle of the night to come help you out," he said. "Twice in three days."

"And I appreciate it," I said, bewildered by how upset he seemed. "I thought we were in this together."

"Together? Well, you might be having fun on some kind of vicarious superhero adventure, but in case you forgot, I'm the one who lost my brother. I'm the one who's grieving here." My heart twisted in my chest. I wasn't thinking, and as always when I wasn't thinking, my blades cut.

Eric's expression grew pinched, and he stepped away from me. "That's right. Because I have no idea what it feels like to lose someone." He had to collect himself before he could continue. "I think I need a break. Maybe we should give each other some space for a while." He limped slightly as he made his way back to the car, holding one hand on his hip as he got in.

I watched the car drive off down the street, my stomach churning.

That's why Tyler kept trying to make you into someone else, I told myself. I walked up the porch stairs and dragged myself to my room with all the ease of walking through water. My phone was in my hand, and I was trying to come up with the best way of apologizing to Eric via text when a message came in.

It was from Nathan. No explanation, only a link. I clicked it, and it took me to a YouTube channel called The District.

I scanned the list of videos hungrily, clicking on title after title, too eager and nervous to watch any one all the way through. The videos were in lots of different formats: short newsy pieces, longer documentaries, silly ones where kids from DC, Maryland, and Virginia tried to understand one another's slang.

Tyler had made a whole series of videos he called Luxury Tax, where he went into bedrooms and garages and basements in McLean and shot videos of these extravagant collections of stuff: paintings and liquor and books—I saw Kyle's dad's watch collection in there too. Then he tallied up the total worth of those objects and estimated what that money could do in real terms: pay a teacher's salary for five years, add ten beds to a women's shelter in Arlington, restore AP classes at three budget-cut DC schools.

But most of the videos the three guys had made together. There was one that started with a teenage girl standing in front of a parking lot in DC—a parking lot that used to be the housing complex where she grew up.

"The city promised us a new apartment," she said. "Never delivered. Now they're making money off people parking here?" The girl shook her head. "That's just not right." She pointed to the sign advertising monthly parking rates. "Wish I could find us a place for two hundred dollars a month."

Then Tyler, Nathan, and Cedric sprang into action. The video cut to them pulling into the parking lot in a pickup filled with stuff. They unloaded it all into a single parking space: a fancy sofa and chairs, a coffee table, a couple of lamps. They set up false walls with wallpaper on them around three sides of the spot, and they put up a sign: *The District Needs More Affordable Housing. Not More Affordable Parking.* They invited the girl in and served her a drink in a fancy glass.

People came by, laughed, and took pictures. Eventually the attendant tried to kick them out. "We rented this spot for the whole month," Cedric said. "Do you want to talk to us about affordable housing, sir? Where do you live? What's it costing you?"

I got it. In a way, the videos were the YouTube equivalent of the parties Nathan and Cedric had been throwing. They bridged the gap that separated one part of DC from another. They brought together people who might never have known one another and put them to work to achieve a common goal.

When I couldn't keep my eyes open another minute, I crawled into bed with my phone, tucking it close to my chest. Clearly this political activism had been important to Tyler—the videos were passionate and partisan and carefully made. But why had he kept this whole project a secret? Maybe he didn't want to tell Bobby, or the other guys from the team, but why hadn't he felt he could share the videos with me, or with Mom and Dad? And how long had he been planning to go on pretending?

CHAPTER 15

THE FIFTH DISTRICT POLICE STATION HAD A STERILE, modern design, with tall vertical windows that bore an unfortunate resemblance to prison bars. The triangular patch of lawn out front might once have been green, but that color had faded badly, a fugitive pigment that didn't stand the test of time.

I stood on the sidewalk, staring at the building and mentally preparing myself to talk to Detective Johnson. It had taken over an hour and a half to get here after my mom had dropped me off at school, including a painfully long Metro ride and a bus that took thirty minutes to go three miles. I felt frazzled and apprehensive and a little bit sick, and I wished Eric were here to walk through those doors with me. I'd texted him several times that morning to apologize, but so far, he hadn't responded.

I took a deep breath, tugged at my clothes, and walked into the station. At the far end of a lobby scattered with blue plastic chairs, a clean-cut young officer sat behind a bulletproof glass window. He looked up politely when I approached.

"I'm here to see Detective Johnson."

"Please sign in and—" He broke off and gestured behind me.

"You have good timing. Here she is now."

Detective Johnson walked through the station doors, followed by an Asian couple, a white guy in a pinstriped navy suit . . . and Nathan Lee.

Johnson's eyes widened when she saw me, but I brushed past her to grab Nathan's arm, my heart pinballing around in my chest.

"Oh my god, Nathan," I said. "What is going on?"

All of Nathan's vivid colors had lost their intensity. His face was blank, his voice emotionless. "They're bringing me in for questioning in connection with Tyler's death." He winced, and I saw him dart a quick glance at the couple, who were obviously his parents. His mother looked sleek and polished, with sunglasses obscuring most of her face. She twisted a battered tissue around her fingers. His father, who was a full foot taller than she was, rested a hand on the small of her back. Nathan shifted uncomfortably, as though he was in pain. "They think I've been moving drugs back and forth between the DC crowd and the kids in McLean."

Tears blurred my vision, and my throat clenched. I knew Detective Johnson had been looking for Tyler's dealer; I should have guessed suspicion might fall on Nathan. "No," I said hoarsely. "No, no, no." I turned to Johnson. "You can't do this to him." My voice grew louder, echoing off the bare walls. "Please. He didn't have anything to do with this."

She rested a hand on my shoulder. "This is a routine part of the investigation. No one has been arrested. Mr. Lee has his parents and an attorney present."

I held tight to Nathan's hand and looked up into his face. "I know you didn't want any of this to happen. And I'm sorry," I said. "I'm so, so sorry."

The glow I recognized returned to his eyes. He lifted his free hand and ran his fingers down the streak in my hair. "It's okay, Red," he said.

Another officer appeared through a door to my left and held it open for the Lees. Nathan's parents went first, followed by their lawyer. Nathan held on to my hand for a few more seconds; then he let my fingers slip from his grasp and disappeared into the recesses of the police station.

Detective Johnson and I were left alone. The last time I'd seen her, she'd been sprinting down a dark alley after me, and I'd barely escaped. I searched her face for any sign that she had recognized me that night, but I found none. "Please don't do this," I said.

"I'm just doing my job. We've gotten reports of illegal activities at these parties—drugs are only part of that. We need to identify the person at the heart of that activity and figure out whether they're connected in some way to Tyler's death." She paused to consider me. "Why are you here, Megan?"

My answer stuck in my throat. I couldn't decide what to do. Should I go through with my plan to tell her about the stealing? Would that make things look better for Nathan, since he wasn't involved? But Tyler and Bobby had been selling stuff at the parties, and Nathan was responsible for the parties. With Johnson already investigating Nathan, would he come under suspicion for those crimes too? I grabbed a fistful of my own hair, tugging on it until my scalp hurt.

"I'm here to tell you," I said at last, "that Nathan had nothing to do with Tyler's death, and you should let him go."

Detective Johnson sighed and rubbed a hand over her face. "Okay. Why don't you sit here for a little while? I need to deal with the Lees, and then I'll come back and find you. We can talk." She pointed to the chairs. "Wait. I'll be back soon."

She gestured to the officer behind the glass, and he buzzed her through the same door Nathan's family had used. Her face was sympathetic but serious as she left, closing the door behind her.

I collapsed into a blue plastic chair. Had I made the right decision? What should I do now? I couldn't bear the thought of Nathan being put through the police machine, but how could I help him? Guilt twisted my stomach, even though I wasn't sure how any of this was my fault.

My phone rang, and I fished it out of my bag. Dr. Brightman's name came up on the display. I hesitated, staring blankly at it for a few seconds before I answered. "Hello?"

"Hello, this is Ms. Charleston, Dr. Brightman's assistant."

My brain spun, struggling to shift gears from my confrontation with Detective Johnson. I stood and walked around the lobby, hoping to clear my head. "Yes?"

"Dr. Brightman would like you to meet him at Ford's Theatre on Thursday at ten a.m."

Dr. Brightman was clearly not used to dealing with teenagers. "Well, I've got this little thing called school. . . ."

Ms. Charleston didn't miss a beat. "Shall we look for a more convenient time?"

Did I even want to see Dr. Brightman again? I pushed open the door of the station and walked outside. I blinked, overwhelmed by the blazing sunlight and the pure ultramarine sky. The air smelled of diesel exhaust and freedom. I couldn't bear the thought of sitting in that police station for one more second. And I hadn't been able to see any memories for days, not since the night of the party. Maybe Dr. Brightman could help with that. "How about right now?" I asked. "Is he available right now? I can be there soon."

"Let me check his schedule and get back to you."

I tapped my phone against my lips, considering. I didn't know what would happen when I met with Dr. Brightman. It could be good; it could be bad. The wild, self-destructive voice in my head whispered that maybe bad was better. My phone rang again. "Yes?"

"Dr. Brightman can meet you in an hour," his assistant said. "He'll wait for you in the museum at Ford's Theatre."

"Did he say what he wants to see me about?"

"I'm not privy to that kind of client information. But I'll tell him you're on your way." The line went dead. I pulled out my wallet. I had to dig through every pocket and sleeve until I found the emergency credit card that my parents insisted I carry. I had never used it, but at this point, I had skipped school and spent hours getting to the police station for nothing. If I was going to get busted anyway, I might as well go down big.

I took one last look over my shoulder at the police station. Then I called a cab.

I asked the driver to drop me off a block away from Ford's Theatre. My mother's office window overlooked the street, so I shielded my face as I walked down Tenth Street, just in case. A school group was gathering outside, field trippers piling off the bus. I made my way to the center of the crowd and tried to blend in as they walked through the lobby and down to the museum.

I didn't see Dr. Brightman, so I wandered around the exhibits, pausing in front of a nearly life-size bronze statue of Abraham Lincoln. His clothes were rumpled, as though he'd been up half the night writing speeches and charting the future course of the republic. The museum lights cast his face in shadow, but his lips curled in a tiny smile, as though someone had promised to tell him a really great joke.

Who are you, anyway? I asked him silently. A cardboard cutout of elementary-school patriotism? Destroyer of the American nation, a villain to be stopped at any cost? A great man? Or just the excuse for a million-dollar industry of artifacts and textbooks and cheap souvenirs?

It depended on who was telling the story.

As if to drive that fact home, a few feet away from Lincoln's statue, I watched a video about his friendship with Frederick Douglass, the former slave who had fought hard for emancipation. Despite the respect he had for Lincoln, after Lincoln's death, Douglass still said, "You, my white fellow citizens . . . are the children of Abraham Lincoln. We are at best only his stepchildren."

I checked my watch and walked over to the derringer. The entire wall where the gun was mounted was covered with an enlargement of a famous drawing of Lincoln's assassination. Booth stood behind Lincoln's chair. In one hand, he held a wicked-looking knife; in the other, the gun, which was still smoking. His heavy eyebrows met evilly in the middle, and his mustache formed a dark frown above his mouth. He looked like a sinister, comic-book version of the man I had seen in my vision. Lincoln sat in front of him, his expression slightly surprised, as though he had only just realized he'd been shot and was becoming mildly alarmed about it.

"They say that, actually, he was laughing." I turned to see Dr. Brightman, wearing his sunglasses, his gloved hands clasped in front of him. "The play he was watching the night he was assassinated—it was a comedy." He came and stood beside me. "But then, you saw that when we touched the fragment of Clara Harris's dress."

Clara was there in the drawing too, her face like a doll's, pretty and puzzled. No screaming. No blood. At least, not yet.

Eric's face flashed into my mind. "So what's your origin story?" I asked. "I mean, how did you figure out that you could do . . . whatever it is we do?"

Dr. Brightman didn't answer. He simply stared at the derringer, floating in its transparent box. "My wife and son," he said at last. "They were killed. In an automobile accident. Three years ago."

I nodded, afraid to interrupt him.

"After the accident, I avoided everything that reminded me of them. I thought that would make it easier. But one day, I found myself in my son's room. I picked up a stuffed giraffe. My son's favorite; he used to carry it everywhere." His bitter smile made me shiver. "And I tore it to pieces. Eviscerated it. And then there he was, standing next to me. I found that the more I touched his things, the more I got to see him. As he used to be. I began to see my wife, as well."

"Was it . . . terrifying?"

"At first it was a joy. And then it became a curse." He leaned against the wall beside the derringer. Booth's face loomed behind him, frightening in its intensity. "I lived for the moments when I got to see them again. But before long, I started to wonder what was worse. Never seeing them again . . . or being forced to see them every single day—but never holding them. Never talking to them. And never knowing when it would stop."

I swallowed past the lump in my throat. "Did you understand what was happening?"

He shook his head. "I thought I was losing my mind. But then I went back to work, and some of the Lincoln artifacts had the same effect. The more violent the history of the object, the stronger my response. The bloodiest objects, the ones associated with the assassination, they produced the most pain. But they also, I guess you could say, *blinded* me temporarily. For a little while, after I touched them, I didn't see any visions. I loved my wife and son, but to be honest, not seeing them was a relief. If I could take a little bit of pain, I could have a little bit of peace."

I stared at him, transfixed. "Then what happened?"

He reached up with one gloved finger to tap the sunglasses he wore. "It backfired. Instead of staying blind, I started seeing more. And more. And more."

"You said you'd met others . . . like us. That didn't happen to them?"

He shook his head, his smile knife edged. "I don't think so. But then, I don't believe they were handling blood artifacts on a regular basis."

"What do those glasses do, exactly?"

He took them off, and it was both comforting and uncomfortable to meet his gaze. He held them out so I could take a closer look. "They're something I had built for myself. The camera feeds directly to the screen in the glasses. They're like virtual reality goggles, but I'm seeing what's around me, in real time. I find that if I'm not looking at an object directly, I don't get a vision from it."

"Do you have to wear them all the time?"

He settled them back onto his face. "It gets a little inconvenient to see the history of almost every object that you touch. Every door handle. Every pen. Every chair in every office."

"But you wear gloves," I said.

"They worked for a little while. But soon they weren't enough. Especially for the strongest memories. Before I had these glasses made, I stumbled across other people's terrible memories everywhere I went: in the Metro, at the grocery store, on the street. The only way to prevent it was to walk around with my eyes closed. Not exactly conducive to leading a normal life, or to keeping my job at the Smithsonian. Which I lost rather quickly." He shrugged, his expression harsh. "It's a cruel punishment in many ways. But no worse than I deserve. You see, that night my family was killed? I was the one driving the car."

With his sunglasses on, Dr. Brightman was almost impossible to read. His description sounded agonizing, but his face was blank. "What about . . . people? I mean, do you get visions when you touch people?"

"No," he said. "But then, I've had very little occasion to test that theory."

My heart twisted sympathetically in my chest, but still, his expression betrayed nothing.

He stepped closer to the derringer, suspended in its almost invisible case. "Now this"—he gestured to the gun—"is my Holy Grail. The ultimate blood artifact. I always believed that if I touched this derringer, the memories it holds would be strong enough to turn off my visions for good." He turned toward me. "That is, if I survived the experience."

"Why the derringer? Aren't there bloodier artifacts out there?"

Dr. Brightman tapped a finger on the plexiglass. "This gun is as important as any object in American history," he said. "It drove North and South further apart, fueled the terrors of Radical Reconstruction, and turned Lincoln into an American martyr." He smiled. "But you're right, there are bloodier artifacts in this city. Trust me, I've handled a lot of them. This one, though"—he rested a hand on the case—"is personal. It didn't just shape a nation. It shaped *me*. All my research, my whole life's work, has centered around Booth, this gun, and the one bullet that it fired."

I examined the derringer with fresh eyes, mentally comparing it to the photographs I'd seen in Dr. Brightman's book. I walked around the side of the clear box so I could look down the barrel of the gun.

I was so absorbed in my study that I jumped a foot when I heard a woman's voice call out behind us. "Megan Brown?"

Genevieve Herndon strode toward us across the exhibit floor. Her forehead creased with suspicion as she looked back and forth between me and Dr. Brightman.

I'd been caught.

"What a surprise to find you here today, Megan. Don't you have school?" Mrs. Herndon's eyes grew cold as she addressed Dr. Brightman. "David."

Dr. Brightman's voice was smooth and sharp. "Always a pleasure, Genevieve."

Mrs. Herndon smiled at him without warmth, then turned to

me. "Megan, may I speak with you?"

"Sure," I said, anxiety creeping up into my chest.

"I'll be right here," Dr. Brightman said as I followed Mrs. Herndon's retreating back.

She paused beside a re-creation of war-torn Richmond and rubbed at a muscle in her neck. Something in her posture reminded me of Emma smoking outside school, the line of her arm curving up and away from her body. "I know this might sound strange, coming from someone you hardly know," she said. "But I value your mother very much, and I know what she's been through. And I hope someone would do the same thing for my child." She paused and looked me in the eye. "Stay away from that man."

My thoughts stumbled to a halt. "What?"

"He's been a colleague of mine for years." Her lips narrowed to a thin line. "There was even a time when I considered him a friend. Both him *and* his wife. But . . ." She paused, thinking before she spoke. "He's changed. There's a darkness about him." She shook her head impatiently. "Of course, I work at an assassination site, so I'm okay with a little darkness. But sometimes . . . people get stuck there. They're happy to live in the darkness."

Her sticky-sweet concern sent a bolt of spite straight through me. "Bad things happen. The darkness is *real.* Maybe we can't all brush it off so easily."

She reached out to me, her face full of pity, but I stepped away. "All right, then." She curled her hand back into her chest. "You're not . . . spending time with him, are you?" Her head tilted, and I could tell from her expression that she was worried about more than just my mental health.

"No," I said roughly. "We're just talking. Okay?"

Before she could answer, I turned my back on her and returned to Dr. Brightman. My body hummed with resentment, and I couldn't stand to be cooped up in this museum another second. "You wanted to meet with me about something. Whatever that is, can we talk about it somewhere else?

"Yes. I have a car outside."

"I'll meet you there." I forced myself to smile at Mrs. Herndon as I walked past her and out of the museum.

On Tenth Street, Dr. Brightman made a phone call, and his car pulled up in front of the theater. It came with an actual driver, who opened the back door for us. His suit must have been custom-made; it fit his heavily muscled arms and shoulders to perfection. Thick black tattoos, barely visible against his dark skin, curled down his neck and disappeared under the collar of his shirt. He gave me a friendly wink as I got into the car. Dr. Brightman handed him a piece of paper, and he entered an address into an old-school GPS system mounted on the dashboard.

"Are we going to look at an artifact?" I asked.

"Yes. An extremely unusual one."

"Is it, like, murder-a-blah-blah?"

"Murderabilia?" He smiled. "Oh, I sincerely hope so."

Well, crapdogs, I thought. *Maybe Emma's mom was right.* "Isn't that a little . . . dark? Don't you ever want to focus on the good stuff?"

"Which do you think sounds more profitable?" he asked. "The exhibit of artifacts from the Crime Museum, just blocks from here, where the morbid multitudes can visit serial killer Ted Bundy's death car? Or your hypothetical National Museum of Good Stuff?"

I shifted uncomfortably in my seat. "Where exactly are we going?"

"A self-storage facility in Bladensburg, Maryland." He saw the look on my face and chuckled. "Don't worry." He gestured to the driver. "I always bring Mr. Wendell along. Just in case."

In case of what? I thought, but did not say.

Instead, I stared out the window for a while, watching the homes and businesses blur past, before I spoke again. "You're a historian and everything, right? It might be a strange request, to touch the gun that shot Abraham Lincoln. But couldn't you arrange it?"

Dr. Brightman snorted. "You may have noticed that Genevieve Herndon is not my biggest fan. And to touch it without gloves?" He shook his head. "Almost impossible. But I'll find a way."

I thought back to the gun, unable to let go of something that had been nagging at me. "It looks different."

"Different from what?"

"Different from the photos in your book." I reached into my bag and produced Tyler's copy of *Disasters in the Sun*, flipping through it until I found the page I wanted. "Look. It's really clear in this picture from the 1950s. The pattern of wood grain on the handle—it's not quite the same."

Dr. Brightman squinted at the photograph. "I'm sorry to burst your bubble, but the FBI's best scientists authenticated that gun, back in the late nineties. Any changes you see are the result of restoration."

"Why would the FBI do that? Authenticate the gun?"

He sighed. "Because of a hoax. A man came forward and said he had stolen the original derringer, way back in the sixties. The park service was so concerned about the rumor that they took the derringer to the FBI, who tested it and declared that it was genuine."

"Restoration. Huh." I closed the book. "I guess I thought artifacts like that were sacred. That you couldn't fix them up, or whatever. It seems wrong."

We pulled into the driveway of a run-down self-storage facility not far from the Maryland state line. A man stood in front of an open unit toward the back of the property, waiting for us: a white guy in a worn plaid shirt and baggy sweatpants. His gray hair was muddled with brown, and it fell in greasy waves, as though he hadn't taken a shower that morning. Or the morning before that.

"You were so eager to meet today," Dr. Brightman said. "We're lucky our friend here was available on short notice."

"What do you need me to do again?" I asked.

"When I touch an artifact like that, I can't see anything specific. Nothing but pain and white light. I'm too sensitive." He tapped his glasses. "I'm hoping you can get more detail than I can."

"You know, I haven't seen any memories for days. Maybe it won't work."

"I guess we'll find out," Dr. Brightman said as Mr. Wendell opened the car door.

"You the authenticator guy?" asked the man.

"I am indeed."

"Who's that?" He nodded at me. I stepped closer to Mr. Wendell.

"My assistant," said Dr. Brightman. "I understand you have something for me?"

The man walked into the storage unit and came out with a shoe box. He set it on the trunk of Dr. Brightman's car, then opened it and reached inside. "Guy wrote a lot of letters. And drew some pictures, if you like that kind of thing. But the real jewel is this little baby." He pulled out a deck of cards, held together with a disintegrating rubber band. He removed the band, set the deck down on the trunk, and fanned out the cards.

I let out a soft hum. "Tarot cards." The multicolored images of the traditional tarot deck stared back at me: a blindfolded woman with two crossed swords, a man walking off a cliff, the devil. Many of the cards had writing on them, blue ink in the white areas around the pictures. I looked at Dr. Brightman, puzzled.

"Well," he said, "go ahead."

I felt cold all over, looking at those cards. I had no idea what secrets they would hold. With great reluctance, I reached out one hand, laying it flat across as many cards as I could touch.

With a deafening squeal, a blue sedan spun into the parking lot, the sun flashing off its windshield and into my eyes, dazzling them. The barrel of a gun peeked through the open driver's window. I cried out and ducked my head, covering it with both arms, as a gunshot rang out.

With a sickening thump, a man fell to the ground at my feet.

At first I thought it was the owner of the tarot cards, but this man was younger, with a dark mustache—and blood pouring from a wound in his stomach.

I screamed and screamed and screamed, curling into a ball, trying to make myself as small as possible.

"Miss Brown. Miss Brown!" Dr. Brightman shook my shoulder gently. "You're all right. Calm down."

Both men stood above me, unharmed. The simple act of tilting my head sent pain through my jaw and into my neck, and I winced, grabbing my head with both hands.

"What did you see?" Dr. Brightman prodded.

"A car . . . a man shooting from his car." I spun around, looking for the body. "Oh, god, where is the guy he shot? Is he okay?" The owner of the cards took a few steps backward, staring at me with a damn-shame-that-kid's-crazy look on his face.

Dr. Brightman addressed the man, all business. "Your object appears to be genuine. I'll take it. Mr. Wendell, please handle the final details and put the items in the trunk." Dr. Brightman helped me to my feet and got me into the backseat of the car. Then he went around to the other side and joined me.

"What was that?" I rubbed my neck, my head still pounding.

"A deck of cards that once belonged to the DC sniper, John Allen Muhammad. You may recall—or are you too young?"

"I heard the stories." In 2002, Muhammad and seventeen-year-old Lee Boyd Malvo had shot thirteen random people in the DC area with a long-range rifle. Ten of them died.

"Muhammad left a tarot card behind at more than one of his shootings. Judging from the number of cards in that deck, it's fortunate they caught him when they did."

"And you want to *own* that?"

"I do not. But someone else most certainly will."

I leaned my head back against the seat, struggling to catch my breath. The sound of my own screams echoed in my ears. I thought of Clara Harris, the blood on her dress, the terror in her eyes. And I heard that bright, ringing laugh—Lincoln's laugh. No matter what Dr. Brightman said, I wished there was a museum where we could keep that laugh, and not the gun.

I squinted over at Dr. Brightman. "Whatever happened to Clara Harris?"

"Ah, Clara." He sighed and stared out the window for a moment at Mr. Wendell talking with the man in the plaid shirt. "Not a happy story. I do have a theory about her, though—and about the other two who were with Lincoln the night he was assassinated. Would you like to hear it?"

"Okay," I said, not entirely sure I did want to hear it.

"I think they all ended up like us."

I turned my body so I could see Dr. Brightman more fully. "What do you mean, 'like us'?"

"I already told you that Clara saw visions of the president. And her fiancé, Henry . . ." He sighed. "He was treated for constant headaches—and for hallucinations. Finally, one night, he lived the assassination all over again, but as the killer this time. He shot Clara in the head. Killed her instantly. Then he stabbed himself over and over, exactly as Booth had done almost twenty years before. When the police arrived, Henry said he saw people all around him, hiding in the walls."

A sick dread settled in my stomach. "And Mrs. Lincoln?"

"Mary always saw 'ghosts,' but after the assassination, her visions got worse. She even spent time in a mental institution." He shrugged. "I think that night changed all of them, left them haunted by memories no matter where they turned. And they had no way to understand what was happening to them."

I stared miserably at Dr. Brightman, wondering if he realized that his theory didn't bode well for either of us, or for how *we* would end up.

"In the end," he said, "Booth's derringer claimed more lives than just the president's."

Lucy Hale's blue eyes flashed through my mind. "But Booth's fiancée," I said. "She was fine, right? She got married, grew old, and everything."

Dr. Brightman held up a finger. "Thank you for reminding me. I brought you a gift. An object I thought you might like." From an inner jacket pocket, he pulled out a small black jewelry box. "A memento, from Lucy herself." He handed it to me.

I took the box, holding it only by my fingertips.

"It has no provenance. I couldn't authenticate it by any of the normal methods, so monetarily—even historically—it's worthless. But I thought you might appreciate it."

I turned the box over in my hands, but I didn't open it. Then Mr. Wendell slid into his seat behind the wheel, and we were off.

"Mr. Wendell," Dr. Brightman said, leaning forward to speak to him, "you can drop me off and then take Miss Brown"—he glanced back at me—"wherever she would like to go."

A sudden thought struck me. *Mrs. Herndon.* She had probably gone straight to my mother and told her all about our conversation. I pulled out my phone. Yep. Three missed calls and four angry texts, all from Mom. I texted back.

I'm okay. Heading home.

I knew I should feel terrible for worrying her, but mostly I just felt numb.

Less than fifteen minutes later, Mr. Wendell pulled up in front of Dr. Brightman's brick row house. Before he got out, Dr. Brightman said, "I hope this won't be the end of our relationship, Miss Brown. I would still love to look at that Lincoln cigar box. And I'm sure we could work out some kind of fee for your authentication services, if you're interested."

I stared back at him blankly. The jewelry box sat unopened on the seat beside me.

"Think it over." Mr. Wendell held the door as Dr. Brightman stepped out of the car, then stuck his head back through the doorway. He tapped his wired sunglasses. "I keep an extra pair of these in my desk, and one in my car. If we move forward, let me know if you start to need them."

After he disappeared into the house, Mr. Wendell took his seat behind the wheel and turned around to face me.

"You okay, kid?"

"I'm really not sure."

He reached into his wallet and handed me a white card with his last name and a phone number on it. "You ever need help, you let me know. I got a daughter about your age. And what happened back there? That was truly effed up."

I nodded in agreement, tucking the card into my pocket.

"Where to?" he asked.

I gave him my address, but then I paused. There was one place I hadn't gone to the last time I was in DC. One last place I hadn't been able to bring myself to visit. But right now, I felt an overwhelming desire to see it. "Would you mind if we stopped somewhere else first?"

Knee-high grass and weeds surrounded the building where my brother had died. A chain-link fence, several feet taller than my head, circled the large, almost empty lot. Inside the fence, one brownstone was still standing, but all that was left of three other houses were concrete foundations and front steps leading up to nowhere. On one side of the lot, a stretch of attached row houses ended abruptly in a windowless wall, an ugly scar where its neighbor had been torn away. A metal sign on the fence clattered in the breeze. Across the street, a construction crane towered over the frame of a large, half-finished building, with signs promising *Luxury Condos, Coming Soon.*

I left Mr. Wendell in the car and walked up to the fence, curling my fingers through the chain link. I couldn't see any way through, and I wasn't going to try and climb over with Mr. Wendell watching from the car. So I just stood there, breathing.

What is happening to me, Tyler? I asked silently. *Why did you leave me here like this?*

After a few minutes, I pulled the sleeve of my sweater down over my fingers, reached into my back pocket, and pulled out a tarot card. I had stolen it earlier, during the commotion that followed my vision. It was the moon. Stern and cold, its cobalt-yellow face shone down from the heavens on two snarling dogs. Or maybe one of them was a wolf. A road disappeared into the distance, stretching through barren land and across a choppy ocean.

Even through all my confusion and struggle, I felt a jolt of satisfaction; taking the card was exactly what Tyler might have done. I took out my art journal and tucked the card between two empty pages. *Raw materials,* I thought. *For later.*

Finally I pulled out the jewelry box that Dr. Brightman had given me and opened the lid. Nestled inside was a wide gold band: a man's ring, etched with an intricate design. I didn't know what memories it held, or what I would see when I touched it, but I knew one thing: Dr. Brightman liked dark objects, and I'd seen enough for one day. I snapped the box shut and gave one long last look at the empty lot before making my way back to the car.

CHAPTER 16

THE MOMENT MR. WENDELL TURNED ONTO MY street, I spotted it: a police car, blocking our driveway, silent but instantly terrifying. I felt my breathing speed up. This was going to be worse than I had imagined.

"Keep going," I said, ducking down in the backseat. "Drop me off up there."

Mr. Wendell didn't hesitate; he drove smoothly past the house and didn't stop until he was around the corner and well out of sight.

"You good to handle this alone?" he asked.

I nodded, trying to look confident as I stepped out of the car. "Yeah. I think so."

"If you change your mind about that, call."

As I turned the corner, I saw my parents and a uniformed police officer walk down our front steps, headed toward the patrol car.

"Thank you so much for coming," my mother said. "I'm sorry that we . . ." She spotted me and trailed off. She took two deep, shaky breaths, and then she grabbed my father's arm and burst into tears.

The sight of them unwound me, and I rushed over and put my arms around her. "I'm sorry," I whispered into her hair. She smelled of honeysuckle and oranges, a scent that made me feel five years old again, and I clung tighter. She stood stiffly against me, tears still running down her face. "I'm so sorry," I said.

"You are grounded *forever*."

"I know."

"Let's go inside," my father said. "We need to talk."

The police car drove away, and I thought the law-enforcement portion of the afternoon was over. Instead, I found Detective Johnson on our sofa. She was becoming a regular fixture of the room, like my mother's favorite porcelain lamp. She stood as we entered.

"You're home safe," she said. "I'm glad to see it. When I realized that you left the police station, I called your parents. We've been looking for you."

"How's Nathan? Did you arrest him? Is he okay?"

"He's fine. We talked, and then he went home." She looked over at my parents. "I'll get out of your hair in a minute, but I have a few questions for Megan before I go."

I perched on the back of the couch and dug my fingers into the texture of the fabric. I couldn't bear the tormented look on my mother's face. My heart was pushing outward on my chest so hard, I thought my body might give way. I wanted to reach into my bag and grab that tarot card, to use the pain it held to kill all the other thoughts in my head, no matter how much it hurt.

"We understand you were at Ford's Theatre today with David Brightman. I need to ask . . . Megan, are you involved with Dr. Brightman in some way?"

"Am I . . . ," I began. Then I realized what Detective Johnson was asking. "*What?* No! Absolutely not. That's . . ." I shook my head.

"No." I looked away from her and into my parents' worried, trusting faces.

"But you were with him?" she asked me.

"I was . . . talking to him," I said. "I met him at the exhibit two weeks ago. He recognized me in the museum. We were just talking."

"But you left with him."

"I may have left at the *same time* as him," I hedged. "But we don't have . . ." I searched for something that was true but not incriminating. A relationship? An inappropriate relationship? Ugh, at this point we might have both. "We don't have the kind of relationship you're talking about."

"But what were you doing at Ford's in the first place? And the police station?" my mother asked. She shook her head, her face creased with sadness and confusion. "Why did you skip school?"

I closed my eyes and saw Nathan's face, sapped of color and grim with the knowledge that all his worst fears had come to pass. I saw his parents, bleak and frightened. I could tell them all that I'd gone to the police station to say that Tyler had been a thief, making money off his friends' parents and using the cash for god knows what. But who would that help, and who would it hurt? And I asked myself . . . did I really want to uncover the truth about Tyler? Or did I only want to prove that Tyler was the person I thought he was? Because, as it turned out, I couldn't do both. And maybe not knowing, however hard that was to swallow, would be less devastating to the people I loved than the truth.

I opened my eyes again. "I just . . . felt really depressed. I didn't want to go to school."

My mother looked at me expectantly. "That's it? That's all you have to say for yourself?" She threw up her hands in frustration. "You told me that if something was wrong, you would talk to me!"

"No one in this family talks to anyone else," I snapped, "and no one listens! This house is like an echo chamber, and all I can hear is the sound of my own voice." I stood. "Can I go now?"

My parents exchanged a guilty look. "Go," my father said quietly, breaking their shared gaze.

I could still hear their urgent whispers as I went upstairs to my room. Before I sat down, before I even took off my backpack, I took my phone out of my pocket and called Eric's number. The call went straight to voice mail without ringing once. Had he blocked me? Since this whole thing had started, we hadn't gone more than a day without talking, and now, nothing.

I heard a knock, and my mother cracked open the door. "You're still grounded. But I couldn't seem to turn this guy away." She opened the door the rest of the way. Eric stood in the hall, his face anxious, one hand twisted in his hair.

"Are you okay?" he asked.

I started to cry. A big, ugly cry, the kind that came with sobbing. The kind I hadn't given in to since Tyler's death. Eric rushed into the room, and I bear hugged him with all my might. I caught sight of my mother's startled face over his shoulder.

"Hey," he said, patting my back, "deep breaths. It's gonna be fine."

My mother coughed, and we broke apart. "Okay, you two. You have ten minutes." Her gaze darted back and forth between us, lingering on our hands, which were still linked together. I don't think she'd ever seen me hold hands with a boy before, much less fall all over one like I'd just done to Eric. "How about I leave this door open?" she said, backing out of the room.

"What was all that about?" Eric asked.

"Oh, she's afraid we're going to make out."

Eric dropped my hand and propelled quickly away from me. "I'll sit over here, then." He flopped into the chair by my worktable. "So you're not hurt?"

I shook my head, lowering myself down onto the bed. My neck and jaw still hurt from the aftereffects of my vision, and the dull ache refused to fade.

"Thank god," he said. "When you went missing, your mom called my mom, then my mom pulled me out of school. I got over here as quickly as I could."

"You should have called me."

"I didn't have my phone." Seeing my puzzled look, he continued, "Don't laugh—my sister tried to Bedazzle it."

I laughed. Of course I laughed, even though it sent a fresh stab of pain across the back of my head.

"It's not funny," he said. "She cracked the screen into a million pieces. Mom will be docking her allowance until the day she goes to college."

I grinned, rubbing at my neck. "I thought you didn't want to talk to me."

"Oh, I didn't," Eric said. "You were a real asshole."

"I'm sorry. You were right—we're in this together." I rested a hand on his arm. "Forgive me?"

He shrugged. "Done. So tell me . . . you saw the box in Bobby's locker?"

I nodded. "He apparently came for all the things he and Tyler had stolen."

"That lying weasel!"

"He must have used the spare key to get in and go through our things—" I shot to my feet, despite my body's protests. My senses still tingled from the vision I'd seen at the self-storage unit—the gun, the body bleeding on the ground. Right now, while I still felt so raw and sensitive, I wanted to try touching more of Tyler's things.

I rushed down the hall to his room, with Eric right behind me. Tyler's personal effects, the ones the police had returned to us, lay scattered across the bed, and all the things I'd taken from his locker were still in a bag in the corner. I dumped it out and sifted through it.

In the pile of things on the bed, I spotted a plastic bag full of money—coins and bills—that the police must have gathered from Tyler's pockets or his car. One of the coins was different from the others: dark bronze, with a hole in the center. I opened the bag and fished around until I had it in my hand.

"Are you sure you're okay?" Eric asked. "You seem a little"—he waggled his hands up and down—"off balance. What happened today?"

I examined the coin. Asian characters clustered around the square hole in the middle. It didn't take superpowers to figure out where this had come from. I wondered what Nathan would think if he knew that Tyler had stolen from his house too.

Eric touched my shoulder. "Megan. What's going on?"

I shook my head to clear it. "Sorry. I guess I'm not myself." I turned the coin over in my hand. "I went to see Dr. Brightman today."

Eric's eyes popped. "And? What happened?"

"I touched a seriously hostile object." Not this coin, though. It had a friendly sparkle, a golden gleam that called to me, and it buzzed, ever so slightly, against my fingertips. "I think I'm feeling a little . . . hypersensitive," I said. "To the visions. Because there's a memory attached to this coin." I held it up. "I can tell."

"Well, can you try to, I don't know, find it?"

I stared at the coin, striving to see beyond it as Dr. Brightman had taught me, looking for the light.

The brightness rushed over me, shocking but painless this time. Then the blaze telescoped down to the glare of a lighting instrument, set up in Nathan's family room. Tyler was kicked back on the couch, flipping a coin in the air—the very coin I now held—and catching it with the same hand. Cedric sat beside him, leaning forward, his elbows on his knees. Nathan stood over a digital camera, adjusting settings and pushing buttons.

"Red, dude, these cameras your folks sprang for are awesome," Nathan said. "They're going to take The District to a whole new level."

Tyler shifted on the sofa, a guilty look in his eyes. I was certain my parents had *not* bought video cameras for The District.

"Yeah, but we can't seem to crack a thousand views per video. We need to draw more attention to ourselves."

"Bring the sunshine," Cedric said, nodding.

"Ooh, I know." Nathan snapped his fingers. "Get Idris Elba."

Tyler shook his head. "You're not taking me seriously."

"You're right. If my gorgeous face isn't reeling in the viewers, nothing will." Nathan struck a model-worthy pose, one fist under his chin, lips pursed.

Cedric blew a breath out through his teeth, smiling. "Fool," he said. "But for real, you think we can keep this thing going when you're both off at college?" He looked hopefully at Nathan. "Unless you're choosing Howard?"

"Oh," Nathan said. "I don't know yet."

Cedric's face fell, and he turned back to Tyler. "I mean, I can keep shooting in DC, bring some new people on board, but without you guys . . ." He shrugged. "It won't be the same."

Nathan flopped down on the couch beside Cedric. "Huh. I hadn't really thought that far ahead."

Tyler caught the coin one last time, clenching it in his fist. "Something big. That's what we need. We could take this channel from kid stuff to national news. Something to be proud of."

Nathan made a face. "Hey! *I'm* proud of it."

"No, we can make it bigger. And I think I know how." Tyler shook his head. "But right now, let's shoot."

The vision faded, leaving the coin warm in my palm. I looked up at Eric. "I found it." I rubbed the coin, feeling its edges.

My mother called up from the bottom of the stairs. "Five more minutes!"

"I'd better go," Eric said, moving toward the door.

"Wait. I want to try something else." I looked around. "This whole room is full of Tyler's memories. It's like a gold mine."

"Or a minefield," Eric countered. "Maybe you should take a break."

"Five more minutes," I said. "Let's try that George Bush bobblehead."

Rolling his eyes, Eric handed it to me. I stared at it until my eyes crossed. I rubbed it as though a genie might pop out. Nothing happened.

"Okay, maybe the laptop?"

I tried. Again, nothing. "Maybe another time," Eric said.

"A few more. What's that thing on the shelf over there? The glass thing?"

Eric passed me a green glass heart flecked with gold, and as soon as it touched my fingers, I found myself in the bedroom of a girl with a spill of dark hair and freckles across her face and chest. Her *entire, naked* chest. I dropped it like a hot potato. "Well. I found something that time."

Eric gave me a questioning look.

"Let's just say it's a souvenir of a very particular kind."

"Sexytimes?" Eric asked.

I snorted out a laugh. "You did *not* just say sexytimes." He shrugged. I laughed harder.

The more memories I experienced, the giddier and looser I felt: an intoxicating thrill, like the best part of being drunk. But at the same time, the pain grew worse and worse. My temples throbbed. Even my teeth hurt. And the pain mixed with elation left me feeling unbalanced. Volatile. An element in some in-between state, teetering on the edge.

I wheeled around, looking for the next object I wanted to touch. My outstretched fingers landed on the leather of Eric's belt, and I was yanked away from Tyler's room in a sudden tunnel of light, only to be deposited beside the hospital bed of a painfully thin man. It took me a few seconds to recognize him, even though I'd known him since I was a little girl. Eric's father. His face was slack, but his eyes seemed alert. A white plastic tube extended from a collar around his neck. Eric was there too, with his mom. She tenderly wiped her husband's mouth and kissed him on his cheek, while Eric turned away and leaned on the bed rail for support, his jaw clenched with suppressed tears.

I slumped to the ground. "I'm sorry," I said, looking up at Eric. "I didn't mean to . . ." A bitter taste filled my mouth, and I smelled burning plastic. Enough visions for one day.

"What the . . . ," Eric seemed confused. Then he rested his hands on his belt, and realization changed the shape of his face. "Oh. This was my dad's. I started wearing it when he got sick." He sat down beside me on the floor, his face apprehensive but full of hope. "You saw my dad?"

"I think so. I'm really, really sorry, I didn't—"

"It's fine. What did you see?"

"Him in the hospital, with you and your mom." I wasn't sure whether I should intrude further, but I pushed ahead. "I know he was sick for a long time, but I never really knew what he had. What disease, I mean."

Eric took a deep breath and let it out slowly. "He had ALS. Lou Gehrig's disease?" He looked down at his hands. "Turns out he had a cousin who had it too, so it might be genetic. Kind of messed me up when I found that out. Like, you go your whole life thinking you're one thing, but something else was lurking inside you all along."

Lurking inside you all along. That was the same phrase Eric had used when we were talking about origin stories.

And with that tiny shift, a whole pattern emerged. My mind

went smooth and focused, and suddenly I could see us, all lit up like cities from an airplane, all the people like me—the historians and artists and archaeologists and antique-store owners—the ones with this ability lurking inside us all along. Maybe we got broken. Maybe we broke the very things we loved. But maybe that was what it took to let the ability out.

I saw Eric in a whole new way too—how much he'd been through, and how kind he'd been to me, even in the face of all that.

My mom appeared in the doorway. "Time's up." Her eyes narrowed. "Why are you sitting on the floor?"

Eric bounced up like a Slinky and helped me to my feet. "Just talking. Seriously. That's it." He patted me stiffly on the shoulder. "Okay, so, see you at school?"

I wanted to say something profound, something about origins and destinations and all the amazing things I knew Eric had lurking inside him—not only the potential for disease. But the moment passed, and he was gone.

Over the next few days, my grounding went into full effect. My parents made a big show of cutting up the emergency credit card I'd used to pay for the cab in DC. The terms of my grounding were laid out. Dad would drive me to school and pick me up. There would be no visits with friends (their use of the plural felt exaggerated), no television or video games (I didn't play video games), and no internet time. They turned off the data to my cell phone, but I could still make calls (which meant I could still text, but I neglected to point that out). No end date was mentioned for this grounding; it would be in effect "as long as we feel like it."

But when we sat down to eat dinners together, they made an effort to hold a normal conversation, as though they had taken what I'd said to heart. And yet by Thursday I was only half listening. I was tapping my fork on my dish—part of a set that had belonged to my grandmother. We'd used them for every meal as long as I could remember, and my grandmother had used them before us. They'd outlived her. Come to think of it, they'd outlived Tyler. Maybe in a hundred years, long after I was dead and gone, some other girl would tap her fork on this dish, her life so foreign from mine I could not even imagine it.

"The gala tomorrow night is going to be the end of me," my mother said. "Four major donors have RSVP'd at the last minute, and trying to juggle the ticket requests and the dinner seating has been a nightmare."

The Ford's Theatre annual gala was a massive fundraising event that my mother helped to coordinate every year. Lots of rich people and politicians, and even some actual celebrities, got together to watch a performance, eat tiny food, and give someone a medal for carrying on the legacy of Abraham Lincoln. My mother had been asking me for months to go with her this year. She had even tried to tempt me by describing the entertainment for the evening, which featured some singer I had never heard of performing songs from some Broadway show I didn't care about. That was one good thing to come out of being grounded—no more pressure to attend the gala.

My father looked up from his food. "I was thinking. The Mid-Atlantic Historical Association is having its annual meeting at American University this week. I might try to catch some of the sessions." He paused. "Before I join you at the gala."

Mom sat back in surprise. "You're feeling up to that? That's . . . great. I'll be at the theater all day, so you can join me there afterward." She looked over at me. "That means you'll be on your own tomorrow night, Megan. You can get a ride home with Eric, but you're still grounded."

I nodded absently, and my parents lapsed into silence, seemingly exhausted by the effort of conversation. I kept staring at my dish.

I could hardly believe that I had to go to school the next day. The routine of classes and lunches and teachers had moved way past boring and into the realm of torturous. My father dropped me off, and I pulled out my phone as I walked into school, missing Elena, mentally composing the perfect *Groundhog Day* quote to send her. I was so caught up in my own thoughts that I almost ran straight into Detective Johnson.

She didn't belong here, in this place, and for the span of a few heartbeats, I didn't even recognize her.

"I was hoping to see you," she said. "You want to step outside with me?"

"I don't know. Will there be handcuffs involved?"

She actually laughed. It transformed her face and turned her into someone I hardly recognized. Someone's friend. Someone's mom. "No," she said. "I have something to tell you, and I wanted to do it in person."

We walked out to the picnic table where I'd brought the things from Tyler's locker on my first day back at school. It seemed like an era ago. An eon. Something that could only be measured in geologic time. Johnson sat on the table and propped one foot up on the bench. Her face had turned serious again.

"We're seeing a lot of each other lately," I said, trying for a joke.

But her smile from earlier was nowhere to be seen. "It's going to be soon. A matter of days."

"What's going to be—" I stopped. "An article? About Tyler? And the drugs?"

She nodded. "I got a call from a friend at the *Post.* They're fact-checking it, trying to get it in on Sunday. But it probably won't hit till Monday at the earliest."

My stomach dropped, and I rubbed my face with one hand.

"You wanted to know," she said.

"I did."

Johnson stood and put a hand on my shoulder. "Megan, you came all the way to the station to see me, and you left without saying a word. Are you sure there's nothing you want to tell me? Nothing at all?"

I couldn't bring myself to meet her eyes.

She sighed. "It's not too late. You know where to find me."

As she walked away, I thought, *It's not too late.* But once this story broke, Tyler's legacy would be sealed. Most of us don't live on in lengthy biographies and museums dedicated to the tiny minutiae of our lives. Most of us get the memory of our family and friends, and that's it. Maybe a newspaper clipping or two. Maybe a work of art. What would Tyler have?

In a rush, I made up my mind: I wanted the truth. Even if no one else ever knew, even if I never chose to tell my parents or the police, I wanted to know exactly what had happened to him. And there was still one card on the table, one piece of the puzzle I hadn't explored: the Lincoln cigar box. Whatever memories were trapped inside, they were so painful I couldn't even touch it. The objects in Tyler's room didn't have as strong an effect. But blood artifacts did.

I needed to take it to Dr. Brightman, and I needed to do it today.

I took out my phone to call Eric before I remembered he had no phone. So I went straight to Bobby's locker instead. I waited there until the bell rang for first period, but he never came. As the hallway emptied out, I sat down beside the locker. If some teacher wanted me to leave, they could physically pry me off this square of linoleum.

When I reached into my backpack for a book to sit on, my hand brushed against the black velvet jewelry box Dr. Brightman had given me, with Lucy Hale's ring still inside. I took out the box cautiously and popped it open. The ring glinted warmly, even in the cool fluorescent light. Whatever memories it held, I didn't want to wait anymore.

I held out a single finger and ran it across the golden surface.

A dead body lay beside me.

I yanked my hand away. Booth. It had been John Wilkes Booth. Dead. Lying on a wooden bench, covered by a thick gray blanket. Except for his face.

I took a deep breath and touched it again.

With a blur of light, I was in a tiny, cramped room with Booth's dead body. A woman knelt beside him, shrouded in black from head to toe. She lay across his legs, weeping. Beside her stood a gray-haired man with a paunchy stomach and a deeply ingrained crease between his eyebrows.

"Enough," he said. "It's time to go."

The woman struggled to push herself to her feet. When she was finally standing, I could see that it was Lucy.

The older man reached into his pocket and handed her the ring. "My influence bought you this ring back." He waved it in the air between them. "Someone could have traced it back to you. It was retrieved from a dead man's body, along with your reputation. See that you never, *ever* threaten it again."

All the spirit and fire I'd seen in Lucy during my last vision—sitting at a hotel restaurant, tossing quips at her fiancé—all that was gone now. "Yes, Father," she whispered. "I promise."

He left the room, and Lucy gave the gold band a single kiss before dropping a dense black veil over her face and following him out the door.

I took my hand off the ring, and instantly I was back in the school hallway, sitting doggedly in front of Bobby's locker. Lucy might have lived a long life, but I felt confident from what I'd seen that every last day had been spent trying to live up to that promise to her father.

The bell rang again, and I didn't have much longer to wait before Bobby emerged from the between-class crowd. I scrambled to my feet.

His chin dropped to his chest and he shook his head in disbelief as he spotted me.

"Seriously?" he groaned. "Just go away."

He turned his back to me and opened the locker. The moment it swung open, my hand caught the door, keeping it from closing again.

"You've got to be kidding." His voice turned mocking, and he leaned in closer to me. "I'm sorry, but sometimes, when a guy says no, he means no."

The hallway was packed with students. I looked around, making eye contact with as many people as I could, and then I channeled Elena's loudest, most obnoxious voice, never removing my hand from the locker door.

"Students of Westside!" I announced. "Bobby Drake is a slimy liar and a sexual harasser!"

A few people stopped to stare, and Bobby's eyes went wide. "You are a *freak*," he whispered. "What are you doing?"

"Oh, do you care what these people think?" I asked, feigning surprise. "Because I don't."

"Let your freak flag fly, girl!" someone yelled.

I kept going. "He has worn the same Yale shirt every Tuesday for a year!"

Two girls burst out laughing. A crowd was starting to gather, and Bobby's face had taken on a distinct sheen of panic.

"Don't trust him around your girlfriends! Or your wallets!"

Bobby had stepped away from the locker now, trying to talk to a few of the people who had gathered around. The Lincoln cigar box was unguarded.

"And worst of all," I said, "he kisses like a starving, toothless St. Bernard!"

As the crowd hooted with laughter, I pulled my sleeve down over my hand and took hold of the Lincoln box. I shoved it into my back-pack as quickly as I could.

Bobby grabbed my arm, and I yelled at the top of my lungs.

"He's laying hands on me! He's laying hands on me!"

Bobby let go instantly and backed away.

I gave him a thin smile. "Sorry, Bobby. Nothing personal." I pushed my way through the crowd and left him to his fate.

As I broke through the last few people standing by Bobby's locker, I came face-to-face with Eric. His expression was frozen in an almost comical look of shock.

"I have only one thing to say." He paused for effect. "Cooler than Captain America."

"I've got the box."

"Let's go." He turned without question and headed toward the nearest exit.

We rushed out into the parking lot, the cigar box in my bag bouncing heavily against my back with each step, and we jumped into Eric's car.

A shot of adrenaline surged through me as he started the engine. Maybe we'd point this car west and keep driving. Drive and drive until the road ended in an ocean. San Francisco. Or Los Angeles. A whole city full of people who'd run as far as there was to run.

But today, there was Dr. Brightman. And, hopefully, some answers.

By the time Eric found parking on Capitol Hill, I was second-guessing myself. No one had answered Dr. Brightman's phone when I called—what if he hadn't gotten my voice mail? What if he wasn't even home? He wasn't the sort to appreciate random visitors.

Eric started to unbuckle his seat belt, but I stopped him. "Stay here? I really think I need to do this alone."

He nodded. "I'll stay here. But you're not alone."

I hesitated, not sure whether I should ask what I wanted to ask next. "So I've been wondering . . . can you get tested? For the ALS?"

Eric leaned his head back on the car seat and blew out a long breath. "When I'm eighteen. But the test's not clear-cut; it can't predict whether I'll get symptoms. So I don't know."

My stomach twisted. "Well, if you ever do, and you want . . . I don't know. Company? Just say the word."

Eric snorted. "It's a date." He swatted my shoulder. "Now go."

To my relief, Dr. Brightman's assistant answered moments after I rang the bell. She was . . . beige. A solid wash of sandy brown extended from her hair to her suit to her "natural"-colored pantyhose. "If you'll give me a moment," she said blandly, "I'll let him know that you're here." And she left me standing in the entryway.

It was the first time I'd been alone in any part of Dr. Brightman's house, and I immediately began looking around for some raw materials, some memento of this place I could take with me. The only thing I saw was the set of car keys hanging on the wall, complete with the goofy Lincoln keychain. They looked like they hadn't been used in years. The plastic was cracked and faded, and a tiny cobweb connected Lincoln's head to the wall.

The compulsion I felt was inexplicable. And irresistible. I removed the keys from their hook and held them tightly in my hand. They buzzed slightly against my bare skin.

I thought of Bobby's horrified, embarrassed face in the hallway earlier, and I felt a stab of genuine remorse. In the last hour, I'd stolen the Lincoln cigar box and Dr. Brightman's keys. The moral high ground I'd thought I occupied was sinking rapidly.

I heard footsteps, and I shoved the keys quickly into my backpack just as Dr. Brightman came down the stairs. His face was bare, no glasses in sight, and he wore a slim-fitting black suit. His pant legs stopped at his ankles, revealing dress shoes and azurite blue socks.

"Miss Brown. A pleasure." He gestured me in. "Please, have a seat. I got your message. I can't wait to see what you've brought me."

I perched on one of the leather couches in his office, dropping my backpack on the floor between my feet. "Before we start," I said, screwing up my courage, "I want you to know that this is my last visit. I don't want to continue . . . authenticating things. I just want to find out more about this box, and then I'm through."

He seemed disappointed but not surprised. "I'd hoped for a different outcome." He rubbed his gloved hands together. "But I suppose we should get started."

I covered my hand with my sleeve and reached into my backpack for the box.

Even through the fabric, it sent a jagged bolt of pain up my arm and into my left eye. I dropped it, clutching my aching face.

Dr. Brightman made a *tsk* sound. He went to his desk and retrieved a pair of gloves, sealed in a clear plastic bag. "To touch that kind of object, you need fabric with a much tighter weave. I order these specially—they've never been touched by human hands."

Whatever the reason, once the gloves were on, I was able to remove the cigar box and set it on the glass coffee table.

Dr. Brightman went to his desk and opened a drawer, taking out his sunglasses. He put them on and sat opposite me. Carefully, he lifted the cigar box, turning it around in his hands, examining the brass hinges and running one gloved finger over the carved swirls on the lid. He spent some time examining Lincoln's image before opening the clasp on the front of the box. In my vision, I had seen cigars inside this box, but I'd never been able to open it for myself. I leaned forward eagerly.

It was empty. Dr. Brightman ran a hand around the inside of the box before setting it down on the table again. "Well. It's a cigar box." He looked up at me. "Probably early twentieth century, made long after the assassination. Other than that, I don't see anything unusual about it . . . yet." He paused. "Are you ready?"

"Not really." I took a deep breath. "Okay, yes."

Dr. Brightman took off his glasses and set them down on the coffee table. Beads of sweat clung to his brow, although the room was cool. He pulled off both his gloves and set them beside the glasses. Then he looked up at me expectantly.

I took off the gloves he'd given me, reached out a hand, and held it above the box. Dr. Brightman did the same. Together, we rested our palms on the wooden lid.

The pain came first. Shooting up the back of my neck, it settled sharp in the center of my forehead. I forced myself to keep my eyes open. A constellation of lights surrounded me, some brighter than others. I leaned toward the brightest one and allowed myself to be consumed by its glow.

When the world coalesced around me again, Dr. Brightman's office was completely gone. It was night, and I was standing near the building where my brother's body had been found. Dr. Brightman stood beside me, his hand in mine. I spotted Tyler coming up the sidewalk, hobbling on his crutches, his leg in its cast. The cigar box was nowhere in sight. Tyler wore jeans and his letter jacket, with his backpack on both shoulders and his ever-present baseball cap tipped back on his head. He glanced around as though looking for someone; then he paused under a streetlight and checked his phone.

Emma Herndon emerged into the light. She looked like a flower in winter, alone here after dark in a pair of white pants and a bubblegum-pink blouse.

"Do you have the box?" she asked.

"It's still inside." Tyler gestured to the row of houses inside the fenced lot. "My friends let me leave things here sometimes. It's their secret drop spot for party supplies." He glanced around, craning his neck to look up and down the darkened street. "Does your dad know you're here? It's not the safest neighborhood. You should have let me bring it to you."

"Yeah, well, maybe *you* should have thought of that before taking it in the first place." She ran a shaky hand through her hair. "Something about that box. He . . ." She paused. "I probably shouldn't tell you this, but he lost it. I've never seen him like that, Ty. I thought he might . . . I don't know."

Tyler grabbed her hand, his face solemn and intense. "Did he tell you why? What made it so important to him?"

"No. He told me to act like it was no big deal. Why?"

After another quick glance over his shoulder, he let out a long breath. "Come on. I'll show you."

Tyler hobbled over to the fence and ran his hand along it until he found a loose section of chain-link that swung free at the bottom. "Can you help me here?"

Emma held up the fence so they could go through. He led her over to the house and around to the cellar doors on the side—big metal doors set level with the ground, with handles on the top.

Tyler handed Emma his crutches so that he could open a dented padlock and swing one of the doors open, revealing a set of steps leading down and out of sight. The doors were damaged and uneven, and the hole in the ground gaped like a mouth full of rusty teeth. Precarious-looking concrete stairs ended in total darkness. As far as I could see, they led down to the center of the earth.

"Yeah, I'm not going down there," Emma said.

Tyler laughed. "No problem. Wait here."

She held up his crutches. "How are you going to manage that?"

"Did you know that after he shot Abraham Lincoln, John Wilkes Booth broke his leg? He evaded capture for ten days. I think I can manage a flight of stairs."

"Then he got killed, you moron."

Tyler shrugged. He hopped over and lowered himself down into the cellar. A soft glow appeared inside—he must have turned on a light. Moments later, he pulled himself back out again, a bulge beneath his jacket. Emma dropped his crutches to the ground and moved toward him eagerly. He unzipped his jacket, pulled out the Lincoln cigar box, and placed it with some ceremony in her hands.

"Okay." She looked up at him, puzzled. "So what's the big deal about this box?"

"It's not the box itself," Tyler said. "It's what's hidden inside. I found a secret compartment in the lid. With papers in it."

Her eyes narrowed. "What kind of papers?"

"Solid proof," Tyler said, "that your dad's been hiding a stolen artifact worth millions of dollars."

Emma's mouth worked, but no sound came out. "Come on," she

said at last. "My dad's a lot of things, but he's not a thief."

"He's *worse* than a thief." Tyler was all venom. "He's a menace."

Emma sneered. "You're lying. You're still mad because you think he made me break up with you. He didn't. I came up with that brilliant idea all on my own."

Tyler's mouth was an angry slash. "You're the whole reason I've been sitting on this. I could have gone to the newspapers—or the police. But I didn't want to destroy your family." He shook his head. "I kept looking for another way. But this is about more than just your dad. It's about what he symbolizes. Him and everyone like him. They're tearing this country in half. Rich people over here. Poor people over there. Wealth inequality: it's the new segregation—and it's about class *and* race. And the walls keep getting higher and higher. Almost no one can make that leap anymore, thanks to people like your dad, who would like to think they own this entire country." He gestured to the box. "Even its fucking history." He stopped, breathing heavily.

Emma was unnaturally still. "So what are you going to do?"

"I can't keep quiet anymore. I'm going to break the story *myself*."

"Are you talking about your YouTube channel?" She gave a watery-sounding laugh. "How will you fit this big story in, between all your cat-fail videos and dumb pranks?"

"The District is a major idea, Em. It's not cat fails. It's journalism. It's community building. It could spread beyond DC and become a pilot program for channels all over the country." He held his chin high. "And once this story hits, it'll be profitable too. I'll be able to take the year off from school to work on it without living in a cardboard box."

She held up the box. "You mean you'll be able to work on it without *stealing* from me and all our friends. Who's the real thief in this scenario, Tyler?"

Still without his crutches, Tyler adjusted himself on his one good foot. "Okay, sure. I enjoyed the irony. Having the ultra wealthy bankroll the project, with some left over. We didn't get our hands too dirty. A few cigars here. A bottle of wine there." He shot her a wry smile. "Like crowdfunding."

Emma's face was red, and I could see the cords in her neck. "Except for the part where you ask first, you enormous hypocrite."

"It did get a little out of control." He hopped a step closer to her. "But it's nothing compared to what your dad has done." He held out his hand for the box. "Here, let me show you. I'll prove it to you."

She shoved the Lincoln box into his hands, pushing it so hard he teetered on his good foot. He struggled to keep his balance. "Take it, then! But don't pretend you care about me. You're going to target my dad? And you think there won't be consequences for me?" She smacked him on the shoulder. "Everything's so easy for you, isn't it? Everything's just a game." She started doing an exaggerated impression of Tyler. "'I'll drop out of school for a while! Make some videos! Save the world!' You total prick."

"Hey," he said, reaching for her.

Emma slapped Tyler's hand away, and he swayed backward, dangerously close to the open basement door. "You never worry about anything, do you? And I always have to think and plan and calculate every stupid thing I do. And now you are trying to ruin my goddamn life!"

She turned away from him, and Tyler leaned to one side, trying to see her face. "Listen to me, Emma—"

She spun back toward him, a flourish of movement, clearly ready to lay into him again. He hopped back in surprise, the cigar box still in his hands, and stumbled on the lip of the cellar doors. As if in slow motion, he wavered back and forth, back and forth, until he lost his balance and fell.

I cried out, instinctively moving toward him, but Dr. Brightman's hand tightened around mine.

I saw my own horror reflected in Emma's face. She tried to grab Tyler's arm, but he slipped free of her grasp, smashing his head against the metal doorframe and disappearing from sight into the darkness.

She screamed, tripping over her own feet as she ran through the open door and down into the basement.

Hot, painful tears ran down my cheeks. I wanted to force my way over there, climb down those steps, and help my brother. But I knew what I was seeing could not be changed. Emma came out of the basement a moment later, clutching the Lincoln box, shaking and white-faced with shock. She leaned against the side of the house, staring off into the distance.

The growl of a car engine and the flash of headlights snapped her out of her trance. She startled like a prey animal and froze, staring at the box. From the street, a car door slammed. Then another. Emma's head jerked up and she spun from side to side, paralyzed with indecision. Finally she squared her shoulders and went back down into the basement.

Two figures came down the sidewalk. As they passed through a pool of light, I saw with surprise that one of them was Senator

Herndon; the other was Matty. They stopped at the fence, looking around.

"Emma!" Senator Herndon called. "Are you here?"

Emma emerged from the mouth of the stairwell, empty-handed. She spotted them and ran over to the fence, curling her fingers through the chain-link exactly as I had done a few days ago.

"Well? Where is it?" the senator asked.

"Did you do it, Dad?" Emma's voice was shaking. "What Tyler said you did?"

The senator hissed out a sharp breath. "Damn," he said. He took hold of the fence with a fierce grip, and his words cut through the quiet like knives. "Where is my box?"

Emma broke down in tears.

"Where?" her father insisted.

Emma had to choke out her answer. "He didn't have it."

The senator's face grew stony. "What do you mean?"

"He left it with a friend." Emma lifted a tear-stained face to look her father in the eye. "And I guess it was stolen."

"Where is he now?"

Emma twisted her fingers in her hair, then pointed back toward the house. "He . . . fell." She started to cry. "It was an accident! But I think he's . . ."

The senator swore viciously, and then collected himself. "Matty, I'll need you to go down there and check it out."

Emma helped the men through the fence, and she took out her phone.

"What are you doing?" the senator asked her.

"Calling 911."

He plucked the phone from her hand. "Wait," he said. "Let me get the lay of the land." The senator swung into action. "Emma, you talked to this kid on the phone, right? You called to set up this meeting?"

"Yes."

"If this seems suspicious, they'll come looking for you."

"It was an accident," Emma whispered.

"There's no such thing as an accident. There's only a story." Senator Herndon paused to think for a minute. "We can fix this. Matty, go down there and get the kid's jacket or something. And his cell phone."

Matty hesitated, rubbing his hands on the legs of his pants.

"We're family, Matty," the senator said. "That means all of us. We take care of our own."

Matty jerked his head in a nod. He took off his suit jacket and hung it carefully on the open cellar door before descending the steps. He emerged soon after, Tyler's letter jacket and baseball cap bundled in his arms. But he didn't have the Lincoln box. Emma must have left it hidden somewhere in the darkness, down where Tyler was.

The senator took out his wallet. "Okay, look. Walk over to the McDonald's on New York Avenue. They've been trying to crack down on drug activity there for years; we might as well get some use out of it." He pulled a wad of cash from his wallet and held it out to the young man.

"What are you doing?" Emma asked, her eyes glassy, as Matty took the money. "Matty, don't take that. What's going on?"

Senator Herndon crouched down beside her and smoothed her

hair away from her face. "I have my insulin kit in the car," he said. "Matty is going to get us everything else we need. We're going to make this look like an accident."

"It *was* an accident," Emma cried. "Please, Daddy, please let me call an ambulance."

"We will. When we're ready for it." Senator Herndon reached down and grabbed the cellar door, closing it with a slam that made me flinch.

And with that sound, I was back in Dr. Brightman's office, staring at the box beneath my fingers. I snatched my hand away and cradled it to my chest, looking up into Dr. Brightman's stunned face.

I sat back on the couch, my mind spinning. My hands buzzed and my head ached, but I could barely feel the pain with all the adrenaline singing through my system. I put the gloves back on and clawed at the lid of the box, trying to find the secret compartment Tyler had mentioned. I opened and closed it, pried at its corners. Nothing.

"May I?" Dr. Brightman asked, pulling on his own gloves.

I handed it to him, and he turned it over in his hands.

"There's often a key mechanism in these old boxes— Ah." With a gentle twist, one of the metal feet came off in his fingers, revealing a long brass pin. Dr. Brightman examined the lid, finally locating a tiny hole in the diamond that surrounded Lincoln's head. He inserted the pin, and a false bottom on the lid popped open.

With trembling fingers, I reached into the opening and removed three folded, tissue-thin sheets of paper, which I laid flat on the coffee table.

I struggled to understand what I was seeing. The first page looked like a receipt from a bank transfer, dated November 1997, from James Herndon to a man named Thomas Marshall. The amount stunned me; it was nearly ten million dollars. The next page was a report on Marshall, who had apparently been an FBI scientist. The final page was a signed statement from Marshall himself. I read it quickly, then read it again, then pushed the papers aside in shock.

Dr. Brightman picked them up and quickly scanned through them. "Your brother was right. Senator Herndon *was* sitting on a valuable stolen artifact. One of the most valuable in American history."

"So this James Herndon—"

"Senator Herndon's father."

"Paid off someone at the FBI to switch John Wilkes Booth's derringer with a fake one?"

"It's brilliant, really. He never could have taken the derringer from the museum. Much easier to orchestrate a rumor that it had been stolen, so that the *park service* would remove it from the museum." He laughed softly. "You were right. The gun did look different, after all."

"So why keep all this evidence? Why would he make the guy who stole it sign a statement confessing that he did it?"

"Leverage, I suppose." Dr. Brightman said. "So he could be sure this Thomas Marshall wouldn't betray him or turn him in." He flipped through the pages again. "And of course, it also gives him provenance. An artifact like this is completely worthless without a paper trail that shows who owned it and how you got it."

"Is he still alive? James Herndon?"

"No," said Dr. Brightman. "But his son obviously is." He took the papers and brought them over to his desk. Then he pulled out his cell phone and dialed. "Gary? It's David Brightman. I've come across something that belongs to you."

I sat forward in surprise.

Dr. Brightman continued. "Well, let's just say that I am smoking a cigar right now in the company of the sixteenth president of the United States."

By this time I was standing, stunned and unwilling to believe my own ears.

"I'm sure we can work something out. I don't want to take the derringer from you. I only want to see it. Examine it, as a scholar." He paused. "What can I say? It's been a lifelong dream. And I'm sure you'll agree—it's not too much to ask in return for my silence. Shall we meet tonight?" He paused again, then laughed harshly. "No, I don't think I'll be meeting you in private. I'll be at the Ford's gala, and so will you. A rather poetic place for this exchange, isn't it? I'll meet you in the theater after the performance." He hung up and put his phone back in his pocket.

I sputtered in disbelief. "How . . . What are you doing?"

Dr. Brightman folded the papers, his hands shaking so badly that the pages made a fluttering sound, and he tucked them into the breast pocket of his jacket. He walked around the desk and toward the door. "It's time for you to leave. As you said when you arrived, this marks the end of our association." He opened the door.

"You can't take those papers."

"Why not? It's clear they don't belong to you."

"But what am I supposed to do? What about my brother?"

One bead of sweat dripped down his face, and he wiped it away impatiently. "You have my condolences."

"You can't do this."

Without responding, he pulled his phone out of his pocket and dialed. "Yes, hello. This is Dr. David Brightman. I want to report a trespasser in my office." He listened briefly. "This person came in for an appointment, but she began behaving erratically and is refusing to leave." He leaned back against the wall as he gave his address, right beside the spot where his keys had once hung, but he didn't appear to notice they were missing. "Thank you very much." He hung up, his expression fierce. "Go now, before the patrol car arrives."

I stood frozen for a few seconds, unable to do anything but stare at him. Then I lunged toward him, with some half-formed thought that I could physically wrestle the papers from his jacket.

Dr. Brightman reached into his pants pocket, pulled something out, and tossed it to me.

It was the deck of tarot cards he had bought last week—the sniper's cards. Even as I realized what I was holding, the light from the open doorway became blinding. The shadow of a man with a rifle emerged, a dark blur against the brightness, moving rapidly toward me. I stumbled backward and tripped over the coffee table, the deck of cards falling from my hands and scattering across the floor as I landed, a bolt of pain lancing through my hip and shoulder.

He'd used them as a weapon against me.

I looked up at Dr. Brightman, my right side throbbing, trying to see through the headache that gathered like a storm behind my eyes. "Please," I managed. "This is my only chance to help my brother."

"I'm sorry," he said, his voice barely above a whisper. "But this is my only chance to help myself."

"Touching the derringer might kill your visions, but it might just kill *you* too."

The muscles in his jaw clenched. "At this point, I'll take one or the other."

Now I could hear sirens in the distance. Pedestrians on the sidewalk looked curiously through the open door as they passed. I lurched to my feet and shoved everything on the table into my backpack. Then I stared at Dr. Brightman with as much defiance as I could muster.

I was careful not to touch him as I walked out the door.

CHAPTER 17

I STAGGERED DOWN THE STREET TOWARD WHERE Eric had parked, but before I had gone more than a few steps, it became clear that something was terribly wrong. The world around me was tinged with gallstone yellow, as though I wore amber-tinted sunglasses. I rubbed at my eyes, but I couldn't clear them, and soon I was squinting hard against both the light and the color. When I reached Eric's car, I could barely make out his hazy form sitting behind the wheel.

I opened the passenger door, and the sun overhead grew blinding, so bright that I had to cover my face with the back of my hand. Silhouetted against the burst of light, I saw a healthy, robust version of Eric's dad holding the car door while two little kids climbed inside. They laughed and pushed each other, and he pretended to kick their behinds to get them in the car. I thought, perhaps, that one of them was me.

I crumpled to the curb and sat there for a moment, breathing heavily.

Eric came rushing around to my side of the car. "Are you okay?"

I shook my head. "I don't think so."

"God, Megan, you're bleeding again!"

He dug through the glove compartment for tissues as I wiped vaguely at my nose with my fingers. The blood wasn't red; it was a deep burnt sienna. I stared at it, dazed, until Eric waved the tissues in my face. I took them gingerly, afraid of what would happen when I touched them. But nothing did.

Eric helped me into the passenger seat. "What's going on?"

"I think it's happening to me. What happened to Dr. Brightman."

He squatted down next to me. "What do you mean?"

"I'm getting too sensitive. Losing control of what I see."

"And he let you walk out of his office like this?"

Tears buzzed behind my eyes. "Oh, Eric," I choked out, "I have something to tell you."

Eric didn't say a word as I described what had happened in Dr. Brightman's office: what I had seen, what Dr. Brightman had done. But his body language spoke volumes. He reared back in shock. He stood and paced the sidewalk beside the car. And finally he shoved both hands into his hair and slumped down onto the curb.

"Oh my god. I can't even . . ." He sat up straight. "Wait, are you okay? I mean, do you need to lie back? Can I . . . do anything?"

I shook my head, sending a jolt of pain down my neck.

"But . . . hold on." Eric shook his head, his face a picture of confusion and anger. "You mean Brightman's going to hand over all the evidence? Tonight?"

I managed a small nod.

He threw up both hands. "You have to stop him!"

"Can't," I gritted out.

"Of course you can!"

"You don't understand." My throat felt tight and painful, and my whole body tensed. "I only wanted to find out what happened to him. Tyler. To put the pieces back together." I leaned my head back against the car seat, tears leaking from the corners of my eyes. "And I've done that. I know what happened. And now I'm . . . broken. Maybe forever." I held both hands up in front of me, turning them front and back. "What if I can't even have a normal life now? What's going to happen to me?"

Eric squatted down beside me again. He rested a hand on my knee. "You're right," he said. "This sucks. And you might not want to hear this right now, but I'm the only one here, so I have to say it." He paused. "This is your hero moment."

"Oh my god!" I cried. "No more. Let that go."

"I'm just saying . . ."

"You don't even like superheroes!"

"I like *you*," he said. "And this is the moment when you rally. When you dig deep and overcome."

My chin sagged to my chest. "But why? To achieve what?"

"There's this other little thing I came across in my superhero research. It's called *revenge*. You go all *Kill Bill* on Dr. Brightman's ass!"

"What am I supposed to do, *authenticate* him to death?" I demanded. "Even if I got the papers back, what would I do?"

"Hand them over to the police! Say that you found them in Tyler's things. Tell them the senator knew that he had them, and he would have done anything—including kill someone—to get them back."

I thought about that for a moment. "Except he didn't kill someone to get them back."

"What do you mean?"

"Senator Herndon didn't hurt my brother to get those papers back. He did it to protect Emma. And his own father, in a way. To protect his family."

Eric scoffed at this. "To protect *himself*."

"No, wait." I held up a hand. "Listen. Maybe the way to get to Herndon is through his family. I can go talk to Mrs. Herndon—get her on my side." I stopped and looked at Eric. "Even if I can't prove he killed Tyler, maybe I can prove he's been hiding the real derringer. Make sure he faces some kind of justice for what he did." A thought occurred to me, and I smiled a self-satisfied smile. "You know what? Tyler wanted to take Herndon down—play Booth to his Lincoln. Well, maybe I can do that. And I'll take him down with Booth's own gun."

"Okay, that's dark hero stuff, but we can work with it."

"So I have to talk to Mrs. Herndon tonight. Before the senator gets those papers back."

"There's one small problem with that plan," Eric said. "You suck at talking to people."

A sarcastic comment rose immediately to mind, but I swallowed it. He was right. I rubbed my face hard with both hands, then reached up and slapped the ceiling of the car in frustration.

Just like that, the vision was back, slamming into place around me like the blade of a paper cutter. Eric's dad was in the driver's seat, and he was singing classic rock. Off-key. I yanked my hands back to my chest, dizzy and breathless, and he disappeared. I could see Eric's face again, the fear in his eyes. Then darkness closed in around me, telescoping my field of vision down to a tiny, bright point. I fumbled desperately for Eric's hand.

"This might be the moment when I rally," I said, "but it's also the moment when I pass out."

And the world went black.

Through the darkness, I could hear voices. Boys' voices. Arguing.

"We have to take her to the hospital."

"And tell them what?"

"How about 'She's passing out and bleeding all over the place'?"

"If we take her there, she's stuck. For hours. Maybe days. Let's make sure that's what she wants."

I struggled to open my eyes, to lift my head, but it was like moving through water. My eyes felt superglued shut, my mouth full of foam. I made a sound low in my throat.

"She's awake!"

I felt the rush of air as they came close. Then a hand gently touched my hair. I cracked one eye open, flinching at the light.

"Quick, turn off the overhead."

Finally two blurry faces came into view: Eric and Nathan. I glanced around. Even that tiny shift of my eyeballs hurt. I was on the big couch in Nathan's family room. Nathan continued to stroke the top of my head. His vibrant colors were back—his shirt was a deep dioxazine purple, and the embroidered cat on the breast pocket was drinking a martini. With a smile, I instinctively reached up to touch it, but before I made contact, I remembered what might happen. I curled my fingers into a fist. Would I never be able to touch him again?

"Glad you're back." Nathan smiled. "We were worried about you for a minute there."

I forced myself to speak. "I found out what happened to Tyler."

Nathan's eyes widened. He looked up at Eric.

"We hadn't gotten to that part," Eric said.

Nathan turned his attention back to me, and his fingers stilled in my hair. "Okay, what happened to Tyler?"

"Drug overdose."

"But . . . you knew that."

"Not self-inflicted."

Nathan was stunned into silence.

As Eric filled Nathan in on all the details, I shifted on the couch, struggling to sit up without touching it with my bare hands.

"Gloves," I said, remembering. "I think there's a pair of gloves from Dr. Brightman's office in my backpack."

Eric found them for me. I slipped them on, their black silk sliding across my palms, and sat up straight.

"First things first," Nathan said. "Let's get you to the hospital."

"The gala starts in a few hours," Eric protested, "and when it's over, there won't be any evidence to back up her story. Thanks to Dr. Brightman." His face twisted with concern. "And Megan, are you sure the hospital can help you?"

"No," I admitted. "That's why Dr. Brightman wants the gun so badly. He thinks touching it is the only thing that can help him turn off the visions for good. Burn them out of his brain or something."

"Like going blind if you stare at the sun," Eric mused.

A realization swept over me. "He said the derringer was personal. That it changed his life. Well, it sure as hell changed *mine*. Maybe it can help me too." I didn't mention the other half of Dr. Brightman's theory: that he might not survive the intensity of the memories the derringer held. That the cure might be worse than the disease.

Eric's face lit up. "Two birds with one stone, then. We help you, we stop him."

We both turned to look at Nathan, whose face was serious. "If you really think this is what you need," he said at last, "I'm in."

"Yes!" Eric said. He jumped up, asked to borrow Nathan's phone, and started typing away madly.

Nathan rolled his eyes. "Updating your mom, are you?"

"Why, yes." Eric's smile was surprisingly sly. "Actually, I am. And if you'll excuse me, I need to make a call." He took the phone and left the room.

"That was weird," I said.

When Nathan and I were alone, I felt the temperature in the room ratchet up a few degrees. I couldn't figure out where to look or what to do with my hands.

He sat beside me on the couch, so close I wanted to move away, and yet somehow not close enough. "I'm sorry about the other night."

"*You're* sorry?"

"No, I mean, getting drunk was really stupid. And showing up at your door like that, without even being invited?" He winced. "Awful. And as for the rest of what happened that night—"

"No, don't apologize for that." I squeezed his hand. "What happened with the cops? And with your parents?"

"I think it's going to blow over," he said. "The cops have no evidence against me. I was just the perfect candidate, in their minds. The ideal middleman." He shook his head. "Mom and Dad . . . they're freaked out, obviously. But they stuck up for me." He smiled.

Relief, almost palpable relief, glowed from him. "I told them the truth, about the parties. They were confused at first. But they weren't disappointed. I even showed them the videos. I hadn't done that before. Thought it would . . . I don't know . . . hurt them somehow, to know I was in touch with Cedric. But it's good. It's all good." He glanced at his watch. "We don't have long to get to the theater," he said. "What do we need to do?"

My stomach flipped. "We don't have tickets."

"Can't we crash?"

"Um, no. The president goes to these things."

"Well, I think you might know someone who works there," Nathan said.

Mom . . . right. Not a call I wanted to make, but I took out my phone.

My mother answered, sounding breathless and overwhelmed. "Hey. Is everything okay?"

"Can I still come tonight? To the gala, I mean. I'd really like to come."

I heard her blow out a sharp breath. "I begged you for weeks to come to this event. I wheedled. I bribed. And *now* you want to come? When you're *grounded* and I'm up to my ears in silent auction items? I'm sorry. The answer is no." I heard someone talking to her on the other end of the phone. "Just a minute," she told them. "Listen, I've got to go."

"Sure, Mom," I mumbled, and she ended the call.

Nathan looked at me expectantly. "Well?"

I shook my head.

He jumped to his feet and began pacing. "Okay, we can still do this," he said. "What if we stop the senator *before* he goes into the theater? We can figure out what kind of car he drives—"

Nathan broke off when Eric came strutting back into the room, bouncing his head to music only he could hear. We watched him groove for a moment.

Finally Nathan spoke. "You planning to share the beat?"

"I'm gearing up for the big party tonight," Eric said. "Practicing some moves."

"A, it's not that kind of party," I said. "And B, we're not going. We don't have tickets."

Eric did a spin with a little flourish at the end. "Yes, we do."

I took several steps toward him. "Are you serious?"

"I am serious, and I am cised!"

Nathan shook his head. "Enough with the DC slang."

"Then I am merely serious."

"How did you . . . You were gone like five minutes. Do you know how much those tickets cost?"

"I do not, but apparently the members of the McLean chapter of the Daughters of the American Revolution do, as they purchased an entire table two months ago. They have made room for us in their group."

Nathan gave Eric a look. "You're a member of the Daughters of the American Revolution?"

"No, but . . ."

". . . your mother is," I finished for him.

Eric pointed to me. "Correct!" He did a little victory robot dance, and Nathan covered his face in embarrassment.

"My mom likes me to have life experiences," I remembered Eric saying.

I got it now, after seeing what had happened to her husband. She wanted to guarantee Eric a lifetime of brilliant memories, no matter what came next.

Eric paused in his dance. "Speaking of the shindig, what exactly should I wear?"

"It's black tie."

"Perfect! I have exactly the thing." Eric tossed the phone back to Nathan and headed for the door. "Give me five minutes to run home for my tuxedo." He left, and Nathan and I were alone.

I thought for a moment. "I actually *don't* have anything to wear."

"Aha," Nathan said. "Then perhaps Nai Nai Lee can be your fairy godmother for the evening."

Nathan's grandmother sat on her bed, hands folded in her lap, watching silently as Nathan's mother pulled plastic garment bags out of her closet. Mrs. Lee handed the bags to me, and I hung them from the bedroom door. She opened the bags one by one, revealing a gorgeous palette of fabrics: silky manganese blues and naphthol reds, textured viridian and gamboge.

Despite the rich variety of colors, my eye was drawn immediately to a white dress with a black lace overlay. The fitted bodice was sleeveless, with a neckline that cut straight across from one shoulder to the other, and the back dipped down in a deep V. It looked like a gorgeous postcard from another time. Nathan's grandmother gestured to her daughter-in-law to bring it over. She reached out a hand and touched the fabric, speaking to Mrs. Lee in rapid Chinese.

"She says she made this dress in 1965," Nathan's mother explained with a smile. "She wore it to the first party she ever attended at the office where her husband worked as a translator."

The older woman touched the dress reverently, lost in the light of other days. Mrs. Lee asked her a question, and she responded with a nod.

Mrs. Lee turned to me. "I asked her if you might wear this tonight, and she said yes." Nathan's mother took the dress off its hanger and held it out to me.

"Are you sure?" I asked.

"Try it on," Mrs. Lee insisted.

Nathan came into the room. Over his purple shirt, he wore a skinny tuxedo about two inches too short in the legs and arms. He held his hands out in front of him. "Is it a lost cause?"

Mrs. Lee flipped up the end of the sleeve. "Looks like it was altered for your grandfather. I can get more length out of it." She stepped back to look at him. "You're lucky the waist fits. Take it off and let me get to work." She shooed me out of the room. "You, go try that on."

I hesitated. So far, I'd seen visions only when I touched objects with my hands, but if I slipped this vintage dress over my body, touching all that skin, what would happen?

I walked down the hall to the bathroom. With the gloves still on, I removed the rest of my clothes and stepped into the dress, my eyes squeezed shut, bracing myself for the worst.

Nothing happened.

I cautiously opened my eyes and caught sight of myself in the dress. The waist hung a little loose, the bust cinched a little tight, and it wasn't as long as it probably should be. But it was perfect. I didn't have to see a vision to feel all the good memories attached to this dress.

There was a knock at the door. Nathan's mother stood in the hall with a big rustling half slip in her hands. She looked me over. "Not bad." She handed me the slip. "Try this crinoline with it." I put on the stiff, puffy underskirt, and she fussed with the fabric at my waist. "We may need to adjust those darts a bit, but you look beautiful." She slipped a straight pin into the fabric where my waist was narrowest.

I swallowed hard. "Thank you so much for this. I know how special it is."

With a smile, she stepped out of the bathroom. "It's good to see Nathan so happy."

I blushed and shut the door. I smoothed my gloved hands over the lace, hating the thought of taking the dress off, even so she could alter it. But I brought it back to the bedroom, where Mrs. Lee sat at a table by the window, ripping the hems out of Nathan's tuxedo pants.

I draped the dress across the end of the bed. When Nathan's grandmother saw it, she asked Mrs. Lee another question in Chinese, and the two had a brief conversation. The older woman picked up the dress, turned it inside out, and started pinning.

Mrs. Lee turned to me, tears in her eyes. "She wants to do the alterations for you. I haven't seen her this alert in quite a while." We watched her deft movements as she found a white spool and threaded the sewing machine. "It's amazing," Mrs. Lee said, "the memories your body holds on to. Even when your mind forgets."

She reached into the top drawer of a dresser and took out a long white box. Inside, wrapped in layers of tissue paper, was a pair of black elbow-length gloves. "I thought you might like something more formal than the ones you're wearing." She hadn't even asked why I was wearing gloves in the first place, and I wondered what Nathan had told her. "If these will work for you," she said, holding them out to me, "you're welcome to wear them tonight."

I took the gloves gratefully, but I didn't put them on yet. I waited until the alterations to the dress were complete, until I was wearing it again with the stiff crinoline and a pair of borrowed, too-tight shoes, until the look on Nathan's face as I came down the stairs made me feel like a kid on her first roller coaster, until all three of us stood in the entryway of Nathan's house, ready to leave for the theater.

When we got to Nathan's car, I peeled off the gloves I'd taken from Dr. Brightman and dropped them into my backpack. I slipped my fingers into one of the opera gloves, smoothing it up my arm and over my elbow. It was so long and graceful, the satin warm against my skin.

Then the lights began to flicker, and a bright burst like a camera flash dazzled my eyes. *No,* I thought. *Not now. Not again.* But the light carried me along like a wave, and I was helpless to resist it.

I found myself in the hallway of an office building, where a young couple argued in Chinese. The scene warped and burned around the edges, like rubber melting at the fringes of my eyesight. The woman—Nathan's grandmother?—was wearing this same dress, with the same long black gloves. Looking back and forth between her and the women inside, I quickly understood her frustration. She'd made a cocktail gown, but the other women were wearing casual skirts and tops. Judging by her body language, she felt embarrassed and wanted to leave. But her husband only smiled. He pulled his fedora down low on his forehead and tugged her into his arms, leaning close to whisper in her ear. Her anger dissolved, replaced first by a giggle and then by a glow.

The burning edges spread, until the whole image warped like melting film, distorting the figures of the man and woman. Holes opened in my vision, and beyond was only blackness. I found myself stumbling and falling, and I plummeted down into the dark, while somewhere, voices called my name.

CHAPTER 18

"MEGAN! MEGAN, CAN YOU HEAR ME?"

I forced my eyes open, my throat screaming for water. I lay in the backseat of Nathan's car. Outside the windows, everything was dark. I shot up, afraid I'd missed it all, afraid that the gala was long over, the derringer long gone. The rapid movement left me light-headed, and I crumpled down onto the seat.

"Whoa there," Nathan said. "Take it easy." He had been standing by the open car door, and now he climbed into the seat beside me, lifting my head and resting it on his lap. "We put Dr. Brightman's gloves back on you, but don't take any chances."

"What time is it?"

"It's barely seven thirty," Nathan said. "Don't worry. You didn't miss anything."

Eric spoke up from the front seat. "He started talking about the hospital again."

"Can you blame me?" Nathan snapped. "You're getting worse, aren't you?"

I struggled to sit up again, and Nathan didn't try to stop me. "Let's just get to that gun before Dr. Brightman does."

I forced myself out of the car, emerging into the sickly sodium light of an underground parking garage. I was grateful for the dim, since the dull ache behind my eyeballs seemed to have taken up permanent residence.

"Did you bring my backpack?" I asked.

Eric gestured to my vintage cocktail dress. "I don't think it goes with your outfit."

I glared at him. "I want the cigar box. Just in case."

Nathan retrieved my backpack from the trunk, and I slung it over my bare shoulders and started walking. When Nathan and Eric didn't follow, I turned to see them exchange a look that was all furrowed eyebrows and unspoken fears.

"We don't have time for this! Let's go."

We emerged from the parking garage a block away from Ford's Theatre—and directly across the street from a storefront exhibit of artifacts from the old National Museum of Crime and Punishment. A poster on the front of the building showed a car riddled with bullet holes, while lettering made to look like crime-scene tape announced *For a limited time only!* Here it was, a whole building full of blood artifacts.

I froze in my steps. Maybe I didn't need the derringer to stop my visions. Maybe this would be enough.

I stepped off the curb and into the street, headed straight for the exhibit.

"Hey!" Nathan called. "What the . . ."

I could hear car horns and angry voices, but they didn't deter me from my course.

I walked into the bright lobby of the exhibit, dizzy with fear and anticipation. Right there, by the lines of tourists waiting to buy tickets, was a car. Not the one from the photo out front, that sexy gangster sedan. This was a beat-up Volkswagen Beetle, its white paint spotted with rust. One door stood open. I moved slowly toward it. A sign above the car read *Theodore Bundy's Volkswagen: Instrument of Crime*. It was, in its way, a murder weapon, the site of possibly dozens of deaths.

How could it be real? How could it be sitting here, in this crowd of bored and distracted tourists? It looked like art, like that Kienholz assemblage *Back Seat Dodge*, where he altered an old car and put a tangle of legs and arms in the backseat, creating something ominous and sexual and terrifying. But this was real. Almost unimaginably real. And we, the multitudes, had come to gawk and stare.

Eric and Nathan caught up to me. "What's going on?" Eric asked. "I thought we didn't have time for this."

I stepped even closer to the car. Only a stanchion made of handcuffs separated us now. If I touched it, would it quiet my ceaseless thoughts? When I imagined the pain it would cause, I shook with a bone-deep fear that was almost . . . longing. Part of me yearned for it, for a pain strong enough to black out everything but itself, a pain that could wipe away everything crooked and sharp and struggling inside me. A pain that would end my grief.

But what if, as Dr. Brightman had suggested, I didn't survive the experience? If I died, what would happen to all the things that *I* had marked? Would anyone find them? Would they have the power to tell my story?

The people around me seemed to fade, and all that existed was me and the car. It hunched there, terrible and tempting. I curled my fingers at my side. Thinking. Debating.

I pulled off one of my gloves.

Nathan took my bare hand in both of his and turned me around to face him. His eyes shone. "Please," he said, "come back to us. Please don't go." He brought my hand to his lips and kissed my fingers.

I blinked at him, the spell of the car broken. "What am I doing here?"

"Scaring the ever-loving crap out of me," he said.

"Me too," I replied.

As the day sped toward its end, my fears only grew. I was losing control. Maybe even losing my mind. Certainly on the brink of losing everything. And Dr. Brightman had lived like this for years? My anger at him faded somewhat. But not my resolve.

I looked down at Nathan's hand, still holding mine, skin to skin. It caused no pain, forced no memories on me. In fact, it did exactly the opposite: it pulled me into the present, grounded me in the right now. I sent up a silent thank-you for all the things I had in my life that Dr. Brightman did not.

"Can we go now?" Nathan asked. Eric nodded vehemently.

I backed away from the car. For better or for worse, this wasn't my artifact. Mine was waiting for me a block away, at the social event of the season, along with the man who'd killed my brother.

As we moved down Tenth Street, heading toward Ford's Theatre, the air turned electric. The sun was still up, but the street shone doubly bright with photographic lights and flashes as attendees walked the red carpet of the gala. People packed the sidewalk across from the theater, angling for a glimpse of the new arrivals, and security vehicles blocked the street from car traffic. Secret Service officers canvassed the area, muttering into their white earpieces, while other security personnel checked IDs and searched our bags.

As Eric spoke to a hostess about our tickets, I spotted a familiar car parked beyond the barricade—Dr. Brightman's black sedan. I gripped Nathan's arm. But it looked like the backseat was empty. Mr. Wendell leaned against a nearby building smoking a cigarette. I had a sudden memory, one not brought on by an object. The special glasses that Dr. Brightman wore, the ones that shielded him from the visions. He'd said he kept an extra pair in his car.

I took a step toward it, but Nathan held me back.

"No way. Not again," he said.

"It's okay." I looked him in the eye. "I'm still here. Come with me."

We walked over to the barricade, and Mr. Wendell quickly spotted us.

"Hey, Cool Hair Girl!" He crossed the street and met us at the gate. "The professor is inside. I dropped him off a half hour ago."

"I don't think he'd be very happy to see me, anyway."

"You two have a fight?"

"You could say that."

"Who's this?" Mr. Wendell jerked a thumb at Nathan.

"Oh, sorry. Nathan Lee." Nathan held out a hand.

Mr. Wendell shook it, but he looked Nathan up and down suspiciously. "Like Robert E. Lee?"

"More like Bruce Lee."

Mr. Wendell hooted with laughter, then turned to me. "This your boyfriend?"

"I . . . don't . . . ," I stammered. I could feel my face heating up.

"I'm still working on that, sir," Nathan said.

My brain hit overload, and my mouth gave up completely. *He was?*

"Good man." Mr. Wendell cuffed him on the arm. Nathan staggered a bit, but he smiled.

"I came for Dr. Brightman's glasses," I said.

"His what?"

"His sunglasses? He has an extra pair in the car, and he said I could use them if I ever needed them."

Mr. Wendell studied me carefully for a moment. "What did you two fight about?"

"He stole something from me, and I want it back."

"He *stole* something from you?"

"Yes, sir," I said.

"Wait right here," Mr. Wendell walked over to the car, opened the passenger door, and leaned inside. Seconds later, he emerged with the glasses and put them in my hand. "You never saw me, okay? We never spoke." He winked at me and walked off down the block.

I added the sunglasses to the growing collection of items in my backpack, and we rejoined Eric at the ticket table.

"Megan Brown!" a voice called from the crowd.

I tried to duck behind Nathan, but my mother's coworker Maureen was making a beeline straight for us. She wrestled a large, unwieldy cardboard box with one arm and wheeled a dolly with the other.

"You here with your mom tonight?" she asked.

"Um, yeah. Just helping out."

"You're like a gift from God." She thrust the box she was carrying into Nathan's arms. "Extra programs. We're so packed in there tonight, we had to dip into the archive copies."

I looked around. Getting stuck with Maureen would be a disaster. There'd be no way I could avoid my mom, and we wouldn't be free to look for Dr. Brightman. "I don't know if I can carry stuff in this dress. . . ."

"Oh, this strong young man and I can handle it." Maureen smiled at Nathan. She pulled a set of keys out of a pocket in her evening dress and held them out to me. "Can you go back over to my office and get the seating chart for the dinner tonight? I left my clipboard sitting on my desk."

The key chain dangled from her fingers, exactly what I hadn't known I needed. With those, we could go anywhere in the building. Access any place we wanted.

"Absolutely." I snatched the keys and tugged Eric with me toward the administrative offices across the street. "See you in there, Nathan!"

Nathan gave me a wide-eyed abandoned look as he followed Maureen into the theater.

I left Eric in the entrance hall of the Center for Education and Leadership while I took the elevator to Maureen's office. I returned to find him staring up at the massive tower of Lincoln books, three stories tall, that dominated the central atrium. He shook his head. "I did not know that there was so much to say about Abraham Lincoln."

"Tell me about it."

With Maureen's keys heavy in my hand, we walked back across

the street to the theater. Before we crossed the threshold, Eric stopped me. "Are you feeling okay?"

I took stock. The pain in my head and neck wasn't diminishing, but so far, it wasn't getting worse, either. "I'm fine."

"Given the history of this place, I hope those gloves you're wearing are industrial strength."

As soon as we were inside, I dropped Maureen's clipboard on a table full of silent auction items.

Eric pointed to it, horrified. "Wait, what are you doing? Doesn't she need that?"

"Yes, but if I give her the clipboard, I also have to give her back her keys." I held them up and jingled them. "Which I'm not planning to do."

Eric whistled. "It's been nice knowing you."

I let my hand drop. "Even if I make it through tonight with my brain in one piece, I'm totally screwed, aren't I?"

"Totally and completely," he agreed.

Eric and I moved along the outskirts of the lobby, where the atmosphere sparkled with wealth and privilege. Even though sunlight still glowed through the glass doors, evening gowns and tuxedos were out in full force, and I boggled at all the false eyelashes and real furs. I craned my neck, trying to spot Mrs. Herndon, terrified I might catch sight of my mother or Dr. Brightman.

I saw Emma instead.

She parted the crowd like a boat through water, moving with the poise of someone twice her age. Her dress was strapless, black, and unadorned. She was alone. Neither of her parents was in sight, and if she had a date, he wasn't with her.

"Did you know she would be here tonight?" Eric asked.

"No, but this is even better than finding Mrs. Herndon," I said. "Emma already knows what happened. Maybe I could win her over, convince her to confess."

Eric cracked up. I stared at him until he stopped laughing. "I'm sorry, were you serious?" he asked.

"She's alone now." I tugged Eric along with me. "You keep watch for my mother."

Emma's cool facade slipped when she saw us coming, and I could tell her veneer of control was paper-thin. She abruptly changed course, heading toward the ladies' room, but we intercepted her.

"Megan, hello." One trembling hand flew up to smooth the already perfect twist in her hair. "That's an amazing dress." She took in my battered backpack, the short black gloves that were slightly too big for me. "You really do make a statement."

"I have something for you." Shifting my backpack onto one shoulder, I pulled out the Lincoln cigar box and held it out to her. "Told you I'd return it."

Emma made a sound like the air had been knocked out of her. She staggered forward, all her poise gone—she moved in fits and starts like a frightened child. "Why would you bring that here?"

I considered a moment, then handed it to her. "It's worthless now. The papers hidden in the lid were stolen, unfortunately."

Her gaze shot up to mine. "You know about them?"

"We know more than that," I said. "We know what happened to Tyler."

Emma froze. Then her face crumpled, and her chest began to heave with rapid breaths.

"We're here to find your mother. Tell her everything. We thought you might come with us."

Emma fought to get her breathing under control. "I . . . I can't."

I stepped closer to her. "I've met your mother," I said. "Like, twice. It's not like I know her. But she was willing to go out of her way to try and keep me safe. And you're her kid. I'm betting she'll fight for you."

"It doesn't matter."

"Why not? You made the anonymous 911 call, didn't you? You hid that box from your father."

She gasped. "How did you know that?"

"So you must have hoped all this would come out, one way or another. Part of you wanted to see that justice was served."

Emma shook her head. "I was fooling myself. Things always go my father's way in the end. I don't think there's anything he ever wanted that he didn't get. Except maybe a son who made the Virginia all-state football team."

"I thought you were an only child."

"Exactly. There are *generations* of Herndons counting on me not to screw up."

I felt a surge of anger. "Too late."

Eric laid a hand on my arm. His look reminded me that we were trying to convince Emma to help us out, and nasty comments might not be the best way to go about it.

Emma's spine straightened, and she forced her features into something like indifference. "You know what?" she said. "I could be someplace else right now. Like, anyplace else." She lifted her chin high and turned to walk away from us.

Another image of Lucy flashed into my mind. "I might have been at six or seven other engagements this morning," she'd said to John Wilkes Booth, on that day her life would change forever. Clara Harris's life too, and countless others. One act of violence, so many people caught in its undertow. I thought about Lucy and Clara—and Emma—all three the daughters of senators, all three trying to balance their own lives against the expectations of their families.

"Hey!" I called after Emma. "Here's something you might not know. My brother didn't die of a head injury."

Emma stopped in her tracks.

"It's going to be in all the papers tomorrow. The head injury didn't kill him. He died of a drug overdose."

"No." Emma turned around. Her face was ashen, her eyes wide. "That's not possible."

"Funny, that's exactly what I said."

Eric spoke up. "Come with us, Emma. Help us make this right."

Emma was visibly shaking now. "I *can't*."

"Please." Lucy Hale's face flickered in my mind, sitting in that candlelit restaurant, watching Booth walk away from her forever. "If you let your father make your decisions, then nothing in your whole life will belong to you. Not even your mistakes."

Emma took a few steps backward, the cigar box wobbling in her hands. Tears ran down both cheeks, marring her flawless makeup.

I reached into my backpack, pulling out Detective Johnson's card and resting it on the cigar box. I tapped Johnson's name with one finger. "This detective will hear you out. She'll be fair."

Emma studied the small white rectangle. A tear dropped onto the cigar box beside it, quickly soaking into the wood. Finally she looked back up at me. "I'm not sure I can live with what happened. But there's no way I can fix it." She disappeared into the crowd.

For a few seconds, Eric and I stared at the spot where Emma had been standing.

I could see the path stretching out before her, the long and lonely path Lucy Hale had followed: consumed by guilt, never able to escape the gravitational pull of her father, her obligations, her reputation. I'd seen it before, when I'd touched Lucy's ring. "We need to tell Mrs. Herndon about this," I said. "I'm scared for Emma."

Then Eric's face changed, and his hand closed around my arm. "Incoming. Two o'clock. It's your mom."

CHAPTER 19

MY MOTHER HADN'T SEEN US YET; SHE WAS TALKING to a woman with a blue dress and a head of puffy blond hair that, together, made her look like a dishwashing wand. "Crapdogs," I said.

At that moment, Nathan appeared beside us. "Found you. What did I miss?"

"Scatter!" Eric shielded his face and made a beeline for the men's room.

I grabbed Nathan's arm and tugged him around a corner. We squeezed into a tiny alcove, pressing our bodies up against a water fountain. I could hear my mother talking a few feet away, and I could smell the faintest hint of cologne on the crisp white front of Nathan's shirt. I closed my eyes and stepped a little closer to him, so that my nose was almost touching his chest. He swallowed hard.

"What's going—" he whispered, but I cut him off with a hand over his mouth.

Around the corner, my mother and the woman droned on, but in our little alcove, Nathan's breath warmed my gloved fingertips. He caught hold of my wrist, brought it to his mouth, and kissed the bare skin right below the glove.

My mouth went dry, and my breath hitched in my throat.

"Is that your boyfriend?"

"I'm still working on that."

"Oh, hi!" Mom's voice cut through my scattered thoughts. "Thanks for getting those programs, Maureen."

Nathan dropped my hand. Judging by the look on his face, he'd figured out why we were hiding here.

Mom laughed. "I'm impressed you could carry all those boxes."

"I was lucky Megan and her boyfriend were there to help."

Double crapdogs, I thought.

"You saw Megan?" And then, in a slightly higher-pitched voice: "And her *boyfriend*?" I couldn't see her face, but I knew that tone intimately.

"Yes, he was right over— Huh. I don't know where he disappeared to. But Megan has my keys, so I'm sure she's looking for me."

"If you see either of them again tonight, please let me know *immediately*."

"Oh, you haven't met the boyfriend yet," Maureen replied, a smile in her voice. "Don't worry, he's completely adorable."

Nathan sent me a cocky smile.

"Seriously," Maureen continued, "if I were thirty years younger, I would be all over that." A look of horror crossed Nathan's face, and I stifled my laugh in the buttons of his shirt.

Their voices faded away, and we poked our heads around the corner.

I let out a long breath. "She's going to kill me. I'm so totally and completely dead right now. I am the walking dead."

"You're a zombie," Nathan agreed. "So you better make tonight count."

I took a moment to admire him in his tuxedo. The arms and legs were still a tiny bit too short, and beneath the jacket, he had on an ordinary white dress shirt. But his personality shone through, pulling everything together and making it look like a fashion statement. The adrenaline that had been coursing through me since I'd first spotted my mother was draining away, and I could feel the pain returning behind my eyeballs, the tight fist of tension gripping the base of my skull. Like Nathan had said, I needed to make tonight count. Because who knew what would happen next?

Eric joined us again. "All clear?"

I stood on tiptoe to look around. "Mom's gone. But I haven't seen Mrs. Herndon anywhere."

"Should we look inside the theater?" Nathan asked.

I glanced over at the ushers and shook my head. "I don't want to get stuck in a seat for the whole show. What if she leaves before we can get back to the lobby?"

Suddenly Eric turned his back on the crowd, blocking me from sight. "Dr. Brightman. At the far doors."

I peeked around Eric's shoulder and spotted him, immaculate in a mandarin-collar tuxedo, his sunglasses firmly in place. His face seemed composed, his body language ordinary, despite the fact that he was hours away from having the derringer in his hands. He handed his ticket to the woman at the door and entered the theater.

As the lobby started to empty, I realized how conspicuous the three of us would be, standing out here all by ourselves. "We can't hang around in the lobby during the show."

"Know a good place to hide?" Nathan asked.

I thought for a moment, jingling Maureen's keys in my hand. "Let's try the family circle."

We used Maureen's key fob to take a back elevator up to the second balcony level. Once upon a time, the family circle had been the theater's cheap seats, but now it was mainly used for lighting and sound equipment—and tonight, an elaborate television setup, as well. We perched on wooden benches at the top of the balcony and watched the TV people scuttle about, taking care of last-minute details as the rest of the audience found their seats far below. Behind a set of glass windows, the stage manager and her crew sat in the control booth, prepping for the performance. A charge of excitement ran through the room when the president and first lady arrived, and the audience stood as the orchestra played "Hail to the Chief." Then the lights dimmed and the show began.

A shiver ran through me in the dark, and Nathan leaned toward me. "You okay?"

I took a deep breath, trying to calm the creeping dread in my stomach. "We're running out of time. And this plan is never going to work."

"When the performance is over, we'll find Mrs. Herndon."

"What if we can't?"

"Then we'll find your mother," Nathan said, "and *she'll* find Mrs. Herndon. We'll tell them everything we know. We'll ask for their help. If worse comes to worst, I'll tackle Senator Herndon and you can grab the gun."

"Well, nothing could possibly go wrong with *that* plan."

He bumped my shoulder with his own. "Nothing will go wrong."

His face grew serious. "We're doing this for Red. I think, somehow, he'll be watching out for us."

"I thought I knew him," I said. "Tyler. I saw him every day of my life for fifteen years. I knew what he ate for breakfast every morning, what kind of jokes made him laugh." I leaned my head on Nathan's shoulder, my gloved fingers creeping up to find his hand and hold it tight. "But it turns out he was someone I only thought I knew."

He rubbed his thumb across the back of my hand. "You might not have known everything about him, but you knew him. And you loved him. That's important too."

I shifted on the bench, too nervous to pay attention to the performance, even if it had been the slightest bit interesting. I scoured the backs of people's heads below, hoping I could spot Mrs. Herndon, but when that failed, I pulled out my phone.

Eric gave me a scolding look. "No cell phones."

"Are you seriously lecturing me on theater etiquette right now?" I whispered.

"Do you want someone to see the light and come looking for us?"

"Point taken." A door off the second balcony led to the theater's boardroom, and I used Maureen's key to unlock it. A long wooden conference table dominated the space, and an oil painting of Lincoln hung on one wall. He was seated, his head resting on one hand.

"Lincoln, Lincoln everywhere," I muttered, studying the portrait.

Huge windows overlooked the street, and the lights outside were the room's only illumination. Music filtered through the doors to the balcony: a woman's voice, high and pure. Phone in hand, I pushed aside a heavy gold curtain to sit on a windowsill and stare down at the street below.

I started typing a message to Elena. But after a few seconds, I changed my mind and dialed her number. I needed to hear her voice.

"You're calling me on the phone?" she said by way of greeting. "Is this the apocalypse? Look around. Do you see horsemen?"

"I love you. You know that, right?"

There was a moment of dead air before she spoke again. "Oh my god. Where are you? What happened?"

Tears filled my eyes. I'd kept everything from her. The visions, Dr. Brightman, everything. She'd been like a refuge, the one good place in my life that none of this could touch. But what if something truly awful happened to me tonight? I couldn't even say good-bye.

"Okay," Elena said, when I didn't answer right away, "enough bullshit. This calls for video chat." She ended the call, and seconds later, her face appeared on my phone.

She looked so different from the last time we'd done this. Her hair had grown out enough that it almost touched her shoulders, and she'd cut it in a messy shag. Her eyebrows had been plucked thin and penciled into place, and her lipstick was an aggressive red. Her devious grin, however, was the same as ever.

"You look amazing," I told her.

"I take it you have *not* been following me online." She fluffed her hair.

"Social media? Not since Tyler died." I shuddered. "Sympathy overload."

Elena craned her neck. "And what are *you* wearing? Tilt down! I want to see!"

I showed her the dress. "I'm on a date, actually. With New Boy."

"No way! Where did he take you?"

"To the theater."

"Very nice," she said approvingly. "So how's the show?"

"Um, it's pretty scary, actually." I held my eyes wide, trying to keep the tears in. "I'm kind of freaking out about what's going to happen next."

"Wait a minute. Are you crying?"

"Maybe a little."

"Oh, honey, it's just a play."

Tell that to Abraham Lincoln, I thought, and I choked out a laugh that turned into a sob.

"Okay, spill," Elena said. "Is this about Tyler? Tell me what's really going on."

I studied Elena's face, which was every bit as strong and gorgeous as I remembered. "Can I ask you a personal question?"

"You're my best friend. I damn well hope so."

"How did you do it?" Realizing that probably wasn't enough information, I kept going. "I mean, with everything that happened before you left, how did you end up still being you?"

Elena squinched up her face, considering me. "Why are you asking me this?"

"Because I'm scared," I confessed. "All the time. Even though I shouldn't be, because nothing really happened to me, it happened to you. But I am. I'm so, so scared." I was openly crying now. "How do I turn it off?"

She paused a moment. "You can't turn it off. You just have to find the things that make dealing with the fear worth it."

I took a deep breath and wiped the tears off my cheeks. "Okay."

"Man, I wish I was there with you. I really do."

"I'm fine. I just needed to hear your voice. And see your face." I heard applause from beyond the theater wall. "I'd better get back."

"I want to see you again soon, okay? And Megan . . . one more thing?"

"Yeah?"

"You tell New Boy if he breaks your heart, I'll break his face."

I laughed.

After the final curtain call, Eric and Nathan and I split up. Eric went to look for Mrs. Herndon, while Nathan took the lobby, to make sure that the senator and Dr. Brightman didn't leave through there. I stayed in the back of the balcony as the cameramen powered off their machines and coiled up their cables. When the light went off in the stage manager's booth, I went down to the balcony railing and stayed there, half hidden behind a lighting instrument that clicked and popped as it cooled. If I was lucky, Mrs. Herndon would walk in any second now. Otherwise, I'd have to come up with some way to keep the senator and Dr. Brightman here until she did.

As the final patrons filtered out of the theater, Dr. Brightman made his way to the front, glasses and gloves in place, straightening his tuxedo sleeves. He stood near the stage and waited, tucking his hands into his pockets. Around him, ushers cleaned up programs and the house manager urged people out into the lobby.

Senator Herndon entered through the rear doors, with Matty trailing at his heels like a cocker spaniel. Matty handed the senator a wooden box, similar in size to the Lincoln box. The senator continued down the aisle while Matty stopped the house manager and spoke to him briefly, passing him a long white envelope. The house manager nodded and gestured the ushers out of the theater, closing the doors behind them. Matty stayed, standing behind the last row of seats.

I ducked down a little lower behind the balcony rail, consumed with a sick curiosity to hear what they would say to each other.

The senator walked up to Dr. Brightman and clapped him on the shoulder. "David. It's been too long. I don't think I've seen you since the accident. Genevieve and I were so sorry for your loss."

Dr. Brightman froze. He stared stiffly at Senator Herndon but didn't speak, and I had the sudden thought that he might be in over his head. Mrs. Herndon had told me they'd been friends with Dr. Brightman, once upon a time, and I wondered if the two men had sat in the Herndon study, smoking cigars and bonding over obscure Lincoln manuscripts.

Herndon checked his watch. "Well, David, the house manager won't be able to give us more than a few minutes in here, and he didn't come cheap. So we should get a move on."

Dr. Brightman finally spoke. "Yes. Let's get this over with." He reached into his pocket and took out the folded papers we'd found in the lid of the cigar box. He held them up between his thumb and forefinger. "Fascinating story. A prominent lawyer, the father of a U.S. senator, involved in a plot to steal a major national artifact. Did your father want the derringer that badly?"

Herndon shrugged slightly. "It's the most sacred Lincoln artifact in the world. And my father was Lincoln's most faithful disciple. If anyone deserved to own that gun, I suppose it was him." He reached for the papers.

Dr. Brightman tucked them back into his pocket. "As soon as

you show me the contents of that box."

The senator's calm demeanor slipped just the tiniest bit. "Let me remind you that we're in this together now. Once I show you this gun, you will be an accessory to theft." He stopped to let that sink in. "And if you ever reveal my family's secrets, you and I will keep each other company on the way down."

Dr. Brightman nodded once.

Herndon undid the clasp and swung the box open. The interior was lined in maroon velvet. From my perch in the balcony, I caught a glimpse of the gun inside, so tiny and yet so deadly.

"An original case," Dr. Brightman said. "What a lovely touch."

"Do you need to take a closer look?"

"I believe I will." He pushed his sunglasses up on top of his head. "Do you mind if I remove my gloves?"

"Do I have a choice?" Senator Herndon asked.

Dr. Brightman slid off his right glove, dropping it to the floor.

I was running out of time. There was still no sign of Eric or Mrs. Herndon, and in a matter of seconds, this entire exchange would be over. Senator Herndon would disappear, and with him, all the evidence of his crimes. I leaned forward, not sure exactly what to do.

Dr. Brightman took off the other glove and dropped it carelessly beside the first. I covered my face with one hand, peeking through my fingers. I wasn't sure what would happen to him when he touched the derringer, but if it was bad, I was pretty sure the senator wouldn't be sticking around to help out.

His fingers stretched toward the gun, and before he could touch it, I stood and called out, "Dr. Brightman!"

Both men jerked their heads toward the balcony. The senator

snapped the box shut. Even from where I stood, I could see the glint of confusion in Dr. Brightman's eyes.

"Megan, what are you doing here?"

"Friend of yours?" the senator asked him.

"I'm Megan Brown," I called out. And then, before I could stop myself: "I know what you did to my brother."

CHAPTER 20

THE AIR CRACKLED, AS THOUGH A BOLT OF LIGHTning had shot through the room. I could almost smell the tang of ozone. "Matty," the senator said, "perhaps Miss Brown would like to join us."

After a moment's hesitation, Matty trotted up the aisle of the theater, heading my way.

For a split second, I considered running away. But I needed to keep them talking until Mrs. Herndon arrived. And even if all else failed, if I couldn't reveal what the senator had done and get justice for my brother, I still wanted to touch that gun.

So when Matty appeared at the top of the second balcony, I didn't argue. I didn't even look him in the face. I simply followed him down the stairs.

As we pushed through the door into the lobby, I lost my balance in the unfamiliar high heels. I caught myself, resting one gloved hand on the outside wall of the theater.

A shock of blinding light fell around me like a glowing curtain, but the pain it brought was secondary to the inferno of noise that accompanied it. People were screaming—hundreds of people.

Groans and curses surrounded me, and I flattened myself against the wall to avoid the panicked, thronging crowd.

"Hang him!" someone was yelling.

"Shoot him!" screamed another. "Lynch him!"

Beside me, a small door marked *Box Office* flew open, and I could see four men inside. Their backs were to me as they peered through a window into the chaos that was the theater itself.

"My god, then, is John Booth crazy?" one of the men asked, turning so I could see his massive mutton-chop sideburns and sparse mustache. Two others pushed past him and ran out into the lobby. I could almost feel the air move as they rushed by me, leaving Mutton Chop behind with an older, distinguished-looking gentleman. The two shared a look. Then they started snatching money out of the box office drawers and shoving it into a cash box—and into their pockets.

The mood of the crowd in the lobby grew darker and more frightening. "Burn the place down!" one man shouted, his face twisted into a mask of fury. The men around him picked up the chant. "Burn it down! Burn it down!"

I pulled away from the wall, but nothing changed. I wasn't touching anything, but I still couldn't escape the vision. As the noise of the desperate crowd grew louder and louder, the sound seemed to take on color and shape. Bright brushstrokes streaked across my field of vision, covering the world in gold ocher and permanent green. I crouched low to the ground, screwing my eyes shut and covering my head with both arms until finally, blessedly, the darkness consumed me.

And then Nathan was there, cradling my head and shoulders and looking searchingly into my eyes. He'd been waiting in the lobby, watching for Brightman and Herndon, and he must have seen me collapse.

"How long was I out?" I whispered.

"Only a few seconds."

"That's good." I looked up, glassy-eyed, to see Matty standing above us, more than a little freaked out.

"What's wrong with her?" he asked.

"She's got . . . a condition," Nathan said. "She needs a minute."

Matty glanced instinctively toward the doors to the theater. For the first time, I could see the beads of sweat on his forehead, the knot of tension in his jaw. "Can you . . ." He lowered his voice, his eyes overly bright. "Can you please hurry?"

Nathan helped me sit up, and I fought through a wave of nausea and disorientation.

"I'll be okay," I reassured him. "That one wasn't so bad."

"But Megan . . ." His face was grave. "You're still wearing the gloves."

I looked down at my hands. Worse than any physical pain was the sinking, inescapable fear that consumed me. The visions *were* getting worse, breaking through all the barriers I'd put in place to keep them out. Tears burned in my eyes, and I fought to keep my breathing steady. If the only way to put an end to all this was to touch the derringer, I had to do it. No matter what the risk.

"Come on," Matty said. "Let's go."

I looked into Nathan's face. What if these were the last few moments I'd ever spend with him? What if our "us," all the time we would ever have, had been this tiny window between Tyler's death and my own? I slid my hands beneath his tuxedo jacket, wrapping my arms around his warm body. He held me close, his open jacket falling like a screen around me.

"You told me nothing would go wrong," I murmured.

"Clearly I had no idea what I was talking about."

I pulled back a few inches so I could see his face. "Are you my boyfriend?"

He laughed gently. "You want to have the talk? Right now?"

"Everyone keeps calling you that tonight. And . . ." I swallowed hard. "I don't know what's going to happen to me when we go into that theater. I might not get another chance to ask."

His arms tightened around me, and pain slashed across his face. "I'm whatever you want me to be," he said.

I pulled him close and kissed him, pouring all my dreams for what we could have been into this one moment.

"Okay," Matty said, his voice strained. "That's enough."

Nathan broke the kiss and looked at me. Then he smiled. "More of that later. I promise."

Together we struggled to our feet. Nathan supported me with one arm, and we started walking toward the theater.

"Not you." Matty gestured to Nathan. "You're staying here."

Nathan shook his head. "I'm not leaving her."

Matty looked around nervously.

"Senator Herndon is in that theater with a stolen artifact," Nathan continued. "Either I come in with you, or I walk out those doors and go straight to the police."

After a moment, Matty gestured for Nathan to go ahead.

"Dr. Brightman's sunglasses," Nathan whispered in my ear. "Where are they?"

"In my backpack."

He paused to retrieve them. As Matty led us into the theater, Nathan looked them over, pushing a small button on the frame before settling them carefully on my face. Seeing the world as an image in a viewfinder was dizzying, disorienting. I felt like the main character in a video-game version of my own life. I made my way unsteadily down the theater aisle with Nathan at my shoulder.

Senator Herndon and Dr. Brightman had moved up onto the stage, where they stood beside a large wooden podium emblazoned with the Ford's Theatre logo. Matty motioned for me to join them. The senator was all stony control, impossible to read, but Dr. Brightman watched me with dread etched across his face.

"Did you bring her here?'" the senator asked. "Who else knows about this?"

"I promise you, I didn't breathe a word to anyone." Dr. Brightman turned to me. "You have my glasses."

"You did say I could use them," I choked out.

"You're getting worse, aren't you?" He breathed out a bitter laugh. "I'm sorry. It's like looking in a mirror."

Senator Herndon stared pointedly at Nathan. "Matty, you seem to have acquired some additional baggage."

"He's her boyfriend," Matty said.

Nathan gave me a sideways smile, and despite our surroundings, my heart did a flip.

"Megan, is it?" Herndon asked. "You're clearly confused. Your grief has gotten the better of you."

I ignored him and spoke to Dr. Brightman. "You would let a man get away with murder for this?" I gestured to the box in Senator Herndon's hands.

"I have no choice." Dr. Brightman's jaw clenched, and he ground out his words with great effort. "I need to be able to forget."

I lifted my chin. "Well, *I* don't want to forget."

"Just wait." His gaze met mine, eyes full of sorrow. "You will."

Senator Herndon cut us off. "If you keep throwing around words like 'murder,' you'll be looking at the wrong end of a lawsuit."

"I saw it." I clutched the straps of my backpack. "I saw everything that you did. You and Matty. And Emma."

The senator took one threatening step toward me, but Dr. Brightman stopped him.

"She's just a kid, Gary," he said. "She's not a threat to you. And we're running out of time. Let me examine the derringer, and you can deal with her when we get out of here." Dr. Brightman gestured for the senator to put the box on the podium beside them, and the senator complied.

"Open it, please," Dr. Brightman said, and he did.

Up close, I could see how cozily the derringer rested in its velvet nest. The box had a second compartment, clearly designed to hold a partner gun, but it lay empty. Arranged around the derringer was a variety of tools that looked like something you'd see at a dentist's office—in a horror film.

Dr. Brightman looked up at him in surprise. "You've got powder here. And blasting caps."

Herndon raised his eyebrows. "We fired it. Once. A poetic gesture, my father said. To mark the passing of the legacy from him to me." Dr. Brightman looked faintly aghast, and Herndon snorted out a laugh. "Come on, David. You clearly understand the power of a poetic gesture." He waved an arm at the theater around us.

Dr. Brightman ran a hand across his face, thinking hard. Then he pierced Herndon with a look. "I want to load it."

Even through the viewfinder of the glasses I wore, Dr. Brightman's face chilled me. In a flash, I understood his plan. If the derringer didn't work as he hoped, if it didn't kill his visions, he was going to use it the old-fashioned way. On himself. He was, as the senator had pointed out, a fan of the grand poetic gesture.

Senator Herndon hesitated. "This room will be swarming with theater staff again in a matter of minutes."

"I'm not talking about firing it. Just loading it." When Herndon paused, Dr. Brightman patted the papers in his pocket. "Or I can just send these to a friend of mine at the *Washington Post*."

Herndon nodded once.

I flinched as Herndon's fingers curled around the handle, afraid the derringer might have some violent effect on anyone who dared to touch it with their bare hands, but his expression didn't change.

He pulled the hammer back and used a bronze tube, about the same diameter as a ballpoint pen, to pour a few grains of black powder into the barrel of the gun. Then he dug through a side compartment of the case. "Sorry to disappoint you, David, but I don't seem to have any bullets."

"Ah," Dr. Brightman said. "But Megan might." He held out a hand to me. "Don't make me go through your bag," he said.

I'd had them in my pocket, I realized, the first time I'd visited his house. I'd showed them to him, and he knew I'd been carrying them around with me. Unsure what else to do, I dug around at the bottom of my backpack until I found one of the antique bullets Tyler had taken from Senator Herndon's study. I handed it to the senator, who looked at it suspiciously before he finished loading the gun. Maybe he recognized it as one of his own. When he was done, he returned the derringer to its case and backed away from it.

"Very good," Dr. Brightman said. He ran his bare hands down both cheeks, his eyes never leaving the gun. Then he rubbed his hands together.

With a painfully slow movement, he reached for the derringer.

My mind raced. Part of me wanted to see what would happen—to use Dr. Brightman as a test case to see if the derringer would work for me too. But once he had the gun in his hand, he was going to use it one way or the other. Could I really watch him shoot himself?

Dr. Brightman stood between me and the podium—there was no way I could get to the gun first. I could try to push the whole thing to the ground, but the gun was loaded. What if it went off and hurt someone?

Then I remembered how Dr. Brightman had knocked me flat with that deck of tarot cards and the memories they held. My mind flashed instantly to the keys in my backpack . . . the ones I'd taken from his office, on the Abraham Lincoln key chain. They were the only thing in his sterile home that had looked like an artifact from his former life, and they'd buzzed when I'd touched them. Did they hold a strong enough memory to stop him now?

And if they did, could I help him find it?

As quickly as I could, I stripped away everything I was using to protect myself. I pushed the sunglasses on top of my head. I yanked off the gloves. Then I grabbed the keys out of my bag and stepped forward. And before Dr. Brightman could touch the gun, I slipped the keys into his outstretched hand and held on tight.

The pain was different this time, heavy and compressing, pushing down on my chest so I couldn't breathe. Even the light felt weighty, like I was drowning in it. When my eyes adjusted, Ford's Theatre was completely gone. Instead, Dr. Brightman and I were sitting in the backseat of a moving car. Beside us was a car seat with a little boy in it, maybe two or three years old. He was asleep. In the front, another Dr. Brightman was driving, and an elegant woman sat in the passenger seat, her long brown hair twisted up into a knot on the back of her head. She turned toward him, laughing at something he said.

Beside me, my Dr. Brightman began to panic. *Oh, god,* I thought, *his family was killed in a car accident.* He tried to free his hand from mine, but I clamped down harder. This artifact might not have changed the course of a nation, but if it held the memories I thought it did, then maybe it could still give him what he was looking for.

Outside the car windows, the twilight faded quickly into darkness. We were on the Fourteenth Street Bridge, driving across the Potomac River, heading from DC into Virginia. The trees on the riverbank, leafless and bare, shivered in the wind, and where the moonlight hit the river, its serene surface broke into ripples.

With a violent blast of sound and movement, the driver's side of the car blew inward. Glass flew toward me, a sudden shower of crystal, and the ground under my feet fell away. The car careened to the left and ran up onto the concrete barricade, two wheels off the ground, teetering. Time froze for an instant. Then another car hit us from behind. It pushed us up and over the edge of the bridge, and we began to fall toward the river below. Fear shot through my veins, a rush of pure ice. I covered my face with my free hand and braced myself.

But nothing came. No shock of impact, no wrenching pain as my body came apart. I looked up. Dr. Brightman and I were no longer in the car. My eyesight was murky, and everything was brown and distorted. In a flash, I realized we were underwater. My chest heaved with panicked breaths. *It's not real,* I thought, forcing slow air into my lungs, trying not to hyperventilate. Beside me, Dr. Brightman had lost all emotion. His face was a blank mask, his eyes hollow.

About twenty feet away from us, I saw the car, moving slowly and inexorably toward the bottom of the river. The entire passenger side had collapsed, but on the driver's side, the other Dr. Brightman began to move. He was trying to free his family from the vehicle, his movements slow but desperate. Eventually he opened his door and swam around to the other side, where he pulled uselessly on the twisted metal, as though his mere strength could unbend, unbreak, uninjure. Gradually his movements slowed and then stopped completely. His lifeless body floated toward the surface of the water, arms and legs extended in a slow-motion farewell to the car below.

I felt Dr. Brightman's hand slip from my own. The keys clattered to the wooden floor of the stage, and I heard a thud as Dr. Brightman's body followed them. This time, I didn't lose consciousness. Instead, in a blink, Ford's Theatre rushed around me again, and I stumbled to my knees.

Nathan crouched down beside me. "Are you all right?"

I nodded.

"What in the hell just happened?" Senator Herndon said.

Dr. Brightman's face was pale and shocked. Tears ran down his cheeks. "I didn't know," he said. "I couldn't remember what happened. I never knew how I got out of the car, or why I survived when they didn't." He looked me in the eye. "I *fought* for them."

"Of course you did," I whispered.

Dr. Brightman reached gingerly for the keys. He touched them briefly, as though they might be hot. Then he picked them up, weighing them in his hand. "Nothing," he said. "I don't know how long it will last, but I see nothing."

A new voice rang out from the back of the theater. "What's going on, Gary?"

Mrs. Herndon had arrived at last. She walked down the aisle of the theater, Eric right behind her. He sent me a double thumbs-up.

As Mrs. Herndon climbed the stairs to join us on the stage, Senator Herndon snapped the derringer case shut. "Nothing at all." He looked at Dr. Brightman. "I think our business here is done." He reached out a hand to Dr. Brightman, who gave him the papers in a daze. Then Herndon tucked the case under his arm and started to leave.

Mrs. Herndon turned to me. "Tell me what's going on."

"It's my brother," I said. "No one meant to hurt him, but Emma and Senator Herndon—they were involved. And they've been trying to cover it up."

Color rushed to Mrs. Herndon's face. "That's impossible. What a disgusting thing to say."

"You have to believe me," I said. "Emma needs your help. My brother needs your help."

"This is ridiculous." The senator offered Mrs. Herndon his hand. "Let's go."

"Mrs. Herndon, please," I said. "You can think whatever you want about me. But do me one favor. Look in that box."

Doubt and anger warred in her face as she looked back and forth between me and her husband.

"I'll tell you everything, Gen," Herndon said. "But not here."

I remembered what Emma had said—that he always managed to get his way in the end.

Mrs. Herndon took her husband's hand.

I couldn't believe it. It was over.

Dr. Brightman lifted his head. "You carry an insulin kit in your car now, Gary?" He struggled to stand, and I helped him to his feet. "I've never heard you mention being diabetic. Is it a recent development?"

I froze. That was something Dr. Brightman had seen in our vision, from the night Tyler died. What was he doing?

Mrs. Herndon stopped. "How does he know that?"

And then I realized: Dr. Brightman was trying to plant a little seed of doubt in Mrs. Herndon's mind. Make her wonder whether Dr. Brightman might know something she didn't.

"They're medical records, not top-secret documents," the senator said. "Let's go."

Mrs. Herndon hesitated. The senator held the box out to Matty, signaling to him to take it away. But Nathan was faster. He body-checked Matty, grabbed the box, and handed it to Mrs. Herndon.

She flipped the clasp and opened it. "Is this . . ." She picked up the gun and turned it over in her hand. "This can't be . . ."

"I believe that is indeed the genuine artifact," Dr. Brightman said.

"But how did you . . ." Mrs. Herndon trailed off as awareness dawned in her eyes. She looked up at her husband. "How long have you had this? And you never told me? *Me?*"

The senator didn't respond.

"Gary, tell me you didn't have anything to do with the death of that boy."

Senator Herndon was silent, his jaw clenching.

Mrs. Herndon closed the box and tucked it under her arm. She gave the senator one last look, then turned to leave.

"Where are you going?" he asked.

"I'm going to find Emma. And if she's done something wrong, I'm going to encourage her to confess."

"Don't be foolish, Genevieve. You're making a terrible mistake."

Ignoring him, she walked back up the theater aisle.

"Technically," the senator said, "it was Matty who hurt that boy."

Mrs. Herndon stopped. Matty's mouth flew open, and he shuffled back a few steps. He grunted out an incoherent word.

"I think he wanted to protect me," Senator Herndon went on. "Maybe he thought it was what I wanted. But Emma didn't have anything to do with it."

"How can you . . . ," Matty sputtered. "I only did what you asked!"

"I guess that's a question for a judge to decide," he said. "At least, if Genevieve decides to go to the police. What do you think, Genevieve? Do you want to ruin this young man's life?"

Something in Matty's face snapped, and he lunged for the box in Mrs. Herndon's arms. He pulled out the derringer, letting the box and all the metal instruments inside fall to the floor with a crash. Once he had the gun in his hand, he didn't seem to know what to do with it. He spun wildly from side to side, and Nathan leaped onto the stage and pushed me behind him.

"Eric, get down!" I called. "The gun is loaded!"

Eric threw himself to the floor between two rows of theater seats, but Genevieve didn't make any move to protect herself.

"Matty, I don't think you want to hurt anyone," she said. "Hand me the gun, and this will all be over."

Matty's whole body shook, and his voice took on a hysterical edge. "It won't be over. He's right. I was the one who gave Tyler the drugs. But they weren't supposed to kill him."

Mrs. Herndon stepped toward Matty. All of a sudden, Matty's whole demeanor changed. His body went still, and his face turned deadly calm.

"I thought you said we were family," he said, his gaze moving to the senator.

Terror coursed through me, making my limbs shake and my knees weak. I wanted to hold on to Nathan for support, but my gloves lay on the stage floor, several feet away.

"How about this?" Matty said. "I walk out of here with this gun, and you make all of this disappear. You tell the cops it was your fault, and you make sure my name doesn't even get mentioned. Otherwise . . ." He pointed the gun straight at Mrs. Herndon.

"Gary, what have you done?" Mrs. Herndon said.

"You mentioned family, Matty?" Senator Herndon said, walking slowly and deliberately toward him. "Did I ever tell you about my family? We're directly descended from William Henry Herndon. He was Abraham Lincoln's law partner. One of his first biographers. And a founding member of the Republican party. We're part of the very fabric of this country's history."

Matty looked confused. His gun hand wobbled, but he didn't

lower it. Senator Herndon walked down the steps and off the stage, his eyes fixed on Matty as he descended.

"I don't necessarily agree with the way my father acquired that pistol, but I think he was right about one thing. Our family has built a legacy that stretches back generations, and we deserve to hold on to it. All of it. It's our inheritance. Our birthright. And I'm not about to let anyone take it away from us."

He was almost on top of Matty now.

"You're just a footnote, Matty," he said. "Is this really how you want to go down in history?"

Matty wavered, lowering the gun slightly.

Then a scream exploded through the tense silence in the room.

"Daddy!"

Emma Herndon stood at the back of the theater, Detective Johnson beside her. In a heartbeat, Johnson pulled her own gun and aimed it, with true badass intensity, directly at Matty.

"Drop the weapon," she said.

Bewildered and glassy-eyed, Matty swung the derringer from Senator Herndon toward Detective Johnson—and by extension, toward Emma, who froze, her eyes hollow with fear.

The senator lunged at Matty, grabbing his arm and forcing the barrel of the gun away from Emma. Mrs. Herndon let loose a shrill scream, and I pushed Nathan to one side, trying to move us both behind the podium, hoping it could act as some kind of shield.

A single shot rang out.

In the theater, the sound was deafening.

My ears filled with a loud buzzing noise. I felt as though I had been plunged into a bubble, separated from everything around me by an invisible pane of glass. I could see what was happening, but it all felt distant and far away, like a scene viewed through the wrong end of a telescope. The room was filled with movement. Matty was lying on the ground. Senator Herndon stood over him. Mrs. Herndon fled up the aisle toward Emma, while Detective Johnson ran in the opposite direction. Ignoring the steps, Eric was frantically climbing the front of the stage, struggling to hoist himself up from the ground. Dr. Brightman had frozen in horror, and right beside me, Nathan's mouth was open in a scream.

I tried to reach out a hand to comfort Nathan, tried to speak up and ask what was wrong. But my mouth didn't seem to be working. I became aware of a pain in my shoulder, and I forced my hand up to touch it. My fingers found ragged skin surrounding a small round hole, with something hard inside. I looked down at the wound in surprise.

I'd been shot.

As this realization dawned, the stage lights blazed on, blinding me. The seats in the theater seemed to disappear, along with the people around me, and all I could see were the lights.

I squinted and blinked my eyes. At the edges of my vision, hazy figures shimmered. Lincoln, his smile sad. Booth, eerily calm, the gun in his hand. Then others: Clara Harris with her fiancé, Mary Lincoln, Senator and Mrs. Herndon, Matty, and dozens more I didn't recognize. Slowly, one of the figures walked toward me, emerging from the glare.

It was Tyler.

He had a wry smile on his face, and he was shaking his head. "Wake up, Brown. You don't want to sleep through all the fun."

The lights went out with a bang, and suddenly I was in a tiny bedroom, lit only by a bedside lamp. Tyler sat on the bed beside the figure of a sleeping girl, curled up on her side. "She's totally out, Nathan. I've never seen her drink so much."

I realized with a little jolt that the girl on the bed was me. There was only one night, only one party, when I'd actually gotten drunk: the party where I'd kissed Bobby, maybe six months ago. This must be that night.

Nathan emerged from the shadows. His hair was a little shorter, and his eyeglasses were different from the ones I'd always seen, but his fashion sense was exactly the same: he wore a funky argyle sweater and a bow tie. "You need some help getting her home?"

"Yeah, thanks, man," Tyler said. "Sorry about this."

"Whatever. It happens."

"Hey, Brown." Tyler shook me gently. "Wake up."

Drunk Me mumbled something and covered her face with both hands.

"Okay," Tyler said, "this train is leaving the station." He hauled me up to a seated position, and together he and Nathan helped me to my feet.

"I'm coming, I'm coming." I blinked fuzzily up at Nathan. "Who are you?"

"I'm Nathan."

"I'm not." I bent over laughing. Drunk Me found herself hilarious.

"Yeah," Nathan said with a smile, "I figured that out." He hooked one of my arms around his shoulders.

Tyler and Nathan helped me down a flight of stairs and out the front door of a house I only vaguely remembered. Outside, they loaded me in the backseat of Nathan's car. Before he closed the door, Nathan leaned down to talk to me. "Everything good back here?"

"Yeah, it's great. Come on in."

"I'm going to ride up front. But thanks anyway."

"I like you." I patted his cheek. "Can I paint you sometime?"

Nathan laughed. "Sure, whenever you want."

I studied him closely. "I'm gonna need some brighter paints." I slumped back against the seat and closed my eyes.

Nathan was still grinning when he climbed into the driver's seat beside Tyler, who was watching some video footage he'd shot on his phone.

"Your sister's a kick," Nathan said. "What does she think of the videos?"

Tyler shut off the screen and shoved his phone into his back pocket. "She doesn't know about them."

"What? Why not?"

Tyler pulled three of the round bullets from his pocket and rolled them in his hands. "Art is her thing. She'd think I was trespassing on her turf."

"Aha." Nathan nodded wisely. "You're afraid they suck. And she'll be able to tell."

Tyler scoffed. "That's ridiculous."

"Oh, no. I've got your number. You, my friend, *suck* at sucking."

Tyler waggled his eyebrows. "The ladies seem to disagree."

"I mean it. You *hate* when you're not good at stuff. This video thing is important to you, but you're not good at it yet. And you're not willing to have anyone in your life look at you differently."

Tyler threw his hands in the air. "Kick me in the balls, why don't you?"

Nathan laughed and started the car. "Prove me wrong, then. Show your sister the videos."

"Nah," Tyler said, grinning. "She'll think they suck." He looked over at me, crashed out in the backseat. "I only wish she wasn't so scared all the time."

That statement staggered me. And then it enraged me. He didn't want me to be scared? If there was anything I could see now, it was how scared Tyler had been, and how scared he had made me. All his rules, all his advice—I'd spent years trying to shove myself into an invisible box that he'd created. And it hadn't been for my own good. It had been a reflection of how he'd treated himself. Everyone had loved Red Brown, and he had never been willing to take the chance that they might not love this new person—the person he'd wanted to be. Or at least, they might not love him quite as much.

From the backseat, Drunk Me lurched forward and wrapped both arms around Tyler's neck, and both guys jumped, startled. "Aw, I'm not scared! I know you'll always be here to look out for me."

Tyler half gagged, half laughed. "You're choking me, Brown," he forced out. "You've got to let go."

"Nooooo! I won't let go! I'm lever netting go!" I shook my head and tried again. "I am never letting go."

As Tyler tried to untangle my arms from his throat, the vision started growing dim. I reached out toward him, desperate to hold on to him for one more second. But my fingers closed around empty air. He was already gone.

When my vision cleared, I found myself back on the stage of Ford's Theatre, amid a swarm of sound and movement. I lay on the ground, with Detective Johnson putting pressure on the wound in my shoulder. "Hang on. The ambulance is on its way."

Eric sat beside me, holding my hand with both of his. "You're going to be fine. You're going to be fine," he chanted.

People poured into the theater, but I couldn't make sense of all their faces. Men in tuxedos. Uniformed police. Maybe my mother, but I might have just imagined her.

I looked out over the theater, my gaze lingering on the elaborate paneled balconies, the golden curtains that hung in the presidential box.

I wondered if this was it—the very spot where Booth had landed when he'd jumped from the box after the assassination. Had he knelt right here with his broken leg and Lincoln's blood on his hands? And had he felt regret? Was there any part of him that wished he could turn back time and undo what he had done?

I realized there was a part of me, a tiny, hidden part, that had believed I could undo what had happened to my brother. That if I could figure out what happened to him, if I could put all the pieces together, a magic door would somehow open, and Tyler would swagger through it, whole and mine once more.

But it wasn't true. The brother I thought I knew—I'd destroyed him myself, trying to recover him. And the brother who had loved me was never coming back.

Whatever I did, whatever people thought of him, whether his death ever made sense to anyone but me, none of that would change the permanent, unalterable fact at the heart of all of this: he was gone. Forever.

And in that moment, he died all over again—for the last time.

I closed my eyes, held tight to Eric's hand, and cried.

EPILOGUE

A WARM INCANDESCENT GLOW SPILLED FROM THE windows of Atlas Fine Art out onto the sidewalk where I stood, fanning my face with a postcard in the sticky July heat. A streetcar rattled up H Street Northeast, temporarily drowning out the sounds of the gallery opening inside.

Eric paced the sidewalk beside me. "Come *on*. How long does it take to walk here from Twelfth Street? It's been at least ten minutes since he texted you."

I patted his shoulder. "Impatient, are we?"

"You've been working on this piece for months!" He pointed to the building behind us. "And now there are like seventy-five strangers in that gallery who've seen the finished product before me."

"Even when Nathan does get here, we still have to wait for my parents."

Eric groaned. He plucked the postcard from my hand and used it to fan himself instead.

An older couple passed us to enter the gallery. When she saw me, the woman did a double take. She leaned over to whisper to her husband as they went into the building.

Eric watched them go. "Did you see the news in the *Post* today?"

"Why, yes," I replied. "I never miss my morning *Post*." Eric nodded and didn't say any more. I let out an exasperated sigh. "Dude. I did not see the *Post*. What did it say?"

Nathan came up behind us, wrapping an arm around each of our shoulders. "Herndon officially resigned his senate seat."

A smile started in my chest and spread through my entire body as I turned to hug him. Since the day I'd been shot, I could touch things again without fear, and I indulged myself in the feel of his jacket under my fingers. My shoulder protested as I reached up to pull him close, but I was rewarded with the warm smell of tea and sunshine.

"It's about time too," Eric said. "They've been pressuring him for months, ever since he was arraigned."

A blast of sound escaped into the night as the gallery door opened and the owner emerged, a distinguished-looking black man with close-cropped hair and a beard shot through with gray. He glanced around until he spotted us, then adjusted his glasses. "Megan, I've got some people I'd like to introduce you to. Come find me when you get a chance?"

"I've got someone I'd like *you* to meet. This is Nathan Lee—he's one of the creators of the videos I showed you. Nathan, this is Mr. Parish."

Nathan's face went blank with shock, and he barely recovered to shake the man's hand.

"Excellent," Mr. Parish said. "Let's find a time to talk. I'd like to explore the possibility of building an exhibition around your videos. Local work, young work, politically engaged work. It's very interesting to me."

"Yes, sir." Nathan gulped as Mr. Parish disappeared back into the gallery. He turned to me, eyes wide. "What did you . . ."

"Bringing some sunshine to The District," I told him with a grin, and he gripped my hand tight.

A car pulled up on the street in front of us, and my mother opened the passenger door. "We're here! Sorry we're late."

My dad ran around from the driver's side to help her. She'd been a lot more fragile since the truth about Tyler's death had come out. She leaned heavily on Dad's arm as she got out of the car, and he gave her a long look to make sure she was okay before letting go. She hugged me in a cloud of perfume.

"Did we miss it?" Dad asked.

"Of course not," I said.

My mother took both of my hands in hers, and her face turned serious. My stomach did a nervous flip.

"Your father and I . . . ," she began. "Well, we've arranged something for you. As a surprise."

I cocked my head to one side. "A good surprise or a bad surprise?"

Mom let out a short laugh. "Good, I hope. . . ." She paused.

"Mom, spill it!"

She walked over and opened the back door of the car. Elena stepped out.

Instant tears clogged my throat, and I felt frozen in place. Two years since we'd been together in person. We stared at each other for a long moment.

Mom rested a hand on the shoulder of Elena's neon-pink shirt. "Surprise!"

She stepped back to avoid my windmilling arms as I ran at Elena. I grabbed her in a massive hug, and we tumbled into a clumsy pile on the sidewalk.

Elena screamed with laughter. "Let me go, wild woman!" She rubbed my short hair. "It's even better in person."

Eric raised his hand. "Can we *please* go see the collage now?"

While Dad drove off to find parking, the rest of us made our way into the gallery. In the entryway, tall silver letters spelled out the name of the exhibit: *Speaking with New Voices: Emerging Mid-Atlantic Artists.* The artwork hung on raw brick walls; above us, exposed pipes and electrical conduits gave the space an industrial feel. Before we entered the alcove where my piece was being shown, I stopped and addressed my little group.

"Ladies and gentlemen, family and friends, gathered together today, are you ready?"

"God, yes, get on with it," Eric said. Elena laughed and took his arm.

I ushered them all into the space.

The finished artwork was about three feet high and five feet wide. On a ground of pages torn from Dr. Brightman's book and washed with watercolor, I had used a blend of wood chips and brown paper to create a box with a lid, standing open. From within the box, a swirling chorus of colors and shapes erupted: bits of photographs and ticket stubs, beads and fabric, plastic and guitar string. The memories surged like music; they spun like light. Across the top of the piece, I had painted the words *the mystic chords of memory.*

No one spoke. My mother wiped away tears.

As we stood examining the artwork, a solitary figure entered the room behind us, lingering on the outskirts of the space.

It was Dr. Brightman—but a Dr. Brightman transformed. Gone

were the dark sunglasses, the black gloves. His face and hands were exposed, making him look strangely young and vulnerable, and his piercing black eyes met mine.

I touched Nathan on the arm. "I'll be right back."

Nathan's gaze followed mine, and he scowled when he saw who I was looking at.

"It's fine," I told him, my eyes never leaving Dr. Brightman's, and I crossed the room to greet him.

"You came," I said.

Dr. Brightman broke eye contact with me and looked over at my collage. "You know, that first day you showed up in my office and I really understood what you could do, I thought . . . why her?" He smiled slightly and shook his head. "I thought, *I'm a historian.* I'm trained to evaluate artifacts, to use them to unlock the past. The others I've met like us? All historical experts in their own way. But you? You were just some teenager." He gestured to my artwork. "But now I understand," he said. "Same skills. Different medium."

"How are you doing?"

He held up his bare hands. "As long as this lasts, I'll be fine."

"But the senator? He hasn't come after you?"

"There are regular messages from his lawyer. The phrase 'We will bury you' has been thrown around. But they have Emma's confession. And as long as the prosecuting attorney finds me valuable, I expect I will be fine."

"You seem very . . . peaceful," I said. "It's kind of freaking me out."

He laughed, the first time I'd ever heard that particular sound.

"See, like that." I pointed at him. "Very freaky."

"I should let you get back to your family," he said. "But before I do, there are two things I wanted to say to you. In person."

"Okay," I said. "And what are those?"

He held up one finger. "I'm sorry." He held up another. "Thank you."

My eyes flooded, but I blinked the tears away. I stood for a moment, nodding at him. Then he turned and walked away, disappearing into the crowd.

As I rejoined Nathan, I noticed two girls staring at me. They whispered to each other behind their hands, and when they saw me watching, they exchanged wide-eyed glances and quickly left the room.

"Does that bother you?" Nathan asked, taking my hand.

"What? That they're only here to see my art because I'm the girl who took down Senator Gary Herndon?"

"That they point and stare."

"I can't stop them. At least now what they're staring at is what I want them to see."

Nathan held me at arm's length, looking me up and down. "You are definitely sassier than you used to be."

"Oh, yeah?" I traced a finger over the cosmic bowling pins on his shirt. "You think I'm sassy?"

A slow smile spread across his face. "Gutsy. Brassy, even."

I stepped closer. "Are you speaking Sinatra to me right now?"

"That depends," he said, running a hand up my sleeve and curling it around the back of my neck. "Do you like it?"

I kissed him in answer.

"All right, all right, get a room," Eric said.

"Are you kidding?" I moved away from Nathan so that I could spread my arms wide and take in the whole gallery. "This *is* my room."

Laughter sounded from the gallery entrance, and Nathan's head popped up.

"Awesome," he said.

"What?"

"I invited Cedric and some of his friends. I have a feeling that might be them. I can't wait to tell them what Mr. Parish said." Nathan planted a kiss on my cheek before rushing from the room, passing my dad as he went.

Dad joined me in front of my collage, putting both hands on his hips as he stared at it. "It's amazing. I can't quite get over it. Is that what it's called? *The Mystic Chords of Memory*?"

"I guess so," I said. "It's a quote from Abraham Lincoln."

"Megan!" He turned to me with his mouth slightly open. "I'm impressed! How did you . . ."

"Google, Dad," I said. "Duh."

My mother came over and linked her arm with mine. "So all the original pieces came from things that belonged to Tyler?"

I nodded. She stood frozen, staring at the collage. Tears ran down her cheeks. She tried to wipe them away, but they came faster and faster, until she heaved a giant sob. My father put an arm around her shoulders.

"Mom, I'm sorry," I said. "What can I do?"

She clung even more tightly to my arm. "Nothing," she choked out. "It's good. It's beautiful." She sobbed again. "It will always make me remember him."

I pulled my hand free of my sleeve and touched the collage, tracing the length of a guitar string with one finger. Looking behind my mother, I caught a glimpse of Tyler's red hair, a copper-colored glow in the light. He laughed at me. "When it starts to sound like actual music, you'll know you're getting somewhere."

I took my finger off the string and used it to rub the sharp pain that lingered behind my eye. "It'll make me remember him too," I said. "Always."

ACKNOWLEDGMENTS

I MUST ACKNOWLEDGE FIRST AND FOREMOST MY extraordinary editor, Viana Siniscalchi. She saw straight to the heart of this story and found the keys to unlock it. I couldn't have imagined a better collaborator or guide. Thank you. My deepest gratitude to the entire editorial team at Balzer + Bray, especially the incomparable Alessandra Balzer and Donna Bray. I'm thrilled and honored to be one of your authors. And to cover designer Sarah Creech, copyeditor Renée Cafiero, publicist Stephanie Hoover, and the marketing team of Bess Braswell and Sabrina Abballe, "I can no other answer make but thanks, and thanks, and ever thanks."

My agent, Lana Popovic, is a superhero in false eyelashes. I've benefited more than I can say from her brilliance, insight, and super-keen advice, and I'm so lucky to have her in my corner.

I'm supremely grateful for the generous and masterly input of Kate Karyus Quinn, who was mentor, dramaturg, and good friend to this novel—and to me. Thank you to Brenda Drake and her Pitch Wars contest for connecting us. Thanks also to my PW teammate, Tracie Martin, and to the entire PW2014 Table of Trust. You guys make a writing life livable.

Many friends gave their time and support to this process. Thanks to my CP, Mara K. Heil, for never letting me get away with any of my excuses not to write this book. Thanks to my beta readers—Jeff Hirsch, Karen Ann Daniels, Lena Jones, Jamal Douglas, and Solomon Hailie Selassie—for your invaluable thoughts and input. Thanks to Patrick Pearson for touring me around backstage at Ford's Theatre and answering all my nosy questions. And thanks to my biggest personal supporters: Eric Louie, Bernadette Hanson, Shana Wride, Marcus Flathman, Lara Gable, Shelley Orr, and my incredible in-laws, for believing in me and in this book.

My family is my heart. Without Dom and Arleen Amato, I never would have had the courage to think of myself as a writer. Without Joe and Brian Amato, I never would have known what a good friend a brother can be. Without the love of my gorgeous girls and the tireless support of my husband, Phil, I never would have had the fortitude—or the time. My dearest Phil, I carry your heart in my heart, now and always.

When I was writing the first draft of *The Hidden Memory of Objects*, a former student of mine passed away suddenly in his early twenties. As the community came together to memorialize him, I realized that a character I'd written resembled him in many ways. My humble thanks to his family, especially to his mother, LouEllen, for giving me their blessing to name that character in his honor. My Eric Bowling isn't based on the real person—none of the details of his life or family are the same—but I hope a little of Eric's kindness, tenacity, and indomitable spirit live on in this book, as they surely will in the hearts of those who knew him.